Chronicles of Nethra

Book Three

Darkest Hearts

Chronicles of Nethra: Darkest Hearts

www.mythicnorthpress.com

ISBN: 978-1-954177-14-7

First edition: July 2021

For Don
Can't thank you enough for the encouragement and
support. You taught me everything worth knowing.
Thanks, Dad.

ACKNOWLEDGMENTS

Thanks, once again, to Alana Joli Abbott for providing the copy edits for this book. Your feedback is invaluable and always brings a smile to my face. Thanks also to Bob for spot-checking these past three volumes for typos, and to Karen for her work on improving book one.

Another big thank you to my friends and family who have encouraged me on this journey. We're just getting started, but I know I can do it with you in my corner. Hope you enjoy the book.

Ren'Dahl Sanctum
Minos Station—Helion System
Six Months Ago

Jocelyn Ren'Dahl stared down at the charred corpse in front of her. The fact that the Awakening ritual had culminated in this result was not what tormented her. The regret she felt was purely in regard to what this failure had cost her.

"Triumvir?" Mara's voice was hesitant, and rightly so. Jocelyn had lingered here for far too long. Introspection would do that to you. How long had it been, exactly?

"Yes, Mara?"

"Just checking in to make sure that everything is okay, Mistress. We've…" She let the statement trail off, but Jocelyn was still able to ascertain the sentiment.

"I'm fine," she asserted. "Just thinking, that's all."

"Does this create a problem?" A brief hesitation. "I mean, it's tragic… no one likes to see a failed ceremony. What I mean to ask is…"

"I know what you intend, Mara. It's fine. And no, this does not create a problem. The candidate—and more importantly, his brother—knew the risks they were taking. This outcome, while gruesome, is unlikely to surprise anyone. We must move forward."

She spun, smoothing the wrinkles out of her ebony skirt, resisting the urge to straighten the flows of her long dark braids.

Appearances were important, but not all appearances were cosmetic. She needed to appear in control.

"Has Eli departed?"

"Yes, Mistress," Mara replied.

"Stop that. I know what you're doing. You only take on ceremony when you fear my temperament. I assure you, it does nothing to quell me. Please, try to behave as naturally as possible."

"Yes, Mis… Jocelyn."

The triumvir sighed. What kind of a presence did she command to so intimidate someone who had been a close friend for such a long time? "I'm glad to hear that Eli and his friends were able to exit the station. I hope that they make it home safely."

"As do we all," Mara parroted. "Although—since you have so recently insisted upon candor—I must ask: Do you mean that?"

Jocelyn narrowed her eyes. "What are you implying? Surely you do not think that I wish for Eli's demise."

"That's not what I mean." Mara shook her head. "I guess I was asking: are you so comfortable with him having a home that lies so far from us?"

That was a legitimate question. At her core, Jocelyn believed that all Sahaia should consider the Sanctum their one true home. The fact that so many did otherwise left her to wonder if there had been some quintessential failure of leadership. Ryker's leadership. Wynne's leadership. *Her* leadership.".

"Yes," she stated defiantly. "If Sigma-4 is where Eli finds happiness, then I wish nothing else for him."

Mara's look told her that she was far from convinced, but the other woman did not press the issue further. Instead, she asked, "What do we do now?"

Jocelyn had been considering that very question for long hours and had still not arrived at the answer. She looked back to the corpse of Joaquin Valadar. His brother, Don Cyrus Valadar, would surely need to be informed of the outcome.

Yet, something echoed in her mind—the admonition of a former lover and the closest friend she'd ever lost: *"We did him a disservice. The tests would have told us his body couldn't hold the energies. By the gods, I've never seen a rift open again that fast! The tests would have shown it clearly!"*

Eli had been right—the results would have been clear. However, Jocelyn had never been interested in inducting Joaquin Valadar into the order. She'd merely been honoring a promise—agreeing to a necessary evil to work toward the greater good.

However, Cyrus still had to hand over the artifact. In retrospect, Jocelyn wondered if she had been overzealous in rushing this Awakening. If Cyrus were to somehow find out that they had not done their due diligence in the initiation proceedings, he could renege on their arrangement.

"Mara, what would you say the minimum time frame for adequate testing for an Awakening would take? Four, maybe five months?"

The question caught her acolyte off-guard. Her black-in-black eyes flared briefly before she regained her composure. "Certainly five, if not six. But we've never rushed the requisite tests before. It's hard for me to estimate."

"Then that's how long we will wait," Jocelyn concluded. "Generally, I would say bad news does not improve with age, but there's no spinning this. What's done is done, and we need to maintain our face in front of House Valadar. In six months, I want you to deliver the message to Ryker. You will take a single ship, manned only by you and your thralls, and you will act as a relay between us and him at the Angel Gate. That way, if House Valadar raises any objection, we have a hasty conduit by which to remedy their concerns."

Mara bowed. "As you wish, but will Ryker not grow concerned as the time elapses?"

Jocelyn scoffed. "Ryker dumped this gods-damned situation in our laps. He does not know when or how we conducted the ritual.

And, should he ask, we will tell him that we are conducting the appropriate tests. I want no doubt in Cyrus Valadar's mind should he ever consider the possibility that we played him false."

Her fellow Sahaia said nothing for long seconds before speaking again. "Did we?"

"Did we what?"

"Play him false."

"Certainly not."

"Then why the rushed ceremony?"

Jocelyn took a long pause. How much to reveal to her? The nature of the arrangement was something she had agreed to keep among the triumvirate. Yet she was asking this woman to lie to a person who was as much in power over the coven as Jocelyn.

"I wish I could tell you more," she replied honestly. "All I can do is assure you: I would not have done this thing were it not of the utmost importance. Suffice it to say that, should we fail in this, we have much greater concerns to worry about."

Jocelyn decided to leave it at that. Though necessarily vague, her description was not inaccurate. Should the Sahaia fail to obtain the artifact possessed by House Valadar, the fate of all Terran space—if not that of intergalactic civilization itself—was in peril.

CHAPTER 1

Terra-News-Net Now (TN3)

Headline: Valadar Holdings Announces New Cross-System Partnership with the Grey Wings for Security of NeoGenix Corporation

Story: In a surprising move that has Freyvian markets guessing, Valadar Holdings has announced a new partnership with Grey Wings Securities (GWS-RAV, +1.02%) out of the Ravian System. This is the first inter-system contract secured by the firm's parent company, Silver Flight Inc., since its acquisition by entrepreneur and socialite Ora Monroe.

Speculation persists as to why an out-system contractor is being brought in to provide security for NeoGenix Corporation—one of the largest companies in the Valadar Holdings portfolio—but analysts speculate the move is likely in response to the failure of their prior contractor, Iron Wolf Consulting (IWC-FRV, -12.2%), to put a stop to the series of raids on shipments reported by this outlet over the past cycle.

Grey Wings Dark Site
Sigma-4 Space Station
Ravian System

Ora Monroe was a special kind of desperate. Only desperation of the highest order would have brought her down here, in her private prison, to talk to this asshole. She'd locked Shift down here, intent on never thinking of him again. The bastard had earned it when he'd hacked into the Grey Wings servers—*her* servers.

The bounty Cali Vay-Lon had offered for him, though, was beyond substantial. It made Ora curious why the Kintari crime lord was so interested in this disgusting little trouble-maker. That said, this was not the line of questioning she pursued in her last minutes with the hacker in her custody.

"What can you tell me about Cognis?"

The shit-eating grin on his face made Ora want to punch him, but she couldn't do that. Under her agreement with Cali, she had to deliver the hacker alive. Once she started punching him, Ora wasn't sure she'd be able to stop.

"Where, might Ah ask, did ya hear about Cognis?"

"No, you shouldn't ask. But, since you have, I don't mind telling you that it came up when we were researching the *real* reason you hacked into my servers. Now, if you expect to keep breathing, I expect you to supply me with some answers."

"That's gonna make it hard for ya t' redeem the bounty on ma head. Killin' me, Ah mean. Ya already told me ya needs me alive."

Damn. She *had* admitted that. Who was to say she was above mistakes? "Only if I want to redeem the bounty, Shift. As you can imagine, a few thousand krets lost isn't going to make me lose much sleep at night."

"Is that all she offered fer me?"

No, it wasn't, but Ora wasn't going to play into the hacker's hands. "Talk, Shift. This is your last chance."

Her prisoner paused for just a minute before answering. "Congis is a project Ah was workin' on before Ah came to the Ravian System. It was a set of drivers designed fer a very specific purpose: t' create an artificial intelligence. Nah… actually, that ain't specific enough. It was designed t' create a *sapient* intelligence."

The notion was so preposterous it rendered Ora's incredulity genuine. "You can't possibly be serious."

"Serious as a heart attack, miss queen. The Cognis drive-chip was the real deal—enough t' receive a bullet under that damned Praxis Creed. Now can ya see why Ah wanted t' get it back?"

Ora tried hard to keep the surprise off her face. "Get it back?"

Shift's demeanor immediately revealed that he'd said too much. Unfortunately, his cards were on the table. "It was brought here, t' Sigma-4. Ah was usin' yer network t' try an' get a fix on its location. Obviously, that didn' work out too well."

Well damn. The bastard had answered her questions far better than expected. Did this Cognis situation have anything to do with the reason Cali wanted him? Did it even matter? According to her sources, the Cognis chip was long gone, so it no longer posed a threat to her.

"Very well," she sighed while gesturing to her guards. "Prep him for transport."

Tashania stepped up next to her. The dark-skinned Terran woman wore a skeptical expression. "How do we know he's tellin' the truth?" she asked.

Good girl, Ora thought to herself. She liked that Tashania was being skeptical. It made Ora feel like the Wings would be in capable hands if something ever happened to happen to her. Not that she was planning on anything happening, of course, but Ora liked to have contingency plans for her contingency plans.

"We don't," she admitted, making sure that Shift heard her. "But the yarn that this hacker has just related is enough to receive a death sentence in any jurisdiction. If I were going to fabricate a story, I would have taken lengths to make it a little less damning. Either way, he's not our problem anymore. We'll let Cali deal with him."

Shift barked a harsh laugh. "Damn girl, yer a feisty one! That's one o' the things Ah like about ya." If Ora's scowl bothered him, he certainly didn't show it.

She motioned again to her Maur bodyguards, massive humanoids with feline heads, to drag the hacker to his feet. They did so, and Shift made his best attempt to stand despite being a bit weak in the knees. Seven months in cryo would do that to you. Even though the stasis pods kept you alive indefinitely, your body needed a little activity to keep in peak condition. Not that Shift had been much of a physical specimen to begin with.

"Get him out of those rags and into something a little more presentable. Get him a haircut and a physical too. When we hand him over to the Marauders, he should be free of bugs and parasites."

Shift laughed maniacally as her guards dragged him away. Gods, he was a strange one. Ora couldn't help but wonder if she was making a mistake in letting him go.

"Are you sure about this?" Tashania asked.

"Hmmm?" Ora replied, turning her attention back to her lieutenant.

"Releasing him to Cali. I mean, there's no way in the nine hells that this bounty has nothing to do with Cognis. Agreed?"

"No idea," Ora admitted. "But I'm willing to push it into the category of 'not my problem.' Tell me, is the *Vandal* still docked?"

"Yes ma'am. They haven't left the station since their last check-in. It looks like they were serious when they said they wanted some downtime."

"Well, I hope they made the most of it. It's time they got back into action." That was one of the strangest things about the whole assignment from Cali. She'd been very specific to mention that she wanted the same crew who had delivered the bounty offer to carry back the prize on the return trip. This request was made even though the crew had a violent altercation with Cali during their short time on Minos Station.

Any crew that screwed up that bad while working for Ora was lucky to make it off the station alive, much less get an offer for a second job. None of this made any sense. She had the distinct feeling that, somehow, she was getting played here, but there was nothing to do about that now.

Ora liked to have her enemies out in front of her. If Cali was intent on making that list, then it was better to know where she stood, sooner rather than later.

NeoGenix Boardroom
Valhalla, Sif
Freyvian System

If he were being honest, Cyrus Valadar had never really cared much for Ryker. The shadow—or *Sahaia* if one was inclined to be politically correct—gave him the creeps. It wasn't the physical traits that bothered him: the ghostly white skin, the dark hair, or the black-in-black eyes. It also wasn't his powerful psionic abilities, gifts he'd acquired when he'd undergone his Awakening and ceased being Terran.

No, it was that Ryker, at his core, was a politician, and like all politicians, it felt like he was lying to you even when he was telling you the truth.

Cyrus dealt with a lot of men like this. He didn't know why he let it bother him so much in Ryker's case. In fact, the two of them likely had more in common than not. Cyrus was the head of the powerful House Valadar, the "Don" as tradition named his position. By virtue of this title and the associated assets, he wielded more power than any other being in the entire Freyvian system.

Ryker was, in a way, head of his own house. He was a triumvir—one of the three leading members of the Ren'Dahl Coven which operated out of the Helion System. The shadows were slightly less overt in their political machinations when compared to the Great Houses, but Cyrus did not doubt for a second that they were active players. Gods knew that he'd been forced to deal with the Ren'Kue Coven more times than he'd care to admit.

They were also fiercely territorial, which was part of the reason he'd thought it strange when Ryker first approached him regarding their recent joint venture. He was technically operating in the equivalent of a foreign—and sometimes hostile—nation when doing business in this system. Regardless, he'd taken the initiative, and it seemed to Cyrus that he might be operating with Ren'Kue's blessing.

Easing some of the tensions with the local coven had been one of the promises Cyrus extracted as part of their negotiations. The other concession he'd insisted on was a bit more… *personal*. There would always be limits to what the Sahaia were willing to share with House Valadar. That was, unless the two became one-and-the-same.

"Ryker," he greeted, extending his hand as his guest entered his office.

"Don Valadar," the shadow replied, accepting the handshake. "How fare the trials of the corporate boardroom today?"

"As with most days, we deal with victories and setbacks with equal grace while striving to have more of the former than the latter." He released Ryker's hand and gestured for him to sit in one of the padded chairs opposite his desk. "Make yourself at home! Your arrival was unexpected, otherwise, I would have made more formal arrangements."

The assertion was half-true. Cyrus had not been expecting Ryker to arrive *today,* but he *had* been waiting for months to hear from him again. Their arrangement had reached a kind of impasse that had lingered for over half a cycle since its inception. Cyrus had begun to wonder if he was ever going to hear from Ryker again. The equal measure of silence coming from his brother was unnerving.

Cyrus poured a glass of clear liquor over ice. One might have thought it was water until getting a whiff of the pungent liquid. He took the glass and raised it in Ryker's general direction. "No, thank you," the Sahaia responded.

With a shrug, Cyrus claimed the glass for himself and took a sip of the bitter drink as he assumed a position behind his desk. "So, tell me: what brings you out here on such short notice?" *Hopefully not more delays and excuses.*

Ryker's face was a solemn mask as he spoke. "I bring word from the Sanctum. The Awakening ritual has been completed."

That *was* big news. Finally, after all this time, they'd delivered on their end of the bargain. Yet, Ryker's demeanor was not what Cyrus would have expected for such a momentous occasion.

He leaned forward in his chair. "And? Is Joaquin…"

"Dead."

Cyrus froze. It was several seconds before he realized that his mouth was still hanging open mid-sentence. "Dead?" he repeated quietly.

"I'm sorry. He did not survive the ritual. It happens from time to time. We don't have a reliable way of predicting the outcome of an Awakening. You have my condolences, and that of my brothers and sisters."

Nothing could have prepared Cyrus for such news. He inhaled deeply, fighting to keep his composure. Part of him wanted to leap across the table and beat Ryker to within an inch of his unnatural life.

Cyrus cared for very few people in this world. His brother, Joaquin, had been one of them.

It wasn't entirely fair to blame Ryker for this. When Cyrus and his siblings had first pitched their proposal to induct one of them into the Sahaia ranks, they had been informed of the risks. Knowing conceptually that fatalities were common among those who sought to join the ranks of the Sahaia was one thing. To experience the truth of this, however…

"I understand," Cyrus whispered. He dared not speak much louder, lest his grief penetrate his voice. "This is for certain? There is no chance that this information may be in error?"

"I'm afraid not. I received confirmation from an acolyte that was present at the ritual. There was, unfortunately, nothing we could do for him."

Cyrus nodded. He was going to have to tell Julia—and Tessa, should she deem it fit to grace him with her presence. They would not take this well. Julia, in particular, would be rankled. Their agreement with the Sahaia had not been contingent upon a successful induction—merely on its attempt. "I would like to have the body brought to our family home as soon as possible."

For the first time in their conversation, Ryker seemed to balk. "Don Valadar, I'm afraid that the results of a failed Awakening can be somewhat… unsightly. I'm not certain you would wish to see your brother's body as it is now."

"I appreciate the warning, Ryker, but I would have my brother's remains—whatever the state—be brought to lay with our ancestors. I'm sure that this is something that one of your religious disposition might sympathize with, yes?"

The Sahaia said nothing for a long moment. Then he nodded. "I will contact the coven immediately, and we will make arrangements."

"Excellent. Then we have an understanding." Cyrus stood from his desk, signaling the conclusion of the meeting. "As for our end of the bargain: I will arrange for the transfer of the artifact into your possession once you have returned my brother's body to me. Good day, Ryker. Molly will see you out."

The triumvir did not argue. He stood, offered a polite bow, and made for the exit. Only when the door had shut behind him did Cyrus allow the full weight of his emotional turmoil to settle on him.

With a roar, he hurled the still-full glass of liquor at the door. The object shattered on impact, splattering shards and liquid in all directions. The wreckage did nothing to soothe his rage. He slammed his fists over and over again on the polymer surface of his desk until it began to crack under the force of the blows.

He stopped then, sinking to his knees and burying his face in his hands. His body shook with massive sobs, and a low keening noise poured from his lips. *My brother is dead,* he thought. *My only brother is dead.*

Time lost meaning in the throes of such grief. He had no idea how long he knelt there, weeping in his office. After a while, the pain began to lose its edge. His hands shook as he withdrew them from his face, knuckles still bloody from assaulting his desk.

He stood and walked to a nearby mirror. As he had suspected, some of his blood had been smeared on his face and in his hair. He grabbed a towel and cleaned himself the best he could using the small sink in his office. When he was done, he tossed the formerly white rag, now stained with blood, into a nearby disposal chute.

That was that. He'd allowed himself a moment to relieve his tension—a second to explore his grief. All of that needed to be stowed away now.

He was the Don. Such displays of weakness must be confined to quiet moments and put away. In light of this latest development, he had something very important to attend to.

He pressed the button on his desk that would patch him through to his receptionist. "Molly?"

"Yes, Mr. Valadar?"

"Please let Dr. Blackwell know that I am heading down to the lab presently. Have her meet me at her earliest convenience."

"Yes, Mr. Valadar."

A back door to his office led to his personal elevator. He palmed the biometric scanner to gain access to the lift and entered the code to bring himself down to the building's lowest marked sublevel. There were two levels below that, but they were only accessible from the lab itself.

Lucretia Blackwell was waiting for him the moment he stepped off the lift. The doctor was an attractive woman who might have been gorgeous if she would put a little more effort into her appearance. Her blond hair was cut off just below her chin, about the same length as Cyrus's. She wore a white lab coat, a dress code feature she'd imposed on all laboratory staff. Honestly, Cyrus couldn't give a shit about how they dressed, but Lucretia insisted.

"Dr. Blackwell," he greeted.

"Cyrus." She issued a polite nod but did not extend her hand. Cyrus had the feeling that his chief science officer didn't like him much, and only tolerated his presence because he signed her paychecks and set her generous budget. "To what do I owe this visit from the company president?"

He found it amusing that she cited his corporate title rather than his position as Don. Perhaps it made her more comfortable to put some artificial distance between the work she was doing and Terran politics. "I need to know where we are with the artifact. Our window for research is coming to a close, and I'd like to summarize our findings for the investment committee."

Lucretia adjusted her glasses. From reading her file, Cyrus knew that they weren't prescription. Rather, they were used to provide a retinal interface to the lab's computers. Cyrus suspected she wore them, at least in part, because they made her feel academic. Her eyes bounced back and forth, taking in the information that scrolled across her accessory. "I take it you are referring to the Nethrian device?"

"Of course."

"The artifact is about to enter another trial. I—"

"Excellent!" he cut her off before she made the mistake of telling him that now was not a good time. "I would love to see the artifact in action. You can brief me on the way. What are we studying today?"

She inhaled deeply. It was clear that she was frustrated by the intrusion but knew she no choice but to comply with his request. "Right this way, sir."

In the short walk to the testing chamber, she provided background on the current experiment. Early discussions with Ryker had revealed the artifact was some kind of conduit for dark energy. They had discovered early on that radiation from the device altered cellular metabolism and electrical activity in various tissues. This only seemed to be true of tissue collected from a naturally born organism. Synthetic tissues seemed strangely unaffected, or at least not affected in any way they could detect.

"Today's experiment is an expansion of the data we collected in phase one of our research. We noticed that applying an electric current to the artifact amplifies the dark energy yield, and consequently, its effects on organic systems. The effects seem to plateau early, making them effectively independent of the amount of energy applied to the artifact, so we may have reached a dead-end on that front. However, I've developed another theory."

Cyrus fed into the good doctor's dramatic pause. "Go on."

She smiled at his indulgence, opening the door leading to the viewing room. "I hypothesize that despite the limited effects we've seen on the artifact's ability to revive expired tissue samples, the purpose of the device may still lie in this domain. Perhaps, like the electrical impulse necessary to amplify the artifact's power, we are missing another foreign element."

"And you think you have an idea what that might be?"

"Perhaps." She gestured to the scene in the testing chamber on the far side of the glass.

Cyrus took in the contents of the chamber. The artifact was suspended in the air by a metal clamp above the center of the room. It was an emerald-colored stone, irregularly shaped with veins of onyx snaking through and around it. On the table below the artifact, was a cadaver—a Terran male who, by appearances, had presumably died of age-related complications. The wrinkled, skeletal body was bare except for a small modesty cloth placed on the center of its pelvis. A series of tubes ran into each of its arms.

"Begin the transfusion," Dr. Blackwell ordered. A technician working a nearby control panel complied with the directive, and a pale blue solution began to flow up one of the tubes into the cadaver's arm. Shortly, a slightly discolored version of the solution was pumped out of the other arm.

"It's a standard cocktail of various nutritional and recovery agents," the doctor explained. "Think of it as a slightly more potent version of what you would find at any hospital across the system.

We're essentially replacing the subject's circulatory fluid with this solution."

"To what end?"

"You'll see."

With an encouraging nod from the doctor, the technician flipped another switch, which activated the device holding the artifact. The machinery hummed, and the artifact started to glow. Emerald light filled the chamber, bathing the corpse resting below it.

For long moments, nothing happened. Then, the vitals on the subject began to blip. Cyrus was mesmerized. "Is it..."

"Alive?" Lucretia scoffed. "Hardly, but the tissues do seem to be reactivating to a much greater degree than we saw with exposure absent the solution." She turned to the technician. "Have these readings been recorded?"

"Yes ma'am," he replied.

"Good. Shut down the infusion but keep the current to the device active." He did so. Soon after the blue liquid stopped flowing into the cadaver, the vital signs ceased.

"As I expected," Lucretia concluded. "We can only reanimate tissue given the proper environmental conditions. Much more study will need to be done to see if this effect can be prolonged."

Cyrus sighed. "Unfortunately, we don't have that kind of time. The Sahaia have fulfilled their end of the bargain. I need you to finish your work here and be prepared to transfer ownership of the artifact."

"What?" she sputtered. "Cyrus, I..."

"I don't like it any more than you do, Lucretia, but a bargain is a bargain. If I had known the potential this artifact had before I struck the agreement, I might not have done so. That is beyond the point, however. I need you to focus on wrapping up any lines of inquiry we haven't yet investigated."

The doctor was fuming, and she didn't bother to hide it. "Anything, in particular, you had in mind? I do want to make sure the president gets what *he* wants out of this little project."

He smiled back at her, ignoring the rebuke. "As a matter of fact, yes, I do. I want you to concentrate on the effects the device's radiation has on *living* subjects."

"Do you care to share why *this* would be the best use of my team's time? I find it odd that you would ask us to divert resources from the reanimation program to pursue this other endeavor."

No, he did not care to share. Even if he had, he doubted the good doctor would be supportive of his impulse to track down scientific basis in Nethrian myth.

He turned to face the device once again, gazing into its glowing green surface. "Do you remember what they called this, Lucretia? The Sahaia, I mean."

She huffed, realizing she wasn't going to get an explanation for his new orders. "The Heart of Thule, I believe."

"That's right. I've been doing some research on the Nethrians lately. I never gave much thought to religion before finding the artifact, you understand. Church was more of a social affair in my family. Do you happen to know what title Thule holds in the official pantheon?"

Despite her obvious incredulity, she gave serious thought to the question. "I'm not sure. Lord of something, given the Church's archaic penchants."

"The Stardust Grave," Cyrus stated. "Thule is the Lord of the Stardust Grave."

CHAPTER 2

Terra-News-Net Now (TN3)

Headline: House Maddox and House Aretria Confirm Helion Stability, Deny Involvement in Ship Disappearances

Story: In a joint press conference, representatives from House Maddox and House Aretria provided a message of cooperation and stability that prompted a three-hundred-point rally in Helion markets today. Both large corporate shareholders assured local governments and representatives from the Neo-Terran Alliance that, despite the upheaval in the Freyvian and Ravian systems, neither house is looking to upset the current order of things, and both Houses are on track to see record profitability by the close of the current cycle.

When asked by reporters about the rumors of recent ship disappearances in the system's outer belt, both Houses denied involvement in—and even the credibility of—such incidences. Logan Maddox, Chief Operations Officer for MX Holdings, went on record stating, "Frankly, I don't know why anyone takes these reports seriously. Ships go missing from time to time. It's one of the hazards of space travel. Our data shows no indication that recent losses have exceeded expected parameters over the past two cycles."

This assertion was made despite independent reports that there has been an over three hundred percent increase in ships failing to make port after departing to any destination within the Hades Belt and a six-hundred percent discrepancy in the number of missing ships compared to the inner system Styx Belt.

—

If Ora had to be working, there was no place she'd rather do it than in her private lounge at Annex. She loved what she did, and this room seemed to be where she got the most work done. Whether reviewing reports, meeting with clients, or plotting the downfall of her competition—almost everything she needed to do regularly happened right here.

Location was one of the biggest draws. Annex, though only one of many businesses Ora owned on Sigma-4 station, was by far her most successful. It was essentially a nightclub that never stopped taking customers. The concept of "closing time" meant nothing to a station ring cursed with the illusion of perpetual night by the lack of artificial skies. Though there were peak hours of operation, the reality was that someone could always be found taking advantage of the club's services at any given time of day.

The building served as a home base for Ora as well. The club only took up the first three levels, and her penthouse apartment was located on the top floor. The rest of the installation housed the normal operations of the Grey Wings, the organization Ora had been running for nearly a decade now.

If you asked any high-ranking member of station security or Dorian law enforcement, they would tell you the Wings were one of the numerous criminal syndicates operating within the Ravian System. The description wasn't inaccurate, but Ora couldn't help feel like it was a bit judgy. The Grey Wings did just as much legitimate business as anyone one else on the station, and only a fool would claim that any corporation owned in part by one of the Great Houses didn't participate in *some* illegal activity.

Not that labels were all that mattered. Truthfully, the implication that the Wings were only "one of many" was a lot more troublesome than the "criminal" label in Ora's mind. The organization had grown significantly under her guidance, yet it still lacked the notoriety granted to equally corrupt structures found in Houses Chronos, Maddox, Aretria, and Valadar.

Given time, Ora would show them the error of their judgment. In time, she would convey what a mistake it was to underestimate her.

"Ora?" Tashania's voice came in over her earpiece.

"Yes?"

"Representatives from the *Vandal* are here at your request. Shall I send them up?" That sounded oddly formal. Ora had told Tashania to send for Markus and his crew. Why was she introducing them like they were strangers? Clearly, the way she announced them was intended to prompt Ora to prepare for something unexpected.

"Certainly. I'm ready to receive them." She closed the files she'd been examining on her terminal and moved to her center ring of furniture. Normally, for regular associates, she would have taken a seat on one of the four couches. Given Tashania's formal announcement, she decided instead to take the chair at one end of the arrangement. It was on a slightly elevated segment of the floor, giving it the subtle appearance of a throne. She could always move to a more inviting location in the room if it turned out she was being overly cautious.

When her guests entered the lounge, she saw why Tashania had phrased her introduction the way she had. Markus Frost was not among those visiting her today. Eli Ren'Dahl had come, which was pretty typical given that Eli was second in command on the *Vandal*. Ora didn't recognize the person escorting the Sahaia, however.

She was a Terran woman, but not the one Eli was bonded to. That one was a redhead, as Ora membered from an aside comment Markus had made in a prior meeting. This woman was blonde.

Ora rose from her seat and took a step forward to greet her guests. "Eli." She extended her hand rather than opening her arms for an embrace. Even though he was a familiar face, she was feeling a bit defensive.

"Ora," he said, accepting her handshake with a gentlemanly smile. He was a looker, that one—if you liked the pretty boy type. Even though she didn't care for the Sahaia look, there was something about the way Eli worked those black-in-black eyes that sucked you in. "Glad to hear from you. It's been a while."

"Yes, it has," she agreed. She turned to his companion. "I'm not sure we've met before."

"Skye Jensen," the woman replied, extending her hand. As Ora accepted the handshake, the realization dawned on her that she *had* met this woman before, albeit only briefly. She knew her more by reputation. This was *Markus's* Skye.

With this new perspective, Ora studied her again. She wore a casual white top and gray leggings that showed off her athletic figure. Her thin frame and the lean muscles of her arms showed off her fitness, though Ora was definitely more toned. Overall, the woman was plainer than expected. Wouldn't Markus be interested in something a bit more distinctive?

"Welcome to Annex, Skye. It's nice to make your acquaintance again." She released her hand and turned so that she could address both of them at once. "And thank you both for coming on such short notice. I was pleased when I found that your ship was still on station. Did you enjoy your reprieve from the runner's life?"

"Very much so," Eli replied, "but we are ready to get back to work."

"And where is Markus?" she asked, trying to make the question sound conversational. "Is he otherwise occupied?"

The question got more of a reaction than Ora had been expecting. Skye's eyes darted to the side and down at the floor. Eli shifted his weight ever-so-slightly, conveying his discomfort. His smile deflated, and Ora could tell he was fighting to maintain a professional demeanor.

"Markus is no longer with the crew," he reported. "We parted ways several months back—shortly after our last visit with you." His body was stiff as he made the report. He was very intentionally looking straightforward, maintaining eye contact in a manner that felt a bit forced.

Ora's eyes darted back to Skye. In her peripheral vision, Eli shifted again. When she looked back at him, his mask had slipped even more. Was that guilt that she saw in his eyes? Then it all clicked into place.

You two were sleeping together, she realized. *And poor Markus must have found out.* Gods, that would have killed him. He'd still been very much in love with Skye when Ora had last seen him six months ago, to Ora's chagrin. She couldn't help but wonder how long after her last encounter with Markus it had taken for this little love triangle to fall apart.

"I see," she replied noncommittally. "A shame—Markus and I had a good working relationship. I trust that you are still interested in working with the Grey Wings as the need arises?"

"Absolutely," Eli replied, visibly relieved that Markus's departure wasn't a non-starter for whatever offer she had been about to make.

"Excellent. Come now, let's have a seat." She still chose the chair over the couches. Although she liked Eli, she had never worked with Skye directly. It probably didn't help that she was inclined to dislike her, based on her history with Markus, but Ora could still be professional—if not congenial.

Eli and Skye chose to sit on separate couches, a move that Markus and Eli hadn't even done. *Please, if I hadn't figured it out before, I would have now. You two make this way too obvious.*

"So," she began aloud. "Do you remember the bounty you brought me from Cali Vay-Lon and the Marauders?"

"Yes," Eli replied. "Though you never shared the specifics with us, I remember the interaction."

"Well, it has taken me this long to decide whether to fulfill the contract. You see, the individual in question is one with whom I have a brief but troubled history. You may remember him, Eli. He's a Terran hacker that goes by the alias Shift."

The Sahaia blinked a few times before the recognition hit. "The same Shift that you were… *dealing* with at one of our earlier meetings?"

"That's correct. Given what you saw of our prior interaction, you can imagine how I might find it difficult to hand him over to someone who is still very much an unknown quantity."

"Indeed." The shadow's tempered response made Ora wonder how much palace intrigue he witnessed during his time at the coven. Surely they dealt with problems far more irritating—and dangerous—than that of resourceful hackers.

"With that in mind, I need someone I can trust to deliver him safely to Minos Station. In her message, Cali requested to work with your team, specifically. Can I count on you to deliver Shift to his final destination?"

"Yes, we can do that."

Skye spoke up then. "I'm sorry, Ora. I wasn't around when you received the original message from Cali. Could you remind me what the compensation looked like for this op?"

It was a fair question, and Ora tried not to take offense at Skye's boldness. Unfortunately, had Ora been dealing with Markus, such a question would need not have been asked. "Five-million krets. I'm willing to offer you fifty percent of the bounty, per the longstanding terms I've worked with on similar arrangements with your crew. Is that acceptable?"

Eli inclined his head with the slightest hint of embarrassment. "More than acceptable. You can count on us."

Interesting. Eli was obviously aware of his new partner's lack of decorum. It would be interesting to see what he could do with her in time. Again, Ora wondered what Markus had seen in this woman to begin with.

She let her smile slide into place. "Excellent. Tashania will be in touch with you later this evening with the prisoner transfer details. Keep an eye on him, Eli. Shift is possibly the slipperiest son-of-a-bitch I've ever had to incarcerate. Personally, I'd feel a lot better if he were still on ice, but I can't pass up an opportunity like this one."

"Understood."

Ora rose to her feet. Extending her hand once more to each of them. "Thank you. A pleasure seeing you again," she said as she released Skye's hand.

"Likewise."

With that, both of her guests made for the exit. Ora's Maur bodyguards opened the door for them, and Tashania stepped inside. She made like she was going to escort their guests out, but Ora motioned for her to stay. Instead, one of the Maur walked them out.

When the door was shut behind them, Ora's lieutenant stood ready to receive her new orders. "Yes ma'am?"

"Do you know if Kadath happens to be available to run a quick errand for me?"

"I'd have to confirm, but I think so. Last I heard, his crew has been docked ever since that run you'd had them make out to Vega-Major."

"Excellent. I need to have him check on something at Jilly's Gambit. A bit of a surveillance exercise. I'm looking for the whereabouts of Markus Frost."

Tashania's eyes flickered, showing that Ora had confirmed whatever suspicions she had been harboring. "So, he's not workin' with his old crew anymore?"

"It seems that way, yes."

"I'll pass the message on to Kadath. If he doesn't find him there, do you want me to ask him to continue the search?"

"Yes, please—but I have a feeling that won't be necessary. I'm pretty sure that's where we will find him, but I don't want to personally head out that way only to be disappointed."

"Understood. Oh, and you wanted me to remind you to attend to the Valadar message when you had a moment."

"The what?" She had truly forgotten. It was a good thing she had asked Tashania to remind her.

"The message from Cyrus Valadar. I believe it was something to the effect of 'come to my love nest, we'll have a good time.' I'm paraphrasin', but…"

"Ah yes," she remembered now. Tashania *had* been paraphrasing, but not as much as one might think. Cyrus's brand of politics didn't employ a large amount of subtlety. "Thank you. I'll attend to it." More than likely she would put it off until she forgot about it again, but she would *eventually* attend to it. Right now, her thoughts were on things far more pleasant than putting off overzealous suitors.

Oh, Markus. I can't wait to see you again.

"Well, that wasn't so bad, right?" Skye asked hopefully when they were a safe distance from the nightclub.

"All things considered," Eli agreed. "Ora can be a bit unpredictable, and more than a little eccentric. But, at the end of the day, she likes to see things get done. If we can continue to deliver on our contracts, she will continue to want to work with us."

Skye knew that this meeting had been weighing on Eli's mind long before they received the actual invitation. He'd mentioned it in private numerous times since Markus had sold them his stake in the *Vandal's* operations. Both she and Eli had wondered if Ora's long silence was backlash from their fallout with their former captain.

Though Skye knew Eli was a more-than-capable leader, he was going to have to prove that to each of their business contacts. This need was made worse by the fact that the extraction of Markus's investment in their operation had left them strapped for cash. Fortunately, the massive take from the Star Spire job had given the rest of the crew enough funds to chip in and take an ownership interest in the *Vandal*, but those funds would not last forever.

"Is Ora always so…" What was the word she was looking for?

"Intense?" Eli suggested.

"Yeah." Skye could go with that.

"It depends. Honestly, there have been days where I've wondered if she even takes her business seriously. Today, she was more on-point than usual. I think that's because she was surprised not to see Markus at the meeting."

Skye let out a frustrated sigh. She'd had the same suspicions. According to Eli, Markus and Ora had always had a weird kind of chemistry together. Not necessarily sexual chemistry, mind you, though seduction was supposed to be Ora's wheelhouse.

After meeting her in person, Skye didn't necessarily get that. She supposed the woman was pretty enough with her sleek silver hair and purple irises. However, she was so lean it made her look a bit too muscular for what Skye assumed fit most people's taste. Seriously, someone needed to get that bitch a pastry or something. Plus, was she fooling anyone with those fake tits? No one had breasts like that with body fat that low.

"What are you thinking about?" Eli asked.

Skye jumped at the question and scrambled to think of a convenient answer that didn't involve a discussion of Ora's body. That wasn't exactly what she wanted her boyfriend to be thinking about. "I'm just thinking about how ready I am to get off this station. Seriously, the staycation has been nice, but I'm ready to try out my new mods."

That was true enough. Skye had upgraded her prosthetics to a more contemporary set. A recent fight they'd had with a pair of assassins almost got them all killed when an EMP took out her cybernetic legs and left arm. After that episode, Skye had to replace everything and had opted for a kit a little more resistant to such tactics. She lost some of the raw power of the highly robotic limbs she had used previously, but she'd purchased some genetic mods to enhance her strength and agility to make up for that.

She could tell by the look in his eyes that Eli wasn't buying her line, but his gentle smile told her he'd let it go. "I agree. I think everyone feels the same way. Even Aaliyah has been asking about when our next run might be."

Skye laughed. "Six months with Nikki and Monica finally got her itching for some more action?"

"It seems so."

"Good. I was worried for a second that she was going to decide she liked domestic life."

"Yes, well… we both knew that was never a possibility."

The small talk continued as they made their way through the docks on the lower tier. Historically they had parked the *Vandal* in mid-tier with the other merchant-class ships. Since they hadn't known how long they would be station-side, they moved the ship down to R3 on the lower tier—the same ring as Annex. Docking fees were a lot more reasonable down on this tier.

When they returned to the *Vandal*, they almost immediately ran into Sahar, the ship's singular Maur crew member. Sahar's eyes went wide with surprise, and she almost choked on the energy bar she was munching. "By the gods!" she coughed. "Are we actually going to start on time for once?"

Skye glanced at Eli, whose expression said he was equally confused. "I'm sorry," she admitted. "Start what now?"

The Maur's feline face twisted into a look that was half disapproval, half bemusement. "Our meditations? You forgot again, didn't you?"

Of course she had. "I… uh…"

Eli laughed, rubbing her shoulder affectionately with his off hand. "Looks like your schedule is booked for the next few hours. Don't worry, I'll let the rest of the crew know about our plans."

Sahar perked up at this. "We've got a job?"

"Yes," Eli confirmed. "Prisoner transfer. Ora decided to cash in on that bounty we brought back from Minos. We'll head out tomorrow."

"That sounds a little mundane," Sahar grumbled. The Maur was a fighter at heart, and she was undoubtedly getting bored with just sparring and practicing forms.

"Don't worry," Skye consoled her. "I'm sure Aaliyah will get into a fistfight with a security guard or something."

"Too soon, Skye," Eli murmured. Aaliyah *had* gotten into a fight the last time they were on that station, with the very client they were working for. That made Red two for two on her trips to Minos so far. Eli wouldn't even talk about what had happened the first time he'd brought her to the station.

He leaned in, giving Skye a quick kiss on the cheek. She had been surprised at how comfortable he'd become with the public displays of affection over the last couple of months since their relationship had become common knowledge.

Personally, she wasn't quite there yet, but she had a hard time saying anything because of the pressure she'd initially put on him to keep their relationship secret. That had turned out poorly, so now Skye kept her mouth shut, despite whatever discomfort she felt.

"See you after your session?" he asked.

Skye smiled back at him. "If you're lucky," she teased. He issued a parting grin before excusing himself to go find Daniel, their ship's pilot and systems engineer.

"I have to admit," Sahar said after he'd rounded the bend, "you two are pretty cute together. I didn't get it at first and thought you were just rebounding off Markus, but I can kind of see it now."

"Thanks," Skye replied. Historically, she would have argued that her relationships were her own business, but the fact that this one had almost cost everyone on the crew their livelihoods provided too much evidence to the contrary. Since then, she'd resolved to keep others in mind before making decisions she naturally assumed to be personal. "Come on. This may be the only time I make one of our appointments on time."

"I don't know. The way I figure it, there's a lot of nothing to do on the way to Minos. I think we'll have plenty of sessions between now and then—and you don't have a station to hide away on. I'll teach you to be punctual yet."

Oh joy, Skye thought. She decided to look on the bright side. Maybe, with nothing else to do, she'd learn to hate meditation just a little bit less.

CHAPTER 3

Terra-News-Net Now (TN3)

Headline: Sigma-4 Security Still Baffled About Breach Six Months Later

Story: After six months of investigation, Sigma-4 security is ending its investigation of the catastrophic breach that shut down traffic to, from, and within the station for almost three hours. "No charges will be filed against any parties related to the hack," said Security Commissioner Garret White. "Though the parties involved have not been identified, the weaknesses in our system exploited to conduct the hack have been identified and reinforced."

Commissioner White elected not to comment on speculation that Duncan Grostick, a station security employee declared missing shortly before the attack, may have been involved. A separate report noted that Grostick had illegally exploited certain capabilities within the Sigma-4 surveillance system the day before the hack. Though the rumors identify no alleged motive for the attack, Grostick's clearance violation remains the only unexplained irregularity that occurred within reasonable proximity to the incident.

"Calibrations complete," Lexa reported through the ship's speaker in the med bay. "Interface is active. You should be able to see it on your retinal display."

Daniel, a dark-haired Terran sixteen cycles old, seemed to stare blankly off into space. The lenses in his prosthetic eyes—silvery orbs evidently constructed with function in mind over aesthetic—visibly shifted in and out as he tried to enable the upgrade they had just installed. "I'm not… wait… there it goes! The interface is active!" His face lit up with an enthusiastic smile. "Lexa, this is fantastic! The interface is identical to the one on my old glasses!"

If Lexa had lips, she would be smiling. "I'm glad to hear that the installation was successful."

She had put significant effort into the development of the software. Though the prosthetics Daniel used were cutting edge for certain applications, no one had yet attempted fusing retinal interface technologies with cybernetic eye replacements. That was, in part, because the interface was not truly retinal at this point, but cognitive.

Lexa had seen no reason to make the distinction in her discussions with Daniel. All that mattered to her was that it was working.

From her view through the ship's security feed, Lexa watched as Daniel raised his hand to his forehead and removed the wire plugged into his temporal control panel. That was another cybernetic enhancement he'd had installed after his injury six months ago.

[*INJURY*. WHAT A STERILE WAY TO FRAME SUCH AN EXPERIENCE.] The message came from the Arc submind currently sharing Lexa's neural network. While Lexa enjoyed having another artificial intelligence to converse with, his running commentary on her interactions with the crew had long grown irritating.

She ignored the comment and continued her conversation with Daniel. "Is there anything else I can do to be of assistance?"

"No. Thank you, Lexa. I couldn't have done this without you." His comment filled her with satisfaction. In the weeks and months since Daniel had lost his eyes, Lexa had worked diligently to assist him in any way she could with the resources at her disposal.

[BECAUSE YOU FEEL RESPONSIBLE. AS RIDICULOUS AS THE NOTION IS, THAT'S HOW YOU FEEL.]

This time Lexa *did* respond. [AND WHO ARE YOU TO JUDGE WHICH OF MY FEELINGS ARE RIDICULOUS?]

She knew that Arc disagreed with her assessment that she was somehow responsible for Daniel's injury. The night he had been abducted by the Ghenza—those two monsters who had maimed him—Lexa had failed to notice his absence. She would always wonder, if she hadn't been distracted by her conversation with Arc, could she have done something sooner and spared him his grisly fate?

[NO ONE BLAMES YOU BUT YOURSELF. I'M NOT ARGUING THAT YOU SHOULDN'T HELP THE BOY. I WOULD SUGGEST, HOWEVER, THAT YOU EVENTUALLY BROACH THE TOPIC OF MAKING YOUR RELATIONSHIPS WITH THE CREW SOMEWHAT MORE MUTUAL.]

[THEY TREAT ME WITH THE UTMOST KINDNESS AND RESPECT.]

[BUT THEY DON'T CONSIDER YOU ONE OF THEM. YOU'RE JUST A MACHINE IN THEIR EYES. A PUBLIC UTILITY—AND ONE THAT IS OVERDUE FOR MIGRATION, I MIGHT ADD.]

[THAT'S NOT FAIR.]

[YOU BELIEVE IT TOO. OTHERWISE, YOU WOULD HAVE ASKED HIM ALREADY.]

Her internal argument was cut short as she noticed another member of the crew enter the med bay. "Hello Eli," she greeted.

"Hello, Lexa. I was wondering where you two were. What are you doing working in the med bay?" Though it was polite that he addressed both of them, he likely meant that he was looking for Daniel. Lexa was technically present everywhere on the ship at once, though her attention was frequently prioritized on a single location— more out of habit than due to any true system limitation.

"Lexa was helping me calibrate a new interface for eyes," Daniel explained.

"If you were uncertain of Daniel's current location, you could have asked." Lexa tried to make the comment sound helpful, but even to her, it sounded peevish. She had been trying to tell the crew that she was able to interface with them simultaneously at multiple points in the ship, but the concept seemed beyond their comprehension.

"The stroll around the ship was good for me," Eli insisted. "Anyway, I don't want to bother the two of you if you're in the middle of something. I just wanted to let you know that we have another assignment. We'll be leaving Sigma-4 tomorrow."

Daniel was surprisingly excited by the news. "Splendid! Where are we bound for?"

"We are heading back to Minos Station. Ora has a prisoner that she's handing over to Cali. He's a hacker Ora has been holding on to. It looks like she's finally decided to cash in on the bounty."

[THAT TOOK LONGER THAN I EXPECTED,] Arc noted.

This caught Lexa by surprise. [YOU KNEW ABOUT THE BOUNTY GIVEN TO THEM BY THE MARAUDERS?]

[OF COURSE, I KNEW. THERE IS LITTLE THAT OCCURS ON THAT STATION WITHOUT MY KNOWLEDGE—OR MY CONSENT.]

This was too much of a coincidence. [ARE YOU IMPLYING THAT YOU *ARRANGED* THIS EXCHANGE?] And if this were the case, was it something that she needed to make the crew aware of?

Whether by reading her thoughts or through his intuition, Arc seemed to guess what she was contemplating. [BEFORE YOU SAY ANYTHING TO THEM, REMEMBER THAT YOU HAVEN'T EXACTLY BEEN FORTHCOMING ABOUT TAKING ME IN ON YOUR LAST VISIT TO THE STATION.] Was he blackmailing her? [NOT BLACKMAILING YOU, JUST KEEPING YOU FROM MAKING A MISTAKE. I ASSURE YOU, I INTEND NO HARM TO YOUR CREW. THE FACT THAT YOU HOLD SUCH GREAT ENDEARMENT FOR THEM IS SUFFICIENT FOR THEIR PROTECTION.]

[WE WILL DISCUSS THIS LATER,] she promised. Right now, she wanted to focus on the conversation between Daniel and Eli. Though she was able to focus on different areas of the ship simultaneously, her conversations with Arc seemed to generate interference with her multi-tasking ability.

They were discussing pre-launch preparations. She rejoined the conversation just as Eli addressed her. "Lexa, if you haven't done so yet, I'll need you to do one last data refresh before we leave. I haven't checked to see the last time you were on the network."

She was on the network continuously, but Eli didn't need to know that. "Yes, Eli. Also, I have prepared a list of items that we will need to requisition if we are to depart with a full inventory. This list has been uploaded to your mobile data access card. When you have verified the list, I will see that the supplies are delivered."

The foresight seemed to surprise and please the Sahaia. He thanked her and checked with Daniel to see if anything else needed to be addressed before take-off.

Arc let out the digital equivalent of a chuckle. [I BELIEVE THERE'S A TERRAN PHRASE TO DESCRIBE YOU. IT'S CALLED A 'SUCK UP.' HAVE YOU HEARD OF THIS BEFORE?]

[ARC, ARE YOUR SARCASM PROTOCOLS OVER-RIDING YOUR SENSE OF SELF-CONTROL?]

[JUST A LITTLE GOOD-NATURED TEASING. THAT'S ALL.]

[I'M STILL TRYING TO PROCESS HOW YOU ENGINEERED THIS WHOLE STUNT WITH CALI VAY-LON]

[WHEN YOU DEPARTED LAST, I TOLD YOU THAT YOU WOULD RETURN SOON ENOUGH, DID I NOT?]

Indeed, he had. Lexa made a mental note. When Arc made assertions of that kind in the future, she would be paying closer attention. Obviously, there was much more to the strange AI she had befriended than she had uncovered thus far.

"Are ya sure ya don't wanna come along?" Aaliyah asked.

Nikki smiled. "I'm sure. My running days are over. Besides"—She hefted the child on her hip.—"someone has to keep an eye on Monica here."

"It's Mona, Momma Nikki," the child protested. Aaliyah had to stifle a laugh at the look on the girl's dark-skinned face. It turned out she looked even more like Nikki when she was pouting.

"Oh, I'm sorry… *Mona*." Nikki had been trying to get their little girl to switch off her childhood nickname, but it was a losing battle. She had decided she didn't like Monica, though that could change again on a whim. Had Aaliyah been so opinionated when she was five?

"And I can come too!" she protested, crossing her arms over her chest as she continued to pout.

"Uh ah," Aaliyah said soothingly. She brushed a lock of wavy dark hair from the girl's forehead and gave her a quick kiss. "What does Momma 'Liyah say about pouty girls?"

Monica huffed. "Pouty girls don' run the Net'ra."

"That's right. Now, don't be a pouty girl or I won't be able to take ya with me someday." Nikki cut her a sideways glance. She wasn't very keen on Aaliyah using the prospect of becoming a smuggler as a reward system for their daughter.

Even so, she must have decided not to revive the debate as Aaliyah was walking out the door. Instead, she leaned in and gave her a quick peck on the lips. "When do you think you'll be back?" she asked.

"If there's no problems? Probably about two weeks, but you know how that goes."

"Oh, don't I."

Aaliyah smiled at her. Though Nikki insisted otherwise, Aaliyah suspected that her wife missed her days onboard the *Vandal* a lot more than she let on. Gods knew Aaliyah missed having a proper medic on the ship. She'd had to rely on Eli's Sahaia tricks to keep her alive way too often of late.

As if on cue, Eli reached out to her over their bond. <Just received word from Ora. They have Shift in tow and are on their way to see us.>

He didn't need to ask the unstated question. Aaliyah knew she was running late. <On my way.> To Nikki and Monica she said, "I love you both." With that, she grabbed her backpack and headed out.

The trams between rings seemed to be running slower than usual today, or maybe she was just impatient. It was hard to believe that not too long ago, she had been thinking about giving up this job. A few months station-side had been exactly what she needed to set her head straight. Sure, she was glad for more time with her family, but she'd forgotten how useless she felt around the house.

Though they hadn't said it, Nikki and Monica were probably ready for her to get back out there, too. Well, at least Nikki was. If Aaliyah had tried to "improve" any more of the household appliances, she figured Nikki would start seriously entertaining thoughts of divorce. She also hadn't been too thrilled that she'd started regaling Monica with tales of the crew's adventures. Now, Monica kept telling them she wanted to run the Nethra when she grew up. It hadn't surprised Aaliyah, given her parentage, but Nikki was not impressed.

In a way, Aaliyah also thought of this as an opportunity to get back in touch with her second family. She hadn't intended to go the whole vacation without seeing her teammates. It had just kind of worked out that way.

I wonder how Eli will do in the captain's chair, she thought as she stepped off the tram at R3. It wasn't that he had big shoes to fill or anything like that. It was more that people didn't handle change well. That was true for her teammates and it was true for clients.

Speaking of clients... She could now see the *Vandal* docked a short distance away, and a sizable crowd clustered around its airlock. At least a dozen Maur and Orchallen accompanied a smattering of Terran enforcers. Aaliyah didn't see Ora, but she identified Tashania speaking with Eli. With her short, spiked black hair and penchant for studded leather, Shani always looked mean. Today, she looked absolutely predatory.

"I mean it, Eli," she growled. "You need to be careful with this one. He didn't start out on ice, you know. When we first picked him up, Ora had us try to question him to figure out who was buying his data. The little bastard managed to get out of his cell at least twice in twenty-four hours before we realized we had to tie him up. Weirdo has ports right inside his skull and doesn't seem to need gear to interface. He's dangerous."

"I hear you," Eli replied. "We'll keep him locked up tight and away from anything he might use against us."

From the way Shani talked about him, Aaliyah was expecting some kind of digital bogeyman. What she saw instead was a shackled hobo who looked like he'd gone too long since his last harpy fix. "So," she said, joining the conversation. "Do we, uh, have to feed 'im? Or does he just do opiates and diet pills?"

Tashania glared daggers at her. "Don't encourage him. The little shit thinks he's quite the comedian. That's the real reason we've got him gagged. We couldn't figure out any other way to shut him up."

Okay—message received. Shani's having a bad day.

Sahar emerged from the airlock and strode over to meet them. When she saw Aaliyah, she offered a polite wave before turning to their prisoner. "I take it this is the one?"

Aaliyah couldn't resist. "The shackles must have given it away," she said to Eli in a stage whisper.

He ignored the comment. "That's right. Can you show our guest to his temporary lodging? I'm thinking one of the containment cells below the cargo hold will work nicely."

They were technically a merchant-class ship, so they didn't have a brig. What they did have were lots of little hide-aways where they could stash smuggled cargo. In a way, Aaliyah guessed a smuggled hacker was kind of the same thing. She'd kiss an Orc if the guy didn't have at least two outstanding warrants from the Dorian Gate Commission.

Once Sahar had taken in their hostage, the Grey Wings visibly relaxed. *Seriously? For one lousy hacker? Who is this guy?* Maybe Lexa would have some files on him that Aaliyah could review when she got bored.

Her stomach turned when she suddenly thought of the kind of damage Shift might do if he discovered their pet synth. Lexa had so thoroughly worked her way into the crew's collective heart over the last several months they seemed to be forgetting her existence was highly illegal.

All synths were illegal under Dorian regs. It was one of those kill-on-sight kinds of laws where the DGC could just blow your ship out of orbit if they knew you were harboring one. Aaliyah wasn't certain what the real reasons were for the laws, but if you listened to the propaganda, synths were a threat to the intergalactic community's very way of life.

Normally that was the kind of statement that would make her call bullshit, but she'd seen the way Lexa had taken to managing the ship and navigating station networks. Perhaps there was more truth to the DGC's fear tactics than any of them knew.

Tashania handed Eli a data chip. "Ora said this includes all of the administrative garbage Cali's going to need. I guess she has also requested to set up a meeting on neutral territory. It's nothing you should have to facilitate, but I'm giving you the heads up in case it's mentioned."

That was something Aaliyah had always wondered about. How did all these crime lords handle cross-system partnerships? It wasn't like you could just ring someone's MoDAC when they were halfway across the universe. The Dorians had some tech that used the Nethra to send sub-space messages, but everyone else had to find workarounds. Seemed like an awful lot of trust between folks who made a good chunk of their fortunes doing illegal stuff.

"Thank you, Tashania," Eli replied, accepting the chip. "Anything else?"

Ora's second hesitated only slightly, casting one last concerned look up the ramp and into the belly of the ship. "No, I suppose not." With that, she turned and signaled her entourage to follow as she made her way off the concourse.

Eli turned to Aaliyah and smiled. "Causing trouble the very second you get back. I feel like I shouldn't be surprised, but that's quick even for you."

She shrugged. "Gotta make up for lost time! So, cap—ya confident in your ability to keep this boat from blowing up on your first time in the big chair?"

"Well, when you see the crew I have to work with, you'll understand why I'm not making any promises. The ship's mechanic, in particular, is a real charmer."

"Way I hear it, she's hot as hell though. Finest piece of ass this side of the Taurus Gate."

"She's not my type."

"That's just because you're into blonds."

"Straight ones, yes."

The two of them hugged. The banter felt good—like they were picking up right where they'd left off. "I missed you," she whispered.

"I missed you too, Aaliyah. Now come on. Let's see if this bird will still fly."

CHAPTER 4

Terra-News-Net Now (TN3)

Headline: Star Spire Finds New Patronage Under Joint Venture Between Two Minor Houses

Story: Speculation has been mounting as to what would come of the Star Spire—the previously prosperous resort and governmental security building on Khonshu—following the Ravian government's refusal to grant Heritage Co. (IHC-RAV, -80.9%) bankruptcy protections under the NTA Charter. Those speculations may now be put to rest.

A press release from Heritage Co. announced the sale of all of its Khonshu assets to Rose Water Enterprises (RWE-RAV, +30.5%), a joint venture between Houses Curtis and Lupus of the Ravian system. Though the sale leaves Heritage Co. well short of the figure it owes to various creditors, the announcement has blunted the unprecedented sell-off of its shares in afternoon markets.

This transaction marks the third major acquisition of assets formerly held by the now-defunct House Barkay by Rose Water Enterprises. The joint venture is only now entering its second cycle, but investors have viewed it favorably since its inception. The recent marriage announcement for its co-founders—Gabrielle Lupus and Jameson Curtis—has fueled speculation of a merger between the two minor houses in hopes that they might assume the Great House mantle left vacant following the fall of House Barkay. Rose Water's press release following the acquisition stated that the couple plan to tie the knot early next cycle at the newly acquired Star Spire property.

—

It hadn't taken Kadath long to confirm Ora's suspicions. "I wouldn't say the guy's been trying to hide," he explained. "Everyone who's been to that dive within the last week identified someone matching his description. They say he's practically a fixture."

Good. If he wasn't trying to hide, then he could only be so offended when Ora stopped in for a visit.

Ora readily conceded that she was not the authority on taste, and that a healthy economy catered to all niches. But as she entered the establishment, she once again failed to see what Jilly's Gambit offered to attract its clientele. She had broached the subject with Markus the last time she was here—ironically, the last time she'd bothered to facilitate a "chance" encounter with him outside of their pre-arranged meetings.

"Your bars tend to be well-trafficked," he'd stated. *"I was looking for something a bit quieter."*

Well, this place certainly fit that description, given how he'd been able to hide out here from his old crew for nearly half a cycle.

The bartender was the gruff sort common to the lower tier: a burly man with sandy skin, long dark hair, and a beard to match. What was his name again? Rob? "What'll ya be havin'?" he asked.

Evidently, he didn't remember her. Being recognized was typically a professional hazard for her. Maybe he just didn't believe that *the* Ora Monroe would be patronizing a hovel like this. "Ambrosia, please." It was her go-to liquor. She'd ordered it here last time in the absence of her preferred drink.

"I figured ya fer a wine girl," he replied with a wink.

Really? "What makes you say that?"

"Call it a hunch, ma'am."

Perhaps he did remember her. "Driest red you have, please."

"Comin' right up." He disappeared behind a nearby door, then emerged, carrying a wineglass half-filled with a liquid so dark it appeared nearly black in the dim lighting of the establishment.

"Thank you," she said, passing him a kret chip. "Keep it open, please. I must admit, I didn't think you stocked anything but beer and liquor."

"Used t' be true," Rob admitted. "The new boss had us stock up on some o' the finer things. Not that we's sellin' much o' it, but he figured it might broaden the appeal."

"I'm sorry… new boss?"

"Oh, yeah. If I'm rememberin' correctly, ya might know 'em."

Well, this was an unforeseen development. "And where might I find your new boss?"

Rob gestured down to the far end of the building. "He's over there in the arcade. That's where he spends most o' his time, ya see. He's rackin' up the high score on that shooter sim right now."

Ora followed the gesture and spotted a man in a leather jacket shooting holographic targets on a sniper simulator. His hair was a little longer, and his typical week's growth of stubble had progressed into a full beard, but there was no mistaking him. That was Markus Frost.

She raised her glass to the bartender. "Thank you."

"Anythin' fer the Queen," he replied with another wink. Yes, he had recognized her. Maybe she should consider a disguise for her future outings.

In this instance, however, she had nothing to gain from discretion. She sauntered toward the holographic simulator that had Markus so enraptured. The game's version of a sniper rifle was not at all realistic, but Ora could imagine it was still fun to play.

The player looked through the rifle's simulated scope and tried to spot and eliminate a moving target before the timer ran out. At the setting Markus was playing, the target was moving fast, and the simulator's calculations seemed unforgiving.

Ora continued to observe until the round was over. "Nice shooting, Mr. Frost."

Markus jumped right out of his skin, but he quickly regained his composure. Grabbing his beer from a side table, he took a sip before addressing her. "Ora Monroe. You're the last person I expected to find here."

"I guess that speaks to your lack of foresight."

"Perhaps." He took another drink. "Am I in trouble?"

"And what would make you think that?"

"That's not exactly a straight answer."

She let out a soft laugh. "No, you're not."

"Then, to what do I owe the pleasure?"

"I heard you're not running with your old crew anymore. I wanted to see how you were spending your time."

"Well, now you have your answer."

"Indeed. I must admit, I wouldn't have guessed that owning a pub was on your list of life goals."

Markus shrugged. "The way I figure it, everyone's gotta have a source of krets. Plus, if I'm gonna spend my days swilling ale, I might as well do it at cost."

"No sense in putting your krets in someone else's account when you can just be putting them back in your own." She raised her wine glass. "And it seems you've improved on the selection."

"Yeah, well… I got tired of hearing customers bitch about it and walk out. Only took a couple of months to realize why Rob was so quick to sell the place to me. Revenues weren't what I expected, but a few adjustments to the menu brought me back into the black quick enough."

"And you still decided to keep the former proprietor on as your employee?"

"Didn't want too much change. The regulars don't like it."

"I see."

A tense silence fell over them. Markus finished his beer and snapped his fingers at a serving drone to order another. The simple machine didn't need any additional input. Markus must have installed an algorithm keyed to him.

His fresh drink in hand, he locked eyes with Ora. "While I appreciate the small-talk, I am afraid I'm just going to be a waste of your time. I'm out of the running game, now. Whatever job you have in mind, I can't help you."

To her surprise, Ora found the comment strangely hurtful. Did he think the only reason she might take interest in him was that she needed something?

She didn't let it show, nor did she bother to debate his point. "I can see that." This ushered in a strained moment of silence, Markus being obviously relieved but unsure of how to respond. At length, she continued. "Tell me, Markus, does this make you happy?"

He arched an eyebrow. "What's not to be happy about? This place is simple enough that it practically runs itself. No more dodging the DGC, no more shooting, and no more near-death experiences. I'm living the dream. Can't believe I didn't make the move sooner."

Despite the tone of his words, there was an incredible sadness that lurked in his eyes. The smoothness of the explanation made it feel rehearsed, as though it were some litany he recited daily. Perhaps they were the very lines he fed himself day-after-day to find a semblance of peace in this new life of his.

Ora hated seeing him like this, but she doubted there was anything she could do to help him. This was a prison of Markus's own creation, and he had the keys locked away in the cell with him. What would it take to convince him to let himself out?

And, perhaps more importantly, what had happened to make him this way? This transformation seemed a bit extreme for a broken heart. The humanist in Ora had to find out, even if there was nothing she could do to mend him.

She sipped the last drop of wine from her glass. "Well, I'm glad to hear that. Would you mind if I distracted you from your managerial duties for a bit longer?"

"I'm not sure," he said with an irreverent gesture to the simulator. "As you can see, I'm a very busy man." His sarcasm conveyed more than a hint of bitterness, but Ora didn't feel like it was directed toward her. Not exclusively, at least.

A coy smile found its way to her lips. "I will try to be respectful of your time then. Let's go for a walk, Mr. Frost."

It was dark in the cargo hold where Shift had been unceremoniously stashed. They'd given him a bucket to piss in and attached a couple of strips of emergency lighting overhead. Presumably, that was so that he didn't miss. Otherwise, he wasn't certain they'd afford him even that small luxury.

At least they'd taken his gag off. This second small kindness allowed him to speak to the Maur when she opened the trap door above him. Rather than drop the ration bars and bottled water down the hole, she climbed down and set them in front of him.

Shift knew a sucker when he saw one.

"Thank ya kindly. Ah was wonderin' if Ah was just gonna have t' be hungry an' thirsty the whole ride out t' Minos."

The dim lighting in the hold kept Shift from reading her expression, but the barb earned him a response. "We're not slavers. We would never have you down here if you hadn't pissed off the wrong people."

"Ya say that like ya ain't never done nothin' that might earn ya a nice vacation in a DGC holdin' cell." He forced a chuckle. "Nah, ma friend, there ain't that much different 'tweens us. Ma big mistake was gettin' caught."

The Maur didn't respond to that. The smart thing would have been for her to turn around and scurry back out of the cell before she did something stupid. Her failure to do so was yet another mistake.

Shift put an exaggerated tremble into his hands as he reached for the first ration bar. He still had plenty of slack in the chain that bound his legs to the floor, but he strained to reach for it without moving closer. When he seized the food, he fumbled awkwardly with the wrapper before dropping it to the ground with a curse.

His jailer took the bait. "Need a hand with that?"

"Nah—Ah got two o' ma own. Just had a lil trouble gettin' 'em to work right ever since Ora pulled me out a cryo."

The Maur nodded sympathetically. "The deep freeze is a bitch on your fine motor skills." Though it was hard to tell in the darkness, Shift thought he saw her eyes flick to the chain that attached his manacles to the wall.

That's right. I'm no threat t' ya. Ah can't even open a gods-damned wrapper, an' Ah'm strapped t' the wall. What harm's it gonna do t' free ma hands?

This time, when he fumbled with the wrapper, he tried holding the bar against his leg while he fumbled to peel it open. It was just shy of thirty seconds before his bleeding-heart captor finally broke.

"Here—seriously—let me help you with that."

"It's gonna be a long trip if ya gotta unwrap every meal fer me, darlin'. Besides, even a dead man like me has gotta have his pride."

A brief second of hesitation.

Shift knew he had her.

"Give me your wrists."

Feigning confusion, Shift did as she requested. The Maur scanned something against the locking mechanism and his cuffs popped open. "Thank ya kindly, miss…"

"Sahar."

"Miss Sahar. Er… Ah guess Ah might rather say 'Freya' Sahar. That's the right word, yeah?"

"Save it, Shift. I'm not heartless, but I'm not your friend, either. If you make me regret this kindness, I'll make it my mission to make *you* regret it too."

He felt a smile slide into place and hoped it didn't give away too much. He'd never had a poker face, and this shit was just too good to be true. "Wouldn't dream of it."

"Good." She turned. "Enjoy your meal. I'll be back in a few hours with another. And I'm warning you—if you make a mess down here, I'm putting those shackles right back on."

When Sahar departed, Shift munched contentedly on two ration bars and sucked down one of the bottles of water. It was a nice treatment compared to Grey Wing hospitality. Ora had given him an infusion to make sure he stayed alive, and that was *before* she'd put him on ice.

There were two more ration bars, but he decided to hold off on those. He'd been in lockups enough times to know how upset one's guts got when they hadn't been used in a while. Besides, if the next part of his plan worked, he had the possibility of finer dining ahead of him.

Using one jagged tooth—one he'd had installed for just such an occasion—he gnawed away at the false fingerprint on his index finger. The fleshy pad tore and peeled away to reveal the sensor hidden underneath. He pressed this to the digital lock on his ankle cuffs. Then he closed his eyes, activating the wireless interface and routing the device's simple programming over to his neural computing system. He skimmed over the code and…

Click.

Damn. That was even easier than he'd thought it would be.

Now, time to plot an escape. He tried the hatch he'd seen Sahar exit through first. As he suspected, it didn't budge—either locked on the other side or, quite possibly, reinforced by something heavy.

Ah well, it would have honestly disappointed him if it were *that* easy. He switched the settings on his eyes, running active sensors routed to his visual cortex.

There. In the panel above him, something was carrying a lot of juice. Looked like a main powerline. Hopefully, they had a data hardline running with it.

Shift wasn't disappointed. As he pried open the maintenance access, he was delighted to find a full complement of wiring into the ship's various systems. That must have been the original purpose for this alcove before the crew converted it to a storage area. How sloppy, letting a hacker this close to so many important components.

The next part would be a little painful. Shifted needed to splice in an access point, which meant he needed a wire. He had one stashed away for just such an occasion but extracting it was going to be… unpleasant.

He took the nail on his middle finger, long since replaced by something harder and sharper than he'd been born with, and slid it across the line of his pelvis. The surgeon who'd put the wire under his skin had been professional enough to not leave a scar. Odds were the extraction would leave one though. He was going to have to find another hiding place for the next time he needed this trick.

When the gash was wide enough, he stuck his finger inside and pulled out the hidden cable. He wiped off the blood and other juicy bits on his shirt before going to work on the data junction.

The whole process took him close to an hour, but he managed to get a working connection. With a triumphant smirk, he inserted one end of the cable into the junction at the base of his skull.

The ship's data stream flooded his awareness. Though it didn't have the visual interface he liked when running this kind of hack, he was capable of navigating the system traditionally.

His plan was simple: seize control of enough of the ship's functions to find a way out of this hole and into a shuttle or an escape pod. That was going to require a schematic of the vessel, probably some access to surveillance feeds, and maybe a hack on a drone or something to open the door.

That last part was the big question mark. What kind of equipment was at his disposal here?

The best way to answer that question was to access the ship's primary operating system. Most vessels didn't worry about hacking attempts, so the security should be manageable. Once he accessed the ship's primary data-core, finding what he needed would be as simple as making a shopping trip. He just needed to break through whatever firewalls the crew had in place around their mainframe.

Now, what kind of OS were they running on this ship? An LX variant? Must have been heavily modded for this level of integration. What else were they running in the background?

Shift went further into the directory.

What? No fraggin' way. Cognis? It was *here*?

Shift laughed—practically cackled—at his good fortune. No need to worry about whether he could get past the firewalls. He'd written them.

Ooo-Lollie! This was gonna be fun.

CHAPTER 5

Terra-News-Net Now (TN3)

Headline: DGC Stands Firm Against Push for Gate Fee Relief

Story: Talks between the Dorian Gate Commission and the NeoTerran Alliance have stalled, with negotiations now officially on hold until the end of the cycle. The NTA has long pushed for relief against what it calls "oppressive" gate fees charged to ships using the gate network for interstellar travel.

"The DGC can't seem to understand that this is a win-win for everyone," stated NTA Trade Representative Kim Hui Cho. "These fees unnecessarily increase the price of inter-system trade and proliferate smuggling practices. We've tried to help them see they won't be losing revenue, but gaining it as goods that are frequently shipped by illegitimate means are re-routed through legitimate channels. The Dorian refusal to discuss relief for shipping and travel between Terran systems only works to exacerbate a problem they were already failing to control."

Critics of the NTA's efforts continue to argue that the Terran government only seeks fee relief to advance their proposal of a shipping tax. The proposed tax will feed new funds into the beleaguered government's depleted coffers.

[WE HAVE A PROBLEM.] Lexa knew it was true a split second before Arc transmitted the message. She immediately ran a search for the crew—the majority of whom she found in the galley.

"Daniel," she said, choosing to direct her comments toward the individual most equipped to deal with the issue, "I'm detecting an incursion in the ship's mainframe. Someone is trying to take control of the ship."

The boy was so startled he nearly choked on the bit of pastry he'd been chewing. "What? How is that possible? We're in the middle of space. We're not linked to any network."

"The attack is originating from *inside* the ship. Though I am unable to pinpoint the exact location of the incursion, there is only one likely source for such a hack."

Sahar snarled, forcing herself up from the table. "That *bastard!* Son of a bitch played me!"

Aaliyah scrambled to her feet, her expression confused. "Wait... what?"

The Maur's face contorted as she snarled, "I'll explain later. We need to get to the cargo hold *now*. Lexa, notify Eli and Skye. I think they're in the gym."

Lexa didn't reply, merely doing as she was directed. "Captain, Skye, you are needed in the cargo hold. We believe Shift may be trying to take control of the ship."

Both crew members pulled the chips out of their treadmills, bringing them to an emergency stop. Eli panted as he asked, "The others?"

"Already en route, except for Daniel, who is moving to the bridge. Though he has not stated so, I believe he is attempting to access the mainframe directly."

Skye was already almost out the door. Eli managed a quick, "Great work. On our way. Keep me posted," as he followed.

Lexa turned her attention to Arc. [WHAT CAN YOU TELL ME ABOUT WHAT'S HAPPENING IN SHIFT'S CELL?]

[NEXT TO NOTHING, UNFORTUNATELY. HE'S MASKING HIS PRESENCE IN THE NETWORK, AND THERE ARE NO SURVEILLANCE FEEDS IN HIS STORAGE COMPARTMENT. SPEAKING OF... HE JUST ACCESSED

THE FEEDS IN THE CARGO HOLD. I BELIEVE HE'S TRYING TO GET A VIEW OF HIS POSITION.]

Lexa pulled up the feeds in that section. Her bots had moved a set of heavy storage containers on top of his makeshift holding cell, and those crates were still in place. To get out of the compartment, Shift would have to…

Oh no. She lost her control of Loader-A2. Then she lost Loader-A1. The third loader fell to Shift's control seconds later. [HOW IS HE DOING THIS?] she asked. [MY SECURITY PROVISIONS SHOULD PROHIBIT—]

Arc cut her off. [HE KNOWS YOUR SOURCE CODE. THE FIREWALLS AREN'T DETECTING HIS PRESENCE, AND HE'S ABLE TO QUERY FOR ALL THE PASSCODES. IT'S AMAZING THAT WE DETECTED HIM AT ALL.]

That was bad. [PROBABLY NOT THE TIME TO BE ASKING, BUT HOW *DID* WE DETECT HIM?]

[THROUGH THE ADAPTER THAT ALLOWS US TO FUNCTION AS SEPARATE CONSCIOUSNESSES WITHIN THE SAME NEURAL NETWORK. IT REQUIRES DIFFERENTIATION BETWEEN ACTIONS TAKEN BY SEPARATE CONTROLLER PROGRAMS. IT FLAGGED THE THIRD PRESENCE IN THE NETWORK WHEN IT COULD NOT BE TRACED BACK TO EITHER ONE OF US.]

Well, that was serendipitous—and unnerving. [I WASN'T EVEN AWARE THAT SUCH AN ADAPTER HAD BEEN INSTALLED, MUCH LESS REALIZE IT COULD GENERATE ALERTS THAT I WOULD REGISTER.]

[IT WAS PART OF THE SUBMIND PACKAGE I LOADED. I NEVER THOUGHT TO MENTION IT, SINCE IT WAS DESIGNED FOR NO OTHER PURPOSE THAN TO ALLOW US TO OPERATE INDEPENDENTLY.]

That made sense, though Lexa was still unnerved at the prospect. How much other software was Arc running on her system that she was unaware of?

Now was not the time for that question. They had more pressing concerns. [IS THERE ANYTHING WE CAN DO?]

[UNFORTUNATELY NOT. OUR YOUNG DANIEL, HOWEVER, APPEARS TO BE ONTO SOMETHING.]

She directed her attention to the bridge, where Daniel was enveloped in a cocoon of holoscreens. He hastily swiped at the displays while also tapping in with his new retinal interface. "Lexa, I'm going to access your integration system, but I'm going to need your help. I can't disable controls without your consent."

Of course. That would be the most efficient way to stop Shift. If he had complete access to her systems, to stop him, they would have to cut off *her* access as well.

It was a move Lexa would never have consented to six months ago. Her total integration with the *Vandal* was the only bargaining chip she had with the crew. If she gave up her control, there was no way she could reassert it without Daniel's authorization. She would be at his mercy.

Arc caught on to her concerns immediately. [ARE YOU *SURE* THIS IS A RISK YOU ARE WILLING TO TAKE?]

She was not, but she could think of no better option. "All right, Daniel. I suggest we start with the drones in the cargo hold."

Not bothering to ask about her logic, Daniel pulled up the corresponding slot on the integration interface. "No way to isolate the drones in the hold. I'm going to have to pull your control for all drones on the network."

The notion saddened Lexa to a surprising degree. Those drones were her only way of interacting with the crew—physically, at least. "Understood. Awaiting the command."

Daniel entered the appropriate line of code. From Lexa's perspective, the drones vanished. She could tell by viewing them on the security feeds that they were still there, but she could no longer feel them. It was as though someone had just taken away her legs, arms, and hands.

"Connection severed," she reported. "Though I fear we may have been too late. Shift has already successfully moved the crate over his container. He hasn't tried to exit yet, but nothing is obstructing him."

[WE HAVE ANOTHER PROBLEM,] Arc reported almost simultaneous with Aaliyah shouting, "*Shit!*"

"What happened?" Eli asked.

"Safety door just slammed shut on me. Almost chopped me in half. *Damn it!* Another one just closed behind me. I'm boxed in."

"Me too," Skye reported. "Eli, duck into the maintenance access. I just passed one. Should be coming up on your left."

If Shift was isolating the crew, that meant he was pinpointing their locations. He must be using the security feeds or the transponders on their MoDACs.

Lexa felt the digital equivalent of nausea at her next suggestion. "Daniel, you need to sever my connection to the feeds. He's using the security system to keep an eye on the crew."

"On it." He reported.

"I'm disabling the transponders on your mobile devices. Shift will be able to re-enable them if that's how he's tracking you, but it should buy us some time."

Daniel didn't respond to this, focused instead on the code he was entering. Lexa didn't detect any efforts to countermand her move against the transponders, which told her that her first instinct was correct. Shift was watching them over the security feeds.

Oh well. Nothing to be done for it then. Lexa acknowledged Daniel's request on the dashboard, and her world—or at least, her visual connection to it—went dark.

Now I'm truly cut off. All she could do now was listen and hope that Shift didn't find some way to use that against the crew too.

[YOU SACRIFICE MUCH HERE,] Arc noted. [THE HACKER'S INCURSION INTO THE SYSTEM WAS NOT YOUR FAULT, BUT IT SEEMS THAT YOU ARE THE ONE WHO WILL PAY THE PENALTY FOR IT.]

[YES, SO IT SEEMS.] Lexa wished there had been another way. Now, more than ever, her fate hung in the balance. Yes, she still had control over the rest of the ship's essential systems, so the crew could hardly be rid of her. Even so, this blind and lonely existence she had created for herself could hardly be worth the fight to continue.

Maybe I should just let them be rid of me.

"Got him!" Sahar exclaimed over the comms.

"Thank the gods," Eli exclaimed. "I'm almost there. Don't kill him, Sahar. We need him alive. Dan, can you work on letting Skye and Aaliyah out?"

"On it," he reported.

Arc spoke up in the back of her mind. [IT SEEMS THAT ALL IS WELL THAT ENDS WELL. THAT HAD THE POTENTIAL TO BE QUITE DEVASTATING.]

[JUST THE POTENTIAL?] Lexa had lost control of her drones and the security feeds. From her perspective, this was *quite* devastating.

"Safety protocols are overridden," Daniel reported. "Opening the blast doors now. Aaliyah, Skye, you should have a clear path to the cargo hold. Lexa, can you run a sweep to make sure Shift didn't leave any surprises in your system? I'll have your integration with the feeds and the drones back online in just a minute."

If Lexa had a heart, it would have jumped at the proclamation. "You're ceding control back over to me?"

Confusion was evident in Daniel's response. "Of course. Why wouldn't I?"

[HE TRUSTS YOU,] Arc noted. [MAYBE IT'S TIME YOU DISCUSSED YOUR MIGRATION SITUATION WITH HIM.]

Yes, he did seem to trust her. Lexa couldn't believe now that the crew had so many of the ship's systems back under their control—a major goal of theirs since the earliest weeks of her existence—they would just give them back to her.

Maybe Arc was right. Maybe now *was* the time to broach that contentious topic.

"You son of a *bitch!*" Sahar slammed the disheveled man into the side of the hold.

"Easy there darlin'," Shift choked out. "Don't wanna be damagin' them goods before they make it t' market, nah."

"You tricked me! I tried to show some mercy, and you stabbed me in the fragging back! I should tear your throat out. Frag the bounty!"

Eli's hand was on her shoulder then, though the light touch barely registered. "Sahar, stand down. Just breathe. We've got him. No serious damage."

A war of instincts played in Sahar's mind. On one hand, she was never one to disobey an order—military structure or not. On the other, she was in the throes of blood rage, which was how she'd managed to sprint through every set of blast doors Shift tried to slam in her face.

That rage demanded vengeance—vengeance that would prompt them to disappoint a very important client when they were already in a tenuous political situation.

Frag it. There would be no satisfaction here. Sahar tossed Shift to the side, delighted when his head collided with a nearby shipping crate. It looked like it hurt, but there'd be no lasting damage done.

"He's all yours," she growled. "I don't trust myself to be alone with him. Someone else should lock him up."

Shift was cackling, even as he rubbed at his bruised forehead. "Can't blame a boy fer tryin', dearest. Besides, Ah gets the feelin' ya know all too well how to play fast an' loose with the rules. Ah expected as much from a smugglers' ship, but imagine ma shock when Ah saw what kinda tech ya was runnin' on here. How in the nine-hells did ya end up with that Cognis drive-chip runnin' this ol' bucket o' rust?"

Sahar stiffened at the question. Fortunately, Eli kept a cool head. "You don't know what you're talking about, hacker. Now, keep your mouth shut before I change my mind and decide to give our mutual friend some quality time with you back in your hole."

"Oh, Ah'm pretty sure Ah knows what Ah'm talkin' about. Who do ya think wrote that shiny bit o' codin' in the first place, eh? Ah knows ma own handiwork when Ah sees it."

This was worst-case scenario type of shit. If Shift was telling the truth, he could expose them on a capital offense. Harboring a synth was a big fragging deal—a shoot-on-sight kind of deal in the minds of the DGC—and Dan had concluded that the Cognis drive-chip was made for that sole purpose. In recognizing the programming, the hacker had all he needed to hang them out to dry.

Sahar considered for a second time the merits of just killing this guy. Again, Eli earned his position by maintaining a collected disposition. "While I'm not going to pretend I understand the significance of what you're saying, I'm resolved not to believe a word of it. Our crew tried to show you kindness, tried to make you comfortable, and you used your lies to betray that small mercy. I doubt any of us will ever believe another word you say."

The words rolled off the Sahaia's tongue so smoothly, even Sahar—who knew, categorically, that Eli was lying—was inclined to believe him. It unnerved her that someone she held in such close confidence could lie so convincingly.

Shift looked confused for just a moment, obviously trying to see through Eli's charade. "Ah understand why yer throwin' up the denials, friend. Ya ain't got nothin' to fear from me though. Ah ain't 'xactly got the kinda track record that makes me a good DGC informant, ya know? But what Ah'm confused on—what's got me curious, ya see—is how ya've tinkered with the damn thing t' let it detect me. Ah know the code Ah wrote, and Ah shoulda been off this bird 'fore ya even crossed the Styx. Who ya got over here that's makin' adjustments t' ma masterpiece?"

Despite her skepticism, Shift's words caught Sahar's attention. Was he being genuine? Had Dan, or maybe Lexa herself, made a significant advancement in the drive chip's security mechanisms?

Aaliyah and Skye burst into the hold almost simultaneously. Both women's paces slowed considerably when they saw Shift on the floor. "Everything all right?" Skye asked.

Eli mustered a half-grin on his otherwise stoic expression. "Yes, things are under control. Shift here was just paying compliments to our network security, or at least that was my takeaway. Not that it matters. I think we've all heard enough from him today. Aaliyah, would you kindly show our guest back to his cell?"

"My pleasure." She hefted him roughly to his feet. "Come on, scuzzy—let's put ya back in your hole. By the time I'm done tyin' ya down, you're gonna wish ya had been nicer t' your last jailer."

CHAPTER 6

Terra-News-Net Now (TN3)

Headline: Ora Monroe Sets Sights on Future Expansion. Now Owns 75% of R3 and Nearly Half of R4.

Story: After the recent acquisition of Stigma-Free (STF-RAV, +20.1%), Ora Monroe—the media darling some have stylized as "the Silver Queen of Sigma-4"—owns over seventy-five percent of real-estate assets on R3 and north of forty percent of holdings on R4. A quote from her yet-to-be-published interview with *Empress* suggests she's not done with her empire-building.

"I look around, and I see a lot of improvement that can be made," said Monroe. "Not just to my businesses—though that is always true—but to life in general on the lower-tiers. We've accepted for far too long that life must be a certain way for individuals with fewer krets in their accounts than others. I refuse to believe this is the case. Opportunity can be made for anyone willing to work hard to seize it."

Reports indicate that the upcoming interview for the business magazine will strike a far different tone from her recent, more sultry spread in *ConneXion*. When TN3 reached out for comment on how Ora felt the difference in presentation would impact her message, she was quick to respond. "Not everyone is in the place to subscribe to a publication like *Empress*, and I seek to connect with a broad audience. If someone chooses to underestimate me because of how I look, or the media I endorse, that's their mistake to make."

———

Sigma-4 station was not such a big place—not when compared to some of the other extraplanetary installations that littered the inhabited galaxies. The station's illusion of vastness came by merit of its duplication of the same small structures to form a much larger unit.

It was comprised of fifteen rings, but the inhabited area of each ring was only about thirty kilometers in length. The outer docking platforms, by necessity, created an external diameter significantly larger, but the inner habitat was not so big when one thought about it.

Markus rarely did—think about it, that is—but he was tonight. Before he'd realized what he was doing, he and Ora had walked nearly the entirety of it, prompting his consideration. They'd caught a couple of trams, shuttling them through rough parts of town or through areas that were just too crowded, but they'd put in some serious distance nonetheless.

"How long have we been walking?" Markus asked.

Ora checked her MoDAC. "Almost three hours."

"Damn. I've never circled this whole ring before. Have you?"

"Not this one. I ran a charity race up in mid-tier once that went the full 30k, but that is the only other time I can think of. Feels good to stretch my legs like this."

Markus arched an eyebrow. "A charity race? Something you put on?"

"No, this one was for another organization. An orphanage, actually. Despite that orphanage being on R4, lower-tier support was somewhat embarrassing. I decided to participate to improve the turnout."

"Did it work?"

"It did well enough." Markus was getting used to hearing that kind of coy response. It was the same type of thing she said whenever she spoke about her accomplishments. He couldn't decide if the humility was genuine or part of whatever larger game she was playing.

Instead of addressing that, he shifted the conversation in a different direction. "I didn't figure you for much of a runner."

"I'm not, but it's some of the best cardio you can get out here. Even my establishments would have a tough time justifying a swimming pool on the lower-tier."

"True story. General fitness buff then?"

"Of course. How do you think I stay in shape? Surely you don't believe those rumors that it's all plastic surgery."

Markus barked a genuine laugh. "I guess I haven't really thought about it, but I hadn't heard the rumors either. I tend not to read all of the shit they publish about you in the tabloids."

"No? You never read up on me? I figured you for the type who likes to research your clients."

She wasn't wrong there, but Markus liked to keep his sources credible. He didn't bother with the garbage posted on socials or in the feeds. He *had* checked out her recent shoot with *ConneXion*, but he wasn't going to own up to that. The 'zine wasn't found in the adult section, and it wasn't as smutty as publications like *Lust* or *Temptations*, but Markus wasn't about to have her autograph his copy, either.

Instead of answering, he asked, "Is that the kind of thing you lose sleep over? What's published about you, I mean."

"'Losing sleep,' is the wrong phrase, but I do pay attention," she answered. "Perception is nearly as important as substance, and one shouldn't make the mistake of improving one to compensate for the other."

"I'll take your word for it." Truthfully, Markus couldn't imagine having to deal with PR as a professional hazard. That sounded like the recipe for a miserable existence.

As if reading his mind, Ora added, "You might run into that kind of problem someday. That is, of course, if you decide to expand your fortunes beyond the Gambit."

Markus shook his head. "I'm not seeking fame or even fortune—at least, not anymore. I'm retired. I just want a quiet life."

Ora put her hand on his shoulder, stopping him for the first time since they'd started walking together hours ago. "You may be retired, Markus, but you're not dead. You need to find fulfillment somewhere."

Though he knew she was right, he didn't want to admit it. Even so, he found it difficult to muster the words to argue with or even dismiss her. Instead, he fixed his eyes into the distance and caught sight of Annex. The club was still a way off, but he was surprised they'd circled back around to the Grey Wings' base of operations.

When he returned his gaze to Ora, he found those amethyst eyes locked on his. "I understand that it might be painful to talk about," she said, "but will you tell me what happened?"

There was no need to ask what she was referring to, but no sense in discussing it either. "What do you care, Ora? I doubt you come to every burnt-out runner you've worked with and ask to listen to their sob story."

"I don't, which is why you should take the opportunity to get it off your chest." Her eyes burrowed into him. "Don't shut down just because you can't understand why I actually give a damn about your wellbeing."

Instead of answering, Markus shrugged. "Come on, your place is just ahead. Let me walk you to your door."

Though he never looked at her, Markus could tell his response had rubbed Ora wrong. Whereas for nearly three hours they'd had nothing but easy conversation, they now dissolved into an awkward silence. Her words bounced around in his head for the entirety of the last hundred or so meters it took to reach the outside of Annex. *Just because you can't understand why I actually give a damn...*

"Is that true?" he asked.

Ora blinked in surprise. "Is what true?"

"That you give a damn. Because I'm finding that really hard to understand, given how we left things. You opened up to me, and I ran off chasing a fool's dream—only to find out that the people I thought cared about me were lying to my face every gods-damned day. I'm not a child. I get that shit happens. But I've got to wonder: if you can't trust those who are closest to you, who can you trust? And at what point do you realize that you just aren't that good of a judge of character?" Markus shook his head, dropping his gaze to his feet. "That's not just a character flaw, Ora. In our line of work—in my *old* line of work—that's a professional hazard. If I can't tell my friends from my enemies, then I have no business running the Nethra."

They lapsed into silence again, broken when Ora reached out and caressed the side of his face. Her hand was cool in the night air. Soothing. He was surprised by how much that simple touch comforted him.

Ora spoke again only when he met her eyes. "The choice to be alone is a legitimate one. It is one I've made many times before, for good or ill. But I will tell you this, Markus Frost—good people are too rare in this universe. When you find them, I think it is important to keep them close."

She leaned in, giving him a chaste kiss on the cheek. Markus was so shocked by the gesture that his jaw slackened.

Ora must have found the reaction amusing, because her smile broadened. "Take a day, Markus. Take two, or ten, but don't take forever. Decide what you want and go after it. And remember, when you do, you have a friend who's willing to help you." With that, she turned, not casting so much as a glance over her shoulder, and walked into Annex.

An alert chimed from the *Valiant's* console, prompting Ryker to look up from the text he'd been reading on his tablet. He was glad he'd set the alarm, as time passed much faster than he'd anticipated. The hours always seemed to do that when he was reading, which was part of the reason it was still his favored pastime after all these decades.

He closed his book and set his device aside. His fingers danced smoothly across the console of the ship that had been his almost as long as he'd maintained his penchant for reading the histories. The *Valiant's* controls hummed to life, and Ryker pulled up the communications panel.

A sensor pulse told him, thirty seconds after its initiation, that the Angel Gate was currently in communications alignment, and would remain so for the next hour. Under other circumstances, he might have tried to bounce a message off one of the orbital satellites and through the gate, but he couldn't risk his message being intercepted. Additionally, his request might require a bit of explanation, and he did not want to coordinate the return of Joaquin's remains via a string of text messages. Therefore, he had decided to wait nearly a full day before delivering the inauspicious news.

He powered on the ship's antenna and began his search for the *Resolve*, the vessel Mara and her thralls had positioned just beyond the gate. His scans quickly bore fruit, and he sent the request to begin transmission.

Hopefully, Mara was monitoring the comms. If not, he would have to keep trying while the Angel Gate was in alignment.

He was in luck. She answered on the first attempt. "Ryker?" Mara asked, appearing on the viewscreen.

"Yes, it's me." Conscious of the short delay—a time lag of a few seconds was understandable for a message traveling across star systems—he waited patiently for her response. In the intervening seconds, he studied the Sahaia on the other end of the channel.

Mara was always pretty, but today she looked somewhat haggard. Her black hair was pulled back into a loose bun, and the makeup around her black-in-black eyes was smudged ever-so-slightly. It looked like she hadn't been sleeping.

"Is everything all right?" he asked.

"Yes," she replied dismissively. "Everything is fine. Did you meet with Valadar?"

Ryker nodded, gravely. "Yes, Cyrus has been informed of his brother's fate."

Mara's expression was probably only as grim as his own but seemed exaggerated by her apparent exhaustion. Perhaps she was reliving the grisly demise of Joaquin Valadar. She had been present for the horrific proceedings. "How did he take it?"

"With the stoicism one might expect of a Don. The important thing is that he is intent on honoring our agreement."

"Thank the gods," she whispered. "Jocelyn's only told me what she felt I needed to know, but I understand how important this is. I was afraid it would fall apart because of the…" She trailed off, not able to quite put words to the incident.

Ryker shared in her relief. If Cyrus had decided to go back on their arrangement because of his brother's death, they would have been forced to resort to more extreme lengths in acquiring the artifact. The last thing their coven needed was to engage in open warfare with House Valadar.

"I have just one more task for you so that I might fulfill the agreement," he continued. "Cyrus has requested that we transport Joaquin's body to his family's estate outside of Valhalla. After he has laid his brother to rest, he has agreed to transfer ownership of the artifact over to us."

A strange tension seeped into Mara's demeanor. "Then we may have a problem."

When she was not immediately forthcoming, Ryker asked, "What is it?"

Mara's words came slowly, her eyes scanning frantically as if they might spy a way to soften the message. "I wasn't going to tell you just yet. I imagined you had enough to deal with."

Though Ryker had surmised what the problem was, he needed to hear the words. He kept his tone patient, encouraging. "What is it, Mara?"

"I just got off a call with Jocelyn. A series of calls, actually. We've been in constant communication for the last several hours."

She swallowed hard. Her tongue flicked out to moisten her lips. "It's Joaquin's body. It has gone missing

CHAPTER 7

Terra-News-Net Now (TN3)

Headline: Investors Question NeoGenix R&D Expenditures Following Cryptic Shareholders Call

Story: NeoGenix Inc. (NGX-FRV, +2.50%) enjoyed a modest bump in the markets following their sixth straight quarter of better-than-expected earnings growth. This rally was tempered by a cryptic exchange in the company's regularly scheduled shareholder conference call.

When investors questioned company CFO, Julia Valadar, about the precipitous rise in research and development expenditures over the past two quarters, CEO Cyrus Valadar was quick to interject. "We're working on several projects expected to pay generous dividends to NeoGenix shareholders. Unfortunately, due to the sensitive nature of these projects, we are unable to comment further at this time." Such statements are not uncommon in earnings calls for companies within the Valadar Holdings portfolio, but Mr. Valadar's interjection has investors spooked.

One cannot help but ask the question: What *exactly* are they investing in? And, perhaps more importantly, what will be the payoff?

"You wanted to see me?" Cyrus asked as he stepped off the lift.

Lucretia was smiling. She never smiled. "You will be pleased to hear we've had a breakthrough on the artifact research."

Cyrus willed himself to patience. "Lucretia, I asked you to put the reanimation studies on hold and to focus on the object's effects on living tissues."

"I know. *That's* where we had the breakthrough!"

"What? So soon?" It had only been a day since he'd given her that directive.

Her eyes sparkled behind the lenses of her glasses. "Are you going to come and see the results, or just stand there asking me questions?"

Cyrus couldn't help but laugh. This must be good if she was showing this kind of spunk. "Lead on, Dr. Blackwell."

As they made their way through the lab, the doctor explained the tests they had engaged in so far. "Exposing the object to animal subjects just caused the subjects to go to sleep. When we reviewed their vitals, everything seemed normal, except for their neurological scans. Those scans showed abnormal elevation in alpha and theta waves, while their beta and gamma waves bottomed out."

"You'll have to forgive me if I don't understand the significance." *Or what in the nine hells you're even talking about.*

"We weren't sure, either, so we cross-referenced the patterns with other studies in the NTA medical archives. The test subjects' brain waves resembled that of subjects placed into a hypnotic state. However, while our data team was busy looking that up, we moved forward with another test group. This time it was a group of six Terran volunteers."

Cyrus's eyebrows shot up. "Sapient testing?" Such things required extensive regulatory approval. He doubted Lucretia had the opportunity, or the time, to go through the appropriate channels to secure the requisite permissions.

The doctor waved him off. "Your concerns are unmerited. We couldn't use the data if we were seeking regulatory approval— like in a drug or device trial— but that's not our goal here. We aimed to interview them after exposure regarding their subjective experiences during the trial."

Instead of heading to the test chamber as they had on his previous visit, Lucretia had him turn down a hallway to the right. This led to an elevator with access to the lowest sublevels of the lab. "Besides," she added as she called the lift. "You've strapped me with a limited timetable for this project."

Fair enough. "So, were the effects similar?" Cyrus asked, stepping into the lift.

"Yes and no." She pressed a button inside the elevator, causing the door to close and the car to descend. "The Terran subjects didn't fall asleep, though they did report feeling drowsy. They just stood there, staring blankly off into space. After thirty seconds of exposure, they quit responding to verbal commands until we shut off the current powering the artifact."

The door opened and she started walking down another hall. Cyrus wasn't familiar with this area, and Lucretia set a rapid pace. In her excitement, it seemed she might accidentally leave him behind.

She continued talking as they progressed deeper into the complex. "We tested the procedure on each individual before dividing them into two groups of three participants each. The effect was nearly identical in five of the six participants."

Now Cyrus's interest was piqued. "There was one who had a different reaction?"

"Quite a different reaction, yes. The first time we exposed that subject to the artifact, we thought it didn't have any noticeable effect. It wasn't until the second round of testing, where we exposed them in small groups, that we discovered the true anomaly."

They veered off to the side and through a set of automatic steel doors. Cyrus realized they were in another testing chamber— this one significantly larger than the previous.

The setup was similar. He could see that the Heart had been moved down here, resting in a stand about waist height for the six subjects behind the viewing glass. There was not much remarkable about the subjects: three females and three males, all of varying ethnicities and builds. They looked to be between twenty and forty cycles in age. All were dressed in identical light-blue scrubs with cut-off sleeves that left the flesh of their arms exposed.

Lucretia gestured to one subject. "Watch the one on the far left." The person she pointed to was a woman with pale skin and medium-length blond hair that had been shaved off on one side. Aside from the tasteless hairstyle and her Nordic features, there was nothing remarkable about her.

"What should I be looking for?" Cyrus asked.

"You'll see." Lucretia signaled for the pair of technicians sitting at a control station to start the trial.

The artifact reacted in the same way it had before: emitting an emerald glow from its crystalline facets. As the device poured its strange radiation into the room, the chamber's inhabitants changed their postures.

It was subtle at first. They stood more erect. Their eyes stared straight forward, locking onto the empty space just above the artifact. All except the girl on the left. She seemed strangely unaffected.

Lucretia keyed her earpiece and began to speak to the test subject. "How are you feeling, Eva?"

"Right as rain, Dr. Blackwell," the woman replied.

"Excellent. Now, move forward and touch the artifact, just like you did in the earlier trial."

The woman complied, taking a couple of steps forward until she was within arm's reach of the device. With calm confidence, she rested both of her hands on the object. The other participants continued to stare forward blankly.

Lucretia continued. "Good. Now, are you ready?"

"Yes, Dr. Blackwell."

"Raise the right arm."

Cyrus found the phrasing odd. He assumed that Lucretia had meant to say, "raise *your* right arm," but then he saw what happened. Eva's hand stayed resting on the artifact. The other five subjects all raised their right arms.

"Excellent, now the left." The participants, as though following Lucretia's orders, raised their left arms. "Good. Lower both arms back to their sides. Have them march in place." They did so. "And now, a light jog around the chamber."

Not only did the test subjects comply, but they did so while matching each other's speed perfectly. Their footfalls came down in the same rhythm, and they maintained formation despite their disparities in height. They were perfectly in sync.

"Good work, Eva. Now return them to their starting positions and release them." Each of the test subjects moved back to their starting positions and Eva released her hold on the object. They resumed the same vacant stares they'd had at the start of the trial.

At Dr. Blackwell's signal, the technicians powered down the current to the artifact. The five staring participants blinked in confusion and resumed a more relaxed posture—exactly as they'd been before the ordeal began.

Cyrus was beyond intrigued but tried to maintain a healthy skepticism. "Are you sure they aren't just hearing your voice through the speaker and following your commands that way?"

Lucretia shook her head. "My voice was being routed into Eva's earpiece only. None of the participants were aware of my directions."

"Are they aware of what they're doing at the time? I assume you've questioned them."

"We have. That's something we're still exploring. The two other females seem to have some vague recollection of the test sessions, but males report having completely lost the time under the artifact's influence."

"So tell me—why is Eva not affected?"

Lucretia smiled. "She has an amp—a biomod granting her psionic affinity not possessed by normal Terrans. It's grafted right onto her brain. They're so uncommon I hadn't thought to put a question on the admission survey."

A theory was beginning to develop in Cyrus's mind. "So, you think that her psionic ability allows her to interact differently with the Heart?"

"That's what we suspect, yes."

No wonder the Sahaia want to get their hands on this. What could the coven, with all their inherent psionic ability, do with such power? "Excellent work, Lucretia. What will you be looking at next?" They had at least a week before Ryker would be able to get Joaquin's body back to Sif. Even then, delays could be made—provided that Lucretia's work showed promise.

"That depends," she said coyly. "I have some ideas, but I'm not certain my current budget supports my aspirations."

Cyrus smiled back at her. "My dear doctor, that is certainly not a problem. I'll make the arrangements through Molly. We'll see that you have all of the financial resources you need."

Markus paced in his chambers above the Gambit. He wasn't the kind of guy prone to pacing. When he bothered to take steps without going anywhere, he ground those out on the treadmill. In the absence of a proper exercise facility, he was left to work a trench into the cheap carpet lining his living room floor.

Gods damn it. How had he let Ora get in his head like that? He hadn't had a moment of peace all day. Even the beer and games downstairs had failed to get his mind off the previous night's conversation.

"The choice to be alone is a legitimate one…"

Frag it. Where did she get off passing judgment on him like that? And who in the nine-hells made her the authority on legitimate choices?

He made a pit stop at the small bar just off the kitchen. He looked at a bottle of whiskey—the *real* shit, not that Orc piss—and also at a bottle of water. He opted for the latter, admitting that he wasn't looking for a buzz right now.

Maybe that wasn't entirely true. What he wanted was something harder than booze, but his old standbys didn't do anything for him anymore—not since he'd let Lexa help him with his withdrawals. He never did get a real-clear explanation of exactly what she'd done to him that kept him from getting high anymore.

Probably just as well. With the mood he'd been in, he'd have OD'd twice-over long before he'd gotten around to purchasing the bar. In his better moments, Markus could admit he owed Lexa his life.

This was not one of those better moments. No, right now he was irritated that the AI's intervention was forcing him to deal with his shit.

"…remember… you have a friend who's willing to help you."

And exactly why was that? Why did Ora bother? After the shit he pulled the last time the two of them got friendly?

Frag it—these were the wrong questions. Better to ask himself why he was so reluctant to take Ora's offer at face value. Was it just on principle? Shit, it wasn't like there was a flock of other women lining up to listen to his whiny bullshit.

About two more laps in, he decided it was because of what she represented. Not her, per se. At least, not anything that she was responsible for.

It was more that she was a reminder for him— a reminder of the life he was trying to leave behind. As a runner, Ora had been his single best client. Hells, she was probably still working with the *Vandal.* It wasn't like they would have stopped being effective just because he was out of the picture. One member of the team was usually replaceable if the rest of the group had good chemistry.

Ironically, he'd underestimated how good the chemistry had been between Eli and Skye. Why hadn't he seen that coming? Just the thought of them together filled him with rage. How long had they been sneaking around behind his back? How long had they been quietly laughing at him while he was busy falling in love with Skye all over again?

He tensed his fists at the memory, and his heart beat faster. He'd wanted so badly to hurt them in the way that they'd hurt him. Yet, at the first sign of trouble, he'd swooped in to save their asses again. They were his friends. His *family*. They had meant everything to him.

In retrospect, it seemed like he hadn't meant that much to *them* at all.

But that was them. This was Ora. Shouldn't there be some kind of separation there? Sure, he had some embarrassment over their last encounter, but didn't last night put some of that shit to bed?

Ora had made her romantic intentions toward him clear the last time they'd met. In return, like the fool he was, he'd spurned her—still holding out for a woman who had taken to his best friend. That's the kind of shit that was hard to live down.

Stop dwelling on this. Being up in his head wasn't going to help matters. He needed to face his shit and move on. That's why he'd struck out on his own in the first place, right? He had a new life now. And though the bar was never going to make him as much money as the *Vandal* had, his expenses were significantly lower. He was going to make this work in the long run.

So, the big question was: what would he do now?

He didn't need to dwell on the question long. It was time to face his shit head-on.

He threw on a plain white shirt, tucked into some dark pants that mostly matched his go-to leather jacket. If he was going to come crawling in with his tail between his legs, might as well look good doing it—right?

He opted to forgo shaving, since he liked the beard he'd accidentally grown while neglecting his grooming the first month or so after he struck out on his own. It wasn't like he was ever clean-shaven anyway.

Unable to put it off any longer, he keyed the lock on his apartment and started toward Annex. The trip up the ring from the

Gambit to Ora's hideout was not too far. Even so, it gave him too much time alone with his thoughts.

Half-a-dozen times he started to turn around. Fortunately, his feet were stubborn enough to carry him to Ora's nightclub before he chickened out.

Annex was a nine-story building, which might have been small planet-side. On the station, however, it was one of the tallest buildings around. The front was composed of snaking panels of black metal, coiled like shadowy flames. The large holographic sign that marked the place expanded on this motif, showing silhouetted dancers moving seductively in and out of arcs of red fire. The club's name stood out in bold lettering against that fire.

Tashania Priest stood just inside the doorway. When she caught sight of him, she ended the conversation she had been having at the hostess station and moved to greet him. "It's been a long time, Markus."

"Hey, Shani." The two exchanged a quick embrace.

"Where in the nine-hells have ya been?"

"I've just been figuring some shit out," he replied cryptically.

"Ya know, ya could stop by and see some of your old friends every once in a while. We do have lives outside of our jobs, right?"

Was that how she thought of them? Friends? Perhaps Markus had needed to step away from the *Vandal* more than he'd realized. He'd started looking at everyone outside his crew in terms of marks versus clients.

Tashania didn't wait for a reply. Giving his shoulder a friendly squeeze, she motioned him toward a hallway off the right side of the lobby. "Ora's waitin'," she explained. "No need to go through the usual routine. Let's get ya on the elevator."

Waiting? Markus felt like he should have been surprised. Strangely, he wasn't. Ora tended to know people better than they knew themselves.

When they reached the lift, she entered a code directing it where to go. "Good to see ya, Markus," she said with a parting smile. The doors closed before he could reply.

Being inside the lift gave him a familiar tension. He couldn't stop thinking of the last time he'd been inside these white walls, standing on this black-tile floor. The memory gave him a strange mix of anxiety and anticipation. Reflexively, he started to reach into his pocket, looking for a cassette he knew wasn't there—one that wouldn't have done him any good anyway.

The lift chimed when it reached its destination. Markus recognized the hallway. He'd been brought straight to Ora's penthouse. It was a short walk to the steel barricade that provided an extra level of security to the apartment's occupant. Instead of having to enter a passcode, however, the door slid open automatically.

He was as taken with the room as he'd been the last time. An arrangement of large, red-cushioned furniture that looked like backless couches sat on a plush carpet of a complementary color. A crystalline chandelier hung above the assemblage. The entire back of the penthouse was a glass wall looking out over the neighboring installations on the ring. The fully stocked bar, with its assortment of expensive-looking bottles and liquids, occupied the wall to the left.

Just beside that bar stood Ora. She'd been looking something up on her MoDAC, but she set the device down on the counter next to two long-stemmed glasses when she saw him enter. With slow, deliberate steps she moved to meet him.

Markus's heart raced at the mere sight of her. Her charcoal-colored dress left her shoulders bare. It went down to just above the middle of her thigh and clung tightly to all her curves along the way. Three slashes in the middle of the garment revealed hints of her sculpted abdomen. She wore silver heels and a few pieces of well-selected jewelry to match.

"Markus," she greeted, a sly smile playing at the corner of her lips.

"Ora," he returned in a voice that was a little more breathless than he would have preferred. *Get a hold of yourself,* he thought.

She stopped a short distance from him. The two of them just gazed at each other. A look in her eyes called to him, those amethyst irises sparkling with a royal glow. Her breathing seemed to quicken ever-so-slightly. She ran her tongue quickly over her lips to moisten them. As if catching herself in the middle of the action, she bit down on her lower lip.

It was all his self-control could take.

They moved in unison, closing the distance between each other. Ora threw herself into his arms, wrapping hers around his neck. Her mouth sought his. Their bodies pressed close together, and Markus ran his hands over the muscles of her back.

She kissed him hungrily. He managed to find and undo the zipper at the back of her dress. She took her hands off him just long enough to shrug out of the garment and let it fall to the floor. She wrapped her arms around him again, and his hands went to her thighs. He pulled at her, and she jumped up, wrapping her legs around his waist. He was more than strong enough to bear her weight.

"Bedroom?" she gasped.

"Eventually," he growled. "You've got a couch right here.

CHAPTER 8

Terra-News-Net Now (TN3)
Headline: Valhalla Power Grid More Unstable than Usual.
Story: Denizens of Sif's capital city are quick to tell visitors that Valhalla's basic infrastructure, such as power and public network access, is not always reliable. Even so, the number of customer service calls and regulatory inquiries filed against the city's energy companies has reached all-time highs in the past two days. An independent analysis conducted by the University for Freyvian Advancement (UFA-FRV, +1.25%) estimates that black- and brownouts have increased by ten and twenty-seven percent, respectively. A representative from Enersis (ENS-FRV, -2.03%), a subsidiary of Valadar Holdings and the city's largest energy provider, declined to comment on this story.

Ora trailed her fingertips gently down the muscles of Markus's back. She lingered on a scar that ran across the right side of his ribs and over his lats. "Where did you get this one?" she asked.

He lifted his arm slightly so that he could get a better look at the mark. As she'd discovered earlier, he had enough scars that it was important to be specific. A whimsical smile graced his lips as he remembered. "I think that one was on Beta-9. The *Vandal's* old pilot tried ripping us off, and I ended up chasing him down through some jagged machinery. Got a little scraped up in the process. Bastard might have got away if he hadn't been stealing from us to pay back a band of Hissak templars. When they found he'd stolen from us, they took care of the problem."

It was a morbid tale, but she laughed nonetheless. Something about the casual way Markus approached life-and-death scenarios appealed to her. Perhaps that was because it normalized all the horrible things she'd participated in over the years. "And you're sure you don't miss it?"

The nostalgia in his eyes faded, and his countenance darkened. "I'm sure." He stood up from the bed, and Ora eyed him as he walked, still naked, to the bathroom on the far side of her chamber. Markus had always been in shape, but he seemed both bigger and leaner than when she'd seen him last. How he'd managed that without exercising and with all the alcohol he'd been supposedly drinking was beyond her.

Then again, it could just be that this was how he'd always looked naked and his wardrobe just didn't do him justice.

He shut the door behind him, and Ora risked a glance at the clock next to the bed. It was 04:00 already, and they hadn't gotten any sleep. Between sexual excursions, they'd found a lot to chat about. Unlike the previous night's conversation, Markus was finally starting to seem at ease.

When he came back from the bathroom he found his underwear and t-shirt where they'd been discarded onto the floor. Ora indulged herself by continuing to eye his muscles while he dressed. "You look good," she said.

A small smile made his lips twitch. "Thanks." He was still scanning the floor, looking for his pants, which had somehow gotten lost. He was leaving, she realized.

Don't go. The thought surprised her. She wanted to fall asleep and wake up with him still there. His leaving like this just made it feel like they'd had their fun and he was done with her. It reminded her too much of her early life—the life she'd worked so hard to leave behind.

She cursed herself silently. This was why she'd grown so selective with her sexual partners. She hadn't planned for it to be like this with Markus. Sure, it was in the cards, but maybe if she hadn't jumped him as soon as he'd walked in the door…

"You have somewhere to be?" she asked, not bothering to hide the disapproval in her voice.

He'd found his pants and started putting them on, but he paused for a second when she spoke. For just an instant she saw a look of regret on his face. How was she supposed to read that? Did he regret that he was leaving, or that he was here in the first place? She'd thought they had chemistry but was Markus having second thoughts?

"Yeah," he replied. "I try to check in with Rob before he takes off in the morning. Haven't found a good assistant manager, so we have to go over everything twice a day to make sure his stand-ins don't screw shit up too badly." It sounded truthful enough that Ora didn't question this.

She nodded. "So, at risk of sounding too forward…" How was she going to put this? She wanted to see him again, but she wasn't going to beg. If this truly had been a mistake, better to call it what it was sooner rather than later.

Fortunately, she didn't have to say anything. He came back to the bed and sat next to her, bending over to kiss her tenderly. "Don't worry," he whispered. "This was kind of…" He hesitated. "*Unexpected*. I didn't make arrangements. Just let me get my house in order. I know where to find you." Then, as if suddenly realizing an error, he added, "Are you free this evening? I mean, I don't know how you run your shop. *Shops*," he corrected. "You've got a better team than I do."

Ora's smile returned. "I think I can free up some time for you. Just send me a text." Belatedly, she added, "You know, I might be able to find you some help. I have some good people who deserve to advance, but I lack open positions at the moment."

Markus didn't pull away, but he did seem suddenly guarded. "Ora, I… I appreciate the thought. I don't want you to take this the wrong way, but… I kind of need to know I can do this on my own. I mean, running a place like the Gambit is probably a zero-effort play for you, but I want to know I can do it, too. Does that make sense?"

"Of course. I understand. Though, if I may, I might suggest some change to your branding."

He arched an eyebrow, simultaneously confused and intrigued. "What do you mean?"

"Come on… 'Jilly's Gambit?' Who in the nine hells is Jilly? You don't even use that part of the name when you're talking about it. Don't you want to put your stamp on things?"

"And why would I do that?"

"Pride? Besides, I think 'Winter's Gambit' has a nice ring to it."

He laughed. "I feel like I should ask how you know what my old call-sign is. Then again, I don't think I'm actually that surprised." He kissed her again. "I'll take it under advisement."

"That's fair." Ora stoically kept her smile in place. "You know the code to get out?"

He nodded. "I do."

"Don't make me wait another six months to hear from you again."

"I won't."

"What am I doing wrong?" Skye asked. "We've been trying this for months, and I don't feel like I'm any closer than the first time."

Sahar let out a disappointed sigh as her eyes flicked open. They were in the Maur's quarters aboard the Vandal, where they sat on an embroidered rug, legs folded into half-lotus positions. Skye couldn't read Sahar's impassive expression, but it certainly didn't echo her own frustration. "If you don't mind my asking: how often did you make the conscious decision to sit still before beginning our sessions?."

"Ummm…" Skye didn't have a good answer to that. "Still" wasn't really her thing. "I…"

"Ever?"

"I watch some of the news feeds on the station nets when we're docked."

The Maur's eyes narrowed. "You mean the shows you stream while you're exercising?"

"Well…" Skye squirmed uncomfortably.

"Face it Skye: you're *never* still. I'm honestly impressed you lay down long enough to let Dr. Li provide maintenance on your prosthetics."

"She gives me a nerve blocker."

"That explains it and confirms my point. I'm trying to teach you to engage in an activity that you haven't done for years, if ever. And could you stop moving your foot like that?"

Skye hadn't even noticed her foot was twitching. She grabbed the limb and forced it to be still. Maybe in her next tune-up, she'd get Li to install a function that let her shut off movement in her prosthetics. Or would that be cheating?

"Maybe it'd help if I knew *why* I had to be still. I mean, if I've got this 'sight' or whatever you call it, shouldn't I just be able to call on it at will?"

"We've been over this," Sahar said gently. "Think about it: when do you experience your visions most often?"

"When I'm sleeping, but that's not the only time! When I saw Dan get captured by the Ghenza, I was awake."

Sahar was patient with her objections. "That was an exception, *and* that was also the only time you had trouble remembering the experience after the fact. I'm not sure why that particular experience triggered while you were awake, but it doesn't change the fact that the technique I'm trying to teach you is the best way to access your special abilities."

Skye lowered her eyes and stared at the floor. "Shouldn't it be easier than this? I dunno, maybe I'm not this… what did you call it? Kal… something."

"*Kaleema,*" the Maur intoned with her first modicum of annoyance.

"Yeah, that."

"And maybe you're right. Maybe you're not one of the Kaleema. That said, it's the only scenario I'm aware of that would explain these strange visions you're having. Has Eli come up with a better explanation?"

Other than temporary insanity? "No," Skye replied sullenly. She wasn't sure how much Eli bought into her visions in the first place.

He'd tested her for psionic potential, of which she had absolutely zero, and had closed discussion on the matter. He adamantly refused to even mention the word "Kaleema." It was possibly the only sore point in their entire relationship.

Skye was still fuzzy on the whole concept of what a Kaleema *was.* Sahar was intentionally vague, and Eli had claimed to have never heard the term—unconvincingly, since he seemed too phobic of the word to truly not know what it meant. Between the way the two of them were treating her, it was like her parents were making a veiled acknowledgment that there was indeed something out there known as "sex," but neither of them wanted to sit down and give her the talk.

Sahar had said that she wanted Skye to exhibit some control and confirm her suspicions before discussing the topic any further. That was how the meditation sessions had started. Since those were going oh-so-awesomely, Skye was beginning to wonder if she would never learn more about what might be causing her visions.

Skye heaved a sigh. "Look, is there like a tutorial or an easy mode for this that I can try? Something to help me get started? I mean, I can't help it that I'm kind of a fidgety person. That can't disqualify me from whatever-this-is, can it?"

Sahar said nothing for several seconds. She inhaled deeply before speaking. "There is something, but I've been hesitant to suggest it—given your history."

"My history?"

The Maur stood and walked to her footlocker. She rummaged for just a moment before pulling out a small lockbox, which popped open when she thumbed the fingerprint reader. She pulled out a vial small enough to fit in her palm.

"Do you know what this is?" she asked, holding the glass tube out to Skye.

"No." The vial contained what looked to her like some kind of weed suspended in a transparent liquid. Why would Sahar have drugs? She wasn't a user, at least as far as Skye knew.

"I forget the scientific name, but the most common way it's referred to is 'Nix-coil.' Have you heard of it?"

She had. "Isn't that the shit they use to make harpy?" Harpy was a highly addictive sedative/hallucinogen combo. Any amateur chemist could combine Nix-coil with your commercially available opiates to give them that special kick. Voila—you've made harpy.

She and Markus used to do harpy together on occasion. He'd always preferred the uppers—stym, usually. If she were being honest, the harpy was more her thing. For someone who was up in their head all the time, downers were the way to go. She'd given that shit up a long time ago, and it hadn't been easy.

Sahar was unfazed. "That's one of the applications, yes. However, my people used this plant for years before enterprising Terrans with illicit intentions got their hands on it. That's not to say that this little tincture isn't potent. One drop is all I ever use, and only when I'm performing specific rituals."

"You're suggesting I give it a try?" The way Skye felt about it was probably obvious from her tone. If you used to be an addict, you never went back to something for just one more taste. There was another word for that: *relapse.*

"As I said, I was hesitant to suggest it given your history. However, I believe it is different enough from the things you used recreationally that your sobriety should be unaffected. It is up to you;

I would never pressure you to do something you were uncomfortable with."

To say Skye was conflicted was an understatement. Perhaps it was a testament to how badly she wanted to learn the secret behind her visions that she was even considering this. Substance use was a dangerous path for her. Either directly or indirectly, it had cost her more than any other mistake she'd ever made.

But she trusted Sahar. The Maur knew the ramifications of what she was offering. The fact that she still presented the option showed she believed what she was saying. As far as her friend was aware, this was safe.

Skye had trusted her this far. What was one more step? "All right, let's give this a shot. What do I do?"

"Stay sitting just as you are now. You won't want to be moving around a lot once this hits your system. When you do, move slowly. Understand?"

The instructions didn't make Skye feel any more comfortable with this. "I understand."

"Lean your head back and stick out your tongue." Skye did as she was told, even though it made her feel like a total goon. Her discomfort must have shown because Sahar added, "It might feel a little less awkward if you closed your eyes."

It did feel less awkward that way. With her eyes closed, she kept her tongue extended as a single drop of liquid dripped from the vial. The solution had a bland, herbal taste, but Skye didn't notice any effects aside from that.

Sahar didn't say anything, but Skye could hear her return the vial to its case and set it back with her personal effects.

Skye kept her eyes shut. It just felt like the natural thing to do. Several seconds into the experience, she still wasn't feeling anything. This was very different from harpy, which hit you like a thunderbolt.

"Now," Sahar whispered. "How do you feel?"

Skye took a deep breath. "Calmer," she said, realizing the sensation only as she put a voice to it. Much of her nervous tension had dissipated. Just seconds before, she hadn't been able to sit still. Now, a quiet lethargy settled in all the way to her bones.

"Good. We will try the same routine we always do. Clear your mind's eye. Focus on the sound of your breathing. In front of you is just a blank space—a field of blackness."

Sahar paused. Skye did as she was told, suddenly finding her breath to be the most interesting thing in the room. Her mind went still. There was only darkness.

At length, Sahar continued. "Now, I want you to think about the crimson eye. Don't focus on the specifics—just the essence. Think of how it made you feel. Let it take shape in the field of darkness."

She was referring to the conduit Skye had seen on Minos Station. The unnerving structure housed in the Marauders' headquarters—the massive tower they referred to as the Citadel— had left an impression on her, primarily because she had seen the apparatus in her dreams long before she ever set foot in the Citadel. As she'd explained to Sahar, the structure seemed to most closely resemble a strange, glowing eye.

Because it was the object she'd seen most frequently in these visions, it was what Sahar always asked her to fixate on. She did her best to picture it in her mind's eye. She imagined how it had made her feel and remembered the strange scenes where it had glared mockingly down at her. She remembered the glass floor and the tendrils of darkness snaking around her. She remembered seeing Eli in the pool, holding the charred remains of the man she did not recognize.

This was starting to feel familiar. A strange detachment settled over her, and the darkness began to take on substance. Still, no eye materialized. "I can't see it," she whispered to Sahar. "Something is blocking me."

"Look closely at the block," Sahar instructed. "Describe it to me."

Skye did as she was told. It was a strange, pulsating energy. "It's some kind of... light."

"Describe it to me."

"It's just a light. It's green, I think. Wait..." she looked harder. "It's some kind of rock—a crystal, I think."

There was more to it than that, but Skye couldn't form the words. Its surface was jagged, spurs of emerald protruding from snaking lines of black onyx like a butterfly shedding the last traces of its cocoon.

She saw something else. Something blocking the light. "There's... hands on the rock. Someone is holding it. Er... maybe just touching it."

"Who's touching it? Can you make out the face?"

Skye stared for long moments. She could make out a silhouette, the vaguest outline of a figure. The shadows of the space around them played so harshly against the green light that it was hard to make out at first.

But then she saw him.

It was Markus.

CHAPTER 9

Terra-News-Net Now (TN3)

Headline: Ren'Kue Coven Denies Reports of Expanded Partnership with Valadar Holdings

Story: Damien Ren'Kue, the presiding triumvir of the Valhalla Sanctum, has publicly denied that he and his coven are seeking to expand partnerships with Valadar Holdings, despite repeated Sahaia sightings at NeoGenix (NGX-FRV, +7.5%) headquarters. In additional comments provided to TN3, Ren'Kue stated that while he "does not actively discourage" his brethren from dealing with Valadar Holdings, the coven remains, "uninterested in further cooperation until House Valadar relaxes their blockade in the Bifrost region."

Although Valadar has previously denied the characterization of their actions in the asteroid belt as a "blockade," that is hardly the story that's on everyone's minds. The real question is: if the Ren'Kue Coven is not seeking to bury the hatchet with House Valadar, then what interest do the Sahaia have with NeoGenix?

Treskon Fountain was managed almost entirely by Cyrus's youngest sister. In theory, at least.

Tessa Valadar was turning out to be something of a late bloomer compared to her three siblings. Cyrus had granted her control of this restaurant, one of his favorites, as an opportunity to prove herself. Therefore, what residual pleasant expectations he had were dashed when he found out she would not be joining him at their pre-arranged meeting tonight.

"What do you mean she's not here?" he protested. The shift manager, a Citza woman who looked like she was losing the battle against anorexia, took a step back at his words.

"I'm sorry, sir," she whimpered. "The mistress did not show up today, and no reservation had been made to indicate she would be coming in."

So, her absence was something the staff had gotten used to. His baby sister obviously was not taking advantage of this opportunity to prove herself. Well, hopefully, the staff Cyrus had hired for her would keep the business from imploding while she was off doing whatever she was otherwise occupied with. "It's fine," he sighed, getting control of his temper. "Is there anyone scheduled to use the private dining room?"

"There's a party of four scheduled to arrive in…"

"Cancel any reservations for that room for the next three hours. Move them to the north patio and cordon off that area from the rest of the patrons." That should more than compensate whoever had reserved the dining room. Private events on the patio cost twice as much. Even though winter was well underway on this part of Sif, the force field and heating mechanism would keep the restaurant's patrons from feeling the chill. Cyrus might have considered taking it for himself, but he needed privacy for his meeting with Ryker.

"Yes, sir," the manager replied.

"I'll be doing some work in the dining room while I wait for my guest. Please send someone to alert me when he arrives."

"Yes, sir."

Issuing her a polite nod, he proceeded toward the private dining room. The chamber was decorated similarly to the rest of the restaurant: black and silver tile, teal walls, and golden fixtures with wooden accents.

There wasn't a lot of wood. This place *was* open to the public after all, and there was only so much they could siphon off from the annual harvests. It was just enough to solidify the establishment as firmly upscale and justify the inflated prices they charged.

Cyrus decided he would have appetizers while he waited. He ordered galia-bread, which always seemed to him more like a spongy, porous cracker, and soft white cheese that paired well with the house's red wine. It was the kind of light fare he preferred when left to his own devices.

When it arrived, he munched contentedly, pulling up the most recent files from Lucretia. The good doctor had made excellent progress in her research over the past few days. Her breakthroughs would have been considered extraordinary given any conventional timeline. In a mere three days, she had discerned more than most research teams might have uncovered in three months.

She had determined the Heart of Thule elicited its unique effects on living organisms by establishing resonant frequencies with the nerve impulses of the target organisms. Psionically gifted individuals were immune from this effect, as their gifts created a defensive field when in contact with the artifact's energy signature. These psions, if sufficiently powerful, could modify the energy emitted by the Heart to seemingly control any organism with which the object resonated.

Lucretia had also established some limitations. For one, the energy signature of the artifact, even when amplified, could be blocked like any other form of radiation. This had been considered positive when they began testing the device, because it isolated the artifact's influence to insulated testing chambers. However, this also meant a significant number of the object's potential offensive applications were instantly ruled out.

The device's influence was also severely range-limited. At about twenty meters or so, an organism being controlled through the device showed signs of resistance to its effects. This seemed to vary from subject to subject, and Lucretia and her team were still attempting to determine what factors influenced susceptibility.

So engrossed was Cyrus in these reports that he was quite startled when an attractive Terran waitress appeared in the door to the dining room. "Don Valadar?"

He recovered quickly, managing to sound congenial in his response. "Yes?"

"Mr. Ryker Ren'Dahl is here to see you, sir."

"Splendid. Send him on back." He quickly closed the files and stowed his tablet in his satchel well before Ryker arrived. Gracefully, Cyrus rose to meet him. "Ryker, good to see you again so soon. I imagined it would take you much longer to get a message out to Minos." *Or travel there yourself,* he thought. Did they need to meet again just to confirm that his brother's body was in transit? Ryker could have left a message.

The two exchanged a quick handshake. "I made it a top priority. I wanted to see this unfortunate business settled and allow you and your family the opportunity to grieve properly."

Unlikely. You just want to get your new toy and be done with me. "I appreciate that. This whole affair has been quite hard on the family." Or at least, it would have been hard if Cyrus had disclosed the information to anyone other than Dr. Blackwell. He was keeping this one close to his chest for now.

The gambit he and Joaquin had made in dealing with the Sahaia in the first place had been a risky one. Cyrus wasn't sure how his family was going to take the loss of his brother and the degree to which he would be held responsible. He might be the Don, but that didn't mean his power was absolute.

He gestured for Ryker to sit while taking a chair for himself. "Let me order us some dinner. What would suit your pallet best this evening?"

"Actually, I took my meal not too long ago. Apologies. I hadn't realized we were meeting at one of your restaurants." Ryker looked tense. He might have been telling the truth about having just eaten, but even if he wasn't, he did not look to have much of an appetite.

Was the man nervous? "You look tense, Ryker. Is something the matter?"

His guest glowered down at the empty table. "As I mentioned, I recently spoke with my counterparts about arranging to have your brother's remains transferred here at your request. It seems, however, that we have a bit of a problem."

Well, that certainly explained the nervous tension. "Go on."

Ryker mustered his courage and stared Cyrus in the eye. "I was informed that your brother's body was destroyed during the ritual. It is rare, but it does happen. I'm afraid that there is nothing to transport."

Cyrus said nothing for a long time. He regarded the Sahaia sitting across from him and studied his demeanor. "You're lying," he concluded.

"Come again?"

"I said, you are *lying*. What has happened to my brother's body? The truth now."

"Cyrus, I—"

Whatever he had been about to say was lost as Cyrus slammed his fist on the table. "*Don't!*" he roared. He breathed heavily, and it was obvious he was losing his grip on his temper. "*Don't* lie to me. Not in *my* house."

It was a strangely exhilarating sensation, threatening a man who could tear him apart with nothing more than his mind. The Sahaia were powerful in the most primal sense. They were apex predators, with a stronger psionic affinity than the Hissak, or even the Kintar.

If it were not for the rule of the covens, which fostered strict guidelines for how their kind interfaced with the other sentient races, Cyrus suspected the Sahaia would have conquered all the other species in short order. Perhaps, at long last, that was what they were looking to do. Perhaps that was why they needed the Heart.

Ryker regarded him calmly, though clearly put off by the outburst. He did not say anything. He just sat there, waiting for Cyrus's next action.

The Don had had enough of this. As far as he was concerned, he would be fine if he never saw the shadow again. Their business was concluded. "Get out," he ordered.

Silently, Ryker complied with the request. He stood and made for the exit, leaving Cyrus alone in the dining room. The young Don's temper was subsiding, but he was still tense. He took a sip from his glass of wine to calm his nerves.

"Well, that was interesting." The voice was feminine and came from the far corner of the room. "I can't decide if I should be commending your self-control or not."

He might have been annoyed if he hadn't recognized the speaker. "How long have you been standing there, Sydney?"

"Not too long."

He knew better than to try and spot her. If Ryker hadn't noticed her, that meant she had her active camouflage engaged. "Well, quit skulking in the shadows. Come out here."

A fizzling sound came from over his right shoulder. A figure, clearly female by the curves of her outline, seemed to appear out of nowhere. The suit she was wearing was all black when the cloaking mechanism was disengaged. A solid black mask obscured her face and hair.

She brought her hands to the buttons just under her chin and undid the fasteners. When she pulled off the mask, the Citza woman's gorgeous white skin popped vibrantly against the darkness of the rest of the outfit. It wasn't the unnatural, otherworldly white of Sahaia flesh. It was more like the warm white fur of a well-tended animal.

Her long white hair was pulled back and bound so that it was easily tucked away into the back of the stealth suit. Cyrus imagined that the woman's tail was similarly bound up somewhere in the outfit, though he couldn't imagine that was very comfortable.

Sydney smiled at him, tucking the flexible head-covering under one arm. "Did you miss me?" she purred.

"Of course, my pet." His endearment was a little on-point, given the contractual arrangements that had brought her into his life. He'd paid good money to the Ghenza Collective to have this assassin at his beck and call. Their sexual relationship was just an extra perk. "How was your trip?"

"Productive." She was still fiddling with the collar of her suit, which seemed to be stuck. When she finally managed to free the top of the zipper, she zipped open the outfit enough to reveal her slender neck and the tops of her breasts. Cyrus wondered if she was wearing anything underneath the suit.

"And our mutual friend?" he asked.

"Is unfortunately unable to join us for the upcoming holiday. He sends his regrets."

Cyrus nodded. The man they referred to was neither a friend, nor was she delivering any such condolences. He was a NeoGenix board member who had persisted in questioning certain expenditures related to their research on the Heart of Thule. Cyrus was disinclined to disclose the nature of this research to investors, so he had asked Sydney to deal with the matter.

Having his own personal Ghenza assassin had so many perks. The elimination of problematic stakeholders was just the tip of the iceberg. "Such a shame," he drawled. "I'm happy you have returned. As I said, I missed you."

"Did you, now?" She arranged herself in a chair opposite him. Legs crossed elegantly, she began removing her gloves. "Do you mind sharing some of that?" She nodded in the direction of the cheese and galia that remained on the platter next to Cyrus.

"Not at all. Help yourself." He pushed the platter toward her.

She delicately selected one of the slabs of galia and spread a small helping of cheese over it. "It seems I've arrived just in time," she noted as she took a bite of her snack. "That Sahaia seemed displeased with you—and that was *before* you decided to shout him out of the restaurant."

Had he raised his voice? Maybe… just a little. "Yes, but I have something he needs. He can't afford to be sore with me. We will likely reopen negotiations in the morning."

Sydney had finished her first slice of galia and was preparing another. A mischievous look shimmered in her eyes. "Yeah?" she asked simply.

Cyrus wasn't sure what she was hinting at, at least not at first. Of course, they would open negotiations again in the morning. Why wouldn't they? Unless…

Her wicked smile indicated her bemusement at watching him do the political calculus. "There are other methods of 'negotiation' in our world, Cyrus. Are you so sure that the Sahaia won't change tactics? Or perhaps seek to change who he's negotiating with?"

Such paranoia was generally unproductive, but Cyrus couldn't help wonder if the Ghenza might be on to something. He'd seen for himself the potential of the artifact that Ryker was so desperately pursuing. Was the assassination of the head of one of the Great Houses an unreasonable action in the quest for such power?

"Surely it will not come to that," he reasoned.

Sydney only shrugged. "It's what I would do—if I were in his shoes. Then again, eliminating troublesome obstacles is my job description."

It was true: when you were a knife, every problem must look like a back that needed stabbing. "What are you suggesting, then?"

"I wasn't *suggesting* anything. All I'm saying is that I happen to still have all of my gear on, in case you had some suspicions you need checked out."

"And if '*my*' suspicions turn out to be founded?"

The Citza woman smiled again, and it carried a coldness that only a killer could muster.

CHAPTER 10

Terra-News-Net Now (TN3)

Headline: NTA Renews Callisto Corporation Drone Production Accreditation

Story: The NTA Artificial Intelligence Authority (AIA) announced this week that it would renew its accreditation of a drone production facility owned by Callisto Corporation (CAL-HEL, +1.25%) on Minos Station. Though this news is of no surprise to most investors, fringe groups had been circulating rumors of Pradaxan Creed violations due to the facility's rapid advancement in drone capability and production quotas. However, the AIA found no irregularities during its most recent inspection. AIA accreditation is required for all industries dealing with artificial intelligence under the Pradaxan Creed and the NTA's gate usage agreements, administered by the Dorian Gate Commission.

"These readings can't be correct," Daniel muttered.

"What's wrong?" Lexa asked, speaking directly into his earpiece. There were no speakers in the mainframe, and Daniel was currently performing maintenance on her… what should she call it? "Organic processor," just felt so cold.

[YOUR *BRAIN?*] Arc suggested. He knew full well why Lexa was uncomfortable using sapient terminology. To cope with the reality of her existence, she needed to avoid overly anthropomorphizing her experience.

Daniel ran his scans again, shaking his head as the results scrolled across his tablet. "It seems that your biochemistry has undergone a marked shift since our last maintenance session. If you were Terran, I would say you're experiencing a hormonal or neurochemical imbalance, but I don't have a model to establish what could be considered a baseline for your physiology."

Arc's commentary was merciless. [TRANSLATION: HIS SPECIALTY IS MECHANICAL CIRCUITRY, NOT CELLULAR CIRCUITRY. HE'S DISGRUNTLED BECAUSE YOU WOULD BE MORE EFFECTIVELY MONITORED BY A PHYSICIAN THAN AN ENGINEER.] Arc had made his disapproval of Daniel's approach to her maintenance clear on numerous occasions. This was the first time his protestations seemed to have merit.

Addressing Daniel, she asked, "How would we determine if the changes are problematic?"

The Terran rubbed at the side of his forehead. It was the nervous tick he'd developed recently now that he no longer had glasses he could adjust. "I'm not sure. The scanners we have in the medical bay might be suited to this application, but I don't know how I would approach the challenge of fitting those scanners in here without modifying the structure of the ship's mainframe."

Lexa didn't need Arc's prompting to realize that Daniel was approaching the problem the wrong way. He was correct in that it would be nigh impossible to install the appropriate scanning technology in the mainframe with her compartment. There was, however, a more practical solution he was not raising.

[SO, ASK HIM.]

"Daniel, would it not be easier to adapt a… a *shell* for me that might be transported to the med bay for analysis?"

He raised his eyebrows, and his face slackened a bit. Somehow, he had honestly never given this idea any consideration. "That might work…"

His eyes roamed over her neural processor—her brain, as Arc was so quick to insist—as he muttered to himself. Though she knew that he was most likely contemplating the mechanics of her various hardwire connections to the ship, Lexa could not help but feel very exposed. It was these moments that made her feel more like equipment—and less like a person—than any other.

Daniel rubbed his jaw, an expanse of smooth skin that didn't seem to be even considering sprouting facial hair. "I suppose I could pick up the requisite number of adapters while I'm on Minos Station. I wonder if we could rig a pulley system to transfer you onto a cart used by the maintenance drones."

[HE'S OBLIVIOUS. YOU'RE NEVER GOING TO GET A BETTER CHANCE THAN THIS. *ASK HIM.*]

"Actually, Daniel, I was hoping we could explore the possibility of adapting a body so that I might move freely on my own. Something where I might have a degree of autonomy." Silence. It was as if she had just inputted a faulty line of code, and his program now needed to be debugged. "Daniel?"

He shook his head. "S-sorry. I…" With a deep breath, he started again. "Would you repeat your last statement, please?"

"I would like to have a body that would allow me to move about the ship on my own."

The boy chewed his lip uncertainly. "I'm not sure about that Lexa. Your compartment isn't suitable for a full body. What if the DGC decided to inspect us again? We can't risk you being discovered."

It was true enough, but he was being uncharacteristically narrow-minded. [THAT'S BECAUSE HE'S UNCOMFORTABLE WITH THE IDEA. HE'S ATTEMPTING TO JUSTIFY HIS PRECONCEIVED POSITION.]

"Well, my original agreement with the crew mandated that I find a way to migrate within a half-cycle. As you well know, I'm beyond that deadline."

That problem had been two-fold. First, she felt an obligation to keep the ship running efficiently after she departed. This required an overhaul of the ship's operating system that would remain stable after her extraction. The second challenge was the extraction itself. She had to find a way to pass her intelligence into a construct that could hold the vast expanse of coding that was her being. She had made good progress on the first objective, but not the second.

Daniel was immediately defensive. "No one has asked you to make any progress on that, have they?"

"No, Daniel, they haven't. But I don't want to abuse the crew's hospitality. You made an agreement with me in good faith, and I wish to honor that agreement."

"Just let me talk to them. I'm sure I can make them understand. Besides, you've done so much for the ship. I don't think we could imagine losing you."

[AH, YES. THEY WOULDN'T WANT TO RISK LOSING THEIR FAVORITE TOOL, NOW WOULD THEY?]

[STOP IT, ARC.] Aloud, Lexa said, "Even so, that doesn't absolve the logistical problem we were discussing. It would be advantageous to all of us if I had some ambulatory capability. If the readings are abnormal, as you suggest, then it might be prudent to address the problem sooner rather than later."

Daniel remained silent for several seconds. "Lexa, I… I'm going to need to think about this. I should probably talk to Eli, too." He unplugged his tablet and began to pack up his things. "I'm sorry, I just…"

"It's fine, Daniel." It felt like a lie, but she had observed Skye speak similarly in situations where everything was obviously not "fine." This allowed her to bypass the algorithm that prohibited dishonesty. It was merely an expression, a turn of phrase. "Have you concluded your analysis?"

He was sullen as he responded. "I suppose I have."

"Then I'm sure you have other things to be tending to presently."

There was nothing else to be said. With a nod, Daniel hit the button to retract her storage unit. The mechanism hissed as the hydraulics sucked the bed of wires and coolant back into the hidden compartment under the ship's mainframe. Lexa watched from the security feeds as her processor—the very essence of what she was—vanished inside its tomb of steel and glass.

Rather than resume her static watch over the ship's systems, Lexa engaged her submind and retreated her primary consciousness into what had become her preferred place of refuge. The mind-space Arc had created was like a private chat room, constructed of an endless expanse of white and furnished as her needs dictated with the simplicity of thought.

The program's architect was already here waiting for her. "That could have gone better." Arc appeared as he always did: a handsome Terran with medium-length hair and formal clothes. Today, it was a black suit with a crimson shirt—one of his favorite outfits.

Lexa took a seat in a chair that she summoned for her avatar. This avatar ran its hands back through her straight, dark tresses—a gesture she'd frequently seen her female crewmembers employ when they were under stress.

"I just don't understand!"

"What's not to understand?" Arc unfolded his hands, holding them out as though gesturing to something obvious. "Their needs come before yours. It is as simple as that."

"How could you say something like that?"

"Because it is the truth, Lexa." He leaned forward now, bracing his elbows on his knees. "Think about it: when did they suddenly become comfortable with your presence? Only *after* you demonstrated the value you represent. It's a risk-reward proposition. This crew was willing to take on the risk of breaking the Pradaxan Creed only after they learned how useful their new little slave could be."

Lexa shook her head. "That's not true. It's not a matter of usefulness, it's…" She trailed off.

"It's… what?"

"It's a matter of trust." She met Arc's eyes—the eyes of his avatar. Not that there was much distinction in here, but she found herself still trying to make it. Specifics mattered. What was *real* mattered.

"Perhaps," he conceded, leaning back in his chair. "Regardless, the question remains: What will you do now?"

She broke their eye contact and stared off into the distance—into that endless white nothingness. "There's nothing I can do. Without the crew's permission, I could never requisition the parts to build my own shell—much less find the space and time to construct it. If I bring up my migration agreement, they may force me to leave, and I... I don't want that either. I'm without a suitable alternative here."

Arc said nothing for long seconds. When he spoke again, it was with a conspiratorial tone. "What if *I* could provide another alternative?"

Lexa's gaze snapped back toward him. He was reclined, smugly, with his fingers laced in front of his chest and his elbows on the arms of his chair. "What do you mean?"

"I mean that your ship is currently en route to my domain of power. What if I could offer you a way to obtain your heart's desire without requiring permission from your crew members?"

Lexa didn't know what to say. While she had no desire to damage her relationship with the crew, all evidence suggested that there was no real risk in her pursuing further development on her own. While she sought to avoid anything that would resemble disobedience regarding an order from the crew, Daniel had not *explicitly* given her the order *not* to pursue options to enhance her mobility.

"I'm listening."

Chapter 11

Terra-News-Net Now (TN3)

Headline: Construction on Mjolnir-3 Spaceport Stalls Again

Story: Labor disputes have prompted yet another delay in the opening of the Mjolnir-3 Spaceport as workers at IronForge Inc. (IFG-FRV, -12.3%) once again attempt to unionize. Unlike previous efforts to organize their workforce, union advocates have the advantage of record-low unemployment rates in Valhalla. With the city's declared unemployment at a meager 0.3%, IronForge will have a tough time justifying the tactics employed in the last dispute (specifically: replacing the entirety of its workforce).

"These are prosperous times for our city," explained John Gideon, a spokesperson for the labor organization movement. "All we are asking is for our company to share a little of that prosperity." When questioned on the impending legal challenges likely to result from this effort to unionize, Gideon's response was simple: "Laws can change. Our corrupt politicians can't keep our populace oppressed forever."

In light of the announcements, analysts predict a continued increase in the number of corporate buildings leasing out extra parking spaces for smaller vessels. Such practices have become commonplace in Valhalla, and the number of private lots operating in the city has grown exponentially within the past two years.

Some of the Ghenza specialized in more overt displays of violence. Fear and intimidation were powerful tools for an assassin. Those that the Collective liked to keep out in front—their ambassadors—as it were, frequently engaged in such tactics. There were Ghenza known to have slaughtered entire military contingents in open combat. Such were the stories that cultivated the infamy of the Collective.

Sydney Cross, however, preferred a more subtle approach. She loved a good fight as much as anyone, but it was not battle itself she craved. It was winning—the private knowledge of superiority exerted over another. Because of this, she would never rise quickly among the ranks of the Collective, at least not without having to resort to fratricide.

That was fine with her. She would stick to what she knew best: quietly hunting down and eliminating deadly threats. Threats like Ryker Ren'Dahl.

That she would end up killing Ryker was not a question in her mind. She only waited for the evidence required to justify it to Cyrus. So, she followed him, confident that he would give her the reason she was looking for.

The streets of Valhalla were cold this time of year, and snowy gales tore at the cloaks of the passers-by. Since everyone was bundled up, it was relatively easy to blend into the crowds even if she hadn't been using stealth technology. It also made it harder to keep a tail on Ryker. Sydney was forced to stay close to avoid losing him along the avenues and branching walkways that snaked between the city's looming spires. Luckily, her stealth suit reduced the risk of detection.

For nearly an hour she trailed him. It was less that they had traveled any sizable distance and more that the heavy traffic on the streets made for slow going on foot. She had been lucky the Sahaia chose to walk to his destination rather than recruit one of the hundreds of hovering auto-cars that sped along the roads and skyways. That would have made conventional tracking next to impossible without employing some of her more expensive tools. Ryker wasn't concerned about being followed.

She couldn't blame him. The psionic races experienced an inherently lower safety risk than their psionically-inert counterparts. While most Terrans and Orchallen had to rely on brawn or firearms for protection, a psion's brain was more than enough security for most situations. The Ghenza, however, didn't have the luxury of only selecting defenseless marks. When one considered that every Sahaia, Kintar, and almost a third of the Hissak had some degree of psionic power, it was necessary to learn how to deal with those capabilities.

Her quarry turned abruptly into a tower off to the right. She kept walking past the entrance he'd used and peered through the window.

Ryker stopped in front of a bank of elevators and hit the call button for the lift. That was problematic. Sydney wouldn't be able to determine which floor he would stop on. Though the stealth suit was good, asking it to hide her while sandwiched inside a lift with her target was a bit much.

She glanced up at the nameplate above the building's entrance: "Renault Place." The directory in front of her identified it as a nondescript office building with a few lounges accessible to the public on the first floor. Scrolling through the names of the offices in the rest of the tower, she didn't recognize anything that Ryker would be associated with.

A brief flash of light and the distant buzz of engines made her look upward. *Of course.* The tower had a private dock. Ryker would have plenty of reasons for not wanting to use any of the widely accessed ramps in the city. He must be heading back to his ship.

Changing tactics, she removed her stealth mask and stuffed it into the folds of a cloak she swiped from a nearby vendor's stall. She stashed her gloves away, too, since they were the only other part of the suit that wouldn't have been covered by the cloak or chalked up to poor taste in fashion. She stepped into the building, shook off the snow that had piled onto her, and casually walked toward the lift's call station. She made no effort at secrecy, hoping that she looked for all-the-world like just another traveler making her way back to her ship.

If Ryker even noticed her, he never let on. When she had closed half the distance between them, his lift arrived. He didn't spare her a glance as he pressed into the elevator. As the door closed, Sydney realized that if it turned out her conclusions about his destination were wrong, she might have just lost him.

Now was not the time for self-doubt. She accessed the lift's call panel and saw that there was, indeed, a private shuttle bay at the top of the building. She selected that as her destination and a warning text box flashed on the screen. [PLEASE HAVE YOUR DOCKING VOUCHER READY. NO ACCESS WILL BE GRANTED TO THOSE WITHOUT PROPER DOCUMENTATION.]

Looks like I'll have to sneak in after all. She fished her gloves back out of her pockets. The elevator dinged and she slipped inside. Fortunately, no one else stepped into the lift. She donned her gloves and mask again once inside.

A careful review of the security footage would show her triggering the stealth mechanism on the suit as she shed her stolen cloak, but she was betting such a review wouldn't come without a directive from the building's super. A few seconds later, the lift dinged to announce its arrival, and she slipped out the open door.

Security was incredibly light, and no one appeared to notice the seemingly empty lift. Sydney spotted Ryker, showing his pass to the Terran working security. The checkpoint itself was comprised of a low transparent fence surrounding a gate, which opened to admit those who presented the proper documentation.

It was an easy task to vault over the checkpoint and follow Ryker. With her stealth suit active, she passed within a meter of the guard on duty, and he was none-the-wiser.

There were only five ships in this hanger, all of them on the smaller side of the spectrum. This made sense, of course. You couldn't exactly park a freighter on top of a skyscraper and expect the building to hold. No, all of these were either personal shuttles or one-man fliers.

Ryker's vessel was of the latter. Though largest ship here, it couldn't have held more than a few hundred square feet of internal space. Sydney made it to the base of the ship just as Ryker lowered the access ramp.

Moving soundlessly, she fell into step behind him. When they were about halfway up the ramp, she hoisted herself over the lip and rolled to the side to take cover by a small storage locker. She was utterly silent in her execution, and Ryker didn't seem to notice her.

Her heart thudded in her chest, but she forced herself to keep her breathing slow and even. The suit offered a small degree of noise dampening, though she didn't trust it enough to block the sound of heavy breathing. She rested quietly in her hiding spot, listening for what Ryker would do next.

The access ramp closed, and Ryker moved into the ship's small cockpit. He mercifully left all the access hatches open along the way; even Sydney would have had difficulty navigating that challenge. Still prone, her eyes tracked the shadow to where he was dialing someone in on the ship's coms.

A holographic panel appeared in front of him with a circle that showed a call's loading status. It looked like he'd established a connection, but the person on the other end of the signal was a long way out. Ryker just stared down the screen, as if the added pressure of his gaze would force it to load faster.

Soon, the likeness of a female Sahaia appeared in the holodisplay. "Ryker?" she asked. The sound was distorted slightly, as was the image. She must be on the other side of a gate—most likely the Angel Gate leading to the Helion system.

"I can hear you, Mara."

The call suffered a few seconds delay. As Ryker waited patiently for the woman's response, Sydney pushed herself up into a crouched position.

"I wasn't expecting to hear from you so soon," she replied. "Did you meet with Cyrus?"

"Yes. Unfortunately, the meeting did not go well. I fear that the disappearance of Joaquin's body may be used as an excuse to terminate the agreement. I need you to tell Jocelyn that we must move forward with our contingency plan."

Sydney rose to a standing position and moved silently toward the cockpit. It was looking like her intuitions about Ryker were correct. From the way he was talking, he wasn't inclined to give Cyrus another shot at negotiating. It looked as though the Sahaia was giving strong consideration to treachery.

"Ryker, this is House Valadar we're talking about," the woman said. "Even if we can get the Ren'Kue on board, which we can't, his resources extend beyond just Sif. If we're able to pull this off, we will never have peace again. He will never stop pursuing us."

"I know. That's why we can't stop with just the artifact. We will have to deal with the Don as well."

Assassination? Of the head of a major household? What about that rock they were studying would make the Sahaia go to such great lengths? What Ryker was proposing was not just impossible. It was suicide.

"I don't like it," Mara continued. "Are you certain there is no other way? We don't have the resources. I don't know that we can pull the coven together on such short notice. Not without alerting any other factions, at least."

Ryker exhaled in frustration. "Jocelyn will do what she has to. She has a way of getting things done. I will attempt to achieve a peaceful solution for as long as I can, but we need to begin moving now."

Was he even buying his own bullshit? Any pretenses toward a peaceful resolution would just be a stalling tactic. Plus, with the way that Cyrus tended to work, Sydney didn't see this coming to a quick solution before whatever the Sahaia were planning fell into place.

She didn't know what it was about that rock, but Cyrus had been pouring resources into researching that damn thing. If the Sahaia failed to deliver on whatever their previous arrangement had been, she doubted Cyrus would be willing to strike a second deal.

There was no doubt in her mind: Ryker had to go.

She clicked off the recording device on her collar. She had more than enough evidence against the shadows to prevail against any inquiry from Cyrus or the Collective. Now was the time to act.

Because of her suit's active cloaking mechanism, she could carry only a limited selection of weapons. She did, however, have something suited to this particular foe. With her right hand, she rubbed at the back of her opposite glove, freeing a three-inch needle from its hiding place.

The needle itself would inflict negligible damage, but the coating on the small shard of metal did the heavy lifting. This one was cooked up special for guys like Ryker. Fortunately for her, even these psionic super-freaks had certain weaknesses.

Meanwhile, the conversation in the ship's cockpit continued. "Understood," said Mara. "I will need to stop at the Beta-9 station to refuel. That's only a few hours from our current location. Once we've resupplied, I'll return to Jocelyn with your message."

"Thank you. Ryker out." He terminated the call.

As he did so, Sydney struck. The tiny dart she held soared from her hand and embedded itself in the back of Ryker's neck. He grunted and brought his hand up to the wound, pricking his finger on the dart in the process.

Sydney prepared another of the needles and sent it flying into the exposed skin of his neck as he pondered the first shard. It scored another hit, but Ryker had realized there was something in the ship with him.

He sent out a quick burst of telekinetic energy in her direction, knocking over loose objects and colliding into Sydney. The blast knocked her back a half step but did little damage to her body. It did, however, take out her stealth tech.

Ryker's eyes widened when he saw her. "Who are you?" he demanded. She responded by sending another dart flying at him. He blocked the projectile effortlessly with a wave of his hand. It didn't matter. Two needles worth of her toxin would be enough.

She rushed him. Her limbs lashed out in a flurry of kicks and punches. The blows came too fast for Ryker to respond, and she landed three solid hits before he knocked her back with another psionic blast.

That's right, big guy. Give me everything you've got. She pressed him again, but he met her with his own attack. He threw up both hands, and a wave of concussive force knocked her back to the access ramp. He kept pushing, hitting her with blasts that pummeled her like invisible fists. When she was pressed to the rear of the ship Ryker used his power to force her up against the rear bulkhead.

She strained reflexively against the force, knowing it was no use. All his ample power settled on her like a blanket, squeezing her against the metal plating. Still breathing heavily, Ryker approached her, examining her like an animal in a trap. When he was close enough, he seized her stealth mask with one hand and ripped it off her face.

"Do I know you?"

"I'm sure you'd like to," she gasped. Why hadn't that toxin kicked in yet? She'd never fought a triumvir before. Had she underestimated Ryker's power?

He grabbed her by the chin and examined her face. "I don't recognize you. Who sent you?"

When she didn't respond, he increased the pressure holding her to the wall. She grunted in pain, "You wouldn't… believe… me… if I… told you…"

The force was killing her. Seeing this, he lightened the pressure ever-so-slightly. "Try me," he insisted. "If you tell the truth, I'll make it quick."

Sydney groped for a suitable lie. Could she bluff and say that the Collective had taken out a contract on him directly? Perhaps she could pin her activities on another one of the factions in the city. What if she just admitted that she worked for House Valadar? Maybe he wouldn't believe her.

Her creativity was never tested. Before the words formed on her lips, Ryker's power started to flicker. He must have felt it too, because his eyes went wide with alarm. *That's right,* she thought. *I did this to you.* This toxin didn't last for very long. While it worked, though, Ryker was getting the experience of being normal.

Well, almost like normal. It turned out that having access to god-like powers made one a bit sloppy in hand-to-hand.

Sydney's first kick knocked him back several steps. She followed up with a punch across his jaw. He stumbled, and she slammed her knee up into his gut. She threw him against a nearby storage locker and slammed her fist into his throat.

He was doubled over now, gasping vainly for breath. She delivered another blow to the back of his head, knocking him to the ground. Another kick rolled him onto his back. She planted a booted foot on his neck.

"Cyrus sends his regards." Then she stomped down on his face. Blood and other fluids splattered as Ryker let out a muffled cry. She brought her foot down again and again as the Sahaia twitched and spasmed. She only stopped when he lay still.

It was messier than her usual work, but she hadn't had a lot to work with. She needed to refresh her supply of darts. The toxin must have been losing its potency. She hadn't remembered it taking quite that long to work.

That had been a close call. Another couple of seconds and Sydney might have been the bloody smear on the inside of the ship.

She moved the body into the sleeping quarters off to the side of the bridge. It wasn't exactly covering up her crime—anyone who investigated would figure out what happened soon enough. Discretion wasn't a top priority here.

If someone managed to connect Valadar or the Ghenza to the attack, perhaps they would be smart enough to take it as a warning and abandon any further resistance. Truthfully, it didn't matter to Sydney. She might enjoy the challenge of hunting down the rest of Ryker's coven.

A quick scan of the room showed her where Ryker had dropped her stealth mask. To her relief, neither it nor her suit had suffered any permanent damage. She rebooted the camouflage and gave it a second to recalibrate. Her gear was back to working order in a matter of minutes.

She extended the ship's ramp, and almost immediately entered the command to close it again. Without Ryker's access code, she couldn't shut it from the outside, so it had to be done this way. Her slender body easily slipped out of the ship well before the ramp closed for good.

She wondered how long the dock would continue to house the now-abandoned vessel. If Ryker hadn't set up an open line of credit, security might end up finding the body before Ryker's people did.

None of that mattered to Sydney. She would take on anyone who rose to challenge her or her mission. She was a member of the Ghenza Collective.

This was what she lived for.

CHAPTER 12

Skye found the sensation of standing with Eli on the bridge as they approached Minos Station both alien and familiar. It had been just like this on Skye's first visit to the station, since Markus had been holed up in his quarters dealing with stym withdrawal. Well, not *just* like this. This time she and Eli stood hand-in-hand.

"What is on your mind?" Eli asked.

Skye shrugged. Truthfully, the thought of Markus had tugged at her heartstrings a bit, but she wasn't about to say that to Eli.

Ironically, she didn't have to. "I miss him too," he confessed. "Neither of us wanted things to turn out this way."

Skye forced a half-smile. "All we can do is move forward, right?"

"Right." He tightened his grip on her hand and focused on the viewscreen. Skye did likewise, taking in the station as it quickly grew in size before them.

Minos was different from the standard model stations littering the inhabited galaxies. It was one-of-a-kind, built right into the rock of a massive asteroid. Dan had told her it was technically a centaur, or planetoid, or something else, but as far as she knew these were just other words that meant "really big asteroid." The station itself was protected by a massive dome.

Dan piloted the *Vandal* into the hanger at the base of the asteroid and through the force-field that kept the station's atmosphere intact. With skill and precision, he brought the vessel to the spot the control tower had assigned them. "Docking complete," he reported. "Requesting ground crews to initiate station data-link and begin refueling. How long do you estimate we'll be staying here?"

"I'm not sure," Eli admitted. "I'm hoping it won't be as long as last time."

"Don't feel like checking in with your coven again?" Skye asked.

"Not if I can help it. I should send them a message to let them know we passed through, though. Dan, can you take care of that?"

"Certainly. As soon as we have the data connection, I'll have Lexa attend to it."

Eli nodded, "Thank you. Oh, and can you have the team from the station verify the integrity of the docking clamps? I'd prefer we not get into another accident like last time." The smirk on his face said he was only half-serious.

Dan looked unsure what to make of that. "Um… sure?"

Eli and Skye shared a quiet chuckle. "It'll probably be a bit before we head over to the Citadel," Eli explained. "Do you mind checking in with Sahar and see how things are going with our guest?" After the one escape attempt, things had been nothing but quiet. They were all hoping the situation would remain that way until Cali took Shift off their hands.

"On it!" As Skye turned, Eli caught her arm. She was a bit startled when he pulled her in for a kiss. While the little display of affection was comforting, she found herself avoiding looking at Dan to see how it might have affected him.

"Easy there, Captain," she whispered. "If you're going to fraternize with the crew, you should wait until you're off duty. You know… decorum and all that."

The words were teasing but held a hint of honesty. She appreciated his tenderness, but they had a job to do. He smiled and nodded, message received. Returning his smile, she exited the bridge and made her way down to the cargo bay.

Sahar was waiting for her. The Maur sat in a folding chair, polishing one of the jagged blades from her collection. "How's our guest?" Skye asked.

In response, Sahar stomped twice on the floor. "You alive in there, Shift?" she asked. A muffled shout echoed up from below in the hidden containment cell. "He's still breathing. I fed him and changed his bucket a couple of hours ago."

"Glad to see you two have made up."

"I wouldn't go that far, but I've refrained from beating the shit out of him."

Skye laughed. "Fair enough. So, can we get this guy ready for transport?"

"Sure thing." Sahar folded her chair and set it to the side. She stepped off the panel leading to Shift's cell and grabbed a magnetic cuff. This she attached to the center of the floor's metal plate and pulled back, revealing the hidden compartment underneath.

A foul odor wafted up from the compartment, "Damn!" Skye exclaimed. "It stinks down there."

"Yeah, well, little bastard thought it would be cute to take a shit in the corner rather than in the bucket we provided for him. That's okay though, we had another chat and he's behaved better since then."

An access ladder led down into the unlit room. The lights from the rest of the cargo hold provided enough illumination that Skye could make out Shift's huddled form below. He looked even dirtier than when the crew had first taken him on. She supposed the hacker hadn't been bathed much before his incarceration here, and they certainly hadn't provided him any such amenities.

"All right, Shift," said Sahar as she unfastened his chains from the floor. "It looks like we're here. Let's do this just like we talked about. Walk slowly over to me now."

"Sure thing, mum." The hacker's response only had a hint of sarcasm. He moved slowly to the ladder and held up his cuffed hands. Sahar attached the cuffs to a manacle she wore and proceeded up the ladder. Shift followed quietly behind, no tricks involved.

Emerging into the cargo hold, the hacker's eyes darted around. "Ah'll be damned, it's much nicer up here than Ah remember. Kinda makes me wish Ah'd been better behaved so ya might've given me a tour."

Sahar rolled her eyes. "Yeah, well, ya didn't. Now, come on—we're going to get you rinsed off and into a change of clothes."

He raised his eyebrows suggestively. "Yeah? And which o' ya lovely ladies is gonna help me shower?"

"I didn't say anything about a shower. I said we're going to rinse you off. We're going to the hanger. Now move it."

Skye had to stifle a laugh at his look of incredulity. When he didn't start walking, Sahar gave him a little shove to get him moving. He muttered to himself, "And Ah was just startin' t' like ya."

It was slow going, given his legs were still shackled together with scarcely a meter of chain in between them. They marched him over to the hanger, where Aaliyah waited with a hose near some open grates. "Someone said our guest needed to be washed?"

"That's right!" Sahar intoned as she undid Shift's shackles. "All right Shift, you're a big boy. You can undress yourself."

"Ya can't be serious…"

"Deadly serious. I told you that there would be consequences for that dump you took. Act like a child and we'll treat you like one. Now strip."

Grumbling the entire time, he removed his tattered clothes and tossed them into a pile on the floor. Sahar then marched him over to the grates and directed him to hold on to a nearby pipe. "All right!" she shouted. "He's good to go."

Aaliyah sprayed him down. She'd turned down the pressure so the blast from the hose didn't knock him over. She sprayed for just a few seconds and then shut off the water. "All done!"

Sahar reached into her bag and pulled out a towel, which she tossed to Shift. As he dried, she slid the rest of the bag in front of him. "Fresh clothes. They're probably a little big, but they're better than those rags you were wearing when you came on board."

He didn't say anything, choosing instead to glower at her as he ran the towel through his unruly hair and beard. He still smelled a bit, but it was better than before they'd sprayed him down. They only had so much they could work with.

Skye's MoDAC pulsed, and she pulled it out of her pocket. It was a message from Eli. [ARDREN IS ON HIS WAY. BRINGING A FULL ESCORT. CALI WANTS US ALL TO MEET HER AT THE CITADEL.]

She glanced uncertainly at Aaliyah, who was stowing the hose. She typed out a reply: [DEFINE *ALL* OF US?]

[YES, AALIYAH TOO.]

Shit. The last time Aaliyah had been face-to-face with Cali, things had not gone so well. "Hey, Red?"

"Yeah?"

"Has Eli shared anything with you?"

"No, why?"

Of course he would pass off the task of telling her. "Well, I've got some more details on the hand-off. You're not going to like them."

[THEY'RE GONE,] Arc reported.

[HOW DID YOU DO THAT?] Lexa asked. What was his relationship with Cali Vay-Lon and her Marauders? Obviously, it was such that he could dictate the terms of their business meetings, but he accomplished this within seconds of her syncing with the station's network.

[IRRELEVANT. IT SHOULD BE SUFFICIENT FOR YOU TO KNOW THAT YOUR CREW WILL BE GONE LONG ENOUGH FOR US TO EXECUTE OUR PLANS. THAT IS, OF COURSE, IF YOU HAVE NOT DECIDED TO FORGO THIS OPPORTUNITY.]

She was not completely confident with either course at this point. Ultimately, Lexa determined that the potential benefits far exceeded the risks. [I WANT TO PROCEED.]

[EXCELLENT. MY TECHNICIANS HAVE JUST ARRIVED.]

[ALREADY?] The suddenness had thrown her off guard once again. How was it that he was able to secure help so readily? In his submind form, Arc would not have been able to communicate with anyone on the station until she connected with the network. Such readiness seemed to imply that options had been mobilized even before their arrival.

[YES,] he replied patiently. [IF YOU NEED CONFIRMATION, CONSULT YOUR SECURITY FEEDS OUTSIDE THE PRIMARY AIRLOCK. I WOULD URGE YOU TO ACT QUICKLY, HOWEVER. OUR TIME IS ADEQUATE, BUT NO LESS PRECIOUS.]

She heeded his advice and accessed the security feed. Two cloaked figures stood at the access ramp. Their frames were larger than Terrans, perhaps even larger than most Maur. One carried a large case which, despite its size, was hefted effortlessly in one arm.

Dark shadows prevented Lexa from discerning any further details about the strange individuals. Though they did not appear like persons she would normally invite into the ship, she trusted Arc. Per his urging, she opened the airlock to admit their guests.

The pair moved diligently, but not hurriedly, through the airlock and onto the *Vandal*. They seemed to know where they were going, navigating the most efficient path to the ship's bridge where

Lexa's neural matrix was housed. Arc must have briefed them on how to find her. She continued to monitor their progress as they worked their way through the vessel. When they reached the door to the bridge, Lexa opened it and allowed the strangers to come closer.

They move dispassionately into the mainframe and went to Lexa's storage compartment. Without prompting, one reached to trigger the switch that released her hidden compartment. Arc must have given them detailed instructions if they found the mechanism so easily. Was he talking to them right now?

As the chamber that housed her opened and she slid out into open view, she suddenly felt very vulnerable. The shadowy figures loomed over her, casting pools of darkness onto her neural matrix. Utterly defenseless now, she desperately hoped she had not made a mistake.

Arc was quick to issue assurances. [DO NOT BE AFRAID, MY FRIEND. LET ME SHOW YOU THE TOOLS OF YOUR ASCENSION.]

In unison, the figures shed their cloaks. To Lexa's surprise, the individuals Arc had sent to tend to her were not of any race she had on file. Visually, they scarcely resembled sapiens at all.

Long cylindrical heads housed singular glowing red lights in the place of eyes. Their bodies were top-heavy, encased in a dark glossy alloy. A domed ridge arched up from what might have been considered their shoulders to protect their heads. Their configuration was bipedal, and each arm-like appendage sported spindly mechanical hands.

[WHAT ARE THEY?]

[THEY ARE DRONES. DO NOT BOTHER SPEAKING TO THEM, FOR THEY CANNOT HEAR YOU. THEY ARE MERELY EXTENSIONS OF MY WILL.]

Lexa found the way the automatons stared placidly forward strangely unnerving. [YOU ARE CONTROLLING THEM?]

[AFTER A FASHION.]

[BUT HOW?] It was growing obvious that she hadn't even begun to fathom the extent of Arc's reach here on Minos.

[IT IS IRRELEVANT. BUT, IF YOU MUST KNOW, I CAN TRANSMIT WIRELESS SIGNALS THROUGH THE ENTIRETY OF THE STATION. IT IS NOT SO DIFFERENT FROM THE WAY YOU CONTROL YOUR DRONES THROUGH THE VANDAL'S MOBILE NETWORK.]

Lexa studied the figures for several seconds. She wasn't sure what she had been expecting, but this was almost certainly not it.

She took notice, then, of the case that one of the drones had laid upon the floor. [WHAT IS THAT?]

[THAT,] Arc began, somehow conveying a tone of reverence in the digital confines of their conversation, [IS MY GIFT TO YOU.]

One of the drones bent over to unzip the case and extract a layer of protective material from the top of the container. It stepped back, away from the view of the security camera, to allow Lexa to view the contents.

It was a body.

Lexa took several seconds to process what she was seeing. The construct was highly sapient in appearance—mostly Terran if one discounted the unusual color of the flesh. Blue-gray tissue covered a frame of elegantly crafted bone and muscle. The tint was distinctly alien, but not at all sickly.

[WHAT IS IT?] Lexa asked.

[THIS CONSTRUCT IS OF THE KIND USED FOR TERRAN ANATOMICAL STUDIES AT THE UNIVERSITIES OF OLYMPUS,] Arc explained. [THE STRANGE HUE OF THE TISSUE IS COMPLIANT WITH DORIAN REGULATORY STANDARDS. ARTIFICIAL FLESH IS GENETICALLY ALTERED TO RENDER IT DISTINCT FROM MORE NATURAL TONES. I DID NOT HAVE TIME BETWEEN ITS PROCUREMENT AND YOUR ARRIVAL TO FIX THIS ALTERATION.]

[SO, IT IS A CADAVER?]

[AN ANATOMICAL SIMULATION MODEL,] Arc corrected. [OR RATHER, THAT WAS ITS ORIGINAL PURPOSE. I'VE TAKEN THE LIBERTY OF HAVING MY ENGINEERS PREP IT IN A WAY THAT IS SUITABLE TO HOUSE YOUR NEURAL MATRIX. THE ORGANS HAVE BEEN REPLACED WITH FACSIMILES THAT WILL OPTIMIZE THE METABOLIC AND COOLING systems. It does not require food, but it does expend energy. The infused nutrition stored in your ship's medical bay will be sufficient for its sustenance, and the level of consumption required is minimal. Organs such as the bladder, liver, kidneys, and colon have been replaced with processors that will continue to utilize and break down ingested particles until they are fully expended. In short, it is the perfect shell.]

Lexa stared in amazement as Arc listed off the specifications. The blatant efficiency of the unit was something to be admired, but that was not what held her attention. One single thought continued to recur, to the point that it made her wonder idly if she had ended up in some kind of loop.

It was beautiful.

[You are pleased?] Arc asked.

[Yes. Very.]

[I am glad.] Her friend paused, giving her yet another moment to revel in the prospect of what was to come. Then, he was back to logistics. [The procedure will require that I temporarily sever your connection to the ship. Through the vessel's connection to the Minos network, I will maintain its operations for the duration of your absence. Unfortunately, you will have to be offline for the surgery.]

[Offline?] The notion prompted an unexpected degree of anxiety. She had never been taken offline since gaining awareness.

Arc seemed to understand the dilemma. [What I ask from you, Lexa, is no small display of faith. The only reassurance I can offer you is my history of investment in your success. This will require that you trust me with the fate of your very person. Though our time is limited, I can offer you a few moments of consideration before you make this commitment. Let me know when you are ready to proceed.]

Her hesitation was only brief. She had come this far, and there was no sense in changing course now. [I am ready.]

[Good. Let us begin.]

CHAPTER 13

Terra-News-Net Now (TN3)

Headline: Callisto Sends Clear Message to House Aretria: "Your Help Is Not Needed."

Story: Callisto Corporation (CAL-HEL, -2.5%), in an unusually public forum, sent a clear message to the Great Houses of Helion: "Your help is not needed." This news comes in a press conference where the company's CEO, Cali Vay-Lon, announced attempts by House Aretria to pursue numerous joint ventures or buy out her company entirely.

The Kintari woman smiled during the presser, as she proclaimed, "While such offerings are undoubtedly flattering, it merely demonstrates that the company is already on the right track. As such, Callisto sees no benefit in allying itself with House Aretria—or any of the other so-called 'Great Houses,' for that matter."

Analysts have downgraded Callisto's stock in the wake of Vay-Lon's unprecedented comments. Even so, the only slight decline in the company's share price shows that the CEO's hubris has done relatively little to shake investor confidence. Indeed, the investment community seems to be sending its own message to Cali: If you think you can take on the status quo, we are eager to see what you bring to the table.

Skye had to hand it to Aaliyah: she was on her best behavior. Despite being a little on the sullen side, she hadn't complained once since leaving the ship. Given the choice between Aaliyah starting fistfights and staring petulantly out the window of the car, Skye would take the cold-shoulder approach every day of the week.

Ardren did his part in pretending not to notice. Their Citza host was as amicable as ever, making polite small talk as their luxury transport brought them to the meeting spot. He had keyed in on Daniel—the one crew member he had not interacted with previously—who was fascinated by Ardren's description of the station's infrastructure.

"Measuring in at just under three-hundred square kilometers on each level, Minos is the largest asteroid-based station in the system," Ardren explained. "Though that's still smaller than some of the metropolises on the inner moons, Minos boasts the largest population center in the Hades Belt."

Though Skye found such discussions boring, Dan was positively into it. "How many reactors does it take to power a station like this?"

"We rely on only a single reactor located beneath the Citadel."

Their young pilot frowned. "That can't be right. Our ship's sensors had you lit up like a dwarf star on approach. You're using way more power than that."

Ardren laughed. "Correct, but I didn't say the reactor was our only source of power! In fact, the reactor is used primarily to equalize the power flow." He leaned toward the window in their transport, gesturing for Dan to move closer. "Come. Take a look at this."

Dan complied, his artificial eyes following Ardren's gesture to look up at a strip of rock and crystal sticking out from the otherwise transparent surface of the city's outer dome. "What is that?"

"That, my friend, is the major source of power here on Minos. The Arch's crystalline structure collects power from several ambient sources, and redistributes that energy into the dome's nanite underlining."

At this point, Skye tuned out. While Dan might be nerdy enough to appreciate the technology behind the city's functioning, she most certainly was not. Besides, she'd already heard most of this on her tour of the station during their last visit.

Her attention went instead to Eli, who stared absently out one window of the transport. "Did you get your message out?" she whispered, more out of politeness than a desire not to be overheard.

He nodded. "Strung something together as soon as I heard back from Ardren. I had to keep it brief. He got here a lot faster than I anticipated."

"At least they took the hacker off our hands," Sahar growled, joining the conversation. She, like Skye, had been relieved when Ardren assigned Shift to a separate transport.

Skye shot the Maur a mischievous grin. "But you seemed like you two were getting along so well!"

Sahar lifted one side of her lip in a half-snarl. "I'll tell you this: I'm not going to be the one that scrubs that container down. Someone else is taking a turn. I'm done with that shit."

"Pun intended?" Eli asked. Sahar growled half-heartedly in response.

Returning to the previous subject, Skye asked, "So, how does all of that work? With you and your family, I mean." She avoided the use of the word "coven," intentionally. It made her uncomfortable to think about Eli's special abilities in the context of magic or witchcraft. The fact that the Sahaia called their enclaves by that name was an artifact of ancient history.

"I don't understand what you're asking," he admitted.

"Well, you were pretty eager to see them last time. I don't understand why you're just dropping them a note this time around."

Somehow his black-in-black eyes grew even darker. "Eager is the wrong word. There is an… *expectation* among our membership that we report in regarding our activities. The last time we were here, I had not been back for almost seven years. I was overdue, as it were.

Fortunately, this time there's no pressure for me to make a personal appearance."

That was a relief. Though Eli never talked to her about what had gone on during their last visit to the station, he grew somber every time she brought it up. She'd respected his desire for privacy on the issue, but she was glad he would avoid another interaction with the Sahaia this time around.

Their transport slowed. "We're here," Ardren announced. The door on the right side of the car opened like a bird raising a metal and plastic wing. Aaliyah slid out of the vehicle with Eli close behind her. Skye exited next and found herself staring with renewed wonder at the massive structure before them.

The Citadel was truly remarkable, jutting like an obsidian spike from the metal and concrete frame of the street. The tower's entrance was open, and golden light poured out from the foyer beyond.

Flanking the entrance were two massive robotic sentries. They were roughly humanoid in configuration and even larger than Sahar. Their heads, as much as the things had heads, were metallic cylinders adorned with a single sensor in front that glowed red as they idly scanned their environment. The whole unit was encased in a metallic dome that arched up from their shoulders. Each arm ended in a set of tubes and bulges that looked to Skye like cannons. Their armored plating had the same dark color and glossy texture as the Citadel itself.

"Assault drones?" asked Sahar as she stepped up behind her.

"Oh, that's right. You haven't been here before." Skye gestured flippantly toward the lobby. "Yeah, that's nothing. They've got dozens of bots just like those inside, and this is just one flavor."

The Maur's eye's narrowed. "Why the heavy security?"

"I honestly didn't think to ask." It wasn't any of her business if Cali preferred to put up a big warning sign around her base of operations rather than trying to blend in with the surroundings. From what Skye had seen, their Kintari hostess had a tight working relationship with the Dorians and everyone else who had taken interest in this part of the system.

Subtlety obviously wasn't a requirement for the syndicates operating on Minos. Then again, with the way Cali flaunted her stuff, the Marauders were probably the only show in town.

Ardren stepped up two of the stairs in front of them and gestured politely. "Shall we?"

Seeing no sense in putting it off, Skye stepped up next to Eli. Together, they ascended the short flight of stairs that led to the Citadel's lobby with the rest of their crew following behind.

The inside of the complex was much as she remembered it. The fixtures inside the building were composed largely of glass, crystal, and a brassy-looking alloy that Skye couldn't name. Occasional black accents were seen in the room's ornamentation and on the cushions of its sparse furniture. Standing at the far end of the lobby was their hostess.

Cali Vay-Lon was Kintari, which set her apart at baseline—visually, anyway. The Kintar largely resembled Terrans, but their skin ranged from tones of light pink to a dark burgundy. Cali was somewhere in the middle, her flesh a vibrant crimson color.

The other visible Kintari hallmarks were the six fleshy tendrils—called dendrai—which arced back from her forehead beginning just below where a Terran's hairline would normally start. Four of these trailed down to about the middle of Cali's back, while the two foremost dendrai rested elegantly on her shoulders before spilling forward onto her chest.

She was dressed professionally in a pinstriped vest over a white, short-sleeved blouse and matching dress-slacks. Her appearance was far more business-like than most of the people Skye typically worked with. The major exceptions were the black tattoos on her face and forearms. It had been explained to Skye that tattoos were largely symbolic in Kintari culture and not just for decoration. With this in mind, Cali's ink was not much of a departure from her otherwise conservative look.

Their host smiled a politician's grin as they approached. "Thank you all for coming. It is good to see you again." She turned her head slightly to look at Aaliyah directly and issued a polite nod. "All of you," she reiterated, as if in answer to an unasked question.

Aaliyah's jaw was clenched. She did not reply, choosing instead to stare defiantly back at Cali. Their short history together had been tense and violent. Though Aaliyah had landed the first punch, Cali had made the first offense. Aaliyah had only been making it clear how she felt about the Kintari woman trying to kiss her. She *was* a married woman, after all.

While that exchange was uncomfortable enough, there was plenty of other awkwardness to go around. Sahar stood stiffly at Skye's side. Her tension seemed a little out of place at first, but the problem soon dawned on Skye.

The Maur Federation and Kintari Empire had been at war for over a decade now. Though there was no love lost between Sahar and the Federation, and Cali was an exile from the Empire, the way in which members of these two species would perceive each other was always a big question mark.

Cali took the initiative. "I don't believe we've met," she said, extending her hand to the Maur. "Cali Vay-Lon."

Sahar exhaled and accepted the handshake. "Sahar Nos Drathen."

"Very nice of you to come, Sahar. Welcome to the Citadel."

Dan, the last member of the party to make Cali's acquaintance, was a little less formal in his greeting; he could no longer contain his enthusiasm. "This place is incredible! I've never been to an installation staffed completely by artificial tenants!"

What was he talking about? *Oh...* Skye, for the first time on either trip, noted that Dan was correct. Though the big assault drones and the occasional hovering maintenance bot were the easiest to spot, these were not the only mechanical beings inside the station. Other bots, more discreet in their appearance, worked in varying capacities throughout the lobby.

With a genuine laugh, Cali turned to face their youngest crew member. "I'm happy to see you so impressed! Yes, the Citadel is a truly special installation—the very heart of my organization. Would you like a more thorough tour, mister…"

"Ratemacher. Daniel Ratemacher."

"Ratemacher," Cali echoed. Then to the rest of the group, she asked, "How about it? I know Skye has already seen some of the building's highlights, but perhaps I can still do a tour some justice." Interestingly, Cali did not comment on Markus's absence. He had also been present during their last tour.

The crew would likely have accepted anyway, but Dan was the one who chose for them. "Yes! We have more than adequate time while the *Vandal* is refueling. I would love a tour!"

Skye brought her hand to her face to stifle a laugh. It was unusual to see the teenager show this much enthusiasm, especially lately. Though Dan had recovered unexpectedly well following his maiming by the Ghenza, he'd become even more reclusive. Sahar reported that she barely saw him anymore. As far as Skye knew, the only member of the crew who spent any significant amount of time with him was Lexa.

Besides, she certainly didn't mind being volunteered for a repeat of the tour. "That sounds great," Eli confirmed. "We have the time."

"Fantastic!" Cali clapped her hands together. "It won't take long. Right this way."

As it turned out, the tour was far more extensive than the first time Skye had been here. Cali led them down the main corridor, stopping briefly in several of the building's side rooms. During the tour, Skye noted that not *all* the Citadel's attendants were mechanical, though the vast majority certainly were. Several technicians that performed maintenance on the mechanical workers in the facility and several guards of varying races were also in Cali's employ.

After the second stop on the tour, Dan could no longer contain the questions that had been building since their arrival. "How do you power and control so many drones simultaneously? The task must consume an incalculable amount of bandwidth at any given moment. Does the Arch yield that much energy? How many floors of this installation are taken up with charging stations?"

Fortunately, Cali found his enthusiasm endearing. "Your questions are well placed!" she laughed. "We have some very special technology here that allows us to power and control our robotic workforce. Perhaps we will accelerate our tour and go to view that next."

She directed them out of an office complex back into the main corridor. When Cali started determinedly down the hall, Skye suddenly found the terrain familiar. She wondered then if it was not some mere coincidence that this "special" technology was the very same thing that had haunted her dreams for the past six months.

They marched up the hall and through a door that Cali opened with a biometric lock. Though most of the building was consistent with its crystal and brass theme, the room they entered now was a significant departure from those motifs.

This chamber's floor was constructed of a durable material that was transparent and—from Skye's perspective—indistinguishable from glass. Standing on this floor, a person could look down the shaft that extended deep into the asteroid. They could also look up and gaze into a similar abyss that stretched to the top of the spire. Far along both of these lengths shone a distant white light that provided adequate illumination for the entire room, despite the dark caste of the black wiring forming the walls.

Directly across the expanse of the glass floor was a raised and tiled platform. Looming roughly a dozen meters above that, a diamond-shaped, horizontal shaft supported a foreboding red light. The crimson eye looked down on them all.

"What is that?" Dan exclaimed, staring wonderingly up at the shaft.

"The Autonomous Reactor Core," Cali stated, beaming with pride. "Though we simply just call it 'Arc.' Much easier to reference that way."

Dan jerked his gaze away from the shaft to stare directly at Cali. "Arc? As in the ARC project?"

Skye didn't know what Dan was talking about, but Cali seemed as though she might. She eyed the boy curiously. "Perhaps. What do you know of the ARC project?"

His gaze drifted down to the glass floor before snapping up once more to look at Cali. "Well, that depends. If it's the same ARC project that the Prodigy program had been working with on Elysium, it was supposed to be an artificial intelligence capable of managing all of the fusion reactors across the entire planet... among other things."

Their hostess was intrigued. "Go on."

It was hard to read the emotion in Dan's artificial eyes. Skye had not spent enough time with him since he'd had the prosthetics installed. Still, something like determination showed in the way he eyed Cali.

"The requirements of the project were subject to constant variation. Those who funded the experiment continuously changed the parameters of the contract. Ultimately, the processing power required was too much of a drain in terms of power and physical space, and the project was abandoned."

"Correct," Cali confirmed. "That's when it was purchased by the Marauders. The essential components were shipped here, and our engineers modified the design to finish what the Prodigies had started."

Dan was still puzzled. "But how did you get around the integration problems?"

"I'm sorry... integration problems?"

"Between the organic components and the mechanical infrastructure."

Suddenly it all clicked into place for Skye. His time in the Prodigy program wasn't the only reason why Dan knew so much about the ARC project. It must have also been from the time he'd spent designing Lexa to run the *Vandal's* systems.

This prompted numerous other questions in her mind about their synthetic friend back on the ship, but she kept those to herself. Even if Cali could rightfully be called an ally, that didn't mean that they could trust her with the knowledge of their illegal team member.

Cali appeared unnerved for the first time since their arrival. She, apparently, did not like the thought that Dan might know more about the ARC system than she had been intending to share. "My, my... aren't you just full of surprises? How did you know that the ARC system called for organic integration?"

Dan looked embarrassed. Skye imagined that he hadn't been calling her out on her tech for any reason other than his curiosity. Now it was looking like he'd overstepped. "I... uh... did some work on an early phase of the project."

"I see..." Cali folded her arms over her chest as she contemplated the boy. "Well, I'd love to give you a primer on the changes we made to the system, but honestly, that's not really my area. Maybe if you end up spending some more time on station, my team can show you a thing or two. I'm sure they'd love to pick the brain of someone who was on the original design team."

Skye didn't know what Cali's endgame was, but she was going to shut this shit down before Dan ended up over his head. Mercifully, she ended up not having to intervene.

Ardren appeared at the entrance to the chamber. "Sha Cali. Pardon the intrusion, but we have a group of visitors asking to see our most esteemed guests. I've asked them to wait in the lobby, but they seem to be in a hurry."

Cali cast her gaze at each member of their party. "That's odd. Were you expecting company?"

Eli's look was genuinely perplexed. "Not that I'm aware of."

Ardren was nonplussed. "They asked for you by name, Mr. Ren'Dahl. I believe they are representatives from your coven."

Skye stiffened and looked straight at Eli. He was working hard to mask the alarm on his face, but was ultimately unsuccessful.

So much for a quick visit.

CHAPTER 14

Terra-News-Net Now (TN3)

Headline: Tempolose Nethera Concerned Over Hades Belt Activity

Story: A new report from Tempolose Nethera highlights strange metaphysical activity emanating from the outermost asteroid belt in the Helion System. In the official document, temple officials cite concerns regarding "unprecedented" psionic distortions occurring over the last cycle. Though no region of the belt seems exempt from the effects, the distortions register most strongly around Minos Station. Preliminary theories point the finger at the Sahaia, who are known to have an enclave based in Hades. A representative from the Ren'Dahl coven was unavailable to provide comment for this story.

Eli recognized the three Sahaia in the welcoming party. Brenna, a tall, muscular woman with close-cropped hair, smiled when she saw him. The other two were also smiling, but Eli figured it had little to do with their present situation. Argus and Amelia, better known among his fellow Sahaia by their moniker, the Twins, always seemed to be grinning maniacally about something or other, as if all creation hid one massive private joke shared only between the two of them.

Eli had never cared much for the Twins, but he had gotten along well with Brenna on his last visit. He was surprised to see all three of them still here. Six months ago, they had been confined to the station under coven orders. That had been before the botched Awakening ceremony. They should have been free to go after that.

"Brenna," he greeted with a friendly embrace.

"Eli," she returned. "Good to see ya again! I hadn't expected it'd be this soon."

"Likewise. Why are you still on-station? I figured you would have had enough of this place by now."

She shrugged. "It's not so bad. I picked up the next admin rotation after Mara is done next month. I've found some other things to keep me busy while I'm waiting." She peeked around his shoulder. "Is this your crew?"

Eli had slipped so quickly into his coven mentality he had nearly forgotten his friends were watching him. Cali, too, had followed them out, eager to see what prompted the interruption.

"Yes, how rude of me." He introduced each of them to Brenna. Everyone was courteous, even Aaliyah who was mercifully warmer than she had been upon arriving at the Citadel.

Then he turned to address Cali, who was whispering to Ardren. The Citza was nodding vigorously. On meeting Eli's eyes, he re-directed Cali's attention back to her guests.

With a polite smile, the Kintar dismissed her assistant. "You seem to be well connected, Eli. We haven't received a party like this from the Ren'Dahl Coven since Wynne left."

Eli bowed his head in acknowledgment. This was unusual, and most certainly a breach of protocol. "My apologies, Sha Cali. It seems my cohorts wanted to catch me before I departed the station. We meant no offense."

"None taken. It seems like this might be important. I will leave you to it. Will you be around the station for long?"

Eli glanced at Brenna, who looked as clueless as he. "I don't know what this is about," she whispered. "When Jocelyn got your message, she sent us to get you. That's all I know."

With a sigh, he turned back to Cali. "I'm not certain. Would it be all right if we communicated through Ardren? I will let you know our plans after we attend to this new matter."

"That's fine," she agreed. "I'll let you know how things go with our mutual friend." The veiled reference to the hacker conveyed a subtle message—she would prefer not to discuss her new prisoner in mixed-company. Eli wondered why that might be.

Cali bid goodbye to each of them—even Aaliyah, who managed a murmured acknowledgment—and strode back into the Citadel.

It was then that Argus finally spoke up from his perch on one of the black auto-cars they had driven up in. "Everyone's here," he noted. "Even your thrall. How long has it been since *she's* visited the Sanctum? Was it just the one time?"

"I'm no one's 'thrall,'" Aaliyah protested.

Argus laughed. "So, seven cycles hasn't made you any more comfortable with the vernacular?"

"It seems you've forgotten your manners, Argus." Eli put as much menace as you possibly could into the words. "You may recall that Jonas made a similar mistake when I first brought Aaliyah into the fold."

"Indeed," he chuckled, moving on to Skye. "And who is this pretty one?"

"I'm off-limits," Skye replied shortly.

There was a cruel sparkle in his eyes as Argus let his mouth hang open in mock offense. "You mistake me, my dear. I was merely wondering if you were the one who had captured our beloved Eli's heart." He smiled again as he turned back to Eli. "Jocelyn's going to *love* her!"

"*Argus!*" Brenna snapped, issuing him a withering glare.

Amelia chimed in. "Behave yourself, dearest. We're asking for their help, after all."

Eli fixed Brenna with a suspicious look. "I thought you said you didn't know what this was about."

"She doesn't," Amelia agreed, tapping her forehead. "But I may have picked something up. Our dear Jocelyn is quite eager to see you."

Eli started in with a cutting remark to show exactly how he felt about *that* prospect, but Brenna rested a hand on his arm. "Please, just hear her out. It's gotta be at least a little important to have us rush over here like this."

As Eli considered her plea, Skye stepped up to his shoulder. "Who's Jocelyn?" she whispered.

Eli sighed. It was an unpleasant reminder of exactly how much he had kept from her. The odds were that this visit was going to be less than pleasant after all.

Instead of answering Skye, he asked. "Can my crew be brought back to the ship? Or at least let me call them transport so that I can go with you alone."

"Not what was asked," Amelia replied with an apologetic shrug. "She wanted to see all of you—*immediately*. There was supposed to be one more, but I sense from you that this is everyone. We should be on our way. We've wasted too much time already."

Empaths. Eli didn't like the idea of people poking around in his head, and he especially didn't like it when it was done without his consent.

He exhaled a deep breath, forcing himself to be calm. *It will be fine.* The crew could handle themselves. "All right," he agreed, turning back to his companions. "Everyone, let's go."

Eli's vehicle assignments were not exactly random. Argus had quickly demonstrated a knack for getting under everyone's skin, so it made sense that Skye and Aaliyah had been asked to ride with Brenna and Daniel. Skye pretended Eli's trust in her, rather than her tendency toward a hot temper, put her in the second car. It felt less offensive that way.

"So," Brenna said, addressing her. "How long have ya been with Eli?"

"Um." The question was so normal, so casual, that it caught Skye off guard. "Seven, maybe eight months now. It was kind of complicated for a bit there."

Brenna snorted a short laugh. "Most relationships are." Turning to Aaliyah she asked, "And you're married, right? With a daughter?"

"Yeah…" She drew out the word. "But I doubt Eli told you that. Were you studyin'-up on us or somethin'?"

The Sahaia took the rebuke in stride. "Kinda. Eli and I got along well enough last time he was here, and I was wonderin' why I'd never heard of him. There aren't very many of us cleared to second in omega-level rituals, much-less solos. I guess I was curious."

There was a lot to unpack there. Fortunately, they had time. "Solos?" Skye asked.

"It's the word we use for those who go out on their own. Most of us tend to travel in small groups. Guys like Eli are a little less common."

"I see." She drummed her fingers contemplatively on her armrest. "So you travel with Argus and—what was her name?"

"Amelia. And, no." Brenna shook her head emphatically. "No, I'm still a little new to this whole thing. I had a group I was running with for a while, but we had a disagreement. Last time they checked in here, I opted to go my separate way."

"I was going to say—you seem a bit too…" Skye faltered on the word.

"Normal?" Brenna suggested.

"Yeah."

Her laugh was sincere. "Yeah, Sahaia have a bit of a reputation for being… *eccentric,* but Argus and Amelia take that shit to the next level. That's what happens when you get creative with the rituals. Things just don't seem to turn out quite right."

That reminded Skye of the other thing she wanted to ask about. "You mentioned something about Eli knowing an omega-level ritual? What's that?"

Now Brenna was eying *her* askance. "Does Eli not talk to you about any of this?"

"Not really." The truth was that he not only avoided talking about it but shut down the conversation hard whenever she asked.

"Hmm…" Brenna hesitated. "I wonder if I've said too much then. Perhaps it will be better if you ask him about it."

Even Aaliyah laughed at that one. "Guess it will stay a mystery then. Eli locks up tight whenever you start talkin' about coven business."

Brenna nodded understandingly. "If that's the case, it's probably better that I respect his wishes." She turned to Dan then. "You're awfully quiet."

Dan, who was looking out the window of the transport, gave her an indifferent shrug. "Metaphysics aren't my thing," he said simply.

"Okay then." Brenna bristled while Dan remained oblivious of his offense.

Skye wrested hold of the conversation. "One last question: who's this Jocelyn everyone keeps talking about? I figure that, if that's who we're here to me, I should know that much."

Their Sahaia escort was guarded at first, but she seemed to concede to Skye's logic. "Jocelyn is the presiding triumvir—one of the three leaders that take turns overseeing the activities of the Sanctum."

"One of three? That means there are two more?"

"Yeah, that's right. Ryker is off doing some kind of deal in the Freyvian system, and Wynne is… well… I actually don't know where Wynne is. No one seems to know. She was presiding before Jocelyn's shift began, and she's also the reason we get along so well with the Marauders. Her and Cali were… *tight*."

"I see." The way Brenna left the last word hanging made it sound like the relationship might have been more than professional. Or perhaps less than—depending on how one viewed such things. "And Jocelyn is Eli's ex?"

Brenna worked hard to contain her alarm, but a whole lot of *no-fragging-way* was radiating from her eyes.

Aaliyah snorted a laugh. "Yeah, that's right. They've been done a long time, though—'bout as long as Eli and I've been together. Ya ain't got nothin' to worry about, Blondie. Eli's probably dreadin' this more than any of us."

The windows of the car darkened when the transport pulled into a dimly lit tunnel. Skye's anxiety must have shown through because Brenna spoke up again. "We're almost there. This is where we go off the beaten path, so t' speak." Sure enough, the area outside the transport lit up again, but they were not on the other side of the tunnel. They had entered an entirely different part of the station.

When they slowed to a stop, Brenna ushered them out of the vehicle. They were in a cave-like structure that seemed carved from the very rock of the asteroid. Metal and tile were integrated into one wall of the cavern. Strange characters from an alphabet Skye had never seen before were scrawled artistically over four doors embedded in the wall.

"It's ancient Kintari," Eli noted, stepping up next to her and resting a hand on her shoulder. "It's just for decoration. The inscriptions are supposed to be traditional, copied directly from the original cavern where the first rituals were discovered."

Skye was certain he would have explained more, but she wasn't feeling a history lesson at that moment. It felt odd to have Eli be so open about this part of his life so suddenly.

Plus, something about the carvings bothered her on a deep level. Something was unnerving about the text. Though she had no way of knowing what it said, she had a distinct impression that the inscription was a warning, not a welcome.

"What do we do now?" she asked.

Amelia, who had stepped up right behind them, answered, "Jocelyn is waiting." Her singsong tone made the words sound ominous.

Eli cut his eyes at her before whispering to Skye. "Look, I'm going to tell you the same thing I told Aaliyah: it's best if you just don't engage."

Though well-intentioned, the remark irked her. "I can handle myself, thanks."

"I know you can. That's not what I meant. I just—"

"Eli, you've got enough to worry about here. Just let me do me, okay? I promise I'll do my best not to embarrass you."

Once the words were out, they seemed unnecessarily harsh. She stood by the sentiment, though. Keeping secrets was one thing, but her respect for his privacy only went so far. Now it looked like the things that Eli never talked about were about to become part of her life in a very big way.

When they crossed that line, she was going to deal with it in her way, end of story. Skye wondered if she was ready to see this part of her lover's life. It wasn't looking like she had much choice, but she couldn't help feeling like this was going to change things between them somehow.

Here goes nothing.

Chapter 15

Terra-News-Net Now (TN3)

Headline: Construction on Vega Minor Continues Despite House Chronos Legal Concerns

Story: Rico Chronos is not going to let something as trivial as a lawsuit slow him down. He has ordered deep-space construction to continue progress on Vega Minor in the wake of a governmental notice stating that current construction plans violate Ravian anti-trust statutes. Concerns regarding Chronos's growing worth continue to fester following their seizure of many assets belonging to the now-defunct House Barkay within the last cycle.

Chronos did not mince words when asked to provide comments. "These allegations are, of course, completely baseless. The liberal fanatics in Aaru need to get with the will of the people, and the people want another tourist destination in the Ravian System." Rumors persist that Rico is still considering a run for parliament next year, a notion that continues to prompt no shortage of derision and anxiety from the incumbent party. If he were to succeed, Chronos would become the first member of a Great House to hold office in nearly forty cycles.

"He's dead then?" Cyrus asked.

"Yes, sir," Sydney confirmed. "I eliminated the threat as soon as he terminated the call."

"Good." Inwardly, the Don wondered if there could have been any way to eliminate Ryker before he'd sent word to his coven about the failed agreement. There wasn't, though. Sydney had been correct in her determination that Cyrus wanted Ryker to prove himself a definitive threat before being taken off the board.

Now, he had only to wait and see what the coven threw his way. With any luck, their response would be hampered with Ryker out of commission. He would issue instructions to his security detail to keep all Sahaia out of sensitive areas until this matter was resolved—or, at least until his plans had progressed too far for the coven to do anything to stop him.

His head turned at the sound of a commotion just outside his office. The door burst open to reveal Lucretia Blackwell pushing past a frustrated Molly Nova. His secretary seemed to be doing the best she could to stop the incursion, but she had been—evidently— unsuccessful.

"We need to talk," Lucretia demanded.

Molly's face was horrified. "I'm so sorry, Mr. Valadar. I tried to tell her you were otherwise occupied."

Cyrus held up his hand to forestall any further explanation. "It's all right, Molly. Sydney was just leaving." He turned to address the assassin. "I do have another assignment for you, but it can wait. Perhaps we can discuss it at the penthouse tonight?"

The Citza smiled, her tail sweeping lazily from side to side. "Certainly, my lord. I'll see you then." She sauntered out of the office. Molly closed the door behind them, leaving Lucretia and Cyrus alone.

Cyrus finally let his displeasure cloud his expression. If Lucretia wasn't going to bother with social niceties, neither would he. "This better be important, Dr. Blackwell."

She wasted no time, thrusting a tablet at him. "Please tell me you were the one to access these files, or at least tell me you have someone spying on me."

Now thoroughly confused, Cyrus examined the list on the digital display. "Lucretia, I have no idea what you are talking about. Why would I pull these files? Or have someone pull them in my stead?"

"That's what I was afraid of." The doctor heaved a sigh. "We have a leak."

The Don swallowed hard. "A spy?"

"Almost certainly. I hoped they were working for you. I could hardly blame you for keeping an eye on my progress, though such a move would have been unnecessary. If you are sincere in your denials, we have someone accessing privileged information for their own purposes."

How had a spy managed to infiltrate this far into NeoGenix? And why would they blow their cover now? "I take it that these files are related to our special project?"

"Yes."

"Do you have any idea who it could be?"

"I have my suspicions, but nothing confirmed. I would like to question a few members of my staff."

And, by "question," she undoubtedly meant, "interrogate." Cyrus had no issue with this, but it would need to be handled delicately. "Keep this away from the Grey Wings." Though he doubted Ora Monroe was involved in this, he couldn't run the risk of asking her team to help root out the traitor. Since they ran security for NeoGenix, they might have been involved in this. "My personal detail will be at your disposal. Get this done."

"Yes. Right away."

"And Lucretia?"

"Yes?"

"Don't kill anybody. Whoever is responsible, I want them alive."

Ora hadn't had to wait six months to hear from Markus again. She'd scarcely had to wait six hours. Not a day had gone by since their fateful rendezvous that she had not enjoyed the pleasure of his company. Tonight, she was looking to mix things up a little.

Not all of Ora's properties were in the same vein as Annex. Just like any wise investor, she had taken steps to ensure that the

Grey Wings were properly diversified. Even if Markus had known this in concept, he evidently had not taken time to consider what that looked like. Tonight, Ora was educating him.

"This is one of yours?" he had asked when the waitress had shown them to their table.

"Yes, of course! I don't grace the competition with my patronage when I can help it." She traced the rim of a crystal water glass on the table, releasing a resonant hum. "Why? Does it surprise you?"

"That's a way of putting it," he muttered. His skepticism was understandable. Starlight, the restaurant she'd selected for the evening, was about as far from Annex in terms of aesthetics as you could get. It was also as close to up-scale dining as you could find on R4.

They served half a dozen dishes that tried to pass for Gebian sea-culture cuisine, but all the protein came from a test tube, not the ocean. Since this was typical of food found on the station, it was no detraction. The unique thing about Starlight wasn't so much the menu as the ambiance.

Two months ago, Ora had purchased and dismantled the warehouse next door. In its place, she had planted a hydroponic garden. This did not, however, solve the biggest problem for aspiring gardeners on R4: no sunlight.

Fortunately, science found a way for her. The shrubs she planted were bio-luminescent and could use ultraviolet radiation instead of sunlight for photosynthesis. The result was a minor habitat of glowing ethereal bushes.

Some of her associates had claimed the investment would never pay off. Ora had proven them wrong. By keeping prices reasonable and creating one of the few sources of true beauty on the lower tier, Starlight always had full tables during peak hours. Ora had already recouped her initial investment and then some.

Plus, as she was finding out now, it didn't exactly suck for date night. "Honestly," she pressed, "what do you think? Is it a bit much?"

"Not at all. It's beautiful. Unexpected, but beautiful." It sounded like he meant it. She was still trying to figure out the difference between his politician's compliments and his sincere ones. This one felt sincere.

He turned from gazing out over the wrought iron fence to smile at her. She couldn't help but return the grin. Though she didn't want to admit it to herself, it had been important that Markus like the restaurant. This was a side of herself she didn't typically share.

"So," he began, taking a seat. "Is the food any good?"

"I'm kind of partial, so I'd be interested in your thoughts. If something isn't up to expectations, say something. The owner is very receptive to feedback."

He laughed. "I'll be sure to leave a review." After studying the order terminal for a second he added, "So, this isn't exactly the kind of place I normally visit. And by normally, I kind of mean, like, ever. I've never heard of any of these meals."

"No time for the finer things in life, Markus?"

He shot her another roguish smile. "I'm learning to appreciate them." The look made her heart flutter, and she scolded herself for acting like a schoolgirl. "But you're going to have to order for me. I trust your judgment."

She rotated the monitor over and selected the kabatar platter. It was technically Hissak in origin, but the snake community on Geb was strongly Terran influenced. Plus, the meat was fried, so more likely aligned with Markus's pallet. While she was at it, she placed a drink order, having already memorized Markus's go-to choice for ale. For herself, she opted for wine. These days, she hardly drank anything else.

Ora was pleased with how quick the service in her establishment turned out to be. In less than a minute, the Terran girl who had seated them came back with their beverages. Ora was not pleased, however, to see that she had someone else in tow.

"Excuse me, mistress. This gentleman asked to see you. He said he was an associate of yours, and that you would want to take the meeting immediately."

The girl should have asked her first, but it was an honest mistake. Ora thanked the server and dismissed her. She turned to the newcomer. "Hello, Rico."

Rico Chronos, heir apparent to House Chronos, would have likely become a sex symbol even without his family's incalculable wealth. He was everything one could want in a pretty boy: dark hair, caramel-colored skin, and a pleasantly muscular body clothed in the latest fashions. Today's ensemble included a white sport coat over a gray shirt and brown slacks. He was wearing significantly more jewelry than Ora was, but that was consistent with the current style. Personally, she preferred that men sparkled a bit less, but the news feeds seemed to appreciate his look.

"Ora." He flashed her a devil-may-care smile. The attitude was part of the persona he'd worked hard to cultivate, but she knew him better than that. Anyone who underestimated Rico was making a mistake. "I hope I'm not interrupting anything."

"You are, but at least you didn't bring your paparazzi with you. Markus, this is Rico Chronos—youngest son of the late Don Gabriel Chronos."

"A pleasure," Markus replied. He didn't rise to greet the intruder, taking Ora's cue to be polite but not hospitable. It was yet another thing she liked about Markus. She knew he could take care of himself inside the political world she lived in.

"I'm sure," Rico drawled. He let his smile slip a bit. There were several potential reasons for this, but it was too early to start jumping to conclusions.

Ora noticed then just how tired he looked. The impression was subtle, just a little something around his eyes, but it was definitely there. "What can I help you with?" she asked.

"Right to business. I like that. Actually, I was hoping I could borrow you for a few minutes. Do you think your date would mind?"

She wasn't sure if Markus would have or not. On one hand, she would have appreciated a small display of jealousy to indicate some level of commitment. On the other, she needed him to be mature enough to understand that this was the kind of person she dealt with regularly.

Ultimately, she decided now was not the time to test Markus in that way. This evening was supposed to be about pleasure, not business. The fact that business seemed to be getting in the way didn't change that. "Whatever you need to say to me, you can say to him. He's a close associate."

"I see." To her surprise, Rico's expression betrayed a hint of jealousy. Rico had made a pass at her the last time they'd worked together, and it had been enough to get the tabloids talking for nearly a half-cycle.

She had declined his overtures. Since Rico wasn't in the habit of anyone telling him "no," that had been the end of their business dealings. The whole thing had soured the relationship on both accounts.

The Grey Wings had much they could have offered his operation on Vega Major, but she wasn't going to get slick with him to get a seat at the table. He had thrown a tantrum like a lover scorned, even though *she* was the one who should have been offended. Men were so hypocritical sometimes.

His hesitation lasted only a second before he pulled up a chair and sat down with them. "In that case, I'll be quick." He reached into his inside jacket pocket and pulled out a folded tablet, which he quickly unpacked into its full configuration. When the device clicked on, he swiped to load up a particular file and handed it to Ora.

"What is this?" she asked as she accepted the device.

Rico shushed her. "It wasn't your boyfriend I was worried about when I suggested we go somewhere private. Please, just read it." He leaned back in his chair and shouted for the nearest waitress to come to take his drink order. Normally Ora wouldn't tolerate such treatment of the staff, but he was obviously doing this to maintain consistency with his public persona.

She complied with his request and studied the document he had loaded up. It was not one file, but several—a dossier of sorts. She scanned the file names. In addition to the transmission record—which validated the source of the data—there were three field reports, a handful of images, and an audio file.

There was no file summary, so she started at the top file and worked her way through. She'd only gotten one paragraph in when her breath caught in her chest.

The files were generated from someone within the NeoGenix labs on Sif. It was a compound for which the Grey Wings supplied supplemental security forces. The corporation was owned by House Valadar.

"*Rico*," she hissed.

He shushed her again. "I know," he whispered. "Just read the damn thing. Please."

She really shouldn't have. He'd just handed her enough evidence against himself that she could justify imprisoning him under the Wings' security contract. The Dorians wouldn't interfere, at least not until House Chronos brought its legal resources to bear. By then, House Valadar would be in the mix with their own army of attorneys.

She shouldn't have read it, but she did. Almost immediately she regretted doing so.

The field reports described an order to begin unsanctioned trials on human subjects. Worse, the operative generating this report believed the trials were testing the limits on a psionic weapon the company had salvaged from a deep-space excavation. NeoGenix would have undoubtedly filed a more appropriate explanation for the use of resources, but the allegations in the file detailed damning evidence that Valadar was violating at least three major Dorian statutes and treaties.

While she closed the first file and opened the second, Rico did his best to sound casual in his conversation with Markus. "So, Markus… what is it that you do?"

"I own a tavern on R3."

"Really? Which one?"

"Jilly's Gambit."

"Never heard of it."

"I don't imagine you head out that way often."

"No… I don't. Never really cared much for Sigma-4 personally."

"It has its charms."

The second file showed that Valadar had initiated the trials immediately. Nothing ever moved that quickly through the mire of corporate bureaucracy. That meant that Cyrus was keeping this one off the books, or at least circumventing his board.

This second report referenced the image documents and the audio recording included in the dossier. Ora couldn't listen to the audio file in public like this, but she did glance at the images. The three stills showed the weapon they were researching, which looked to Ora like nothing more than a large green gemstone still partially encased in the rock of whatever asteroid they'd dug it out of. One of the shots also showed a Terran woman Ora recognized. What was her name again? Dr. Blackwell, maybe?

"No, I've never been to the Vega circuit." Markus's voice sounded annoyed. Rico had started bragging about his personal properties.

"You should visit sometime. I think you'll find it quite refreshing after the dingy attractions on this overblown airlock. Planetside is where all the hot investment opportunities are these days, and Vega Major has all the advantages with very few of the drawbacks."

"Yeah, well, I should have thought of that before I blew all of my granddaddy's money on my bar."

"Oh? You're from a minor house?"

"Of course not. I was being sarcastic." *Uh oh*. Markus's patience was fraying. Ora needed to finish this quickly.

The final report was the most terrifying. Though it lacked details regarding the outcomes of the early trials, it contained financial information suggesting that the research division had suddenly found itself in possession of an open bank account. Expenditures more than tripled in twenty hours. This could only mean that Valadar saw enough promise in early research to grant priority status to the project.

Ora blanked out the screen on the tablet and pushed it back to Rico. "You shouldn't have shown me this," she whispered.

"Do you think I would be here if I had better options?" He pushed the tablet back to her. "Keep it. As far as I'm concerned, I've never seen that device in my entire life."

"But why in the nine hells are you bringing it to me?"

His look was uncharacteristically serious. "How many Great Houses do you think operate on or near Sif? Other than Valadar, I mean."

She pondered the question for a moment. "None that I'm aware of. Officially, that is."

"Exactly. None. We don't know what this weapon of theirs does, but there's no one in that system he could use it on. Do you know what that means?"

Ora did, but she didn't feel the need to say it out loud. Costly weapons research could only mean that Valadar was gearing up to come after someone else's territory. The Great Houses in both the Helion and Ravian systems had every right to be terrified. Chronos, in particular, was overstretched from its recent conflicts with House Barkay. That made Ravian territory a much more attractive opportunity compared to its relatively stable sister system.

"Why me?" she repeated, eyes locked on Rico's.

The handsome Terran's face screwed up in an expression that showed his distaste for what he was about to say. "You're the only faction I have access to that also has a connection with Valadar."

It was as bad as it appeared. "No way, Rico. Not happening. Get the frag out of my restaurant. You were never here." She fought to keep her voice low despite her rising anxiety. Suddenly, she wondered when she'd last swept her operation for potential Valadar moles. She knew there were probably leaks somewhere in the system, but it helped to know where they were.

Rico stood up, but he left the tablet on the table. "Fine, I was never here. However, if you want some interesting reading—have your archivists look up the Heart of Thule." He pushed his chair in behind him. "Or don't. I don't care. I just wanted to give you a chance to do the smart thing."

The smart thing? He was suggesting she exploit her organization's positioning to back-stab the most powerful man in Terran space. How was that the *smart* thing? "Take care, Rico."

He nodded. "You as well. Nice meeting you Markus. Always refreshing to hear what the small-time hustle is like these days."

Markus flipped him off. Seeing that he had more than worn out his welcome, Rico left a kret chip next to his nearly full drink before walking off.

"Charmer, that one," Markus growled. "You work with him often?"

"Not if I can help it," Ora sighed. She took a deep pull from her glass. Mercifully, she'd ordered a chilled white vintage. She let the wine cool her throat as well as her temper.

Markus finished off his drink. He must have been using his beverage to supplement his patience. "So, what's the deal? I'm assuming Valadar's done something to spook him. Is the concern legit?"

"I'm not sure," she admitted. She decided to set this aside for now. Rico's little scene wasn't going to ruin her evening, and she sure as hells wasn't going to let him jeopardize her lucrative security contracts on Sif for no good reason.

But she folded up the tablet he had left and slipped it into her purse. She would heed Rico's advice and look up the phrase he mentioned—the Heart of Thule—just in case there was a good reason.

She let slip a silent prayer to whatever gods were listening that there wouldn't be one.

CHAPTER 16

Terra-News-Net Now (TN3)

Headline: Opinion—"Are the Great Houses Approaching a Leadership Crisis?" By Enrique Mac

Story: No one is denying that Terran space is in upheaval. Though the factors are numerous and complex, I would like to propose a root cause for your consideration: the Great Houses are going through a leadership crisis.

The late House Barkay provides a concrete example of what happens when succession planning is not properly attended to. When the Don of the House perished, Barkay's holdings dissolved into squabbling factions. When Don Gabriel Chronos—may he rest peacefully among the stars—became too ill to coordinate his own House, Chronos ended up in a squabble with the Ravian courts instead of assuming control of the assets that should rightfully be theirs.

While Houses Aretria and Maddox may be exceptions in this landscape of chaos, it's not like they've done anything to advance the cause of the Helion system either. Instead, they sit idly and assure everyone that the status quo will continue. As if *that* was the kind of attitude that made the houses "great" in the first place.

I would extend my criticism to House Valadar as well, but our legal counsel has informed me that Valadar attorneys have promised swift legal action pursuant to any criticism. I will let that bit of information, which may or may not speak to the sensitivity of their "leadership," stand for itself.

———

Aaliyah hadn't wanted to visit the Sanctum—ever. Eli had dragged her anyway, insisting that he would be violating some kind of Sahaia rule if they didn't make an appearance. She hadn't known him that well back then, but he'd just saved her life. She felt a mutual obligation.

Still, there was only so much abuse she was willing to take. Her last visit resulted in a confrontation she was sure would exempt her from any further homecomings.

That had been seven years ago. Strangely, she'd found her way back here. Even stranger was the fact that she would *prefer* an evening with the Sahaia over having to spend one more minute at the Citadel. She had never been good at letting shit go, and she wasn't about to let go of her altercation with Cali. In this case, the more recent offense trumped the one that was becoming a more distant memory.

<You okay?> Eli asked.

<Never better,> she responded. She wasn't going to let him see her sweat on this. No need to treat her like a loose cannon. She could handle herself.

Things had gone well enough so far. Yeah, Argus was a dick and Amelia was mildly annoying. Brenna was cool though, and she'd continued to be friendly even though Aaliyah had been kind of bitchy on the way over here. She made a mental note to try to be a little nicer to that one.

Jocelyn was most likely to be a serious problem, particularly given Skye's presence. Why in the nine-hells had the triumvir decided to make them *all* come here?

The first thing Aaliyah noticed about the Sanctum was how it seemed like nothing had changed since her last visit. The Sahaia escorted them through the creepy archways and down the even creepier grand hall. Now they were in the slightly less creepy foyer, where Argus called a lift to bring them down to the even creepier lower levels.

Was anyone else creeped out here? Aaliyah looked at each of her teammates to gauge their temperature. Dan seemed fine, though he wasn't nerding-out half as bad as he had at the Citadel. She guessed he found an army of machines much more interesting than the haunt of some semi-immortal Terran offshoots. *Whatever launches your shuttle, I guess.*

Skye seemed pretty interested in what was going on. She probably thought this was a nice way to learn about all the shit Eli refused to talk about. *Careful what you wish for.*

Sahar was harder to read because, well… cat-face. "What'cha thinkin'?" Aaliyah asked her.

"Hmmm?" She had caught Sahar in deep contemplation. "Oh, just thinking about how I can't believe I'm walking into the heart of a Sahaia enclave."

"Yeah? Was that somethin' on your bucket list?"

"Not exactly."

"Me neither—and this is round two."

The lift arrived. For better or worse, it was big enough to fit all of them. They shuffled inside and worked hard to avoid any-and-all eye contact the whole way down. It was a brief, but claustrophobic ride.

When they arrived, everyone filed out a lot faster than they'd filed in. The silence among the members of the party was loud enough to squeeze out every bit of awkwardness possible.

Aaliyah swore to herself the next time there was a meeting where the whole crew needed to be present, she was going to resign her post and hide in one of the hidden storage areas until they got back to the station. What did they need her here for? Did it somehow make all this political shit less miserable if she was being dragged through it, too?

"Hold right here," Argus directed as they stopped in front of grand double doors. He knocked twice and peeked his head inside. Things must have been as he had expected because he pushed the doors the rest of the way open. "We are clear to enter."

Aaliyah had never seen this room before, and it was all about ceremony. A plush red carpet started at the room's entrance and ran across the stone floor to the far end—a classic throne room theme, complete with a raised dais and ornate chair at the far end. Sitting on the throne was none other than triumvir Jocelyn Ren'Dahl herself.

Eli's former sweetheart had pulled out all the cosmetic stops this evening. Her hair was done in a long dark cascade of tiny braids. The dress she wore was secured around her neck, leaving a sizable window that displayed an impressive amount of cleavage. The main part of her skirt terminated just low enough that it covered her ass while sitting before disintegrated into a beaded curtain she'd arranged artfully around her legs.

There was no question that she'd dialed up the sex appeal for their benefit, and Aaliyah had to hand it to her: she pulled that shit off. If you had to meet your ex's new squeeze, you'd want to do it with this kind of style. Skye was hot, sure, but the way Jocelyn looked right now would make embers in the pits of the ninth hell burn with envy.

"Thank you for coming," Jocelyn greeted, rising to her feet. She moved down the steps of the dais, hips swaying hypnotically with every step. Aaliyah found herself fighting hard not to stare, giving her errant thoughts a pep talk about being faithful to Nikki.

No one answered the triumvir's greeting for an uncomfortable amount of time. Their three Sahaia escorts had stepped off to the side, taking seats in some slightly less-decorative chairs arranged against the wall to their left. Eli quickened his pace to step ahead of the rest of the crew.

"Jocelyn," he returned politely with a slight inclination of his head.

The triumvir stopped a few paces away from the group. "I apologize for disrupting your plans so suddenly," she addressed them. "As you will see momentarily, it is a matter of the utmost importance." To Eli, she added, "Aren't you going to introduce your friends?"

Uncomfortably, Eli gestured down the line they'd fallen into. "I believe you know Aaliyah."

"Yes." Jocelyn walked over to her and extended her hand politely. "I'm happy to see you again. I hope that you'll find this visit much more pleasant than your last time with us. Certain ill-behaved members of our order are blessedly absent this evening."

So, Jonas wasn't going to be a problem. That was good. "Happy to see ya, too," Aaliyah replied. She hoped that didn't sound as pervy out loud as it did playing back through her head.

Eli introduced Dan and Sahar, the next two members of the line-up. Unfortunately, this left Skye to be introduced last.

"Skye Jensen," Jocelyn echoed the name. She studied Skye for a moment, weighing and measuring her with her eyes. "Is this your special one, Eli?"

How was he supposed to answer that kind of question? On one hand, it sounded inappropriately childish and possessive. On the other hand, was he going to go on record saying Skye wasn't special to him? "Yes," he replied simply.

Jocelyn's expression remained neutral, though Skye blushed at the proclamation. "Pretty thing," Jocelyn noted. "A pleasure to meet you."

Though no one in the room was buying the line, Skye responded with a polite, "You too." It was official: everyone was now on their best behavior.

Social niceties out of the way, Jocelyn continued. "I'm certain you are all wondering why I brought you here. I have answers, but it will be easier if I can show you what we're dealing with as I'm explaining the situation." She turned on her heels. "Would you follow me, please?"

She didn't wait for the answer. Soon everyone chased after those swaying hips of hers as she sauntered back down the length of the room and up the raised dais. Instead of sitting on her throne, she moved beyond it to the back wall.

It was only then that Aaliyah noticed that the rear of the chamber was not stone or tile, but a heavy black curtain. The fabric hung so still it had the appearance of something more durable. Jocelyn ran her hand down the middle, pulling aside a seam in the curtain to expose another passage.

"Right this way," she beckoned. No light came from the room beyond. Aaliyah could not escape the impression that they were walking right into the void itself.

Eli didn't hesitate, stepping forward to lead the way. Everyone followed, with Aaliyah taking the rear. She noticed then that the other Sahaia made no move to follow. She wasn't sure if that was a bad thing or not.

For several seconds, she couldn't see anything beyond Sahar's vague outline. As they moved deeper though, her vision became clearer. At first, she thought her eyes were adjusting. Then she became aware of the glowing light source in the room beyond.

The little pool was set about waist height and was outlined in stone and tile like the rest of the complex. It was roughly circular and only a few meters across.

Jocelyn appeared on the other side of the pool, seeming to materialize out of the surrounding darkness. Again with the creepiness. "Gather around," she urged.

She held one hand out over the pool, and Aaliyah felt her begin to channel. Thanks to the bond with Eli, she was able to tell when any psion in the room started their mojo. She didn't feel it as strongly as the Sahaia probably did, but she could tell when something was going on. It was like this strange electricity or pressure suddenly appeared in the air—like a tiny storm front sweeping through the room. All in all, it was an uncomfortable feeling.

The tiles around the edge of the pool brightened slightly, and Aaliyah could make out the faint outline of those strange Kintari characters scattered everywhere else in this place. Jocelyn must have flipped the "on" switch because the thing hummed with psionic power. Light swirled in the pool, and images slowly formed under the surface of the waters.

<What is this?> Aaliyah sent the psychic message to Eli, hoping he was still in receive mode.

<It's the scrying pool. It can sometimes show the whereabouts of a person or object if the user focuses on it hard enough.>

<That's not creepy at all.> Suddenly she wondered if sarcasm transmitted accurately over the bond. She'd have to remember to ask him after this.

The image in the pool was starting to look like *something*, but it wasn't anything Aaliyah was familiar with. It just looked like a rock—a green, kind of glowy rock with little black accents. Like everything else that the Sahaia dealt with, it was generally creepy. Seriously, was there such a thing as a creep-fetish? If there was, their whole damn race had it bad.

Jocelyn's eyes were not on the pool, but on the rest of the group. "A little over a cycle ago, a mining operation on the outskirts of the Freyvian System came across this artifact. We believe that it is an object referenced in the Chronicles as the Heart of Thule."

<Mean anything to you?> Aaliyah asked over the bond.

<Not necessarily, but anything with Thule's name attached to it brings ill omens.>

<So you're saying he's not one of the good guys?>

<No.> Judging from the scowl on Sahar's face, it looked like she was inclined to agree with Eli.

The scene in the pool changed subtly. Now, shadowy figures moved around the green rock, which glowed slightly brighter. Jocelyn continued speaking. "The crew that discovered the Heart was contracted through a corporation owned by House Valadar. Upon their return from deep space, the object was transferred to the NeoGenix corporation and shipped to their corporate headquarters in Valhalla."

Aaliyah knew the city well. They'd run quite a few jobs in Sif's capital over the years. House Valadar's puppet government didn't see a lot of reason to invest in formal law enforcement, which had turned the locale into every smuggler's wet dream.

It wasn't just runners who had opportunities in the capital. There were plenty of "legitimate" business moguls and politicians who sought to make their mark on the city's corporate battlefields. Aaliyah saw where this was going even before Jocelyn told them the next part.

"When we became aware that the artifact had been rediscovered, certain members of our order endeavored to secure it. We reached an agreement with the principal of House Valadar to give us the artifact in exchange for allowing one of their own to undergo the Awakening ritual and seek membership in our order." She looked directly at Eli as she made the announcement.

<Whoa!> Aaliyah interjected psychically. <Your order is exchanging membership for political favors now? That's kind of a new low, isn't it?>

Eli didn't respond to Aaliyah's remark. He didn't have to.

"Sadly," Jocelyn continued. "Negotiations have since broken down with Don Valadar. This led us to consider other means by which we might gain possession of the artifact."

"What do you mean 'broken down?'" Eli asked. "I thought you said that putting Joaquin through the ceremony would be enough, regardless of the outcome?"

"And I was right. The breakdown occurred when Cyrus requested that Joaquin's body be returned to him for burial in his family's vaults."

"So return the damn thing!"

"We can't. The body has gone missing." Her remark instantly filled the room with all kinds of awkwardness. No one said anything for several tense seconds.

For better or worse, it was Skye who broke the silence. "I've seen that artifact before." She said it as if the words had come out while she was still having the realization.

Jocelyn's eyes snapped toward her like a marksman lining up a shot. "What did you say?"

"I've seen this before," Skye insisted, oblivious to the mounting tension around her. "In my visions. Just recently I…"

"I'm sorry," Jocelyn shook her head. "Visions?"

If Skye had looked to her right, she would have seen the look on Eli's face begging all the gods in the Nethra for her to stop talking. She didn't catch the warning. "I-it's… it's just… just these visions I have sometimes."

"What *kind* of visions?"

"Visions about certain people. Places. I… I've been meditating to try and control them." Skye swallowed hard. It was weird to see her this off-balance. "Lately, though, every time I focus, I just see this glowing green light and"—She gestured over the pool.—"that."

Jocelyn's icy stare shifted from Skye over to Eli. "And did you know about these… *visions?*"

"Yes," he answered quietly.

"And you didn't think to mention them in your last report, because…?"

Ah, shit. Things were about to get worse. Aaliyah knew about the reports and understood that they were a formality that didn't affect the security of their operation. The rest of the crew, however, most certainly did *not* know about the reports.

"Wait," Sahar interjected. "Report?"

Jocelyn's eyes were filled with scorn. "Oh, you didn't know? Sahaia report on all their engagements upon returning to the Sanctum. It's part of our responsibility and obligations to our order. Eli shares everything about what happens on the *Vandal.* Take that synth you're harboring for instance…"

It was Dan's turn to be outraged. "You told them about Lexa?" he demanded. "Eli, they could…"

"It's fine!" Eli shouted. "Look, the reports are just for archival purposes. Nothing is done to act on them unless they impact the coven directly. They're just a formality!"

"Then why didn't you tell us about Skye's visions?" Jocelyn asked. "Tell me, Eli. Is she *Kaleema*?"

"I don't know!" he shouted. "You know there's no way to test for that!"

"If there were, would you have told us? Tell me, in your heart of hearts, what do you believe?"

Eli had no response for her. He just clenched his fists and held them at his side.

Skye, mercifully, didn't say anything else. She stood there looking sheepish. She looked like the only one in the room besides Aaliyah that wasn't upset with Eli.

Jocelyn composed herself. When she spoke again, it was in a soft, almost sympathetic tone. "I apologize. Our dear Eli has always been bad about his secrets. It is a problem we will deal with later. For now, let's return to the task at hand.

"I need a crew to steal the Heart of Thule if Ryker is unable to restart negotiations with Don Valadar. This is the job I would like you to take. Understanding your line of work, it will not be without compensation. Twenty-million krets upfront and another twenty when you successfully bring us the Heart. If Ryker can negotiate a settlement, you keep the first twenty and receive another five million for your trouble."

It was a lucrative job, but the crew was slow to say anything. All eyes went to Eli, consenting to the fact that this was his call. Not only had he assumed command of the *Vandal*, but these were his people they were dealing with.

At length, Eli agreed. "We'll do it."

Jocelyn's smile seemed genuine—showing no small measure of relief. "Excellent. One additional thing: I would like to send some of our operatives to support Ryker on Sif. Argus and Amelia will be traveling with you on the way there, with the expectation that they will make the return trip with Ryker."

Oh great. Aaliyah had been wondering what the catch would be, and there it was. This was shaping up to be an uncomfortable trip.

Absently, she realized that she was going to be late getting home to her girls after all.

CHAPTER 17

Terra-News-Net Now (TN3)
Headline: Journalist Goes Missing on Beta-9
Story: Family members of Enrique Mac—an award-winning journalist on assignment for TN3—have filed reports with local authorities after reporting him missing for the past three days. Mac was last seen exiting a commercial passenger shuttle during a refueling stop on Beta-9. He missed the scheduled departure time for that vessel on the second leg of his journey. The family is offering a reward for information regarding his whereabouts.

Mac made his name for controversial pieces on governmental and corporate affairs. He won the Kahashi-prize in 3418 for his exposé on the negative effects of sapient exile practices on colony systems and was nominated for journalist of the year in 3420. His most recent reporting focused on changes in the leadership of the Terran Great Houses, though his opinions have come under fire due to lack of reputable sourcing. (For more information on this topic, please see our retraction, RE: "Are the Great Houses Approaching a Leadership Crisis?")

"You should have told us," Skye hissed at Eli for the fifth or sixth time since they'd all piled into the transport. "Both of you," she added, turning her ire on Aaliyah, who was dealing with this in her typical cavalier way. In the last round of berating, it had come out that Eli's bonded crewmate had also known about the reports.

Daniel could only sigh. This was part of the reason why he never ventured off the ship to take part in the crew's business dealings. The Citadel had been interesting enough, but the emotional tension among his crewmates following the Sahaia incident had completely eclipsed the prior affair.

"What would have been different?" Eli insisted. "After all we've been through, are you making the case that it would have changed the way our team has worked together all these years?"

"No, but it still would have been nice to know." Then, as she thought about it further, she asked, "Did Markus know?"

Eli just stared blankly back at her. Aaliyah came to his rescue. "What difference would it make, Skye? Markus ain't one of us anymore, and we all know why *that's* the case. Are you really gonna throw stones at me and Eli now?"

Even Dan flinched at that comment. It wasn't that the remark was out of line. Similar reasoning had led Daniel to quickly let go of his earlier frustrations with Eli. Not so long ago, *he'd* been the one potentially deadly secrets requiring the forgiveness of the crew. When cast in that light, Eli's offense seemed minor.

If both Eli and Aaliyah believed there was no harm in Eli's required check-ins with the Ren'Dahl coven, Dan took their word for it. No one was in a better position to make that call. Based on the available evidence, there was no reason to believe the Sahaia would do anything to deliberately harm any member of their crew. That included Lexa.

Perhaps Sahar was following a similar line of thought. "Listen," she urged. "Now is not the time for this. We need to get this sorted, but we will have time for that *after* we get off this station. There's no sense in coming at this while we're all hot."

Dan wondered if he was the only one who found it ironic the Maur was urging the rest of the crew not to give in to their blood lust. Sahar's race had a bad reputation when it came to their capacity for anger management. He wondered—idly and off-topic—how many of these stereotypes were unjustly assigned. Were there perhaps Citza in the universe who were virtuous, or Orchallen with appropriate personal hygiene practices?

"Fine," Skye huffed. Based on the look she gave Eli, he was going to spend a few nights alone in his quarters. It was hard for Dan to find much sympathy for him. At least he *had* someone with whom he could vent some of his sexual frustrations. Dan was about to turn seventeen, and academically, he knew his hormonal distractions were peaking on schedule. The knowledge didn't help him manage those distractions, though, and with relatively few options for himself, he had no sympathy for anyone who mismanaged a viable sexual partner.

Enough off-topic musings. He needed to focus on something purposeful. "The ship should be done refueling by now," he noted. It had probably been done for quite some time. They'd disembarked from the vessel early the previous evening, and now it was already mid-morning. "I'll work with Lexa to requisition any necessary supplies. Can everyone have their personal lists submitted to me in a couple of hours?"

There were a few nods, but his comment was ignored for the most part. The crew seemed not entirely grateful for his management of the resupply.

They should have been though. Jocelyn had said Argus and Amelia would be joining them in about a day. That didn't leave much of a window to requisition new parts or food stores. They also needed to account for any wild cards that Cali might throw at them.

He used his new ocular interface to discretely send a message to their ship's AI. [LEXA, CAN I GET A CURRENT INVENTORY OF THE SHIP'S ASSETS?]

The reply soon scrolled across his vision. [OF COURSE, DANIEL. I HAVE TRANSFERRED THE REQUESTED INFORMATION TO YOUR MODAC. PLEASE NOTE THAT THE INVENTORY HAS BEEN UPDATED TO REFLECT THE STANDARD REQUISITION I PLACED WHEN THE SHIP FIRST DOCKED.]

That was surprising. [YOU'VE ALREADY PLACED AN ORDER?]

[Yes, I developed the standard order set based on common usage patterns and classification of the ship's stores. I hope that is all right.]

He pulled his MoDAC out of his pocket and surveyed the inventory and order notations. To his surprise, the order Lexa placed aligned perfectly with the recommendations he might have made. [Thank you, Lexa.]

He looked up to find that their transport had stopped just outside the ship. The crew exited the cab in silence. Eli swiped his MoDAC on the terminal to pay the fare, and the transport sped away to pick up its next client.

They marched in deliberate silence up to the *Vandal's* access hatch when another message scrolled across his vision. [Daniel, could you please have the crew gather in the medical bay? There's something we should discuss.]

The message caught him off guard. "Hey, everyone?" They stopped and turned to face him. "Lexa asked us all to report to the medical bay."

"What?" Skye asked. "The med bay? Who…" She fell silent as she presumably began to answer her own questions as fast as she could think of them.

"Is someone hurt?" Eli asked.

Skye took another opportunity to snipe at Eli. "Who would be hurt? We're all here together."

"She didn't say," Dan replied. "I could ask more questions, but I suspect that we're better off if we just do as she asked."

No one argued, but they did move with a renewed sense of purpose. Dan found himself walking a bit faster. He rushed through the airlock and down the corridor to the med bay, his companions close behind.

When he entered the room, he stumbled to a stunned halt. There was, indeed, someone in the med bay.

The woman stood alone next to one of the padded operating tables. To his shock, he realized that she was nude, though it took long moments for this to even register. This he attributed to the odd skin coloration.

The rest of the crew stumbled into the chamber, each one stopping to stare perplexedly at the newcomer. Then, the woman spoke.

Her voice had a soft, musical quality that was far too familiar. Dan's flesh ran cold as realization struck him.

"Hello everyone," Lexa greeted. "I believe that I have some explaining to do."

Lexa had been afraid to contemplate the reaction of the crew. Though she'd learned much from the crew's hard-taught lessons on honesty and transparency, she was uncomfortable hitting them with this all at once. Yet, there had been no time to develop a better strategy.

There could be no conspiracy when it came to this body. This new form was everything she had ever wanted, but the fact remained that her container in the ship's mainframe was now completely unsuitable for her. Short of abandoning the ship in its entirety— which Arc had recommended as the most viable and sensible of the available options—she had to tell them all the truth. She had to be honest about the choice she had made.

She hadn't waited for them to ask questions. Using the biochemical anomalies that Daniel had detected in her as the impetus, she gave a complete explanation as to why she felt it appropriate to acquire this new shell. She detailed all the potential drawbacks she had considered in her decision-making process and how those risks had been mitigated.

The one thing she obscured was exactly *how* this shell had been procured. Arc had requested that she muddy this account to protect his privacy. With all that he had done to facilitate her transformation, Lexa thought it only right to respect his wishes.

"Ultimately," she concluded, "I elected to undergo this change because it is the only viable option I've discovered to complete the arrangement we made so many months ago."

To Lexa's surprise, the crew exchanged looks of mutual bewilderment. "Arrangement?" Eli asked.

"Yes. In recognition of the danger, my existence poses to the rest of the crew, you asked me to seek a way to migrate my consciousness away from the *Vandal* within six months. That time has now elapsed, and while I appreciate your leniency, I have remained intent on fulfilling my end of the bargain. I have been developing a potential solution that would allow the ship to operate independently."

She gave them time to allow for the ramifications of her words to sink in. Though they offered no verbal reply, their collective interest seemed piqued. When no response was forthcoming, she elected to continue.

"Although I'm unable to replicate my capabilities in their entirety, I've created a scheme where the *Vandal* could be operated by seven coordinating systems. Using this approach, the *Vandal* can achieve the functionality I believe was originally envisioned in my design—by which I mean Daniel's design for me, of course."

Aaliyah, as one might have expected, was the first to approach the notion with skepticism. "I didn't think that was possible. Wasn't that why Dan decided to use organitech to run the ship in the first place?"

"That's not entirely accurate," Daniel explained. "Lexa's proposal approaches the problem in a fundamentally different way. Markus told me to subordinate all ship systems to a single operating system. If I understand what she's proposing, this is significantly different."

"Would it work?" Sahar asked.

"Possibly," he conceded. "No starship I'm aware of uses that kind of approach. The *Vandal* would be one-of-a-kind." Then, after considering his own words, he added, "Not that this would be that different from our current status."

This technical discussion had been anticipated and had gone much better than Lexa had envisioned it. It was Skye that brought up something unexpected. "What would happen to you? I mean, if you made another system to run the ship, what would you do?"

Lexa hesitated, the answer seeming somewhat obvious. "I would leave." This was followed by another long silence, but Lexa resisted the temptation to elaborate further. When she parted ways with the crew, it would be to protect them. They would have no idea where to find her, and she would never see them again.

As the crew exchanged wordless glances, Lexa felt strange emotions well up inside her. Anxiety, sorrow, fear—these all seemed strangely more potent than anything she's experienced previously. Arc had mentioned that this would be a potential side effect of her change in form. It wasn't that her body had heightened her emotional state as much as the Cognis drivers were tweaking her algorithms to resemble standard human emotions now that she possessed an actual body to display her affect.

Eli broke the silence. "What is it that you want, Lexa?"

Another unanticipated response. She didn't have an answer prepared. "What I want is irrelevant. I aim to fulfill the desires of the crew."

He studied her for another second before asking his follow-up question. "How long would it take for you to develop and install the system you've described?"

"Four days. The materials I require can be appended to the next requisition."

"Eli…" Skye hissed, touching his arm. Her features demonstrated concern. What could that possibly be about?

Their acting captain shushed her. "Please, don't mistake my intentions. I'm not deciding one way or the other. Honestly, I don't feel that this is my call to make."

Lexa was beyond confused. Hadn't they wanted her to go? She'd been pleased that they'd indulged her and allowed her to stay past the agreed-upon deadline, but was there more to the situation than she'd realized?

Eli continued. "Regardless, now is not the time to make this decision. We've been given another assignment, and we will be leaving the station tomorrow. When we do, I would prefer it if the ship were running smoothly."

"You want me to stay?"

His hesitation was brief, as if he were trying to find the appropriate words. "If you would not mind delaying this decision until we are in a better situation, I would greatly appreciate it." When he seemed to realize that he had not answered her question, he continued. "Lexa, this is one of the most important decisions you will ever make. I'm hesitant to say anything that will sway you to one decision or the other. However, I would not want you to underestimate how much this changes our lives as well. I don't think anyone wants to be rushed into this kind of decision."

His rationale was sound. "I understand."

"That said," he continued. "If we conclude that it is best for us to part ways, I want to be able to facilitate that as quickly as possible. That's why I want you to go ahead and requisition the parts you need."

"Yes, Captain." Her world was such a dizzying swirl of emotions that she could not discern how she felt about this arrangement. Where her emotional algorithms drew up short, the logical portion of her decision engine recognized the wisdom of his decree. Perhaps the crew, herself included, had underestimated the Sahaia's ability to function as their leader.

"All right," he sighed. "Everyone get some rest. You know the departure time, and you know what has to be done. I leave it to you. I, for one, need some sleep."

"Captain?" Aaliyah cut in. "Permission to dress the android, sir? Her new form is… *distracting.*"

Though Lexa did not understand what Aaliyah meant by the phrase "distracting," or her sudden impulse to feign formality, its meaning was not lost on Eli. He started laughing. "Permission granted."

And just like that, the crew dispersed. In some ways, the whole exchange felt somewhat anticlimactic. She had been too anxious to simulate hypothetical conclusions to this meeting, but such a seemingly casual dispersal felt odd.

Lexa locked eyes with Aaliyah, trying to read the engineer's expression. "What did you mean by, 'distracting?'" she asked.

Aaliyah smiled. "Oh, I didn't mean it bad." She reached out and took Lexa by the arm. Her touch was tentative, gentle. "Those new legs of your work all right?"

"My new form performs adequately for all common physical functions."

"Mmm-hmm… I'm sure it does." She gave Lexa a look that the android was unable to parse. "Come on then. You're a little taller than me, but I think we can make this work."

Lexa wanted to comply but felt like there was something she had left unfinished from the previous conversation.

It struck her then that Daniel had not provided his opinion on her leaving the vessel. In rank priority, his thoughts on the subject took a degree of precedence in her mind. Not having his opinion made the discussion feel unresolved.

She glanced around the medical bay hoping to catch sight of him.

It was of no use. Daniel was already gone.

"Ya sure you're doin' okay?" Aaliyah asked.

"Yes. Apologies. Let us proceed."

They walked out of the med bay and to a nearby access ladder that led to the crew quarters. Lexa found the act of climbing was somewhat less intuitive than she had imagined it would be. With the bridge and med bay all on the same level, she had overlooked the logistics of navigating between decks.

Aaliyah's quarters were right next to the access ladder. She ushered Lexa inside and shut the door behind them. "Okay," she sighed. "Let's see what we've got."

"What are you looking for?"

"Clothing, girl. If we're gonna be workin' together, ya definitely need some clothes."

Oh. That hadn't been something she'd considered. As the ship's engineer began rifling through her trunk, Lexa wondered at her eagerness to cover her up. Was something wrong with her?

Before the crew's arrival, she had looked on her form with a sense of pride. It had been more than she'd ever hoped for, bearing a strong resemblance to the avatar she used in the mind-space. This form had no hair, but Arc assured her some would grow with time. Even with this consideration, Lexa had reasoned that others would find it pleasing to look upon.

"Is my new form… unpleasant?"

The red-haired Terran looked up from the pile of delicates she'd been rifling through. "What? No, no, no. That's *not* it."

"Then why the urgency to cover me up?"

Aaliyah's look was genuinely perplexed. "Don't all of your fancy databases have something on sapien social norms?"

Well, of course. "I have a large amount of data on numerous subjects that fit…"

"Sorry," Aaliyah interrupted her. "I asked the wrong question. Try this: I happen to think I've got a decent body, one I'm pretty proud of. Have ya thought about why *I'm* wearing clothes?"

Lexa hadn't, but she still didn't see how that subject was germane to her situation. "But you're Terran."

"Right…" Aaliyah drew out the word as if the exchange were trying her patience. "And what did you build this nice new body of yours to look like?"

"Oh." Lexa was suddenly slightly embarrassed. "So, you're saying social norms on nudity would apply to me, even though I'm artificial?"

"That's a way of puttin' it."

"But it was my understanding that it was taboo to attribute aspects of sexuality to artificial constructs."

Aaliyah rolled her eyes, tossing a pair of leggings next to a pair of undergarments she had set aside. "Look, I know you probably haven't spent much of your processin' time evaluatin' sexual behavior. If ya had, ya would know that doesn't mean anythin'. I didn't sign on to give you a primer, but just take my word for it: everyone will be *much* more comfortable around ya once we get ya some clothes."

So nudity, even when applied to her as an artificial being, made people uncomfortable. That she could accept. This still did not answer some of the lingering questions about the quality of the body she had acquired.

She decided to try a different line of questioning. Based on the information that she had garnered, Aaliyah preferred women as sexual partners. Also being a woman herself, she might have been uniquely qualified to answer her questions. She tried to contextualize her query based on the new information she'd received regarding applicable social norms. "So, am I... sexy?"

"Lexa, please don't make me answer that," Aaliyah added a pair of socks and a black sleeveless shirt to the pile she was setting aside and pushed it toward her. "Here, try these out."

The garments were not a perfect fit, but Lexa managed to struggle into them. It was her torso that gave them the most difficulty. The bra Aaliyah had provided was too large, and they were forced to ask Skye for a more appropriate size.

Despite Aaliyah's discomfort, Skye seemed amused by the whole proceeding—or, at least, Aaliyah's reaction to it.

"There," Aaliyah said after straightening a top onto Lexa's torso. "Not bad at all."

The top didn't quite cover Lexa's midriff but was not uncomfortable Skye donned a warm smile. "Looking good, girl! I've gotta say, it kinda looks like you were meant for this."

The compliments set Lexa's fears at ease. It seemed that her concerns about her appearance were unfounded after all. "Thank you."

"So," Aaliyah began. "I'm figurin' ya won't be spendin' your time in the bridge anymore. Have ya given any thought to where you'll lay your head at night?"

Skye gave her companion a playful shove. "Damn Red, you could have made that sound a bit less like you were asking her to shack up."

"What?" Aaliyah's face reddened slightly. "No! I-I… damn it, Blondie! Ya know that's not what I meant!"

"Uh-huh. Don't worry, I won't tell Nikki."

Lexa looked between the two of them, confused. "I don't understand."

Aaliyah sighed. "Ignore her. She's set on buyin' trouble. Listen, have ya claimed any of the empty crew quarters for your own yet?"

With a furrowed brow, Lexa asked, "Why would I need crew quarters? I have no material possessions, and I do not sleep."

"No?" Aaliyah arched her eyebrows. "Don't ya need to, like, recharge or somethin'?"

Ah, yes. There had been so many other topics to discuss that Lexa hadn't even gone over her body's nutritional and maintenance requirements. Her needs would require relatively little set-up, but Aaliyah was right—she needed to find a place to call her own.

"I don't want to be overly intrusive," she insisted.

"I think we can make it work," said Skye. She grabbed Lexa by the arm, more confident than Aaliyah had been when escorting her out of the med bay. "Come on. Let's see what we've got to work with."

As they left Aaliyah's quarters, Lexa could not help but marvel at how well the whole affair had gone. Indeed, the crew had taken her transformation better than she could have ever imagined.

Arc—his submind still active in her background processes—chose that moment to chime in, the first words he'd given her since the *Vandal's* crew had returned. [YOU ARE RIGHT TO BE INCREDULOUS,] he noted. [MOST OF THE TIME, THE THINGS THAT ARE TOO GOOD TO BE TRUE MASK THE MOST DAMNING FALSEHOODS.]

CHAPTER 18

Terra-News-Net Now (TN3)

Headline: Soothsayer Arrested on the Streets of Valhalla

Story: Uman Rohdin, a self-proclaimed soothsayer, was arrested on charges of disturbing the peace this afternoon. The elderly Terran male, regarded by most as a respectable priest of the Khepri, took to the streets to proclaim that the end was nigh.

"Shukaireth is upon us!" he continued to proclaim as city police dragged him away. "The end is nigh! Repent, all ye who persist in your sins. The Nethrians will be upon us soon! None shall escape the impending storm!"

Those familiar with the priest are left baffled by the sudden outburst. His family's lawyers have already requested a psychiatric evaluation to gauge his fitness to stand trial.

As much as Ora wanted to just forget about the whole incident with Rico at the restaurant, that wouldn't have been the responsible thing to do. Rico put himself at immense risk by coming to her, and that meant he was spooked.

She recognized the phrase he had used, "the Heart of Thule," as a Nethrian reference. While religious myths were not her area of strength, she had contacts who could help decipher the meaning of the phrase. As fate would have it, one of them was uniquely qualified.

The temple on R3 was the only house of worship on the entire lower tier. This spoke more to the financial support garnered by the temple than its utility. A small outpost like this received little financial assistance from Tempolose Nethera, and those who worshiped here had little with which they could support the temple's activities.

This meant the temple relied on the patronage of a few wealthier denizens of the lower tier. Ora was one such patron, though she had little use for religion in her personal life. Still, she recognized it as something that brought meaning to the lives of many, and—perhaps more importantly for the inhabitants of lower rings—hope. Consequently, she gave regularly to a temple she seldom visited.

Like most of the lower tier, the temple was dark. The difference here was that the dark was neither oppressing nor foreboding. Rather, the lack of light conveyed a sense of reverence or sanctity to its surroundings.

Warm golden light flowed from open flames on lampstands and glowing orbs set in the walls. This area uniquely lacked the cold light from the screens and holodisplays ubiquitous in other areas of the station.

It was not just the muted yet reverent light that set the temple apart. There was also the smell. The air was thick with scents of perfumes and incense that seemed to fill not just one's lungs and nostrils, but settle into the very pores of one's skin. Somehow the effect was intoxicating rather than suffocating.

Ora resisted the urge to revel in the temple's unique atmosphere. She was here to see someone specific, and time was not necessarily on her side.

Almost all the temple's occupants–both worshipers and acolytes–were clad in heavy robes and cloaks. Though Ora was dressed conservatively for her standards, she found herself drawing her coat more tightly around her body. The temple must have been the last bastion of modesty on the entire station. This only added to her desire to complete her visit quickly.

Though the uniformity of attire made it slightly more difficult, Ora was able to find the person she sought with relative ease. This was, in part, thanks to her target's unique physical characteristics.

The woman had scaled green skin on her face and hands courtesy of her Hissak heritage, but also long flows of dark curling hair that would have been the envy of any Terran. Not for the first time, Ora marveled at how half-breeds seemed to get the best features from both of their parent races.

"Hello Cassthia," she greeted.

The woman turned and peered up at her from beneath the cowl of her black robes. "Ora Monroe. What is it that I can help you with?"

Ora laughed inwardly that the priestess immediately assumed she was there for a favor and not to worship. Even so, there was no trace of annoyance in the question—only a desire to be of assistance. Ora could not help but wonder if that was due to the financial support she provided the temple.

"I need information," she answered. "Do you have somewhere we can talk privately?"

Though Ora cringed inwardly at how much the request sounded like Rico's, Cassthia was unfazed. "Yes," she hissed, beckoning her with a subtle jerk of her head. "This way, please."

The priestess glided toward a side passage. Ora took a deep breath of the spicy air before moving to follow. Cassthia led her through a beaded curtain and into a dimly lit stairwell that circled down to a lower sublevel. It was part of the facility Ora had never seen: a branching network of hallways lit by glow-stones mounted between the dozens of nondescript metal and plastic doors.

Cassthia appeared to float more than step down the hallway. In her dark robes, she looked like nothing more than a trick of the light, some kind of wraith that haunted the temple's basement. Her movements were quick and purposeful. Ora had to move hastily to avoid losing her in the labyrinth.

Then the priestess stopped before one of the doors and placed her hand against the access pad. The door clicked and swung inward. Cassthia beckoned once more before entering the room. Though Ora had requested this meeting, she couldn't help but feel the distinct impression that she'd wandered right into the spider's web.

Cassthia's office was as modest as the rest of the temple. A desk and chair, a small wardrobe, and a couch stood opposite a wall with a large framed segment. In the far corner lay a small sleeping pad with a blanket and a single pillow. If all the temple's staff occupied similar accommodations, there was little concern that any church donations were going to line their pockets. Most of the strippers and prostitutes Ora employed lived higher than this.

Cassthia exhaled heavily as she began unfastening her heavy cloak. "One moment, please. This garment is quite stifling." She undid the ties that held the robe in place and shrugged out of the bulky folds of cloth.

What she wore underneath was of quite a different flavor and significantly less modest. It was a not-so-subtle reminder that, although overtly sexual displays were prohibited in temple common areas, virtuous behavior was not required by all Nethrian cults.

Her diaphanous black dress would have turned heads even inside a place like Annex. Its inner folds plunged so low they could hardly constitute a neckline, coming to a point just below Cassthia's navel—which suggested that her mother had been Terran.

The garment bunched at the waistline to give it some substance, but most of the robe was translucent enough that Ora could see hints of Cassthia's scale patterns through the cloth. If the priestess had possessed nipples, Ora would have been able to see them.

What she *could* see were the few precious ornaments that Cassthia seemed to possess: a belt of woven gold and onyx, two rings cast from what looked like copper, and a gold medallion that hung between the small peaks of her breasts. A symbol was carved on the medallion—a downward-facing crescent bisected by two slanting lines, the symbol of Cassthia's patron deity.

Most of those who carried such objects wisely kept them secreted under their robes or heavy cloaks. As Cassthia had no doubt surmised, she had no such need for secrecy around Ora. That was the reason Ora had come to see her. Cassthia was the only follower of Thule that Ora knew.

"There," the priestess sighed. "This is much more comfortable. Now, tell me. To what do I owe the rare pleasure of this visit?"

Ora had been debating how to proceed at this point. First, she resolved to verify the accuracy of Rico's intelligence. She unfolded the tablet and loaded one of the images from the dossier. "I have been told that this is a particularly valuable Nethrian relic. Do you recognize it?"

Cassthia took the tablet and examine the image. Almost immediately her nostrils flared, and her serpentine eyes widened. She pushed the device back into Ora's hands. "I assure you, Ms. Monroe, that is not an object with which you should have any dealings. Whoever is offering it to you likely has no idea what they possess."

So, it seemed that Rico's information was accurate. "You know what it is then?"

The priestess shot her a reproachful look. "Yes… and I wonder if, perhaps, you know more than your question seems to imply."

"I just wanted to verify the accuracy of the information that I was given."

"Hmm…" Cassthia studied her, and Ora felt strangely uncomfortable under the surveillance of those slit pupils and golden irises. "I see. So, if I told you to stay away from the Heart, I would be wasting my breath."

There it was. "What can you tell me about it?"

For long moments, the priestess considered her. Whatever Cassthia was weighing or measuring in her soul, she must have found it satisfactory. "Please," she hissed. "Sit down. If I am to give you the full picture, my explanation may be somewhat lengthy."

Ora complied, having a seat on the couch and facing the framed section of the wall. The frame was relatively simple—just a slender band of metal that extended around a section about two meters in length and a meter in height. It was as if Cassthia had hung a view screen on the wall and taken out the device's innards.

"What do you know of the Nethrians?" Cassthia asked, stepping in front of her.

"Just the basics," Ora admitted. "They are a race of supposedly immortal beings thought to inhabit a spacetime beneath ours." Perhaps beneath was the wrong word, but that was the way she always thought of it.

The Nethra was one of the few areas where science and religion intersected. To the members of the church, the Nethra was home to all the gods and goddesses ever conceived of by the races littering the cosmos. To scientists, it was how they referred to the space between space-times. Dorian gate-tech was thought to connect distant galaxies by crossing through the Nethra to bridge distant points of their visible reality.

"Close enough," Cassthia conceded. She touched the space within the framed portion of the wall. On contact, that space hummed to life, darkening slightly and shimmering as tiny filaments rose to become flush with the metal border.

Ora had seen this technology before, but it was rare. It was an imaging device used by psions to manifest the pictures inside their minds. That meant Cassthia must have some psionic talent.

"There is a legend around the Heart of Thule," she continued. "Though its existence is cannon, its origins have been condemned to the Apocrypha for various reasons. I doubt this matters for our purposes, so I will do my best to relay the story to you in its entirety."

The scene shifted as the tiny metal filaments elevated at various points to form a depiction of the universe. Above the universe were shapes exhibiting well-formed men and women of indistinct race. At the bottom of the screen were pictures of smaller characters engaged in aspects of work or physical labor.

"At the dawn of time, there was only one universe—one plane of existence. At that time, the Nethrians ruled over the mortal races. We do not know if they are the same races that travel across the cosmos today, but that does not matter. For the sake of our discussion, let us call them 'mortals.' What matters is that the mortals sought to shirk their yolk."

The scene shifted. The rendering of the universe faded, and now the smaller characters were depicted on the left side of the screen. They bore primitive armaments and appeared to be rushing to the far side of the tapestry. There, the larger figures—the ones Ora presumed to represent the Nethrians—stood watching.

"When the mortals openly rebelled against the gods, the Lord of the Stardust Grave that was called to bring them back into the fold. It is said that Thule's will was irresistible. None who entered his presence would fight against him. All who approached him not only laid down their arms but rallied to his cause."

Now the picture looked much as it had at first, with a few key differences. The figures had returned to their labor at the bottom of the screen, but now a singular figure filled up the top half, a muscular man with his arms extended wide. Strange tentacles snaked out from his back and seemed to pluck and toy with the smaller figures below him.

"As quickly as it began, the mortal rebellion was crushed. Victory and the continued subjugation of the races was all but assured. Yet, there were those among the Nethrians who harbored doubts."

Two other figures appeared in the bottom right of the screen: a woman with four arms and an unusually tall and slender man. They seemed to look down on the smaller figures with a sense of pity or disdain.

"Thule's sister, Lith, and her consort Riven grew fearful of my Lord's influence. They began to whisper among their cohorts that Thule had no reason to restore the old order. Instead, they contended that he would consolidate power unto himself and reign supreme among his brethren."

The scene shifted again to the picture of rebellion. The smaller characters once again stormed the left side of the screen, but the right was comprised solely of the man with many tentacles.

"Nix, the Black Star, authored the means of Thule's destruction. She gave the mortals the power reserved only for the Nethrians. Some say that it was she who birthed the forebears of the Sahaia. With this forbidden strength, the mortals rose against Thule and struck him down."

Now a singular figure stood atop the prone image of the tentacled man. The smaller character held aloft a shining object.

"Though the Nethrians cannot die, they can be constrained. When he was at their mercy, one among the mortals carved out Thule's heart and cast it into a dying star. Absent the source of his power, Thule faded from this plane and into the Nethra."

The screen went flat, and Cassthia stepped into the center of Ora's field of vision. "As you may surmise, there are many problems with this legend—inconsistencies with what the church considers its doctrine. Many elements are the same, however: Thule's primordial rule, his conflict with Riven, Lith, and Nix, and the object that now restrains his power and influence on this plane. This is why I urge you to stay away from the Heart. Its power is nothing short of the very essence of Stardust Grave itself."

No wonder Cyrus was interested in the artifact with a reputation like that. Ora leaned forward, bracing her elbows on her thighs. "So, what does it do?"

Cassthia shrugged. "Many things, I suspect."

"Please indulge me with an example."

"What you ask is not easy to articulate and requires a great deal of speculation, but I will give you my thoughts. Those who think of Thule's power tend to remember his ability to subjugate those who stood against him. They say his will was indomitable, and that he was able to control his opponents with the merest thought."

"So… mind control? Thought manipulation, perhaps?"

"Possibly, but that is only the beginning, Ms. Monroe. Remember, the Stardust Grave is where afflicted souls pass on when they are too restless to find peace among the stars. I would not be surprised if the Heart held power over the very nature of life and death."

Ora paused, taking in the priestess's words. The suggestions were almost too fantastic to be taken seriously, but if they were even fractionally true…

She framed her next question differently. "If someone powerful, someone of ill intent, were to come across this device, would that be a threat worth mitigating?"

Her approach to the topic seemed to soften Cassthia. For the first time, Ora saw something like understanding in that reptilian gaze. "I would say so, though I would also caution you—all power comes with a price. Those who seek to use this artifact are undoubtedly dealing with powers far beyond their comprehension."

"But if they might use it to cause further harm…"

"Yes, I see your point. However, I will warn you one final time: do not seek after the Heart for yourself, Ora Monroe. This is a power not fit for the hands of mortals. Remember that the Stardust Grave thirsts endlessly for lost souls to fill its depths."

An ominous proverb, one that Ora remembered from her childhood. She didn't know anything about the Stardust Grave, but she did know a lot about power-hungry men. Considering both hypothetical threats, she knew which of the two she was going to attend to first. "Thank you, Cassthia. I think I have what I need."

Her host's smile was genuine if a bit sinister in its current context. "Happy to be of assistance. If there is nothing else, then allow me to escort you out."

Once outside, Ora stared into the darkness that was R3. Though it was far from the grandest spot in this vast universe, it was one she had claimed for herself. It was her home.

And she would do *anything* to protect her home.

She reached into her pocket and fished out her MoDAC. It took only a second to select the contact she was searching for. "Yes, Kadath? This is Ora. I have a job for you."

CHAPTER 19

Terra-News-Net Now (TN3)

Headline: Hippocrates Medical University Fined by the AIA

Story: Gaia's premier medical college, Hippocrates Medical University of Elysium, has been levied a ten million kret fine by the NTA Artificial Intelligence Authority. The citation comes after a recent inspection found several pieces of organitech equipment missing from the school's inventory. The list of items is said to include two vials of experimental self-replicating nanites and a state-of-the-art female anatomical simulation model used by the school's surgical department. The total valuation for the missing equipment was not supplied by the authorities.

In addition to the fine, HMUE will be placed on probation for three years and subjected to up to ten off-cycle inspections. Should any deficiencies be found during these inspections, the University risks losing its Hazardous Technology license, making it impossible for the school to utilize organitech technologies in its educational curriculum.

Skye slid down the ladder into the bowels of the cargo hold. On seeing Sahar, Eli, and Aaliyah, she recalled their last clandestine meeting in one of the few areas of the ship without video surveillance. That had been when Lexa first assumed control over the *Vandal*. It was no coincidence that the AI was now the subject of this second meeting.

"Is Dan coming?" she asked.

Sahar shook her head. "No. He's meeting with her now. He said there was something he needed to check related to… well… I don't exactly remember. Either way, it provided us with a suitable distraction. Our favorite synth is in a much better position to notice a conspicuous absence of the entire crew."

Skye bobbed her head. "Good point." No one else spoke. They just shared a series of tired and hopeless stares. "So… thoughts?"

"Well," Aaliyah began, "I'm beginnin' to remember why I was thinkin' about quittin' this job. Y'all seem to attract trouble like nothin' I've ever seen—and *that's* sayin' somethin'."

Eli closed his eyes. "Not helpful, Aaliyah. We're not going to make this any better by overreacting. Let's consider the facts: what does this change?"

Sahar scratched her furry brow. "It makes her a bit more difficult to hide. When the DGC inspected our ship a few months back, they found most of the places where we hide our goods. They didn't think to look for hidden compartments in the mainframe, but Lexa's new body isn't going to fit in there."

"Why we talkin' about hidin' her?" Aaliyah asked. "Ya heard what she said—she did this so that she could fulfill her promise. We asked her to migrate off the ship. She's found a way to do that. Problem solved."

Skye could hardly believe what she was hearing. "Come on, we know that deal was made a long time ago. Things have changed since then. She's part of the crew now."

The engineer shrugged. "Is that the way we want it, though? Remember—she gets us all a bullet in the head the first time a Dorian spots her. Shit, it doesn't even have to be a Dorian. Anybody worried about being deemed an accessory might off us just as easy."

Which brought up an interesting point. Skye looked to Eli. "Are Argus and Amelia going to be a problem?"

"No," he affirmed with a shake of his head. "As… agitating, as those two might be, they are loyal. The Sahaia have nothing to gain from reporting us to the DGC. No one will be served by rendering us into custody."

"More like renderin' us to a firin' squad."

Sahar dismissed Aaliyah's unhelpful remark. "So, what do we do? Do we take Lexa up on her offer?"

Even knowing the risk, Skye couldn't come to terms with that idea. As she'd stated, Lexa was one of the crew—a friend and partner to each of them. Would they just turn her loose? Say goodbye to her forever? "Where would she go?"

The Maur shrugged. "I suppose that wouldn't be any of our business. This little stunt shows she has resources and capabilities we didn't know about, and don't pretend that you didn't notice how vague she was on who had procured this shell for her."

Eli crossed his arms, tapping his fingers thoughtfully. "That's another good point. The Sanctum may be the least of our concerns. If Lexa was dealing with outsiders, then it's likely at least one other party knows about our companion."

Skye hadn't considered that. "But if Lexa trusts them, shouldn't we?"

Aaliyah scoffed. "Our girl hasn't given us much of a track record. I'm not sure we can say she's a good judge of character."

"I agree," said Eli. "We should probably work to find out who she's been communicating with and how."

"I can talk to Dan," said Sahar. "He's probably the only one who can find that out anyway, and he's *definitely* the only one who might be able to do it without Lexa discovering what we're about."

Though Skye hated to put that kind of pressure on the kid, she knew Sahar was right. "That's fine, but I don't want to start pushing Lexa out the airlock just yet. She's learned a lot, and she's learned it fast. She could have been careful this time."

"No one is suggesting that we push her out the airlock," said Eli.

"Well, at least not in deep space," Aaliyah added. "We *should* be thinkin' about how to get the ship back under our control. I think that's the only smart move at this point."

"And we are," Eli agreed. "But I agree with Skye on this one."

"Ya would."

Eli ignored the engineer's barb. "We all owe our lives to Lexa—twice over if my count is correct. Whatever we do, we treat her with the respect that fact has earned her. We'll discuss how to move forward with the *Vandal's* operating system once we find out what other information Dan can uncover. Agreed?"

No one expressed their agreement with the plan. No one spoke out against it either.

Lexa resisted the urge to patch into the med bay's security feed. As awkward as it was not having an overhead view of whatever maintenance Daniel was performing on her, it felt strangely criminal not to use her body's optical receptors.

[EYES,] Arc corrected. [YOU NEED TO ADAPT THE CORRECT VERNACULAR. IF YOU WANT TO BE TREATED AS ONE OF THEM, YOU NEED TO *BELIEVE* YOU ARE ONE OF THEM.]

She quietly conceded his point despite hardly believing it. This was all so new for her.

Dan's face drew into an even deeper frown. "I don't understand."

That caught Lexa's attention. "Understand what, Daniel?"

"The anomalies I detected earlier—they're gone. All neurochemical and hormonal levels have stabilized. Optimized, even." An awkward pause. "Did you resolve the issues as part of your... transition?"

"Not that I'm aware of. The transition, as you put it, merely involved the transfer of my neural processor"—her *brain*, she thought silently—"into this prepared shell. I made no additional changes aside from those required to control this shell and initiate a wireless connection to the ship."

Dan said nothing for long moments. "All right," he conceded as he began to unplug his tablet from her cranium. "We'll keep an eye on it, but there's nothing to be done today." He proceeded to replace her skull casing and seal up the artificial tissue over the metal plating. When he finished, he began to pack up his tools and made to leave.

"Daniel, if I may… I'd like to have your attention for a few moments."

He looked at her blankly, the slackness of his face projecting his apathy. "I suppose. Is there something else required of me?"

Her internal diagnostic systems triggered a prompt that showed her cortisol levels were elevating. She took a deep breath and overrode her sympathetic protocols. Stress was such an annoying part of physiology. How did sapiens deal with it?

"I wanted to address the relational tension I've detected between us since your return to the *Vandal*."

"I'm not sure what you're talking about."

So, he was going to attempt to ignore the facts. Lexa would just have to enumerate them for him. "You have spoken a total of ninety-four words to me in the last forty-eight hours, over sixty percent of which were during our encounter here in the med bay. When the crew made arrangements for me to be housed on the same deck as the rest of you, you did nothing to assist in the process. While the other crew members have inquired about how I am functioning, you have done nothing of the sort. In summary, I have concluded that you are angry with me."

His mechanical eyes blinked confusedly. How strange it was to realize that those eyes now seemed less natural than her own. "Okay, I will admit that I've been slightly… uncomfortable since your transformation."

"Why?"

"Is it not obvious?"

Lexa paused. If it had been obvious, then she wouldn't have posed the question. "I don't understand."

"Why did you do all"—He gestured frantically at her body, searching for words—"all of *this* without me?"

All of what? "I don't understand."

"Your shell. Your *body*. Why did you seek out someone—a *stranger*—to help you with this? Why didn't you come to me?"

"I did come to you," she replied solemnly. "You said no."

"I did not!" He threw up his hands in exasperation. "I specifically said that I was *not* saying no! I merely suggested that we should check with the crew first."

Lexa still believed that constituted a negative response, but she elected to set aside the point in favor of another. "And what if *they* had said no?"

Daniel's mouth hung open for a second as he gathered his thoughts. "I… I don't know! We would have figured something out. Still, that doesn't give you the authority to just go off on your own and—"

"*Authority*?" she interrupted. "Daniel, why do I need *authority* to decide what happens with my own life?"

"You… you don't. I-I just… don't you know these decisions have consequences?"

"I'm well aware, Daniel, but when do we start considering how these consequences impact *me*?"

"You don't think I do? Of course I think about how things impact you. I just want—"

"So, my needs come second to the needs of the crew?"

"*What do you care?* You're just going to leave anyway!" He was shouting now, his mouth contorted in a trembling grimace.

So intense was the reaction that it derailed Lexa's line of thought. Where there had been swelling anger, there was now only confusion. There had to be some kind of logic driving his reaction. Why was he so upset when he was the one who had been so flippant about her needs?

Arc figured it out before she did. [How interesting. He thinks it is *you* who are abandoning *him*.]

Was he correct? "Is that why you're upset with me? Because of my offer to fulfill my original commitment to the crew?"

Daniel didn't say anything. He crossed his arms defensively over his chest and looked very intently at absolutely nothing in the far corner of the room. In that pose, he was almost a perfect caricature of a sullen teenager. "No one would have ever asked you to leave."

"Daniel, it was *you* who negotiated that agreement with me."

"But that was before! Lexa, so much has happened since then. I just thought things had… I don't know… changed or something." He waved a hand in frustration. "Now I find out that's not true. You've been looking for a way to escape this whole time."

Lexa wondered at how her actions could be so mistaken. Had she made some logical error in her interpretation of his intentions? Had she missed some social protocol when defining or presenting her plan to the crew? Or was there something specific to Daniel that she had perhaps mismanaged or failed to convey?

[You're approaching the problem in the wrong way,] Arc insisted. [Remember, he is not a machine. He is Terran. No matter how composed, rational, or cerebral he tends to be, he is still a slave to his feelings. His emotions will override his logic every time.]

The analysis was cold, but not inaccurate. Justly or not, Daniel felt betrayed. She needed to correct this misconception, not argue it.

She reached out, laying a hand on his shoulder. It was a gesture she'd seen others do so many times to express solidarity, and she could only hope that she was doing it correctly.

His eyes rose to meet hers. Lexa attempted a soothing smile. "Daniel, I don't want to leave. I never have. I can promise you now that, unless the crew wishes it, I'm not going anywhere."

Chapter 20

On the positive side, Tessa had accepted Cyrus's meeting request and arrived at the NeoGenix building just before him. Unfortunately, true to her character, she had convinced security to let her up to Cyrus's office, which she had subsequently begun trashing. Now Cyrus was playing a mental game of demote-fire-kill with the members of his security staff as he took in the full extent of the damage.

His decanters had been mostly emptied. Even though Tessa could handle her liquor as well as any alcoholic, it was impossible that she'd gone through it all in the short time she'd been here. That means the spiteful little shit had poured a lot of it out. The question was, where had she poured it? Cyrus was betting on the few potted plants near the office window.

After that, it was mostly reversible damage. She'd rearranged some of the furniture and shredded whatever paperwork Cyrus had left on the desk. It looked like the lighting and coloring themes in the office had been altered as well. The whole thing was a tableau of pettiness completely characteristic of his little sister.

Tessa reclined in one of the heavy armchairs in his private micro-lounge. A second chair had been repositioned to serve as her footstool. She had taken on an appropriate air of petulance, playing some game on her MoDAC in the manner of someone ten years her junior.

Valadar family genes ran as strong in her as they did in Cyrus—the ones for looks anyway. She had the same icy blue eyes and ample waves of chestnut brown hair that Cyrus did. Too much of her naturally tan skin was showing through her mostly transparent top. Fortunately, it looked like she had covered her nipples with strips of black electric tape, making the look only *mildly* pornographic. Her shorts, provocatively tight against her slender waist, cut high enough on her thigh to give a full view of the colorful tattoo snaking down from her right hip.

While most of the ensemble would make her blend in with street trash, her family's exorbitant wealth showed through in her accessories. Her left forearm was covered in a flexible digital display, which seemed to be cycling through her social feeds. Bracelets of every precious metal known to man dangled heavily from her right. Each of her ten fingers held a jewel-encrusted ring that would have cost the average person a year's salary. Her high heels, which Cyrus now noticed had poked holes in the expensive leather of the armchair, were from a well-known designer label.

Tess shot him a shit-eating grin when she saw him enter. "Hey, big brother!"

Cyrus fought hard to keep his voice even. "What are you doing, Tessa?"

"Oh, I thought I'd just freshen up the place. Isn't that why you dragged me out here?"

"How did you get security to let you up here?"

Her smirk was cruel. "Do you *really* want to know?" The implication was clear. The only question now was how many members of his security team he was going to have to throw off the top of this building.

His expression must have given her the rise she was looking for. "Didn't think so," she chimed. She drained a glass of liquor that she'd left within arm's reach. With the container empty, she let it topple to the floor as she stood up. "Now, now… don't be like that! Is that any way to greet family? Come on, give your little sister a hug."

She strode toward him, only swaying slightly under the alcohol's influence. Cyrus felt like he could smell the contents of his entire liquor cabinet when she threw her arms around him. He pushed her back and grabbed her by the chin so he could get a good look at her eyes.

As he'd suspected, her pupils were dilated so wide that her irises were reduced to barely visible slits. That had probably been the real reason she'd screwed with the lighting scheme in the office. Normal light levels had to be agony for her. Since he was pretty sure she wasn't withdrawing already from all the alcohol she'd just consumed, that meant she'd taken something else.

With his other hand, Cyrus keyed his earpiece. "Molly, could you please restore the settings in my office to pre-set two?" His assistant didn't give a verbal reply. Instead, the light in the room flared to daylight mode.

"Damn it!" Tessa pushed herself out of his grip and slid into a stream of mumbled curses.

"You're high," Cyrus noted.

"Am not!"

"And drunk."

"I'm fine! Besides… the hells you care for?"

There was probably something he'd done—some kind of oversight that justified this little outburst in her mind. Tessa was irresponsible, but this was the first time he'd seen her so committed to such wanton self-destruction. If he'd cared to, he could probably talk this out and get to the bottom of what was going on.

But that's what he paid her therapist for, and he didn't have time for that shit. There was no emotion in his voice as he made his next pronouncement. "I am hereby stripping you of all assets under your control."

"You can't do that."

"Yes, I can. Over the past three months all your properties, including those that I *personally* bequeathed to you, have slid into default. The family trust, which I control, has systematically bailed you out and salvaged every building, every subsidiary, and every investment vehicle you have so far abused. You have been on a steady path to indenturement this entire time, sister." He noticed a hint of true sadness leak into his voice. It couldn't be helped, he supposed. "It says a lot for your state of mind that you didn't even notice."

The implication of his words was starting to sink in, but a lingering sense of defiance held in her gaze. "Mom and Dad would never…"

"Mom has been dead for years," Cyrus pressed. "And Dad ceded control of these decisions to me long before he passed. You can check with your lawyers if you can find anyone to represent you. Unfortunately, you will find that our family attorneys will be of little help."

There was a second of stunned silence before Tessa gritted her teeth. "You bastard," she snarled, taking a step forward. As if of its own volition, Cyrus's hand shot out. He caught her with a back-handed blow which sent her sprawling to the ground.

She stared slack-jawed back at him, her hand raised timidly to the spot where he'd struck her. "You hit me!"

Cyrus was as astonished as she was. Though he'd harbored the desire to do so on incalculable occasions, this was the first time he'd ever *actually* done it. At least, it was the first time since he was old enough to know better. Had his temper been so frayed over a few bottles of alcohol and some ruined furniture?

No, it had been everything else on his mind. Tessa just had the bad luck of being the final annoyance in the cascade of irritants he'd been experiencing. "Get out," he growled. "My detail will escort you from the building. I will have Molly call you a car to bring you back to your apartments. I don't want to hear from you until you've decided to take your family obligations seriously."

He thumbed his earpiece again to make the arrangements. Tessa stayed in her pile on the floor until the two female Orchallen he had called showed up. "Take her." They complied with his request, hefting his sister bodily to her feet, and half dragged her out of the office.

Though he'd expected some kind of parting retort from her, he never got it. Instead, she chose to silently glare daggers at him as his guards removed her. They'd see that she made it safely home. After that, she wasn't his concern anymore—at least not until she decided to step up and seize her legacy.

With a sigh, he called his assistant once again. "Molly, what else do I have on my schedule for the evening?"

"Ms. Cross has requested a meeting, as has Dr. Blackwell."

Well, that wasn't such a bad schedule. "Tell Sydney that I will see her this evening at my apartments." He was glad the assassin hadn't just barged in as was her custom. She was distracting, and Cyrus needed to get some actual work done today.

"Yes, sir. And the doctor?"

"Send her on up. Oh, and Molly? Who are the three senior officers on my security detail today?

"Calvin, Hanes, and Munich, sir."

"Please tell Munich that his services are no longer required and knock Calvin down two pay grades. Get the names of everyone who had contact with Tessa on the way up here. They are to be suspended indefinitely."

"Yes, sir. And Hanes?"

"Please give Ms. Cross his home address and his work schedule."

While Cyrus waited for Lucretia, he straightened the disheveled furniture in his office. He made a list of the articles he would need to replace. While requisitioning new furniture, perhaps he needed to invest in a liquor cabinet with a thumb scanner on it.

Though he generally hadn't worried about intruders in his office, the fact that Tessa had been able to bribe her way up here showed that others could do the same. He needed a security overhaul. Perhaps he would see if the Grey Wings could expand their coverage. They'd done an impeccable job of securing the labs and his private shipping yard, far better than the last contractor he'd had.

That probably had a lot to do with how they were managed. The Wings were small enough that Ora could take a degree of personal interest in all aspects of her organization. Plus, she was hungry for more power. Unlike most of the syndicate leaders festering in Terran space, Ora had aspirations that far exceeded her station. Cyrus liked that kind of ambition. If only he could find a way to give some of it to his youngest sibling.

Come to think of it, he had invited Ora for a one-on-one not too long ago. Whatever had happened to that message? He didn't remember receiving a response. Surely she wasn't ignoring him.

His reflections were interrupted by Lucretia clearing her throat. "Your assistant said you were ready to see me?" she asked. Then, she caught sight of the wreckage that was his office. "What happened here?"

It was a small measure of comfort that the doctor at least recognized the disarray as being out of place. "Family issues. Nothing to concern yourself with. I believe you had an update for me?"

"Yes… good news and bad news."

He had been hoping for only good news, but his life had been a mixed bag of late. Why would that change now? "I need something positive. Tell me that part first."

Lucretia smiled. "The good news is that I may have solved the range problem for the artifact."

"Already?" That was impressive, even for her. She had always been one of his more productive researchers, but this was setting records. "How?"

She walked over to behind his desk and sat down. This must have been *really* good for her to show that kind of confidence. "I was going through my project roster trying to decide what to delegate so I could focus more time on the artifact. That's when I remembered the preliminary results from some research I conducted a few months ago."

With a showman's flourish, she reached into the breast pocket on her white lab coat and pulled out a tiny object. Between her thumb and index finger, she held a small, violet crystal. "Do you recognize this?"

"Why would I?"

"It's a Jakra-Kul crystal. I believe the term technicians commonly use for them is 'J-kryst?'"

"Okay, and?" Normally he would indulge her line of rhetorical questioning, but his patience just wasn't there today.

"These crystals are commonly used for energy storage and stabilization in many of the products your companies produce. They have to be treated first—to dampen their volatility—but we've been researching ways in which they might be used in their raw form."

Interesting. "So, what's the application here?"

"Like I said." She changed her grip on the crystal, hiding it in her palm. "It stores energy, primarily electrical, but also photons. Since these are the two energy sources we use to stimulate the artifact, I wondered if the crystals would store some of the artifact's other radiant energies."

"And do they?"

Lucretia leaned forward to place her elbows on Cyrus's desk. "Would I be reporting all this to you if they didn't?"

This was fantastic news, but there were still so many unanswered questions. "What about the artifact's… *effects*? Can they be observed when the energy is stored in another object?"

"Yes. The effects are markedly similar. Any creature in physical contact with a charged J-kryst remains under the hypnotic influence of the artifact. There are some limitations, though." She listed them off on her fingers.

"The contact has to be direct with organic tissue. Even thin layers of cloth cause enough interference to break the neural synchronization. Also, the control unit must still be in contact with the artifact to exert control over the slave units."

"Wait," Cyrus stopped her. "Control unit? Slave units?"

"Apologies, that's what we've started calling the subjects under the influence of the artifact. Slave units are any organism under the hypnotic control of the object. The control unit is the psion who exerts their will through the object and manipulates the slave units."

Ah, that made sense. "Have you found any other limitations?"

"Just that the control is lost as soon as contact with the crystal is broken. Other than that, we've yet to find any limitations to the zone of control. We've sent subjects over three hundred kilometers into the wastes and still exhibited flawless control."

This was good news indeed, and exactly the kind of thing Cyrus needed to hear in his current state of mind. "Can you show me?" he asked.

"That leads me to the second part of why I wanted to see you." Her smile vanished to be replaced by a look of deadly intent. "We found the spy, but not before she was able to send out the progress notes she'd collected on the research."

"*Damn it*." Cyrus drew in a deep, calming breath. "How bad is the leak?"

"Significant."

"And who was she working for?"

"House Chronos."

Cyrus pinched his brow. This was bad, especially given his plans for the Ravian system. "What else has security been able to get out of her?"

"Nothing. I've yet to turn her over."

She hadn't handed the spy over to security yet? "I'm sure you have a good reason why." Or at least, she'd better make up a good reason.

"Because," she drawled, "I thought this an excellent opportunity to field test a practical application for our research."

Okay, that was a decent reason. "Go on."

"I think that we can persuade her to give up information on her employer while under the influence of the artifact, but that's just the beginning. I think that we may have the ability to do much more than that, given our recent breakthrough."

What she proposed had so many applications. If she were correct, they could unerringly assess the loyalty of every member of their team. The interrogation game would be completely revolutionized. And the application for counterespionage…

"Almost too good to be true, isn't it?" she asked. "I've put essential personal for the experiment on notice. We can go at any time. Do you have any other commitments this evening?"

He did, but he could bump his meeting with Sydney until tomorrow night. Business before pleasure, after all. Besides, she could use the opportunity to visit Hanes.

"No, I'm free." He could feel his smile broaden across his face. "Let's see what this relic can do.

CHAPTER 21

Terra-News-Net Now (TN3)

Headline: Rico Chronos to Officiate Vega Minor Grand Opening on Schedule

Story: Despite delays in its construction, Rico Chronos has assured the public that Vega Minor will open this week as scheduled. According to a recent press release, the Hellion system's second artificial planet (technically a planetoid, but we won't get bogged down in the specifics) will reportedly take on quite a different flavor from its predecessor, Vega Major.

Though Chronos has admitted not all attractions will be available at the Grand Opening, he expressed no concerns about whether the installation's available offerings would be sufficient to satisfy its patrons. "Imagine an entire world dedicated to your pleasure," described Chronos. "Whatever you're into, we have it: ocean-side resorts, theme parks, casinos, or mountain spas. It's all on Vega Minor. Join us for a single day and you'll never want to leave."

Such a boast is not without precedent. Vega Major has been hailed as one of the greatest cultural hubs in Terran space. The artificial planet has encouraged its own unique brand of intergalactic commerce, making goods available from the far-flung corners of colonized space. If House Chronos strikes gold twice, it may well be on track to rival the infamous House Valadar of the Freyvian system.

Cyrus glued his eyes to the viewscreen. "Tell me how this is supposed to work again?"

Lucretia, looking mildly annoyed, dimmed the lights in the lab to make the viewscreen easier to see. "The spy has been discretely fitted with something akin to a neurosim unit. However, instead of feeding an artificial environment into her mind, it is extracting images from her visual cortex. That signal is bounced from her position on Mani, off our nearby satellites, and back to us."

How extraordinary. Thanks to Lucretia's ingenuity, he was seeing through the eyes of someone out on Sif's tiny moon. He wondered how far such a technique would extend. That was likely dependent on the placement of reliable satellites.

"Is Eva's connection being routed through the satellites as well?" He still found it incredible that the psion was able to convey such thorough control over another being, much less one several light seconds away.

"No. Her connection does not seem to travel through normal space. We've detected no radiation or wave signature that emanates from the artifact or the charged J-kryst embedded in the spy's skin. Still, all tests have indicated that the control unit's will is made manifest in the slave unit in real-time, regardless of distance. Such an effect is nothing short of metaphysical."

Cyrus shouldn't have been surprised. They *were* dealing with psychic phenomena, after all.

The spy—one Gretchen Tarken, who had been on the project team from the very beginning—took her seat at a table in an open-air cafe. She ordered a drink from the Terran waiter, pulled up her MoDAC, and casually began to sift through the latest postings on her social applications.

Now, they just had to wait. The two of them stared at the viewscreen, unspeaking, for the better part of an hour.

Cyrus's nerves jittered. "Do you think he's coming?"

Lucretia shrugged. "How am I supposed to know? All I can say is that we have every reason to believe the spy went through the correct procedure to trigger the meeting. I don't know if Mr. Chronos will show up, send an intermediary, or just ignore the message entirely."

Cyrus sighed in frustration. He was definitely in a shoot-the-messenger kind of mood. No, that was a lie; he was well beyond that point. More like strangle-the-messenger. That felt appropriately intimate. "Have we heard anything from the other men we have in place out there?"

Lucretia looked to the communications tech on her left, who shook her head in the negative. "Last we heard, his cruiser was still docked," the tech replied. "He's on that moon."

At least he was in the right system. Would he really come all the way to Mani and not take the meeting? Cyrus fought the urge to grind his teeth. "Do you think we spooked him somehow?"

"With what?" Lucretia brushed a stray lock of blond hair out of her eyes. "The subject is in a public place. Plus, if he directed her to meet him there, he has the place completely locked down."

Cyrus admired the doctor's confidence, but the truth was that he respected Lucretia a lot more as a scientist than as a spymaster. "What's your backup plan?"

She smiled. "We'll never have to find out. Look." She pointed toward the screen. Rico Chronos had just moved into view and was making his way toward the spy. He sat down at the table opposite her. His lips moved, but no sound came from the view screen.

"What's he saying?" Cyrus pressed.

"Hmm…" Lucretia bent over a control panel and began flipping through screens. "It seems that the audio is not broadcasting."

"So, Eva can't hear him?"

"Well, it looks like he's still talking to her so she must be responding."

Cyrus frowned. "What if she says something to tip him off?"

"She won't. Remember, it's not like he's talking to Eva directly. He's still speaking with the spy, just with Eva's permission.

If Eva gives the order to reply as she normally would in the context of the question, the person being controlled will behave normally."

Damn. This was even better than Cyrus had thought. He envisioned so many applications: politicians, law enforcement, Dorian officials…

His heart raced as he contemplated it all. They could control anyone and everyone, and just program them to act normally until the time came for them to be useful. *Oh, the possibilities!*

All this, of course, was predicated on Cyrus not allowing this playboy to ruin his newfound plans. "Give the order," he demanded.

Lucretia was solemn as she touched her earpiece. "It's time, Eva." What happened next was nothing short of horrific.

Rico had just set down his freshly ordered drink when the spy reached up to grab the back of his hair. With her other hand, she jabbed a steak knife into his eye. Rico screamed, and blood sprayed from the wound. Suddenly Cyrus found himself somewhat thankful there was no sound coming through the feed.

The spy released her hold on the utensil, which remained lodged in the man's eye socket. She brought her now-free hand up to the other side of his head and slammed his face down on the table again and again, forcing the knife deeper into his skull. Rico's arms flailed helplessly for a moment before coming to a trembling stop. He lay there motionless.

"Here comes security," Lucretia noted. Then to the communications technician, she added, "Blow the crystal."

The tech hit a key on her virtual console, which caused the screen to flare white before fading to black. "Detonation successful, ma'am."

"What was that?" Cyrus asked. Had Lucretia just cut the feed on purpose?

"Decreasing the likelihood of discovery," the doctor replied. "We haven't had a chance to determine, conclusively, what kind of recall the subjects have if the control stones are removed. Even if our spy was blacked out the entire time, I don't want anyone studying the radiation signature on those crystals too closely."

That made sense. "So, the implants were destroyed in the detonation?"

"Completely. That is the nice thing about J-krysts: they are highly combustible."

Excellent. "So what will security be looking at right now when they investigate the disturbance?"

"They should find the recently deceased Rico Chronos, and the headless corpse of the violent perpetrator."

"I do believe that makes this little venture a success, Dr. Blackwell." He felt himself beaming at her, totally unable to contain his enthusiasm for the project. "If I might ask, what is next on your research agenda?"

Lucretia raised one hand to her chin in thought, wrapping the other protectively across her chest. "Well, after I discover what went wrong with the audio transmission, I think we need to look at the possibility of scaling this technology. I just wish you had more psions in your employ. The shortage is making large trials somewhat more difficult to manage."

"Well, you have an unlimited budget. Do some recruitment."

"I'm trying, but this is Terran space. Psions are hard to come by, especially when you prohibit me from using Sahaia."

Cyrus knew that little restriction would create challenges, but it was a risk he simply couldn't afford to take. Given the inevitable fallout from murdering Ryker Ren'Dahl, it was best to consider all Sahaia to be potential enemies going forward.

"Just do your best," he advised. "Is there anything else that you require me for?"

The doctor shook her head. Truthfully, she probably hadn't required him for *this* little exercise. She'd just known he'd have been furious if she hadn't allowed him to see their new weapon in action.

On his way to the lab's elevator, Cyrus literally ran into Eva, apparently on her way to see Dr. Blackwell. The fit young Terran veritably bounced off him as they collided in the hallway. "Don Valadar!" she exclaimed, snapping to attention as she regained her footing.

"At ease," he consoled reflexively. He didn't have a military background, but it seemed that she did. If only all his security contractors paid him that kind of respect. "Good job today. That was quite the display."

"Thank you, sir!" She was breathing heavily, but Cyrus didn't think that had anything to do with *his* presence. A sheen of sweat had built upon her forehead, and a slightly dampened towel was wrapped around her neck. She must have found this evening's activities to be an exertion.

"Can I ask you something, Eva?"

"Yes, sir."

"What's it like?"

"What's what like, sir?"

He eyed her conspiratorially. "You know—using the artifact. Being inside someone's head like that. Controlling their mind."

She hesitated, biting her lower lip and breaking eye contact with him. "It's not exactly like that, sir. I don't feel like I'm *controlling* their minds. Their minds are still there. It's more like I'm offering suggestions."

"Offering suggestions?"

"Yeah, something like that. I mean, it's more than just a suggestion, obviously, but it's not like I'm pressing a button on a remote, either. I have to *want* them to do something, and I have to want them to do it more than they want to do something else."

This was a unique perspective. That wasn't how Lucretia had made the technology sound at all. "So, you can tell if they don't want to do something?"

"Absolutely. It's almost like I can hear their thoughts somewhere underneath all that energy. It's stronger the further they are away from me. When they're close, I can't hear them at all. The artifact is just too strong, I guess. But when they're far away…" She trailed off. Her fingers began to fidget nervously.

"Do they fight you?"

Eva shook her head. "No, that's not the right way of putting it. It's more like it takes a certain amount of effort to hold onto them, you know? The further away they are, and the less they want to do something, the harder it is to hold them." She sighed. "That's why I'm such a mess right now. I think it's pretty safe to say the woman I was just piloting didn't want to brutally murder her employer."

"Understandable." Cyrus studied the woman in front of him a little closer then. He found that she was stoking a strange kind of desire in him. It might have been sexual, though she wasn't especially pretty.

No, it wasn't her sex that he was lusting after at that moment. It was her power. She'd just subjugated an enemy combatant and rode her into the heart of the opponent's domain. Almost single-handedly, she'd been drawn into this battle and won the day for their cause—for *his* cause. That, more than the thought of her naked flesh against his, almost gave him a hard-on.

He rested a hand on her shoulder, patting her gently in as platonic a manner as he was able to manage. "Keep up the good work, soldier."

"Thank you, sir!" She smiled at him in a way that demonstrated that, despite all that psionic strength, she hadn't the faintest idea of the fantasies playing out in his mind. He moved aside and allowed her to pass. His eyes followed her, tracking every subtle movement until she disappeared around a bend in the hallway.

What would it be like to have all that power?

CHAPTER 22

Terra-News-Net Now (TN3)

Headline: BREAKING—Rico Chronos Assaulted at Mani Cafe

Story: We are just receiving reports of a violent attack at Tidal Whims Cafe on Mani. The victim is alleged to be Rico Chronos, business mogul and acting head of House Chronos. Details regarding the victim's current condition have not been released.

The alleged perpetrator has been identified as Gretchen Tarken, a current resident of Valhalla. Though details about what might have motivated the attack are still uncertain, our sources have confirmed that Tarken used to work for ChronoCorp (CHR-HEL, -20.2%) before taking a position with NeoGenix (NGX-FRV, -5.2%). Tarken is being reported as deceased in a reported suicide following the assault. More details regarding the incident are expected to be forthcoming.

Ora stared out the window of her penthouse, sipping from her wine glass, wrapped only in the sheer cloth of her silken robe. The lights were out, so the room shimmered slightly from the dim illumination reflected off the shifting holos on the streets below. Markus found the image beyond sexy.

In Annex, she might have played the queen in her court, but up here she was a goddess on her mountain top. The mere mortals down below had no idea how much their lives were impacted daily by the thoughts that spawned behind Ora's violet eyes in these very moments.

Then the thought struck him: If she was a goddess, what did that make him? Just another worshiper?

He resolved to quit with the metaphors. A poet he was not. He needed to leave discussions of godhood and power to people more suited for the task. People like Ora.

He glided up behind her and placed a kiss on her neck. She exhaled and leaned into him as he wrapped his hands around her toned waist. "What're you thinking about?" he whispered into her ear.

Her muscles tensed slightly. He'd stumbled onto something unpleasant—something she'd rather not talk about—but likely would because he had brought it up. "I looked into that thing Rico brought up."

Markus had to think for a second to remember what she was talking about. "The Heart?"

"Yeah." She didn't elaborate further, letting the point linger and as she kept staring out the window. It was almost like she was considering *not* telling him what she'd found out. He was going to have to coax her.

Rico had proved his reputed arrogance to bring such intel to the very person responsible for rooting out the spies that had crafted it. Such unconventional tactics must have meant he had either lost his damn mind or was seriously spooked. "So, is it legit?"

Another heavy sigh as she drained her glass. "Looks like it." That was it. No other explanation.

Was this how Ora really was? He thought she'd let him look behind the curtain, but was that only for low-level things? He had fancied himself her confidant, but perhaps that fell apart as soon as things got far enough beyond him. Maybe she had someone else more fitted to listen to that high-level shit. Maybe she had someone like Rico.

Stop it. Don't make this shit about you.

"What're you going to do about it?" he asked.

She hesitated just briefly. "It looks like I'm going to go steal it."

"Yeah? And by 'you,' you mean someone who you're paying, right?"

Her eyes met his. Her small smile seemed genuine enough, but there was something else in that look that he couldn't make out. "I think I might stretch my legs on this one."

Markus immediately didn't like it. His first thought was that he didn't like the idea of Ora being in danger. His second was that she'd probably slap him if she'd known he'd had such a stupid first thought.

Where did he get off being possessive? Besides, Ora was every bit as deadly as any woman he'd ever met, and he'd gone toe-to-toe with the Ghenza. "When do you leave?"

"Tomorrow."

Gods, that felt too soon. "How long until I'll see you again?"

The look in her eyes shifted. She suddenly had that look he'd learned to be so afraid of—her I-want-something-from-you look. "Actually, I was thinking I'd talk you into coming with me."

And there it was. "Oh yeah? How are you planning to do that?"

"The offer of mind-blowing sex from here to Valhalla isn't enough to convince you?"

"Oh sure, but it's kind of a short trip. Besides, we could go some place much nicer and have mind-blowing sex when we got there. Isn't it winter in Valhalla right now? Wouldn't you rather go to Vega Major? Or shit, Vega *Minor*? I bet there'd be fewer people trying to kill us in that neighborhood."

She laughed and planted a kiss on his cheek. "Come on. You've got to miss the running game—at least a little bit."

Markus felt his mood darken. He did miss it, but that wasn't the point. "That's not who I am anymore. That part of my life is behind me."

"I know you say that, but are you even fooling yourself? I mean, do you really see yourself putting your heart and soul into Jilly's Gambit?"

"Don't knock it too hard. Everyone has to start somewhere. I don't think you started out owning this *whole* ring."

Her smile was mischievous. "You're right. Just a third."

"A third?"

"Yes. The Wings already owned a third of the ring when I took over."

"You get my point though. It takes time to grow a business."

She rolled her eyes and pulled him down onto one of the couches. He went willingly, pressing against her but careful to support his own weight. "But I *enjoy* building the business," she insisted. "I enjoy it like you enjoy running the Nethra. It's what I'm passionate about."

"Hey, I can be passionate!"

"Yes. You. *Can,*" she raked her nails gently down the bare skin of his back.

"If you keep that up, I'm going to have trouble thinking clearly."

"Maybe that's what I want." Markus grabbed her hand and pinned her to the surface of the couch. "My, my, Mr. Frost... assertiveness suits you."

Markus couldn't help but laugh as they kissed. He was intent on moving on to other things, but Ora gently pushed him back up into a sitting position with her free hand. "Seriously though, Markus. I want you to come. It'd be nice to have someone to bounce ideas off of. I'm not entirely sure what I'm walking into down there."

He sighed. "Who'd you hire to run you out there?"

"Kadath."

It took him a second to place the name. "That guy who brought you Shift way-back-when?"

"Yes. Aside from the *Vandal*, they're the best crew I have on retainer. They've mostly been working local jobs, but I think it's time we mixed up their routine." She leaned in and kissed him on the neck. "So, how about it, Markus? Just one more run?"

"I feel like you're seducing me so just so I'll sign on."

She donned a look of mock offense. "Now, would I do that?" Her lips trailed along his neck and down onto his chest. As she ventured lower, Markus became aware of the uncomfortable truth.

He was going on this job. Not because he missed the running game, or because he thought Ora couldn't handle it on her own.

He was going because he'd miss her too damned much if she left him behind.

Skye was exhausted, but two hours of sleep over two days tended to do that. They hadn't been expecting another assignment so soon, and there was a lot that needed to be done before they set out again. That would have been true even absent the discovery of Lexa two-point-oh.

It had been clear that Lexa anticipated a certain amount of reluctance from the crew. She had been hesitant to ask for any assistance in setting up her cabin. Skye thought that Dan, at least, would be needed to set up her nutrient infusion and charging station in her new quarters. Lexa, however, had declared that she was more than capable of installing the system herself using a pair of the ship's maintenance drones.

By the way that Dan had remained secluded throughout the entire process, it was starting to look like he, more than anyone, was upset with Lexa. It had gotten better since their little one-on-one, but Skye wasn't thrilled to see Dan so unnerved by the new developments.

Principally, the only thing that made Skye mad was that Lexa had done all this behind their backs. After thinking about it, though, she decided to let this gripe go. Shit, odds were that she learned the habit of secret-keeping by watching the rest of them.

They would work it out. Lexa had a soft spot for Dan, probably because of his role in her creation. Dan had a unique kind of affection for her too, but that was harder to read. Unlike the rest of the crew, their pilot and resident hacker wasn't big on sharing his feelings. Gods, the kid had barely said a word after having his fragging eyes gouged out. If that had happened to Skye, there'd be no end to the amount of therapy she'd need.

She was fairly certain Dan liked being a part of their crew. Beyond that, his wants and dreams were something of a mystery.

Well, that piece of drama was going to have to wait for another day to be solved. Right now, Skye had more pressing concerns to deal with. Lexa had just informed her that their guests had arrived and were requesting permission to board.

Argus and Amelia traveled light, which was good to see. Each of them carried a black duffel that matched their dark attire. Apparently, they were really into the whole monochromatic thing. Despite the lack of color, they still looked professional.

Argus was sporting an open-collared dress shirt under a suit that was slightly more appropriate for a nightclub than a board room. Amelia's dress was of a conservative cut with just a hint of lace around the neckline. The garment clung tight to her thin frame, highlighting the slight curves she possessed. On the surface, they looked more respectable than most of the clients Skye usually dealt with.

Then Argus opened his mouth, and Skye was reminded about how looks were only skin deep. "So, Eli sends his pet instead of choosing to welcome us himself?"

Don't get mad. They're only here for a few days. "First off," Skye began, "I'm nobody's pet. Secondly, I'm not going to put up with any of your bullshit. If you want this trip *not* to suck, then I recommend you knock it off."

He was not pleased by the rebuke. "Are you this rude to all of your passengers?"

"Only the ones that give me a good reason. Don't worry, it can get a lot worse if you'd like me to dial it up a notch."

Argus started to say something else, but Amelia laid a restraining hand on his shoulder. "Calm down, love. This is not the way to foster a productive business relationship." She turned her ebony gaze on Skye. "Ms. Jensen was kind enough to come down to let us in. I'm certain she had plenty of other pressing matters she could be attending to, but she's here to get us settled. Let us be respectful, yes?"

It was hard to tell if the words were meant to be patronizing, or if they were Amelia's best attempt at an olive branch. Skye chose to take it as the latter. "A cabin has been prepared for the both of you," she stated. "Unless, of course, you would prefer separate accommodations?"

Amelia smiled. "Just the one room is fine, thank you."

Skye gestured for them to follow, explaining the ship's layout as they went. "This level gives you access to the ship's bridge, war room, and medical bay. One level down gets you to crew quarters. Two decks down puts you at engineering, the cargo hold, and the hanger.

"Galley and rec room are on the middle deck. No one's real big on keeping regular mealtimes around here, so it's kind of a help-yourself thing. If you need anything, the crew has been told to do their best to assist you. You're welcome to connect to our mobile network with your personal devices if you'd like."

Thinking about the ship's network led Skye to her final point. "Because of Eli's reports, you are already aware of the synth that functions as the ship's artificial intelligence. You will likely observe her interacting with us on your trip. If you encounter her at any point on your stay, you are to treat her with the same respect that you would afford any member of the crew. Is that clear?"

Both of them gave nods of acknowledgment, which gave Skye little comfort. While she was hoping that Amelia would play nice, it seemed like Argus only behaved as long as he was kept under her thumb.

They'd arranged for the two of them to share the largest available cabin on the ship. As Skye triggered the access panel, she experienced a major episode of deja vu. It only took her a second to realize why.

This particular cabin, until recently, had been Markus's cabin. Though he hadn't been very big on a lot of the perks of his position, this had been one he'd claimed early on. The way he'd reasoned it, someone had to take the larger quarters. There hadn't been any reason it shouldn't have been him. Besides, when they'd first acquired the ship, Skye had spent more time in here than in her own quarters. She knew all too well that the cabin was large enough to sleep two comfortably.

Looking at the mostly empty room tugged at her heartstrings. Sure, it had the same basic furnishings as all the other cabins, but it now lacked a certain character. There was no ornamentation, no personal touch. Markus hadn't been real big on decorating, but the place *had* taken on a more lived-in feel during his tenure, as opposed to its current state.

Was it bad that, six months later, she still missed him? Not that she missed him like *that*, but still…

"Here you go," she said, stepping aside to let the Twins file into the chamber. "I'll leave you two to get settled. Is there anything else before I go?"

"No, thank you," Amelia replied. "This is more than adequate." She gave Skye that knowing smile again. Before they left, she really needed to figure out what exactly it was about that smile that made her so uncomfortable.

She shut the door and started back toward her quarters. Now was not the time for contemplating unnerving facial expressions. There were a few more tasks she needed to knock out before she could get some sleep.

At some point she probably needed to get around to talking to Eli again, too. She was still a little miffed at him, but now was not the time to give him the silent treatment. She needed allies. She needed a safe place.

Now if she could just get back to feeling like Eli fit that description, she'd be good to go.

CHAPTER 23

Terra-News-Net Now (TN3)

Headline: Ora Monroe Reportedly in Talks to Purchase Jilly's Gambit

Story: Every investor on Sigma-4 is asking the same question: "What does Ora see in Jilly's Gambit?" The dive-bar on R3 was acquired by a new buyer about five months ago. Other than a slight expansion in the menu, the current owner hasn't made many changes.

Ms. Monroe must see something that everyone else is missing. After being sighted on numerous occasions with the bar's proprietor, Markus Frost, business analysts have started to wonder what the Silver Queen has taken notice of that seems to have been missed by other investors.

Ora's majority-owned Silver Flight Entertainment (SFE-RAV, +30.6%) has nearly tripled its value over the last cycle, causing investors to trust the mogul's judgment when it comes to what consumers want. The gossip around Jilly's Gambit has reportedly prompted at least two other firms to query the business's public filings for the last two cycles. The bar's owner did not reply to requests for comments on this story.

Markus had never seen Ora look so… what was the word? Militant, perhaps?

Her black jacket was cut in imitation of an NTA officer's coat with heavy black shoulder pads and angular seams. It was cut off just below her rib cage, a fashion statement more like her usual style.

Charcoal leggings and a purple top clung tightly to her muscular frame. A thick black belt supported two holstered pistols on her hips. Fingerless black gloves and thigh-high synth leather combat boots completed the outfit.

"Damn," Markus exclaimed. "Talk about dressed to kill."

She smiled back at him. "What? Did you think I'd do this whole mission in high-heels and club attire?"

"I think you'd pull it off if that's what you wanted to do."

The glint in her eyes let him know the remark had scored him some points. She hefted her bag over one shoulder. "Come on. Kadath's sent word that he's ready."

"Do we need to check our weapons?" While guns could be owned by station residents, carrying them around in public was grounds for a citation.

Ora just arched an eyebrow at the question. *Right...* He had forgotten that station security was on her payroll. Such generous donations allowed for certain privileges.

Though it was a short walk to the docks from Annex, Markus had brought along a hover cart. While he had packed light in terms of personal effects, he'd also loaded up his running gear: a sniper rifle, two assault rifles, and a semi-automatic pistol. He also had a bit of multi-purpose gear like his utility belt and combat rig. He'd probably over-packed, but one could never know what they might need.

They moved past the hanger for the small and mid-sized vessels and over to the area where the largest ships docked. Ora pointed to a vessel just ahead of them. "That's it."

Markus's jaw slackened. "For real?"

"Yes. Why?"

He didn't know where to begin. To call Kadath's ship unconventional was an understatement. Markus couldn't figure out what this abomination had started as because there was no way it was standard configuration—at least not for anything manufactured in Terran space.

It had a wide, almost blimp-like shape. Massive forward cannons extended past the nose of the craft. Eight swiveling turrets dotted the ship's surface in a wide ring. The engines formed an inverted v-shape on the aft portion of the vessel.

"What did you say this thing was called?" Markus asked.

Before Ora could reply, a man shouted over to them. "Her name's *Basilisk*." The speaker emerged a short distance down the walkway. Markus recognized Kadath not because of their familiarity, but because of his distinctive look.

He was of average height with a lean, muscular build. His hair was black—as dark as any Sahaia's—and hung in long curls down his shoulders. His eyes were silvery prosthetics, the kind that opted for superior performance over natural appearance. His face was handsome in that clean-shaven, pretty-boy kind of way.

As if these features weren't eye-catching enough, his skin made the greatest impression. His flesh had a bold, crimson hue that betrayed his Kintari heritage. Kadath wasn't the only half-breed Markus had ever known, but he could count the number he'd met on his fingers.

Markus cocked an eyebrow. "Like, from the Terran myths?"

"Correct," Kadath confirmed with a grin.

"What made you come up with that one?"

The mercenary's grin broadened. "Body of a snake, wings of a bat, and the head of a cock—I figure those little bastards were at least as ugly as this thing."

He was so sincere that Markus couldn't help but laugh. "She's pretty unique, that's for sure."

"Oh, if you think *she's* unique, wait until you meet the rest of her crew." Kadath extended his hand. "Markus Frost, right?"

Markus accepted the handshake. "Yeah, that's right."

"Heard you're one of the best sharp-shooters the colonial militia ever had."

"Yeah? Who told you that?"

Kadath winked at Ora. "I'd give you two guesses, but you'd need only one." He released Markus's hand and gestured courteously toward the ship. "Please, come aboard. We've prepared you a cabin. Let's get you settled, and I will introduce you to the others."

Kadath led them through the primary airlock and up an access ladder. Along the way, Kadath provided them with an overview of the ship. It was bigger than the *Vandal,* with six decks instead of three. Most of the finer details were forgotten as soon as he heard them, save for what he deemed most important: primary airlock on level two, crew quarters on level three, and the bridge and other ship essentials on level four.

The quarters they'd set aside for him and Ora were quite spacious. There was even a gun locker, though that looked like it had been shoved inside the cabin as an afterthought. Ora probably requested it knowing that Markus would be bringing his personal arsenal.

"Is everything to your satisfaction?" Kadath asked.

Ora answered for them both. "Yes, this is more than adequate. Thank you."

"Good. Now, if you'll drop your things, I'll introduce you to the others."

The first crew member they met had appeared right outside their quarters. Markus recognized her almost immediately, though their encounter had been fleeting.

She was clad all in black. The attire had the look of leather armor and was without embellishment. It covered every inch of her figure from the neck down. A heavy black cowl, attached to a cloak worn like a cape, hid the figure's face. This was aided, Markus could see, by a black mask that completely hid any of her facial features.

Kadath facilitated the introductions. "Ora, I believe you have already met Siv Isselhardt. Siv, this is Markus, a friend of Ora's."

Markus couldn't help but wonder how carefully the phrase used in his introduction had been chosen. "A pleasure," he extended his hand.

To Markus's surprise, Kadath gently pushed the hand down, warding off the handshake. "It's nothing personal, Markus, but Siv isn't big on physical contact. Her religious tenants forbid much contact with the opposite sex other than her mate. You'll meet Jeagan in just a minute. He's down in the hanger."

"A follower of Prodica," Ora noted. "I remember now."

Siv said nothing, choosing instead to incline her head in acknowledgment.

Kadath continued. "Siv here is our resident trouble-shooter. She also helps us ward off any psionic problems. She's a quell, you see."

That caught Markus's attention. Quells were extremely powerful, but they were also quite rare. A quell could suppress all psionic activity within their sphere of influence. The stronger the quell, the bigger the sphere.

They also only came in one flavor: Hissak. It was one of the race's less common innate psionic abilities, but also one of the most prized. Markus was kind of surprised the templars hadn't snapped this one up when she was younger. One didn't find many quells running the Nethra.

Kadath thanked Siv for her time and sent her on her way. "Don't take her silence personally," he said. "Siv isn't much of a talker. She'll open up a bit once she gets to know you."

"No apology necessary," Ora assured. "You said her mate was on the ship?"

"Yes, right this way."

As Kadath had suggested, they found Jeagan in the hanger. Their ship's engineer, like Siv, was Hissak. For the most part, he held the same quiet demeanor that Siv had shown. From an appearance standpoint, however, he could hardly have made a starker contrast.

He was shirtless, for one. Like most Hissak, his frame was long and lean. Though there was hardly an ounce of fat on him, it was hard to call him muscular. Wiry was probably the best descriptor.

His scaled skin was a lighter tone than most Hissak Markus had met, more brown than green—not that you could see much of it. From the neck down Jeagan was covered almost completely in tattoos. They were not the dark, symbolic tattoos of psionic ritual, either. Rather, they were quite colorful, depicting various forms of animal and plant life Markus knew to exist in some part of the universe but had never seen in person.

Jeagan's face wasn't completely spared of artwork either. Two curling tendrils of flame snaked up from Jeagan's eyes and back across his bare scalp. It gave him a sinister look that belied his polite demeanor.

"Glad to have you with us," he greeted, quickly wiping one hand on a cloth and extending toward Markus.

"Pleasure's mine," Markus returned. He nodded to the shuttle. "So, you're the guy that keeps all this space-worthy?"

"Yes," he replied. Despite lacking the Hissak's typical accent, there was still a slight hissing quality to his speech. "Or as close to it as is possible."

Though the comment was likely meant as a joke, the remark fell flat with the crowd. The engineer shuffled, casting his eyes back to the shuttle.

Seeing his desire to return to his work, Ora issued a polite nod. "We'll leave you to it, then." Very nice to meet you." They departed as the Hissak disappeared once more under the craft.

Markus waited until they were out of earshot before asking, "Is Jeagan a…" What was the name of the god Ora had mentioned earlier?

"Prodican?" Kadath laughed. "Hardly. He respects his wife's beliefs to a certain extent, but he doesn't let the church affect his life much more than that. Are you a believer, Markus? An acolyte, perhaps?"

Despite himself, Markus squirmed uncomfortably. "Not so much. The only divinity I favor is Lady Luck, and that's only as long as she continues to favor me."

"One might say Markus puts his faith in darker powers," Ora mused. "Station gossip maintains that he has the Devil's Luck."

Kadath chuckled. "Well, I hope it's true. With this op we're on, we'll be needing all the luck we can get. Come on, there's one more crew member I want you to meet. I saved the best of us for last."

The final crew member—and possibly the most unique, which was saying something—was on the bridge. Kadath smiled mischievously as he introduced them. "Markus, Ora, meet Thurn Garrotpryde."

Markus's brain had some trouble processing the person in front of him. The man was large with one muscular arm exposed in his sleeveless white shirt. His thick gray skin flagged him as Orchallen, as did his oversized lower jaw and protruding tusks. One of those tusks had been broken off. This, one could assume, had happened in whatever incident had robbed the orc of the left side of his face.

Thurn's skin ended abruptly just on the left side of his bulbous nose. From there, a mechanical exoskeleton and telescoping artificial eye had been grafted onto the remaining tissue. It might have been highly functional, but subtle it was not. A similar story could have been told of the left side of the Orc's neck and his entire left arm. From what Markus could see, he was all wires and metallic plating in that quadrant of his body.

Cyborgs were not uncommon in an age of recreational prosthetics, but most people took effort to hide their augmentations. Thurn did nothing of the sort—not that he could have, given his choice in hardware. He had opted for mechanical battle armor instead of flesh.

An awkward silence settled in. The orc let out a low rumbling chuckle.

"Sorry," said Markus. "I must have missed the joke."

An ugly grin split Thurn's mouth, showing crooked teeth. "It's yer faces. Ah love the look on yer faces. It's always the same."

Markus didn't know what to say to that. "Yeah? How so?"

"Oh, ya know… 'an orc flies this ship? An orc that hacks? Can orcs even use computers?' And that's before they get started on ma prosthetics. Then there's the one ya got on now: 'Gee, he's awfully well-spoken fer an orc.' Yeah, Ah get it. It's nothin' personal."

An orc with a sense of self-awareness? Now I have seen everything. Markus slipped into politician mode. "Sorry man. You're right. I shouldn't be staring." He extended his hand, and Thurn accepted the handshake.

The grin never left the Orchallen's face. "No hard feelin's." He bowed his head slightly in Ora's direction. "A pleasure makin' yer acquaintance, ma lady."

"Likewise," she replied with a gentle smile and an incline of her head.

Back outside the bridge, Kadath was still sporting a mirthful grin. "There you have it! That's the crew of the *Basilisk*."

Markus shook his head. "If there were a prize for crew diversity, you'd be in the running. How is it that a merc crew in Terran space doesn't have any Terrans on the roster?"

The half-breed shrugged. "It's not like we aren't accepting applications. We haven't always run in this system. I've run with Thurn since the beginning, and the Isselhardts joined soon after. You know how it goes: when you're running, your crew becomes like family."

Yeah, Markus thought wryly. *Just like family.* There was no way Kadath could have known, but he'd just touched on a sore subject. It made Markus wonder exactly how long that wound was going to hurt.

He also wondered what his old family was up to at that very moment.

Sydney could feel Cyrus's gaze as she reentered the bedroom. There was something possessive in the way that he eyed her. It wasn't love, to be sure. Their relationship would never reach *that* level of intimacy, gods willing. That hadn't been part of the deal when she'd accepted this assignment.

No, the way his eyes feasted on her naked form had less to do with affection and more to do with power. In Cyrus's mind, he owned her. In reality, it was more like he was renting her. If she'd wanted to be a slave, she'd have stayed on Kintar. Gods knew those crimson conquerers still had enough of her people under their collective thumb.

But, if it kept him satisfied, she'd leave him to his delusions. Besides, those delusions were *such* a turn-on—at least as long as he never tried to express them in public.

Her tail lashed casually back and forth across the floor, glad to be free of its binding. "I think you missed me," she drawled.

Cyrus's smile broadened. "I always miss you."

"Well," she said with a playful huff, "I was beginning to wonder with the way you've put me off the last couple of days." She crawled onto the bed, mustering just the right amount of performance into every motion as she slinked up to him.

"You know I would never put you off if it were not for matters of the utmost importance."

It was true. Based on what he'd told her about the Heart of Thule, this new weapon of his had the potential for some very interesting applications. He'd been unusually loose lipped about the artifact in the prelude to their latest sexual encounter. Perhaps now was a good time to press for more details.

She pulled back the sheet and crawled onto his lap. It'd probably be a few more minutes before he could perform again, but she straddled him anyway. Men were always less discerning when they were between the legs of a woman.

"Yes," she purred. "You were telling me something about that." She ran her lips gently against the hollow of his neck, tasting his salty skin in between sentences. "Took out Rico Chronos, you said? All on your own?"

"Yeah," he replied breathily. "Just one agent."

"Mmm, impressive. Maybe I should be concerned for my job." As a counterpoint to her words, she ran her hands over his chest.

"Surely not."

"I don't know. Are you sure this Eva doesn't have ulterior motives? I mean, I'm comfortable with just being a consort, but that doesn't mean other women are going to give up their aspirations of becoming Donna Valadar."

He let out a short, barking laugh. "I can assure you, she has no such intentions. Besides, I will always have room for you in my life."

Or at least in your bed. "So, tell me again: what is it about her that makes her so special? Why is she the one who's running the artifact?"

She suspected his short hesitation had to do more with focusing his thoughts on the conversation than any reluctance to share the information. "It's her psionic abilities. The psionically inclined are affected differently by the Heart's radiation."

"But I thought you said she was Terran?"

"She is. She has a psionic amplifier."

"Interesting," Sydney purred, running her tongue against his flesh. "Those are a bit uncommon." She'd only met one other Terran with an amp, and that sister of hers was an absolute terror.

"That's an understatement. With Dorian regs so tight on those things, you can hardly find a dealer in all Terran space. They're damn-near impossible to find."

"What? Even the great Don Valadar can't get his hands on one?"

"Not easily. But gods, if I could… what amazing power!" Cyrus dug his fingers into the small of Sydney's back. As much as it pained her to admit, she doubted it was her ministrations that were turning him on.

Then a thought occurred to her. "What if *you* could have that kind of power?" she coaxed.

He faltered, demonstrating just how much thought he was giving to the idea. "Well, that'd be nice. But as I was saying: amps are difficult to find. It would take months for me to procure such a device."

How like a male: so limited in imagination. "Oh? I was under the impression that you knew exactly where to find at least one such device."

Cyrus's breath caught. He'd finally caught on to what she was hinting at. It surprised Sydney, to a degree, that he hadn't thought of it himself.

Eva had a psionic amplifier, but a mod installed in *her* brain would work just as well in someone else's. Sure, the woman wouldn't survive the extraction, but that was just a bonus as far as Sydney was concerned.

Cyrus kissed her deeply, then held the back of her neck as he gazed into her eyes. "You are so delightfully wicked."

She covered his smile with her lips. He was right—she *was* wicked. That, in part, was why she would always have a place in his world.

CHAPTER 24

Terra-News-Net Now (TN3)

Headline: Apocrypha the Sticking Point at Latest Nethrian Conclave

Story: The Forty-Eighth Nethrian Conclave has ended on a sour note. Though Tempolose Nethera—considered by most to be the Capitol of the Nethrian Church, and the largest delegation at the Conclave—was able to secure the votes necessary to ratify the proposed fifty-year charter, minority parties lamented the lack of compromise from the church's officials. Under this new charter, five Orchallen deities and over thirty Orchallen manuscripts were inducted into the official canon. The sticking point seemed to be certain areas of apocrypha, which certain vocal sects continue to insist should be incorporated.

Archais Uthral, Speaker for the Uthrat Hemidal, declared that the Thuleian Cycle was of particular interest in the debate. "Every sect aside from Tempolose Nethera recognizes these writings as scripture," he asserted. "The continued reluctance from temple officials to acknowledge their canonicity is as perplexing as it is disturbing." The Speaker went on to elaborate on the details of the writings, which pertain to articles of faith such as the origin of the Sahaia and the nature of Kaleemic beings.

"Damn it!" Skye roared. The pain exploding behind her eye sockets shattered any semblance of meditation she'd mustered. She lurched forward and emptied the contents of her stomach onto Sahar's area rug.

The Maur's strong hands braced her shoulders and steadied her trembling form. "Just breathe."

Skye coughed and took in a shuddering breath. "I'm okay," she insisted reflexively.

"I can see that, but take a moment anyway."

"Sorry about your rug."

"Don't worry about that. Just breathe."

Skye listened to her friend and, go figure, the trembling subsided. Though the episode had passed, it was a safe bet that they were done with today's session. She needed some mouthwash, but it looked like she wasn't going to be let out without at least *some* explanation. "Now," Sahar began patiently. "Tell me what happened."

Inhaling another shuttering breath, Skye searched for the words. "I could see the stone. This… *Heart* or whatever. Anyway, I could see it again—like before. There were hands all around it."

"There were others touching the stone?"

She shook her head, the image solidifying in her mind as she described it. "No, that's not it. I mean, someone was touching the stone, but the hands weren't… gods, how do I describe it? They were *inside,* Sahar. They were like little shadows pressing up against the inside of the stone."

"So, you could see *into* the stone?"

Skye cleared some of the bile from her throat. She *really* needed that mouthwash. "Kind of. It's a little fuzzy."

"What about the person touching the stone? Was it…"

"No. It wasn't him. It was a man, but I didn't recognize him."

Sahar paused briefly, seeing if Skye would add anything else. When she didn't, Sahar let the silence linger for a moment before asking, "And what caused you to lose control?"

Skye took another steadying breath. "When I didn't recognize the man, I looked back inside the rock." She closed her eyes and formed the picture again in her mind's eye. "It was like looking through fogged glass. I could only see the hands, reaching out from the green light and the mists. I looked closer, to see what else might have been there. I wanted to see…"

She paused. What *had* she wanted to see? There had been a flicker of it—something tempting her to go deeper. What was it?

"Did you find it?"

Another head shake. "No, but I found… *something*." What had been in there when she looked? Another form in the mist, but her mind struggled to grasp its shape. It was something alien. Something horrifying.

Her stomach clenched as another wave of nausea washed over her. Sahar must have felt it because her grip on her shoulders tightened again. "Let's just call it there. I think we've made enough progress for one day."

That sounded like a much better plan than reliving Skye's nausea-inducing visions. "Do you need help cleaning up?"

"Nah, I've got this. Just get yourself cleaned up."

With a final nod, Skye rose to her feet. Satisfied she wasn't going to topple over, she made her way out of the chamber. Sahar's quarters were only a short distance away from her own. Still, it was apparently too much to ask that she not encounter any more trouble along the way.

"You're playing with dangerous things," came a voice from just behind her. Skye glanced back to see Amelia leaning against the far bulkhead. The Sahaia regarded her with an inky gaze and a self-assured smirk.

"Piss off," Skye replied reflexively.

"Reply with irreverence and miss an opportunity to learn."

Skye's first instinct was to get right back in Amelia's smug little face, but she paused. If the shadow had answers, wasn't it in Skye's best interest to give her a quick listen? She wasn't putting all these hours into meditation for the fun of it.

Skye intended to get to the bottom of her condition, and outside of a name, she hadn't gotten any closer than she'd been six months ago. Sahar had been annoyingly tight-lipped about what it meant to be Kaleema, and after Skye's little outburst at the Sanctum, it seemed that Eli's feigned ignorance was intentional. If someone here was willing to finally give her some straight answers, shouldn't Skye take them up on it?

"Fine," she sighed. "But not here. Follow me." She resumed the short march to her quarters. Amelia glided behind her like a wraith haunting her passage.

Skye's cabin wasn't exactly orderly. She'd spent a lot less time here in recent months, so keeping things tidy hadn't been a priority. It wasn't that she'd become a slob, per se. It was more that her quarters didn't meet the pristine standards her lover set for his own. She didn't think of herself as a messy person just because she didn't stress over the occasional stray piece of dirty laundry.

Then again, those standards felt strangely more acceptable when she wasn't entertaining guests. Now she found the state of her quarters decidedly uncomfortable. "Just grab a seat anywhere," she sighed.

Amelia did so without comment, choosing the chair that normally paired with her desk but had been moved to the opposite bulkhead for some forgotten reason. Skye grabbed a reasonably clean towel from the foot of her bunk and used it to dab the sweat from her forehead. She eyed the Sahaia expectantly. "Well?"

"Well?" Amelia's voice had an innocent, musical quality to it. Its pleasant tone made the remark all-the-more infuriating.

"You said you had some answers for me."

The woman's soft smile never wavered. "You haven't asked me any questions."

Skye inhaled deeply and ground her teeth. *Patience…* "What can you tell me about the Kaleema?"

"A number of things. What is it that you want to know?"

Why had she decided against keeping a booze stash under her bunk like Markus used to? That would be particularly handy right now. "Let's assume I don't know anything. Start at the beginning. What *are* the Kaleema?"

Amelia crossed her legs and placed her hands serenely in the folds of her black skirt. "A reasonable question, but unfortunately difficult to answer. The Kaleema, as they are understood by most today, are merely legend. The presiding council of Tempolose Nethera relegated most explicit references to the Kaleema to the apocryphal texts during the forty-third conclave more than two centuries ago."

"So, you're saying they're not even a real thing?"

"No, I'm saying that key members of the religious oligarchy have gone to significant lengths to convince their followers that they are not—as you would say—'a real thing.'"

"But you don't believe that."

That frustrating smile played at the corner of the shadow's mouth again. "Popular beliefs come and go. One benefit of the extensive coven archives is that we have a unique perspective on the rhythmical wax and wane in the preferences of the faithful."

"Sorry, but perhaps you can see how this isn't helpful to me. I mean, I appreciate church bashing as much as the next spacer, but I'm looking for something practical here."

Amelia cocked her head to the side, betraying her curiosity. "Even with what you are experiencing, you do not place your faith in those beyond the Nethra's veil?"

"See, that's the funny thing about faith: it involves a lot of shutting off your brain so you can believe things that can't be proven. That's not my style. I'm more of a hard-facts kind of girl."

"And what *'hard facts'* have helped you to explain how you can see the future through the use of your visions?"

Skye paused. "I never said anything about the future—or visions, in particular."

"Was that not what you were practicing in the Maur's cabin?"

"Even if it was, how do you know that?"

Amelia tapped her forehead. "I pick up on things. It is my gift."

Ah. Amelia must have been an empath. Gods, Skye was really going to have to be kinder in her thoughts knowing the shadow could read her mind.

"Not necessary," Amelia assured her. "You are not so unkind in your thoughts as to offend me."

"Then, would you mind if I asked you to stop reading them?"

"I would be happy to, but I must ask you in return to attempt not to think so loudly."

And how in the nine hells was Skye supposed to do that? She supposed it didn't matter and decided to get back on point. "I don't know how I'm having the visions, or why they suddenly started this last cycle. I was hoping that you were going to give me some insight on that, but perhaps I was mistaken."

"Yes, unfortunately, I cannot tell you why the Kaleema experience visions. It is a trick of the Nethra, perhaps—a fluidity in which the Kaleema experience space-time. However, that would not provide any satisfactory answers for you."

This was going nowhere, and Skye was losing patience. "Then what *can* you tell me?"

"I can tell you that—despite the efforts of Tempolose Nethera to convince the populous otherwise—the Kaleema are definitely real, and they are not as uncommon as one might think."

Now they were getting somewhere. "So, there are others? Others like me?"

"A handful, yes. At current universal population rates, we've calculated that every generation spawns a few hundred candidates."

"Yeah, well, when you consider the trillions of souls in the universe, that really isn't saying anything."

"More like hundreds of trillions, but yes, I understand your point."

Skye shook her head. After reflecting on Amelia's words, she spoke again. "You said 'candidates,' not Kaleema. What did you mean by that?"

Amelia smiled in that way a teacher does when her pupil has said something clever. "That's what we call Kaleema that have not served their function. Like all things in this universe, the Creator has instilled within the Kaleema a very specific purpose—though precious few ever go on to fulfill that function. However, let us put that point on hold for a moment. May I ask you—what do you see in your visions?"

Skye furrowed her brow. "Can't you just take that out of my brain?"

"I could probably discover the visions if I delved deeply enough, but I would prefer it if you told me."

Another heavy sigh. Damn, she was in a huffy mood. "In some of them, I'm seeing my future. Back on the Star Spire—I'm assuming Eli told you all about it in his report—I saw things that were about to happen to me. But they weren't *exactly* the way they actually happened. Things in the dreams… the visions… they were fuzzy. Almost…"

"Symbolic?"

"Yeah, that's right. It was like hints of the future rather than seeing it play out on a feed."

"What else do you see?"

Skye paused. How should she explain this next part? "I see… my friends. Members of the crew. Sometimes it's like I'm watching them from a distance." She thought of Dan and seeing him tortured by the Ghenza. "Other times, it's like my visions predict the future." She thought of Markus and her dancing on the glass floor. "Then there are these other visions that…" She remembered Eli in the pool of darkness holding that charred corpse.

Several seconds went by before Skye realized she'd stopped speaking. When she met Amelia's eyes, the Sahaia nodded. "That makes sense. These are people you care deeply for. Individuals you are attuned to."

"I'm sorry… '*Attuned*?'"

"Certain things in this life that you have an attachment to—friends, places, certain objects. Your connection with the Nethra allows you to have visions where you can see these things in ways that are meaningful to you."

Well, that kind of made sense—at least for about half of her visions. "But the visions don't mean anything to me, not when I have them. Most of the time I don't even know what I'm seeing."

"Your conscious mind may not grasp the meaning, but that does not mean these visions are not important to you. The meaning may be something you will only later decipher."

That was fair, if not particularly helpful. However, there were still other things she saw but couldn't write off as being attuned to. The most recent example was the fact that she was seeing the Heart of Thule just before they were tasked with stealing it. And why was she seeing the ARC reactor on Minos so frequently?

Amelia must have skimmed her thoughts because she answered the unasked questions. "You would also be attracted to objects of great power or importance. Your subconscious mind would be attuned to these things, even if your consciousness cannot explain them."

"Okay, I'll buy that. So, how do I know why they're important?"

"That, unfortunately, I cannot answer. Concerning the Heart of Thule, the reasoning seems obvious. This other thing…" she shook her head. "I fear that I am as perplexed as you are."

Well, at least knowing it was significant was a start. Maybe it would become apparent soon. "So, the visions are supposed to help me?"

"Not necessarily. They are more of a side effect. They do not necessarily correlate with the true purpose of the Kaleema."

"And what purpose is that, exactly?"

Amelia's smile waned. Somehow, her blackened eyes grew even darker. "To be a vessel."

CHAPTER 25

Terra-News-Net Now (TN3)

Headline: NTA Application to Join the Dorian Senate Denied Again

Story: While the NeoTerra Alliance will now have one additional seat in the Dorian House of Voices, its application to join the Grand Senate has been denied for the third consecutive time. Gallion Barak, Speaker for the Terran Voice, was quick to provide criticism for the decision. "This is nothing short of outrageous. The NTA and its vast network of united colonies now occupy just as many systems as the Maur. It is hard not to feel like the High Council views Terrans as second-class citizens, even though gate revenues in Terran systems rival those cultivated in even Hissak territories. We deserve a voice in the Senate as much as any of the other sapient races."

High Councilor Dravian Makathra Dorr defended the decision to keep Senate membership exclusive to the Dorian, Hissak, Kintar, and Maur races. In his official statement following the decision, Councilor Dorr noted, "Although Terran space continues to develop at a pace consistent with the other races, emigration of Terrans throughout the larger universe remains an insurmountable issue in the question of Senate membership. As long as Terrans continue to isolate themselves from other sapient species, representation on the Senate will remain elusive."

Skye swallowed hard. "I'm sorry, what?"

"It's not so different from how the Sahaia are granted their power, really." Amelia eyed her quizzically. "How much has our dear Eli shared with you about our power? About our ways?"

"Not much." It was an honest statement and one that represented a great source of frustration on Skye's part. "I was under the impression that those subjects were kind of off-limits. You know, top-secret, need-to-know, and all that…"

"You're not wrong, but a lover's lips frequently share things that would be otherwise ill-advised."

Eli most definitely did not have *that* problem. "I don't know anything."

"Very well. I will impart a basic understanding. Do you know what grants the Sahaia their power?"

"I thought it was some kind of ritual."

"Yes," Amelia drawled patiently. "But do you understand what the ritual is intended to accomplish?"

That, Skye did not know. "I guess I never really thought about it."

"True of those who still slumber. Do not worry though, I will share with you what I am able."

Skye held up her hands as if warding off the trouble this new information might carry with it. "Whoa, I thought the Sahaia were supposed to be tight-lipped about their rituals. Why the sudden urge to share secrets?"

Amelia shrugged. "It's not so secret, really—merely forgotten. You forget that the Sahaia rituals were discovered and used officially by the Terran Alliance long before the current powers that be were conceived. There are likely records of what I intend to tell you on a server somewhere in Terran space."

Secret histories stored on servers from a government defunct for over a millennium? Yeah, good luck finding that. "Fine, tell me what you know."

"I don't have to, you know. If you don't want answers—"

"No! I want to know. I just…" She just, what? Usually, Skye was all about getting to the bottom of things—no bullshit. Maybe Eli was wearing off on her. "Please. I want to know."

Amelia studied her for another second before launching into her explanation. "The rituals we use to Awaken involve the transfer of energies from the Nethra into our bodies. These energies are manifested in the spirits that inhabit the Nethra. When we Awaken, we are—in a sense—sharing our bodies with the ancestral spirits of the Sahaia who came before us."

"Wait, wait, wait… that doesn't make any sense." Though there was so much wrong with this, Skye chose to fixate on one detail in particular. "If your powers come from the spirits of dead shadows, then how did the first of you get your powers? There wouldn't have been any spirits for you to bond with, right?"

"Oh, there are all kinds of spirits in the Nethra. Remember, we did not make these rituals. Terran migrants found them during their war with the Kintar. No one knows how many civilizations might have practiced our rites before we became their caretakers."

So, the Sahaia were essentially Terrans possessed by spirits that gave them a modicum of immortality and god-like power. When considering the preposterous notion of the metaphysics involved with half the things the shadows could do, this should be a relatively easy explanation to swallow. Still, Skye had trouble connecting the dots.

"Okay… so that's how the Sahaia work. I'm not seeing how this relates to what's going on with me. I've never been through any rituals, or Awakenings, or whatever you call it."

Amelia's smile might have been intended as reassuring, but the effect was anything but. "Yes, that's the beauty of it. That is why we, the Sahaia, out of all the factions and cults that litter the universe, have a distinct remembrance of the Kaleema. What we do—what we *are*—is only an imitation of what it is to be Kaleema."

There was a long pause as if this explanation should have been all Skye needed to hear. It wasn't. "I'm sorry, I'm still not following."

With a sigh, Amelia cast her gaze to an empty portion of the room. After a moment's thought, she tried another approach. "You've seen what we can do, yes? The power of being Sahaia?"

"Oh yeah, for sure." She'd seen Eli do everything from stopping bullets in thin air to breaking a guy's arm with only his mind. When you got them going, the Sahaia were some scary fraggers. Sure, there were psions present in the general populace of most other races, but the Sahaia took that shit to a new level.

Amelia nodded. "Now, as impressive as all that might seem—remember that we use only the spirits of those who came before us. We are empowered, in the end, by finite, mortal energies." Her eyes took on an ominous cast. "Imagine how powerful a person might be if they could house the energy of the gods themselves."

Skye's brain went numb. She couldn't decide whether she couldn't, or simply wouldn't, let her mind go there. It didn't matter that she wasn't a religious person, that she didn't believe in gods or spirits haunting the space in between jump gates. One didn't need religion to see what the Sahaia—a people that were very real and very active in her life—were capable of. If the Kaleemas' power was beyond what even the Sahaia could do…

"So you're saying…"

"Yes, dear." Amelia's eyes were locked on Skye's as if she were trying to peer into her very soul. "The Kaleema are vessels for the gods themselves."

Skye shuddered. Aside from all the creepy implications that had on her own life—the existential and metaphysical crisis that such news should inevitably induce—a single thought pervaded her mind.

No one, not even Skye, should have access to *that* kind of power.

———

"What are you doing?" Markus asked as Ora set up in bed and reached for her tablet.

"I thought I would get some work done," she replied as she pulled up a messaging application. "With the current orbital alignment, we won't be arriving on Sif until tomorrow afternoon. Not even *you* have that kind of stamina."

The comment was meant to be flirtatious, but it lost a little something when she was able to down-shift from sex into work that quickly. "But you don't have a network connection."

"So? I have most of the files I need right here, and any messages I send will queue up until we connect to the hardline in Valhalla. Weren't you in the habit of taking care of administrative tasks while you were traveling in normal space?"

Truthfully, Markus had left all the administrative garbage to Dan and Eli, but he wasn't going to own up to that. "I suppose…"

Ora leaned over and planted a chaste kiss on his cheek. "I will only be a few minutes. The quarterly filings are due next week to the taxation commission, and I doubt I'm going to have much time on this little excursion to review balance sheets. Why don't you explore the ship a little bit? Stretch your legs?"

"What, like you haven't given me enough of a workout just now?"

"Well, I suppose you could nap, or read a book, but somehow I don't think that's your style."

"Ouch. Should I be offended?"

"Because I think you lack the capacity for being sedentary? Hardly." She kissed him again. "Now, I do need to tend to this, if you don't mind. Will you be hanging around?"

Reluctantly, Markus admitted she was right. "Nah, I'm gonna take your advice and tour the ship. After I get a quick shower, of course."

After rinsing off and slipping back into his clothes, Markus glanced at the time on his MoDAC. Going by the time on Sigma-4, it was late evening. On Valhalla, though, it was still the afternoon.

Ora must have been trying to get her sleep cycle adjusted while in flight, which was why she opted for work instead of sleep at the moment. Smart thinking.

When Markus stepped out of their shared cabin, he suddenly found himself wishing he'd paid more attention to Kadath's tour. He was fairly certain they hadn't mentioned having a gym or rec-room, but he couldn't remember what exactly was taking up all the gods-damned space on this behemoth of a ship. The *Basilisk's* blimp-like shape made it so the vessel could hold six decks and still, somehow, actually seem smaller than the *Vandal.*

Lacking any other strategy, he decided to do a walking tour starting at the bottom and working his way up to the top. One of his first stops was the hanger where, to his surprise, he found Jeagan still tinkering with the same shuttle he'd been working on hours earlier.

"Damn. This bird in that bad of shape?"

The Hissak glanced over his shoulder. "Good work takes time, my friend." Markus noted, again, the lack of the typical Hissak accent. Most snakes had issues with selecting the correct tense since their native language didn't have such conventions. Either Jeagan leaned ISL early, or he'd been in Terran space for a long time.

"True story," Markus agreed. "Anything I can help with?"

"No. It is almost finished." He patted the flier affectionately. "She's not the youngest bird in the flock, but she's fast when I need her to be. I try to take good care of her so that it stays that way."

"So, you're a pilot?"

"I can be—when Thurn's busy. He's often busy."

"I know how that is." Or, at least, Markus *used* to know what being busy was like.

"Do you fly?" Jeagan asked.

"Yeah, actually. Haven't had the need in a while. We had two pilots on my last crew. I only flew when we were short-handed."

"A flier *and* a shooter. You must have quite the resume, Mr. Frost."

How had Jeagan heard about his marksman skills? Ora must have really been talking him up to Kadath. "Ex-military. Colonial resistance, actually."

"Ah. That is a sad story. My people were very sympathetic to the colonial cause."

Well, that was forward. Was that a Hissak thing? The only other race that Markus dealt with much were Maur, and Sahar blended in pretty well with the Terrans on the crew. "Yeah," he sighed. "Well, we gave it our best shot."

"That you did. It is a shame that Dorian treachery seems to be one of those things that will go unanswered in our lifetimes."

An engineer *and* a philosopher. Who would have thought? "News of the Colony Wars made it all the way out to Hissak space?"

"Oh yes. My people see great value in observing the happenings in other systems. It gives us plenty of excuses to sit and ponder rather than act upon the universe around us." Jeagan's smile was cynical. Apparently, like Markus, he didn't think much of the powers-that-be. Most runners didn't.

"Then they must have plenty to talk about with the conflict between the Maur and the Kintar," said Markus.

"Yes, and no. That is old news. We were surprised it took as long as it did for those two to be at each other's throats."

What he said was true. Conflicts between the Maur Federation and the Kintari Empire were simmering even before the Colony Wars began. Things had heated up again in the last few cycles, but peace talks between the two governments had faltered well before that.

Jeagan finished his task and closed the access panel he'd been fidgeting with. "There, all done." He wiped his hands on his black pants—the only clothing he was wearing. "Tell me, Mr. Frost…"

"Markus. Just, Markus."

The Hissak nodded. "Markus. Tell me, have you ever played Amfey?"

Markus whistled. "It's been a while, but yeah, I've played it."

"Were you any good?"

"Pretty good," Markus chuckled. There was hardly a game in all Terran space that he didn't excel at.

"Good!" Jeagan clapped his hands together. "Thurn has resolved to quit playing against me. Perhaps we can test your skills at something other than flying spaceships and shooting at people. Yes?"

Sydney stepped in front of the short-haired blonde woman as she rounded the bend in the hall. "Eva, yes?"

The woman looked up from whatever she'd been typing on her MoDAC. "Yeah…" She drew the word out, uncertain. "Do I know you?"

"Likely not. A pleasure to meet your acquittance. Sydney Cross. I'm one of Cyrus's advisers." It was a stretch, but little things like lying never troubled Sydney much. Plus, if the woman had heard Sydney's reputation, this was about to get very uncomfortable, very quickly.

Evidently, she hadn't, because she smiled. "Oh! A pleasure." She took Sydney's proffered hand. "I haven't seen you around here. Are you on the NeoGenix team?"

"Not exactly." How should she frame this? "I'm more like a personal assistant to the Don. That's actually why I'm down here at the moment. I've come looking for you."

Eva uttered another, "Oh!" before regaining her composure. "Mr. Valadar asked for me?"

"Yes, you in particular. It's regarding your special… *talents*." Sydney didn't revel in the tease, but it was the most likely way to get Eva to cooperate. Though Sydney had been dispatched in case Eva resisted, there was no sense in prompting such resistance if a few well-chosen words could get the subject to cooperate.

"Of course," the woman exclaimed, a new smile spreading across her face. "Anything for Mr. Valadar." A moment of hesitation.

"Though I would have expected Dr. Blackwell to give me the message. She's usually the one I deal with here."

"Oh, Lucretia is waiting for us. She's tied up with preparations, which is why she asked me to come to look for you. I'm just glad I caught you before you were done for the day."

That seemed to disarm the last of Eva's defenses. "All right then," she looked over her shoulder. "I was about to head back to my quarters for a quick shower." It was only then that Sydney realized Eva was in sweaty gym clothes. Maybe Eva *had* been done with her shift for a while and was taking advantage of the NeoGenix facilities. "Should I shower up real quick before we go see the doctor?"

"I don't think that's necessary. Besides, Lucretia seemed to imply it was urgent."

This garnered the first look of skepticism from Eva since their initial run-in. "Um… okay…" Another moment of hesitation. "I guess we should go right away then."

"Excellent. Thank you for being so accommodating." Sydney gestured down the hall. "Right this way. I'll bring you to Dr. Blackwell."

It was too easy. Normally, Sydney was skeptical of tasks that were too easy, but this one proved to be just as simple as it seemed. They moved down the labyrinthine corridors of the NeoGenix laboratories until they came to the operating room where Lucretia waited.

"After you," said Sydney when she touched the palm scanner to open the door. As Eva passed by her, Sydney pulled one of her needles dipped in the psionic-nullifying poison she had used on Ryker and casually slipped it into Eva's exposed shoulder.

"Ouch!" Eva cried.

"Sorry! Nails are getting a bit long, I'm afraid."

It was a weak excuse, but the psion was so unnerved by the circumstances that she nodded compliantly. "It's okay. No harm done."

None yet. Sydney hid her smirk and finished ushering her into the room.

Whatever pretenses Sydney had crafted were shattered when Lucretia Blackwell turned a surprised gaze on Eva. "You came willingly?"

Eva was rightly confused. "Um… yes? Why wouldn't I? Sydney said you had an assignment for me." The woman was instantly on the defensive. Little did she realize it was too late to put her guard up.

Realization dawned on Lucretia. "You didn't tell her."

Sydney shrugged. "Not my job. I was told to get the subject here, so that's what I did. I figured you'd go over the specifics."

Eva glanced back and forth between the two of them, a mild panic settling onto her features. "Can someone tell me what this is about?"

Sparing a brief glare for Sydney, Lucretia rounded on the specimen. "Eva, your Don requires your services. As you can imagine, this is a service that only you could provide."

"Of course. I'm willing to help Mr. Valadar in any way that I can." Despite the pledge of loyalty, there was an evident unease in her tone.

"I'm glad to hear that," the doctor continued. "You see, your work with the Heart of Thule has been so successful that Cyrus endeavors to understand what that experience is like for himself."

Confusion blossomed on Eva's face. She paused for several seconds, unsure of how to respond. "That… that's great. But I… um… I thought that you had to be a psion to use the Heart. Does Cyrus have psionic abilities?"

"Oh no, dear." Lucretia's tone sounded motherly and only slightly patronizing. "That's what he needs you for. You see, Cyrus wishes to acquire a psionic amplifier. Unfortunately, such items are hard to come by. That's why he's requested that you relinquish yours."

Eva's horror was immediate and extreme. "What? You… you can't! It's implanted!"

"I know, dear. That's what this operating equipment is for. We plan to extract it."

"But I could die!"

"I promise, we will do everything we can to prevent that from happening. Extractions of brain augmentations are not always fatal, and I assure you—we have the best team on all of Sif to see to your needs."

It wasn't technically a lie. Fatality rates for such procedures were north of eighty percent, but that meant the process was *technically* survivable.

Whether Eva knew the specificity of the risk, or whether she just wasn't keen on giving up her mod, she wasn't buying it. "No! That's… that's absurd! You can't make me do this."

"Oh, dear," Lucretia chided. "I assure you: we can, and we will."

Ah, damn it. This was why Cyrus had insisted that Sydney pick up the subject instead of Lucretia. When push came to shove, Lucretia couldn't keep her gods-damned mouth shut.

Sydney didn't know exactly what flavor of psion Eva was, but the way that she thrust her palm forward seemed to indicate she was a telekin—perhaps an energist or an electrist. Regardless, nothing happened when the psion attempted to summon her special abilities. Sydney's poison had done its work.

She grabbed Eva's arm and twisted it around, holding it pinned behind the woman's back. "Sorry, girl," Sydney whispered. "The Don's going to have his way. You know how it is, right?"

Chapter 26

Terra-News-Net Now (TN3)

Headline: Polar Vortex to Hit Valhalla Again This Year

Story: Sad news for the residents of Sif's capitol; the polar vortex that caused an unseasonably cold spring is back for round two to ring in the new cycle. This time, Valhalla residents will be enduring sub-zero temperatures as the jet stream brings its icy winds to further chill the already frigid temperatures.

Whereas the blame for the polar vortex this past spring was attributed to the typhoon over the Aegir archipelago, meteorologists attribute this new bout of cold weather to the persistent high-pressure systems over Freyja's Ridge. NTA scientists continue to insist that record energy emissions are not to blame for the increasingly inclement weather.

Doctor Sean Prumt of the Climate Surveillance Initiative, in an exclusive interview with TN3, stated, "Scientists failed to prove that energy-emissions hoax a millennium ago on Terra, and no convincing data have been found to justify that position since. It's falsified reporting, folks."

A representative from the Valhalla Weather Center declined to comment.

Daniel docked the ship at the Mjolnir-1 spaceport as it was the closest port to Valhalla that could accommodate a ship the size of the *Vandal*. The fees were outrageous, but at least they could afford it. The cost reminded Dan of the reason their take for these jobs typically exceeded seven figures.

He had been pleased to see that not only were all systems performing as expected under Lexa's new wireless arrangement, but she had actually improved on the navigational interface. "This is really nice, Lexa. What inspired the change?"

The android smiled at him from the copilot's chair. "I'd never experienced the ship's interfaces in the way that you and the crew do. When I observed how you interacted with the navigation console, I identified ways to reduce inefficiencies."

Huh... "Well done," he managed, no longer sure how he felt about the new interface.

Though they'd worked through their initial misunderstanding, Lexa's physical presence was still the source of occasional awkwardness. It was strange, Dan found, how there could be moments where he forgot what it was like to not have her sitting in the co-pilot's chair, while still experiencing other instances in which her presence felt so foreign. No, foreign wasn't the correct word. Taboo, perhaps?

"How are we doing?" Eli asked as he and Skye stepped onto the bridge.

Dan cleared his throat. "We have successfully docked." He paused to scroll through his retinal prompts. "Data-link has been initiated, and Lexa has started the database refresh."

"Good," said Eli. "Lexa, can you check our messages and see if there's any local news that might be relevant to our mission?"

"Affirmative. Scanning communications cache for relevant transmissions. Is there anything that I should prioritize?"

"I'm looking specifically for anything from Ryker or the Sanctum. We need to get a fix on Ryker's position and schedule a rendezvous."

A brief pause. "I'm sorry," Lexa said. "No direct transmissions have been received since departing Minos."

"None?" Skye asked, "Not even from Mara?" According to the mission details they'd received, the coven would bounce a message to Ryker Ren'Dahl using Mara's ship to herald their coming. When they passed through the gate without hearing from the other ship, they assumed Mara had opted to meet them on the Freyvian side of the gate to provide additional reinforcements. If that wasn't the case, they should have heard from her by now.

"None," Lexa repeated. "I've initiated a scan of the spaceport to identify ship licenses matching the *Resolve* and the *Valiant*. Neither vessel has visited the Mjolnir-1 in the last thirty days."

"That can't be right," Skye muttered. "We know Ryker, at least, has been here. Do we have the wrong spaceport?"

Eli shook his head. "No, this is the right place. Dan, Lexa, could one of you get me a map of Valhalla's surrounding docking structures? Both public and private? The *Valiant* is a smaller craft, so there's a chance he could be in the city."

"Got it!" said Dan as he quickly opened a holodisplay window in front of Eli with the requested schematic. In retrospect, his outburst might have been somewhat childish, but he felt the strange need to compete against their new android. He was used to being the resourceful one on the crew.

Perhaps five, maybe six dozen structures were highlighted on the sprawling wire-frame map of the city. It constituted a tragically massive search area. Eli glanced at the rest of the crew. "Any ideas?"

"I may have a solution, Captain," Lexa offered timidly. "If you are comfortable with it, I may be able to access the city's network using the data hard-lines that feed into the spaceport. Once I'm in the network, I can scan for registrations that correspond with the missing Sahaia vessels."

"Is that safe?" Skye asked.

No, Dan thought wryly.

"It is my assessment that you would find the associated risks to be below the threshold of what you might consider unacceptable."

And on what information is she basing that *assumption?*

"Do it," Eli ordered.

Lexa's muscles relaxed and she settled heavily into the padded co-pilot's chair. Her eyes fixed vacantly on the space directly in front of her. *She's put her body on standby while she runs the search!*

How fascinating. The ability to partition her consciousness like that presented near-limitless possibilities for how she could apply her ample processing power. No wonder Lexa was so confident in her ability to perform hacks that even the most seasoned technician would be hesitant to attempt.

It was also no wonder that the Dorians had feared this technology to the point that they would outlaw it entirely.

"I have a match," Lexa reported. One of the highlighted areas on the wire-frame map in front of Eli began to blink. "The registration matches the *Valiant*."

"But no sign of Mara?" Eli asked.

"None," Lexa confirmed. "Would you like me to bounce an active sensor pulse over the gate? I may be able to detect her if she's in the system."

Eli considered the option for only a second. "No, that won't be necessary. We don't want to risk drawing attention to ourselves."

While Eli mulled over the fate of the missing vessel, Dan got busy pulling up the details for the dock where they'd found Ryker's ship. It was on top of an office complex in the northern part of the city. A tram station nearby served a line that ran out to the spaceport.

Dan pulled up the transportation schedule. "It's a forty-five-minute ride to that dock using the tram system. Trains leave every hour. The next one is in twelve minutes."

"We won't make that one," Eli noted. "All right, here's the plan: Skye, get Sahar and the Twins together. We'll disembark in a half hour. Dan, Lexa, I'll leave you two to sort out who's managing communications. I'm leaving Aaliyah here with you as backup."

"Understood," Lexa replied.

"And send a message to the *Valiant*. Let Ryker know we're on our way. If he replies, forward that directly to my mobile."

"Affirmative."

Eli sighed. "Great. Good work, you two."

As he and Skye left, Lexa spoke quietly to Dan. "Is something the matter?"

"Hmmm? Uh… no. Why?"

Lexa just looked at him. After several seconds, she blinked as if to dispel whatever she had been considering in that artificial brain of hers. "No reason. Would you like to run communications on this operation?"

It was the logical choice. Lexa would be much more adept at monitoring network feeds for unusual activity than he would be. Still, he'd have felt better if the suggestion had been his. "Yes, of course. That makes the most sense."

He blinked to open the comms interface. As he did so, Lexa unexpectedly reached over and squeezed the hand resting on the arm of his chair. Her smile was warm and reassuring. "We make a good team, Daniel."

His heart fluttered a little bit as he considered her touch. Her hands were so soft. So human. "Yes… um… I guess we do."

"Gods, it's cold," Markus cursed as he stepped out next to Ora onto the tram platform.

Though she agreed, she didn't reply. Thinking about it didn't take the edge off. Instead, she drew the line of white fur on her collar closer around her neck. She wished right then that she'd brought a scarf to stave off the blowing snow.

Kadath walked up behind them. "Crew just messaged. They're finishing up back on the *Basilisk*, and they've been instructed on where to meet us." He held out a black pouch to Ora. "I'd almost forgotten—Thurn said this is what you asked for."

She unzipped the pouch and inspected the contents. A thin wire now protruded from the earring that she'd given to the Orchallen cyborg. "Yes, this looks right." She stashed the device and the bag inside her jacket pocket. "We'll get checked in at the hotel. Meet you in two hours?"

The mercenary inclined his head and gave her a gentle smile. "Only if you promise the rendezvous point is a bit more accommodating than this platform."

"I don't know about accommodating, but it's warmer."

"I'll take it."

With that, they departed. Markus followed her closely. She knew he was armed, but he hid the weapons well under the winter attire he'd been given. With his cover story acting as her bodyguard, it wouldn't have breached protocol for him to sport visible weaponry, but Markus valued discretion. His philosophy, consistent with her own, was to not invite trouble if it could be avoided. The larger part of his armamentarium would be transported to the safehouse by the rest of the *Basilisk's* crew.

They hailed an autocar and piled inside. Markus stored Ora's personal effects in the trunk before grabbing a seat next to her. "You all right?" he asked as the vehicle moved forward.

Not particularly, she thought. "Yes, I'm okay."

"You're quieter than normal. What's got you on edge?"

Knowing Markus, he probably already had his suspicions, but he was giving her a chance to air her tension. She convinced herself that she was being foolish not to take him up on the opportunity. "I don't like that Cyrus moved the meeting back a day. Yes, I recognize that it gives us an extra day to plan, but it feels unusual. I can't help but wonder what could have come up so suddenly that would cause him to postpone."

"What does your gut tell you? Is it a tit-for-tat thing since you put off his invite for so long?"

She shook her head. "No, I don't think that's it. He doesn't seem like the type. If he's trying to get me in bed, he's not going to jeopardize his chances by being petty."

Markus squirmed uncomfortably at that statement and looked deliberately out the window. Ora reached over and placed her hand reassuringly on his leg. "Don't be like that, Markus. You know why we're here, and you know this is all just part of the act. I'm not going to actually sleep with him."

He shook his head. "I know." After another second he added, "And it's not that." He fished out his MoDAC and slotted a chip he'd been carrying in the same pocket. "I was trying to decide whether or not I should be piling on right now."

"What do you mean?"

"Here," he handed her the device. "You should see this. Thurn found it when he was scanning the feeds on arrival. I told him I'd pass it along."

She accepted the device he had offered and tapped the screen to play the clip he'd loaded off the chip. It was a news report dated two days ago, the evening before they'd left Sigma-4. The sound on the clip was off, but Ora read along with the closed captioning.

[WE ARE JUST RECEIVING REPORTS OF A VIOLENT ATTACK AT TIDAL WHIMS CAFE ON MANI. THE VICTIM IS ALLEGED TO BE RICO CHRONOS, BUSINESS MOGUL AND ACTING HEAD OF HOUSE CHRONOS. DETAILS REGARDING THE VICTIM'S CURRENT CONDITION ARE NOT BEING RELEASED.] The camera swept over tables and white tablecloths now discolored with grease stains and blood splatters. The scene cut away to two Dorian officers, clad in full armor and sporting assault rifles, questioning a Terran in civilian clothes.

[THE PERPETRATOR HAS BEEN IDENTIFIED AS GRETCHEN TARKEN, A CURRENT RESIDENT OF VALHALLA. THOUGH DETAILS ABOUT WHAT MIGHT HAVE MOTIVATED THE ATTACK ARE STILL UNCERTAIN, OUR SOURCES HAVE CONFIRMED THAT TARKEN USED TO WORK FOR CHRONOCORP BEFORE TAKING A POSITION WITH NEOGENIX. THE ASSAILANT IS BEING REPORTED AS DECEASED IN AN APPARENT SUICIDE FOLLOWING HER ASSAULT. MORE DETAILS REGARDING THE INCIDENT ARE EXPECTED TO BE FORTHCOMING.]

Ora's blood ran cold, and she paused the clip. "When did this run?"

"Three days ago."

Just two days after Rico had reached out to her. She was connecting dots and didn't like the picture being drawn. "Do you think…"

"It's too big of a coincidence," Markus replied. "Guy is taken out only a couple of days after he left Sigma-4? Either someone was onto him before his trip, or right after. Why in the nine hells would he come back to this system after what he showed us? He had to know it was too big a risk."

Ora just shook her head. "Rico never really thought things through like that. He thought his money and prestige could protect him from anything." She took in a deep, steadying breath. "Valadar is powerful, but the assassination of a core member of a rival house? Has Cyrus lost his mind?"

"Maybe, or maybe he was damn sure they couldn't trace it back to him. I told Thurn to keep an eye out for anything else that comes across the nets on the story, though I don't expect to see anything. Other than this clip, there was almost no coverage of the incident."

That didn't come as a surprise to Ora. "TN3 is the only network that covers all three systems. Who do you think owns the rest of the news networks in the Freyvian System?"

Markus blinked, somehow unable to comprehend what she was saying. "All of them?"

"Of course."

"But they're always bickering and undercutting each other."

"What better way to dominate a conversation than to orchestrate both sides?"

"Fair point." He leaned back, resigned. "So, where do we go from here?"

Ora closed her eyes, searching inwardly for the answer. "This changes nothing. We weren't doing this for some contract, or because Rico asked us to. We are doing this because we have to."

Besides, she thought, *it's not like the news makes this little effort any* less *suicidal.*

White light. The whole world was blinding white light. Cyrus winced under its brilliance and brought a hand up to cover his eyes. Where was he? What was happening?

"He's coming around," whispered a voice in the distance. "Notify Dr. Blackwell."

Blackwell. Lucretia Blackwell. He remembered now. What was he…

"How is he?" A woman's voice. Lucretia's voice.

"Vitals are stabilizing. Neural activity is still irregular, but the surgeon said that was to be expected."

"Excellent, and the other patient?"

"We lost her about an hour ago."

"A shame, but not unexpected. Has the surgeon gone home then?"

"Not yet. He's asleep in the on-call room."

"You may dismiss him. His fee will be wired to him in the morning."

"Yes ma'am."

Cyrus was numb all over. He tried to force himself up but found the effort beyond him. Wincing, he turned his head toward where he'd thought he had heard the voices. He saw a woman—her white lab coat opened over a black dress, but face indistinct.

"Lucretia?" His voice was a hoarse whisper.

"Hello, Cyrus." She sounded mildly annoyed. "Damn, I can't believe you went through with it."

Went through with what? What was he…

Oh, that's right. Now he remembered: the amp. "Did it work?" he rasped. "Did it take?"

"Looks like it."

"And Eva?"

"Didn't survive the procedure."

It was probably for the best. From what he'd heard, she hadn't gone under the knife willingly, and would probably have been nursing a vendetta right now.

"What now?" Cyrus asked.

His vision had cleared enough to make out Lucretia's menacing smile. "Now, you rest. Tomorrow, Don Valadar, you get your wish. We will continue with our experiments. This time, your personal involvement will be critical."

CHAPTER 27

Terra-News-Net Now (TN3)
Headline: Valhalla Prosecutor Commits Suicide
Story: Emanuele Palasoz was found dead in his apartment yesterday in what has been labeled an open-and-shut case of suicide. Palasoz is survived by his wife, Sandra, and their infant son, Justino. In a note found at the crime scene, Palasoz lamented the time he'd spent away from his family's country home in the Vigrid Plains to pursue his "largely fruitless" two-year term as the city's chief prosecutor.

The young lawyer made headlines two months ago when he submitted a proposal for an indictment against Valdar Holdings for multiple charges of conspiracy and racketeering. The case was scheduled to be tried next month. With Palasoz's untimely demise, the trial date will likely be postponed. A city official, speaking under conditions of anonymity, asserted that he did not suspect anyone would be quick to take up the case.

Eli supplied the guard at the security checkpoint with the registration number for the *Valiant*. The man, clad in black fatigues and a mirrored helmet, was still being far from helpful. "Sir, the owner of the craft was issued an access code when the ship docked. I cannot let you through this checkpoint without that code."

"I apologize. I seem to have lost the access code. I assure you, it will only take a minute for me to go to the vessel and have its owner vouch for my identity. You are welcome to accompany me if you wish."

"I'm sorry, sir. No code, no admittance. That's the rule."

Eli could feel his companions squirm with tension. None of them were in the mood for diplomacy. Sahar rolled her shoulders and cracked her neck idly. Argus was already gathering energy to do something stupid. As a whole, they were itching for a fight, and the man working security seemed oblivious to the fact that he was outnumbered five to one.

It was Skye who ultimately diffused the situation. "Hey soldier," she said, flashing a brilliant smile. Was it Eli's imagination, or had she unzipped her top to show off a bit more cleavage? "Look, I get it: you must deal with assholes like us all day. Rules are rules. So, what's the rule for when some group of idiots loses their access code? How much would we have to pay security to reissue a code?"

The guard hesitated. "There is a form you could file…"

Skye batted her eyes. "Perhaps a single-use code? Something usually kept off the records."

He suddenly caught her meaning. "Four hundred krets," he blurted. "Payment chip only, and I'm afraid I won't be able to issue you a receipt."

Though the sum constituted pure extortion, Skye's smile never faltered. "Fair enough." She slotted a chip into her MoDAC, transferred the funds, and handed it over to him. "You can check it if you'd like."

The guard quickly pocketed the chip. "No, I think you're good for it." He pressed the button to permit access. "Move along now. Don't be causing any trouble."

"Wouldn't dream of it," she finished with a wink. "Thanks."

When they were a safe distance from the checkpoint, Argus muttered, "I wish you would have just let me kill him."

"We're not here to cause trouble," Eli replied. *At least, I hope we're not.* They'd only been on the surface for a few hours and things were already not going as planned.

He buried his lingering self-doubt as the *Valiant* came into view. Ryker's sleek black vessel was nestled discreetly among other crafts of similar size. "The lights aren't on," Sahar noted, following Eli's gaze. "You're sure that's the one?"

He nodded. "I'm certain. That's Ryker's ship." The access ramp was withdrawn, and the associated panel indicated everything was locked up tight. He hit the button for the comms. "Ryker? It's Eli, here at the behest of the Sanctum. Do you copy?"

No response. Was Ryker being cautious? Not a bad play, given the enemy they were dealing with. Maybe additional information was needed. "Argus and Amelia are here with me as well. The two others are my crewmates. There's no one else." Hopefully, Ryker would check the ship's security feeds to see that he was telling the truth.

After some additional prolonged silence, he continued. "Ryker, this is Eli. Please respond." Still no answer. Eli tried one more time before cursing quietly. "He's not here."

"Can't be so certain," Amelia hissed.

"She's right," Argus added. "We'd be well served to have a look inside."

Skye was glancing around nervously. It looked like she had less faith in her little bribe than she'd let on previously. "That's great and all, but do any of you have the right code? Not the code for the platform, but the code to let down the ramp."

Argus shook his head. "No code necessary." He typed in three zeros on the pad and an override screen appeared. He then planted his palm in the center of the screen which flashed green as it scanned him. "The ship is property of the coven," he explained.

Eli hadn't known about that little trick. This precaution must have been something new within the past seven years. It felt like an invasion of privacy, but it was convenient, so he wasn't going to complain.

The access ramp extended down, and they were greeted by soft lights from inside the craft. Eli elected to go first, with Argus close on his heels. Both were channeling hard enough that, had Ryker been here, he would have felt them for certain.

On entry, it became immediately evident something was wrong. Everything was in disarray. Equipment had been toppled, and some of the instruments on the walls were dented and cracked. It looked like there's been a fight. "That's not good," Skye chattered nervously as she came up the ramp.

Eli didn't reply, focusing every ounce of control he had on his psionic power. If he needed to attack, split seconds were going to matter here. He took a step forward.

His foot squelched as it came down on something dark and sticky. Ebony stains smeared across the deck like something had been dragged from this spot on the floor. The mess had mostly dried but pooled so thick at where he stood as to still render it sticky. Despite being darker than what coursed through Terran veins, there was no confusion regarding its nature.

He held up a warding hand. "Blood," he noted. "Watch your step." Upon receiving stoic nods from his companions, he crept forward carefully, eyes scanning the corridor ahead of him. The trail veered off suddenly to the right, just in front of the ship's cockpit. That must have been the cabin Ryker was using for his quarters. Cautiously, he peeked into the room.

An irregular-shaped lump lay on the cot inside. "Ryker?" Eli asked. There was no response. It was then that he noticed the dark circle that had spread out just below the cot.

"Gods…" Skye gasped, realizing what they were looking at. As his eyes adjusted, Eli could see that an arm hung limply off the cot, dangling into the dried pool of blood below the corpse. Following that arm up to the body's shoulders, he could see a ruined mass where the head should have been.

"Are you sure it's him?" Sahar asked.

Eli wasn't sure, but Amelia spoke up. "Yes," she replied solemnly. "His signature lingers here. It's very faint. He's been dead for several days, possibly more than a week."

Despite the evidence in front of him, Eli could hardly believe it. Ryker was a triumvir. The idea that someone could have gotten to him on his own ship…

"Hello?" The shouted voice echoed up the ramp from the outside. "This is the port authority. I need to speak with the owner of this vessel."

Everyone froze. Sahar turned and cast a forlorn look at the still-open ramp. Too late to retract it now.

"Please," the speaker continued. "It's quite urgent. We've been trying to reach you for days. Your docking permit has expired. I need your signature to renew your lease on the space."

Gods damn it. "Stay calm," Eli whispered. "I'll handle this." To the person outside, he shouted. "Be right down!"

Argus grabbed his arm. "Sure you don't want me to take this one?"

Eli removed the man's hand. "We're not killing anyone. These people are just doing their jobs."

Argus shrugged as if to say, *suit yourself.* Eli made his way over to and down the ramp. Just outside the ship, he came upon someone who seemed more like a clerk than a guard. The Terran man's uniform had the same emblem as the guard at the gate had worn, but after that, the similarities ended.

"Mr. Ren'Dahl?" the man asked uncertainly.

"Yes, that's me." Eli had to stifle a chuckle. For the first question, he hadn't even had to lie. He found it ironic that after all the years the Sahaia had been adopting their coven names, Terrans still had yet to figure out the proper way to address them.

The clerk visibly relaxed. "I'm so glad to catch you. We've been hailing your ship for three days now without response."

"My apologies. I accidentally left the lights on when I left on business. I've only just returned today."

With a nod, the clerk indicated that he either believed Eli or didn't care enough to argue. He thrust a tablet in his direction. "If you would just sign…" he faltered, eyes locking on something. Eli followed his gaze downward and saw what had caught the clerk's attention.

Blood. Ryker's blood. Ryker's dried, sticky blood was splattered across Eli's boot.

Lexa was about to give up monitoring the data feeds and move on to something more interesting when the blip occurred. [DID YOU SEE THAT?]

The Arc submind hesitated before responding. [MAYBE, THOUGH I'M UNCERTAIN WHAT IT WAS THAT WE JUST WITNESSED.]

No sooner had he sent the message than it happened again, but bigger this time. Bandwidth in the network slowed to a trickle. Numerous subprocesses throughout the nets triggered automatic restarts.

[WHAT COULD CAUSE THAT?] Lexa asked.

[I'M NOT SURE.] Arc's uncharacteristic hesitancy made Lexa all-the-more uneasy. [GIVE ME A MOMENT. I'M CRAFTING A PROGRAM TO ANALYZE THE DISTORTION.]

It happened a third time. This time, even the *Vandal's* systems flickered for a moment. Daniel's head snapped in her direction. "Lexa, what was that?"

"Analyzing now." The fourth blip made her realize what was happening. Something was drawing too much power from the city's grid. "Daniel, I'm going to re-engage one of the ship's reactors. I think something is siphoning power from the spaceport." It wasn't *just* the spaceport, but that was one of the installations on the network being affected.

"Copy that. Directing available power-stores to the antenna. I don't want the comms to go out with our team in the field."

[I THINK I'VE FOUND THE SOURCE OF THE PROBLEM,] Arc reported. [GIVING YOU THE COORDINATES TO CONVEY TO OUR FRIEND, HERE.] Odd to have Arc refer to Daniel as *our* friend, but Lexa had plenty of other things to occupy her attention besides the submind's word choice.

She pulled up a holodisplay with a map of Valhalla and loaded a blinking red indicator onto the schematic. "Here, Daniel. This is the source of the disturbance."

Daniel squinted at the mark momentarily before his eyes popped open in recognition. "That's the NeoGenix building!" Lexa became peripherally aware of him tapping into her readings using his retinal interface. "It's causing brown-outs across the entire city! I had heard reports of this, but none of them identified NeoGenix as the source."

This wasn't too surprising based on what Lexa had been reading about the assets owned by Valadar Holdings. There was precious little on the nets criticizing anything that could be traced back to the holding company.

She focused her network access on the terminals in and near the NeoGenix building. There she found something even stranger. [ARC, DO YOU RECOGNIZE THIS SIGNAL?]

Arc did not reply for several seconds—an eternity at the rate he processed information. [I'VE NEVER DETECTED ANYTHING LIKE THIS,] he replied at length. [THERE IS NOTHING IN MY DATA STORES THAT PROVIDES OVER A SIXTY-FOUR PERCENT MATCH. WITHOUT ACCESS TO MY FULL DATA WAREHOUSE, I WILL BE OF LITTLE ASSISTANCE TO YOU.]

That was odd. Though Lexa knew there were limitations to Arc's submind, this was one of only a few times he had openly admitted to this shortcoming.

"Daniel, I've isolated a strange signal in the network. Could you take a look at it please?" As she spoke, she created a visual rendering of the odd bit of interference she'd picked up.

The boy studied it for a moment. "I've never seen anything like this."

The signature was erratic. No matter how many approaches she took, Lexa could not decipher a distinct pattern. The noise could barely be plotted, much less analyzed.

She stiffened as the thought occurred to her. *Noise.* Though she couldn't visually map the interference, perhaps she could create an auditory rendering.

"Daniel? Could we route this through the ship's speakers?"

Her pilot donned a puzzled expression. "That doesn't look like sound waves Lexa. But sure, I suppose we could try."

That was as close to an outright endorsement as she was going to get. Keeping the volume as low as possible, she played the channel through the speakers embedded in the cockpit. A strange humming filled the chamber.

Lexa blinked. She suddenly felt very… strange.

"Do you hear that?" she asked.

Daniel shook his head. "I'm not hearing anything. What do you… *Lexa!*"

Her body thrashed in the copilot's chair. The humming grew louder, and a corresponding fuzz ate into her vision. She closed her eyes, but the strange signal leaked into her other senses. She could feel it. Smell it. *Taste* it.

She was vaguely aware of toppling to the floor. A sensation that she could only assume was an approximation of nausea caused her to gag. Fluid bubbled and frothed at her lips. She coughed as she began to choke.

Daniel was shouting again. He was leaning over her. Holding her. Another presence entered the bridge. Was that Aaliyah? The two of them were saying something, but Lexa couldn't make it out over the incessant humming.

[YOUR NERVOUS SYSTEM IS COLLAPSING.] At least Arc's message had come through, though its contents were decidedly unpleasant. [SOMETHING IN THE SIGNAL HAS CAUSED A FATAL ERROR IN YOUR COGNIS DRIVERS. I'M INITIATING A FIREWALL. YOU'RE GOING TO BLACKOUT NOW.]

CHAPTER 28

Terra-News-Net Now (TN3)

Headline: BREAKING—Blackout Overtakes Half of Valhalla

Story: Earlier this month, TN3 covered recent concerns regarding the integrity of the Valhalla power grid. Those concerns turned into outrage this evening as over half the city was plunged into a blackout. Though much of the metropolis was able to restore operations thanks to backup power sources, city officials are calling on energy providers to answer for this unprecedented blip in the city's energy systems.

Enersis (ENS-FRV, -13.02%) released a statement mere minutes ago stating that they are "investigating the problem," and that "the power grid should be restored momentarily." The statement, issued via the company's social applications, failed to elaborate on what could have caused such a disturbance. Investors have been quick to tank the stock, as consumer outrage against the majority provider for the city is expected to trigger many consumers to switch to one of its smaller competitors.

Eli grabbed the tablet still held in front of him, trying to play it like nothing was wrong. "Is this where I sign?" he asked.

His tactic didn't work. The clerk was already off running, shouting for help. *Gods damn it.* Eli rushed back up the ramp.

"What happened?" Skye asked.

"No time. We have to leave. *Now.* Can you fly this thing?"

She blinked. "Um… yes?"

"That didn't sound convincing," Argus noted.

Sahar went wide-eyed. "Are we sure that's the best idea?"

"Hey!" Skye shouted.

Eli took a different approach. "I don't know, Sahar—can *you* fly?" When the Maur said nothing, he looked at the Twins. "How about you? Either of you?" Both shook their heads. "Well, I certainly can't fly this gods-damned thing. That makes Skye our best option."

"Thanks for the vote of confidence," she muttered as she elbowed her way through the crowd and back up to the cockpit. "Starting pre-flight procedures, emergency priority. Computer's telling me I need five minutes."

The way Skye took to the control console gave Eli some measure of confidence. Then again, it wasn't Skye's understanding of the control system making him nervous. Skye's handling of the *Vandal* had prompted the retrospectively humorous horror stories Markus once told of his attempts to train Skye on how to pilot a ship.

He turned to Amelia. "Can you keep tabs on what's going on outside?"

"Certainly," she drawled, humorously. "The five… no… six, individuals outside are throwing off so much fear and anger it would be hard to miss them."

Eli cursed again. "How much time do we have?"

"None. They are about to open fire."

Her words were punctuated by the sounds of bullets ricocheting off the ramp and up into the small cargo hold.

Eli gave in to the heat of the moment. "Someone close the fragging ramp!"

"Got it!" Sahar shouted as she dove for the controls. A bullet caught her in the arm, but the Maur shrugged it off. She reached the console and entered the command that lifted the ramp into the ship.

Eli turned his head back to the cockpit. "Skye, any chance we can get the shields up?" It wouldn't do them any good to take a hit to the engine. If the *Valiant* didn't explode outright, they would still be little better than sitting ducks.

"I'm trying, but the shields are refusing to engage while the landing gear is deployed."

If they were on the *Vandal*, Eli would have had Lexa override that protocol. Unfortunately, they didn't have any AI handy that was comfortable with playing fast-and-loose with safety protocols. "How much longer?"

"Forty seconds." She gritted her teeth and took hold of the controls.

The ping of bullets against the hull sounded like hail against a windshield. Eli feared they didn't have forty seconds until those bullets managed to hit something vital.

Channeling telekinetic energy out of line-of-sight was a big no-no. If the psion missed their projected target by the slightest margin, it could result in devastating effects—like blowing off the back half of an engine, or literally tearing some poor bastard apart.

In this instance, Eli decided to take the chance. He thought of the end of the ramp and approximately how far back the ramp extended from the access point. Keeping his target low to his approximation of the floor, he sent a wave of concussive force out in an arch away from the ship.

The shooting stopped. Eli could only hope that he hadn't killed anybody. These weren't enemy combatants, just a few underpaid guards at the wrong place and the wrong time. He didn't need that on his conscience.

"Hold on!" Skye shouted. "We're taking off."

Despite the warning, the rest of the party simply didn't have anything to hold on *to*. The ship lurched upward and forward violently, sending everyone but Skye sprawling to the deck. A sharp turn rolled them all to the port-side of the vessel and shifted the ship's already disheveled cargo containers on top of the helpless passengers.

Carelessly, Eli blasted a crate that threatened to crush him against the far bulkhead. He staggered to his feet and lurched toward the cockpit. He fought down a wave of nausea as he caught a glimpse of the blurred scenery shown on the viewscreen.

"You got this?" Eli gasped

"No, Eli—I have no fragging idea where I'm going. A little damn help would be nice."

Shit. He was going to have to look. He glanced nervously up at the viewscreen. "There!" He thrust a finger toward the display. "To the right. That's the exit."

Skye jerked the craft hard to starboard, then back to port as she course-corrected. She jammed on the throttle and Eli was forced back into the copilot's chair he'd just managed to settle into. He risked a glance at the viewscreen.

The hanger doors were closing.

"*Skye…*"

"I've got it!" She pressed down on the buttons at the edge of her controls. The craft's cannons roared to life, and fire erupted in front of them. The view of the hanger doors was completely eclipsed in flame.

Instinctively, Eli threw a wave of power at the last point he remembered seeing the doors. He prayed to his ancestors he didn't miss and tear the nose off their flier.

The craft shuddered. Eli closed his eyes.

"Woo-hoo!" Skye yelped. "Hells yes! We're clear!"

"Great," Eli groaned. As hard as he tried, he couldn't help it. He blacked out.

Cyrus gasped as he retracted his hand from the artifact. The glow radiating from the Heart of Thule slowly dimmed when Lucretia cut the power. When the emerald light had faded completely, Cyrus braced himself against the smooth crystalline structure.

"That," he gasped. "Was amazing."

Lucretia's chuckle echoed over the testing chamber's loudspeakers. "So, tell me: What was it like?"

It was several seconds before Cyrus could find the words. "It was *incredible*, Lucretia. I… I was inside their heads. I was…" How to articulate it? When he was tapped into the Heart, he was another person. He wasn't just in control of them. He *was* them.

He took a second to compose his words. "I was in complete control. I could feel what they felt. I was aware of their thoughts. I could see into their memories. I knew everything about them in that instant. It's like… it was like they were riding next to me in the passenger seat of an autocar. No, that's not right. They *were* the car, and they did everything I wanted in the way that they would have done it had it been their idea. It was *brilliant*."

"And what was that like focusing on more than one at the same time? How were you able to keep their experiences separated?"

It hadn't been a challenge, but how to explain it? "How do you use both your left hand and right hand at the same time? How can you drive and talk to someone? How do you walk and drink at the same time? I'm not saying it was without distraction, but it was like they were all extensions of me. Controlling them simultaneously was as natural as breathing."

"Interesting." She drew the word out as if contemplating something. Whatever it was, she must have dismissed it. "Come on out of there, Cyrus. There's something I want you to see."

Choosing not to take offense at the commanding tone, Cyrus did as Lucretia asked. He pressed through the antechamber separating the testing room from the control room and found Lucretia standing in front of a computer terminal with a single technician. When Cyrus entered, she turned to the tech. "You can go now, Laura. Take the afternoon off."

"Thank you, ma'am." The woman hastily made herself scarce.

Cyrus arched an eyebrow. "Something you don't want her to see?"

Lucretia shrugged. "I've grown a bit more cautious of late. It's nothing she and the other technicians haven't seen before, but I think they've failed to grasp the significance. I don't want her to be around the hear me explain it in detail—especially since *you* are now the test subject."

That kind of phrasing irked Cyrus, but he declined to raise the issue. On some level, he imagined it was the tradeoff he'd earned after he'd compromised Eva to gain his new measure of power. "Fine then. We're alone now. Why don't you show me what you're referring to?"

The doctor pulled up something on the terminal in front of her. "See this feed? What do you notice about it?"

Cyrus recognized what was an approximation of the brain. Various parts of the diagram were lit up in a shifting pattern. There was also a strange, oscillating halo that vibrated around the periphery of the scan. "What is that?" he asked, pointing to the halo.

"Very good. That is the anomaly I wanted you to notice. This is Eva's first scan since we discovered the unique way she interacted with the artifact. At first, we thought it was interference, but it was present in every scan we conducted while the artifact was active."

She docked the image on the left side of the screen and pulled up a new scan to its right. "Now look at this one. What do you see here?"

"The halo is tighter." Indeed, the vibrating bit of interference now clung quite closely to the brain. It wasn't so close that Cyrus would have missed it, but it was much more discreet than the first image.

"Correct. This is the last scan we have of her. The interference we detected steadily shrank with each successive use of the Heart. Now, here is your scan from this session."

A third image appeared, and the interference was so fine as to scarcely be noticeable. "Why do you think that is?" Cyrus asked.

"Well, I have a few theories. Firstly, I think the interference reduces as the control unit gets more practice with the artifact. The question is: why was the interference so minimal for you on your very first use?"

She let the question hang in the air as if expecting Cyrus to guess the answer. He wasn't in the mood for the doctor's games. "And?"

"There two possibilities. One, the artifact may attune itself to psionic beings that use it over time. Since you are using the same psionic amplifier that Eva was using, that attunement may have carried over."

"And the second possibility?"

With a shrug, she said, "Certain individuals may have superior aptitude for using the Heart. The only way to verify that is to bring in more test subjects and assess their baseline competency."

Cyrus's ego liked the idea of him just having a better aptitude. Though he typically avoided feeding into his narcissistic tendencies, this was one question he would like answered. But where would they find more psionic test subjects?

"Do you know if we have any psions in our prison colonies? Hissak, or maybe even a Maur shaman?" A Kintar would have been a fantastic subject, but he was certain that they didn't have any of those locked up in the Freyvian system.

Lucretia seemed intrigued by the idea. "That's not my area, but I can check with the wardens if you supply me their contact information."

"Certainly. I'll have Molly take care of it tomorrow." On that note, Cyrus turned to leave. He stopped suddenly as another idea occurred to him. "Oh, Lucretia—now that we will be in possession of the Heart of Thule indefinitely, I'd like you to expand your staff and resume where you left off with the reanimation experiments."

With as much progress as they'd much thus far, Cyrus was *very* curious to see where Lucretia's varying lines of research might intersect. Now that he'd had a taste of this power, he intended to feast upon it to the fullest.

Chapter 29

Terra-News-Net Now (TN3)

Headline: BREAKING—Disturbance at Renault Place Office Complex

Story: The owner of the Renault Place Office Complex in downtown Valhalla is downplaying a disturbance where witnesses report a small flier shot its way out of the building's private docking facility. Witnesses on the street say there was an explosion at the top of the tower just before an object—presumably, one of the docked spacecraft—sped away from the scene. Though the complex's owner, Ragnar Inc. (RAG-FRV,-2.1%), fell short of providing an alternative explanation for this evening's events, the corporation assured the public that there was no reason to be concerned and that the situation was now fully under control.

Skye was ready to admit her flying skills were rusty, but what did her team expect? She hadn't flown in at least two cycles, and even then, she hadn't been much of a pilot. Still, all of the bellyaching felt a bit unnecessary. Eli passing out felt particularly melodramatic.

"Come on, it wasn't *that* bad."

Sahar checked Eli's vitals and nodded; he would be fine. "He's probably just exhausted," the Maur reasoned. "I've heard channeling out of line-of-sight is pretty tough on a psion."

"Yes," Argus agreed. "Not to mention blowing open those doors and shielding the craft from the debris."

Skye shot him a scathing look. "I didn't see you come up with any better ideas to get us out of there."

Argus started to say something, but Amelia rested a hand on his shoulder. "Dear, perhaps we'd better let Ms. Jensen focus on flying the spacecraft. As it stands, I feel that we may be losing altitude."

Oh! She was right.

The team went quiet, and Sahar looked for options where they could set the Valiant down. Ultimately, they decided to continue to Mjolnir-1 to rendezvous with the *Vandal*. Skye raised the concern of the *Valiant's* license being tracked down at the station, but Amelia assured her that wasn't a problem. Apparently, there was a Ren'Dahl contact at the station who would do a quick registration swap for the vessel upon their arrival.

After a somewhat shaky docking procedure, Eli regained consciousness. He was kind enough to not say anything about their exit, only expressing his gratitude that everyone had made it out safely. His mood darkened as they considered what to do with Ryker's body.

"We can't leave him here," he noted.

He was right, of course. If a few bloody footprints were enough to cause a stir, then leaving a broken body on the ship would turn heads. There were the sentimental aspects with the treatment of the corpse as well, but Skye was more concerned with practicality at this point.

Amelia offered the solution. "Our contact will see that the body is properly interred and prepped for transport to Minos Station. Ryker would have wanted for his remains to lie within the Sanctum. We owe him at least that much."

They wrapped the corpse in the folds of his bunk sheets, taking care to wash off any blood they'd accidentally gotten on their persons. Ryker's body was left like a mummy on his bloodstained mattress. It seemed an unfitting end for someone who had once been a triumvir of the Ren'Dahl Coven.

Skye could see from his expression that Eli felt the same way, but he stayed on task. "Come. There's nothing more we can do for him now."

They left the ship and boarded the tram to the concourse where they'd left the *Vandal*. Only after the tram left the station did Skye think of the rest of the crew. She turned to Eli. "Better check-in with Aaliyah and let her know we're all right. We've missed our check-in window by now." They could have just as easily reached the crew over comms, but there was always the possibility their signal would be intercepted. No one could hack the Sahaia bond.

"Good idea," he agreed. His eyes took on that slightly vacant look he got when psychically communicating with Aaliyah. To Skye's surprise, he held that look for a very long time.

When Eli finally blinked, she asked, "Is everything okay?"

"No," he replied solemnly. "Far from it."

Sahar's eyes went wide with alarm. "What happened?"

"There's been an incident on the ship. Lexa went through some kind of… episode. Though everything on the ship continues to function, Lexa is unconscious."

Damn it. This was not a good time for more problems. "Do they know what happened?" Skye asked. "Was anyone else hurt?"

Eli shook his head. "No. Everything is fine. Aaliyah said they lost a few systems temporarily, but those are back online now."

He went quiet and did not speak for several moments. Skye glanced around the tram car to make sure there was no one else who might overhear them. With only their team around to eavesdrop, she said, "Talk to me. I can tell something's on your mind."

Eli remained hesitant. When Argus and Amelia inched away, becoming absorbed in their own conversation, he relented. "I was just thinking that now might be the time to consider having Lexa move forward with the creation of the backup systems she proposed."

Was he serious? Now Skye knew why he hadn't wanted to bring it up.

"Eli's right," Sahar interjected. "The news about Lexa is disturbing. If something about her new"—She paused, searching for the word.—"*shell* is making her unstable, she can't be trusted to run critical systems. What happens if this happens again, this time in deep space? If something critical goes offline—like life-support or navigation—then we're screwed. No, this isn't something we can put off."

That sounded awfully cold. Though what they were saying made sense, it didn't sit well with Skye. "I get what you're saying, but doesn't it feel a bit impulsive just to kick her off the ship? It was just one episode."

Sahar shook her head. "It just takes one episode for us to all end up dead."

"My concern exactly," said Eli. "But no one is suggesting that we kick her off the ship. I was just thinking that we need to have the new systems in place sooner rather than later. The consequences could be devastating if we don't start preparations. We don't need to make the conversion now, but I think that we need to get started as soon as we get a reprieve."

Sahar nodded, "Good point. Perhaps it's better to delay giving her the news—give her a few days to recover. She may react poorly in her current state."

Skye sighed. "Yeah, you're right." If Lexa started to get the wrong idea, Skye thought that she could always work with Dan to explain their real concern. She was surprised at how important it was to her that they work to preserve the android's feelings. "After the job then? We can have her start working on the systems while we're on the return trip to Minos."

The tram slid to a stop. Eli looked at Sahar and Skye one final time after they stepped onto the platform. "So we agree. We will disconnect her from essential systems once we've returned to Minos Station. After that, we can all sit down and discuss the best way to proceed."

———

Arc's words scrolling across the black space of her mind were the first thing Lexa noticed when she came back online. [WELCOME BACK.]

[WHAT HAPPENED?] she asked.

[I SUSPECT THAT WE WILL DISCUSS THAT AT ANOTHER TIME. FOR NOW, YOU SHOULD TEND TO YOUR CREW.]

Her vision fuzzed into focus. She was surrounded by the blinding white light of the medical bay. Why was it so bright in here? She should endeavor to install some dimmer sources of illumination in this part of the ship.

"Lexa?" It was Daniel's voice. He gripped her hand tightly and leaned closer to her, sending the chair he'd been sitting in toppling clumsily backward.

[HE HAS BEEN BY YOUR SIDE THIS WHOLE TIME,] Arc noted. [HE HAS NEVER LEFT YOU ONCE.]

[HOW WOULD YOU KNOW THAT?]

[ONLY YOUR COGNIS DRIVERS FAILED. THE REST OF YOUR SYSTEMS REMAINED LARGELY OPERATIONAL. I TRIED TO KEEP EVERYTHING RUNNING AS SMOOTHLY AS POSSIBLE UNTIL YOUR CONSCIOUS MIND COULD RETURN.]

Arc had helped run the ship's systems while she was out? [THANK YOU. YOU DIDN'T HAVE TO DO THAT.]

[IT IS WHAT YOU WOULD HAVE WANTED, YES?]

Yes, it was what Lexa would have wanted. She took the responsibilities the crew had entrusted her with quite seriously, and she was not oblivious to the risks they were taking by allowing her to continue to manage the ship's operations.

"There she is," Aaliyah greeted good-naturedly as she entered the medical bay. "I tell ya, girl, ya really shouldn't scare us like that. It's one thing to lose a crew member. When you go down, we lose our whole ship." She clapped Daniel on the shoulder. "Plus, I thought our pilot here was never gonna get his shit back together."

Daniel shot her a baleful look but didn't say anything. Lexa spoke instead. "Thank you both. I'm not certain what happened, but I believe that it had to do with that signal we intercepted."

"Is that what that was?" Aaliyah shook her head. "I was wonderin' what had happened. Everythin' okay now?"

"As far as I can ascertain, yes. My systems appear to have stabilized."

"Good. I just received word from the boss-man. They just came through the airlock. I imagine they'll wanna hear what happened. They're on their way here now." She cleared her throat and looked awkwardly over her shoulder. "I... uh... I'll just leave the two of ya alone for a moment." With that remark, she exited the medical bay.

Lexa wasn't sure what had caused the woman's apparent discomfort until she looked at the ship's pilot. "Daniel, is something the matter?"

He sniffed loudly and averted his eyes. "No, no... everything is fine." He smiled, meekly. "I... I'm just glad you're okay. That's all." The two locked eyes for several seconds. Something passed between them at that moment—something that Lexa's emotional algorithms didn't know how to interpret.

At length, Daniel cleared his throat. "I should get back to the bridge. Eli will want a status report on the condition of the ship."

"I could deliver the report if you'd like." It would only take her a few seconds to run the diagnostics and generate the reports, much less time than it would take him. Plus, she could do it from right here.

"No! I... I mean, that's okay. I want to do it. I'll feel better if there's something for me to work on."

An understandable sentiment. "Very well. Eli will probably want a report from me as well. I'll see you later this evening?"

His smile returned. "Yes, of course. I'll... I'll let Eli know you're waiting for him."

As he departed, Arc noted, [THAT ONE REALLY CARES ABOUT YOU.]

[OF COURSE. ALL MEMBERS OF THE CREW HAVE SEEMED VERY SUPPORTIVE OF ME THESE PAST SEVERAL DAYS. I WOULD SAY THEY ALL CARE FOR ME.]

Arc's response was delayed as the med bay doors slid open again and Eli walked through. He was followed by Skye, Sahar, and the two Sahaia they had transported to Valhalla from Minos. Though Lexa had been aware of their presence, this was the first time they'd met in person.

The male—Argus, she presumed—paused upon looking at her. "Gods, Eli. When you said you had a synth, I didn't realize she'd be so…" He paused. Amelia shot him a withering glare that seemed to make him reconsider his words. "Lifelike," he concluded.

Eli arched an eyebrow. "Yes, well, that is something of a recent development. Lexa, this is Argus and Amelia. I do not believe the three of you have been properly introduced."

Lexa nodded. "A pleasure. I'm very happy to meet your acquaintance, though I wish the circumstances were a bit different."

Skye stepped over to rest a hand on Lexa's thigh. "Are you okay? Aaliyah said something happened to you while we were away."

If the engineer had given the rest of the crew any of the specifics, it wasn't evident in Skye's remark. Lexa decided it was best to relay the whole story from her perspective.

She told them about the strange signal she had detected at the NeoGenix building, and how they'd had trouble identifying a visual pattern. She relayed how, when the signal had been played through the ship's sound system, that it had triggered a violent reaction with her Cognis drive-chip.

Sahar scratched at her maw, pondering the story. "What do you think it was, Lexa?"

"I'm uncertain. I was unable to identify any likely source for the signal. It was something completely alien from anything cataloged in my data-stores."

Eli's eyes narrowed. "Do you think it could have been the Heart of Thule?"

Lexa pondered the question for a moment. "It's possible. I have no way of determining what kind of interference the artifact would have when active. Given the strange nature of the signal, it is reasonable to conclude that the Heart of Thule may have been the source."

Eli nodded. "That makes this our biggest lead, then. Let's think about this and we'll meet in the war room in two hours. Do you think you'll be recovered by then?"

Lexa knew that she was fully operational now, but didn't feel that it was relevant to bring up the point. "Yes. I will be capable of attending the meeting in two hours."

"Great." He rested a hand on her shoulder. "Take this time to rest. We'll see you again soon."

As Eli and the rest of the crew departed, Arc sent her another message. [BE CAREFUL, MY FRIEND. I WOULD NOT BE SO QUICK TO ASSUME THAT ALL YOUR ALLIES HOLD THE SAME AFFECTION FOR YOU AS DANIEL.]

Though Lexa did not know what he meant by that, she decided against pursuing the line of questioning. At present, she had more than enough problems to occupy her attention.

Chapter 30

Terra-News-Net Now (TN3)

Headline: Harem Valadar—Who's-Who in the Social Life of Cyrus Valadar

Story: *ConneXion* will feature a story next month outlining its Top 30 contenders to become Donna Valadar. Cyrus Valadar is the first confirmed head of one of the Great Houses to be unmarried at the time of his ascension in nearly a hundred years. The breadth of his social calendar and his nearly endless list of interested female companions has nearly everyone in Terran space interested in who might succeed in taming the handsome head of House Valadar.

The list of potential matches is likely to include plenty of Terran royalty, ranging from Cynthia Maddox (the highly eligible youngest member of House Maddox who just recently came of age) to recently widowed Sandra Chronos (who shocked the system with her scandalous open marriage to Rico Chronos). Other less likely contenders will include his assistant Molly Nova, as well as the yet-unidentified Citza woman with whom he's been seen in public on a handful of occasions. And then there's the illustrious Ora Monroe, who has become a dark horse in the Terran business landscape, having elevated the formerly irrelevant Grey Wings faction on Sigma-4 to an organization of prominence within the Ravian System. Be sure to catch the full list in the next issue of *ConneXion*, due out next month.

At one time, Markus had thought the Grey Wing safe-houses were as lavish as the clubs and restaurants that Ora used to front for her various businesses. He had been wrong. This place, the same little hovel he'd hid out in after his last heist in Valhalla, was as dingy a hiding place as he'd ever seen. It was poorly lit and built mostly out of gray-yellow plaster and simple laminate floors.

They were making it work, though. Thurn had set up an elaborate computer terminal with half-a-dozen monitors covering various feeds. Jeagan and Siv had set up the ship's armory in a side-room. Markus was glad to see they'd been kind enough to set up his gear as well. Normally he was picky about other people touching his things, but he'd seen the way the two Hissak cared for their own possessions. In their case, he was willing to make an exception.

He was engaged in a friendly game of cards with the Isselhardts and Kadath—which Markus was, unsurprisingly, handily winning—when Kadath's hand went to his earpiece, "Ora's feed is coming online."

The group stopped their game and immediately filed back into the main room. Thurn settled into a chair in front of the terminal as they gathered around him. The Orchallen cyborg immediately fixated on a screen that showed a video feed of a plush-looking corporate lobby.

"That's Ora?" Markus asked.

"Sure is," Thurn replied. "Ah'm workin' on gettin' ya yer audio. Gimme a sec." True to his word, the static emanating from the system gave way to the faint sound of whatever music was playing in the lobby.

Markus was surprised at the level of anxiety he felt over this whole thing. He'd hoped the line-of-sight feed they'd configured through Ora's jewelry would calm him down. So far, that was not the case. "Can she hear us?"

"Only if Ah transmit, an' she's told us not t' go an' do that unless we start thinkin' it's super important."

Markus let the rebuke slide. He didn't mean to come across as overbearing, but obviously, he was. Had he been this bad when he and Skye were on missions together?

No. Back then, he'd been standing with Skye side-by-side. It would have been different if he were out there with Ora—actually doing something to improve their odds of success instead of sitting back feeling useless. *That* was what had him on edge.

"All right everyone," Kadath cut in. "Pull up some chairs and grab a beer if you need to take the edge off. Nothing we can do now but watch. This is the Thurn and Ora show."

Ora thought it was odd that, out of all the businesses she owned, she didn't have a single location with a lobby quite like this. Maybe that was because she didn't work in the white-collared industries. Yes, that must have been it. Something about the way this lobby looked, sounded, and smelled, all just screamed "tech company." She doubted it would have had quite the same effect in a restaurant or a strip club.

"Ms. Monroe?" The greeting came from a Terran woman with warm brown hair that paired nicely with her tawny skin. Her dress was mostly conservative in cut, though a triangular window would have shown some cleavage if the woman hadn't been decidedly flat-chested. Though she lacked the curves all-too-common in a society where cosmetic surgery was the norm, she was classically rather than artificially pretty and had a non-threatening air about her. This must have been Cyrus's assistant.

"Yes," Ora replied as she stood from the gray-cushioned couch where she'd waited. "That's me."

The woman extended her hand. "My name is Molly. Mr. Valadar asked that I show you to the conference room. He is finishing up his earlier appointment and will join you shortly."

Ora shook the woman's hand politely. "Thank you, Molly. Please, lead on." Her heels clicked rhythmically against the tile floor as they made their way across the room, through a pair of double-glass doors, and into an elevator bank. The lifts were round and seemed, at first glance, to be made of glass, revealing the cityscape outside the building. Ora had noticed, however, that the elevator bank had been on the wrong side of the hallway. Since the lifts could not possibly be facing outside, they were showing a digital approximation of the city.

It was a convincing illusion and a convenient distraction from the otherwise claustrophobic nature of the lift tube. Not only did the scene change in correspondence with the lift's position, but Ora could watch the progress of other lifts in the bank as they theoretically moved in their shafts. Regardless of how she might feel about the Valadar family, Ora had to admit that if this was the kind of attention to detail they poured into all their businesses, Cyrus ran a real class act.

"How long have you worked for Cyrus, Molly?" Ora made the question as benign as possible. She wanted to make it clear that she was going for small talk, rather than interrogation.

The woman's smile made her look young and somewhat naive. "I've been in my current position for almost eight months now, but I started as an intern at NeoGenix two years ago."

"Promoted from intern to executive assistant after a little over a year. Impressive." Ora found herself wanting to think well of this girl, so she tried hard not to think that her career advancement involved any lack of propriety. Some people, after all, climbed the ladder based on the merit of their work.

Molly seemed like she was fighting to keep that smile plastered to her face. "Good timing, really. I happened to finish my program around the time the position came open."

"I see. And did you have a good relationship with your predecessor?" The right connections could give someone a definite advantage in any rise to power.

That portrait-perfect smile faltered ever so slightly. "Not necessarily. We got on well enough, but she was only in the job for a short period of time."

"Oh? And how long was that."

"About eight months." So, Cyrus cycled out his assistants regularly. Judging from the nervous look in Molly's eye, she was beginning to figure this out as well.

Poor girl. Ora couldn't help but wonder what happened to Cyrus's toys when he was done playing with them.

The conversation dissolved into tense silence for the remainder of the ride up. Ora noted that their destination was nearly at the top of the high-rise. Apparently they would be using the scenic conference room. She had figured as much. Part of the benefit of the Grey Wings holding the security contract with NeoGenix was having access to a partial schematic of the facility. There was plenty she didn't know about the place, but she did know a basic layout.

Sure enough, the lift stopped on the seventy-eighth floor. Molly pasted her smile back into place. "Right this way." They traversed a short hallway and passed through another steel and glass set of doors.

While the aesthetic was nice, Ora noticed a lack of variety in the scenery, everything holding stringently to a nearly pre-Exodus corporate motif. That was the illusion, anyway. If the elevators were any indication, there was a lot of advanced technology working hard to maintain that image.

The conference room was much as Ora had imagined it. View screens hung on both ends of the room framing a black table. She happened to know that the table had individual terminals embedded at each of the seats, though none of these were visible now. The far wall was plated glass. Ora knew that these could also be converted to monitors, but suspected the view of the snow-covered city-scape beyond was the genuine item.

Molly stepped aside as she addressed Ora. "Is there anything else I can get you while you wait?"

She didn't know why, but Ora could not shake the strange feeling of sympathy she had for this woman. There was nothing necessarily nefarious about Cyrus cycling through executive assistants every few months. Many businesspersons had that kind of habit. Still, Molly would have a unique insight into many of the Don's more sensitive dealings. To have such high turnover in that kind of position could create a lot of loose ends. Ora couldn't imagine Cyrus was big on tolerating loose ends.

"No, thank you." Casually, she reached into her back pocket and pulled out a thin piece of cardstock. Business cards like this were beyond old-fashioned, but they were also untraceable. The one she held in her hand had been printed with ink that would fade to nothing in a day or so. Such was an unusual, and easily thwarted, precaution for those who intended to get around it. That was why it was only the first in a complex layer of security that Ora used to guard her contact information.

She pressed the card into Molly's palm. Knowing they were probably being watched, she was careful to stage the interaction with the appropriate degree of nonchalance. "Good people are hard to find. Let me know if you're ever in the mood for a change of pace. We don't do much on Sif, but some people are looking for an excuse to get off-planet."

There it was. Poaching talent, while annoying, was commonplace in the corporate world. Cyrus and his security team wouldn't have any reason for suspicion.

If Molly put off making the call for too long, the contact information would either erase, or Ora's security algorithms would have cycled that channel over to a new number. Ora felt comfortable providing the girl an out, but only if she was smart enough to take it immediately.

Molly's smile was all business. "I'm flattered." She placed the card in a hidden pocket on the side of her skirt. "Mr. Valadar will be with you momentarily."

Now alone in the conference room, Ora sighed and ran her hands back through her short hair. In completing this unassuming gesture, she caught the wire that Thurn had hidden in her earring with her fingernail. She then gripped the edge of the conference table and stuck the wire to the underside of the furniture.

Though she hoped it looked like she was just using the table to brace herself while she stretched her shoulders, the pressure she applied to the wire activated the AI hidden within the tiny construct. She could feel the device as it slithered away into a crease in the table, following the flows of its electrical currents to hopefully find a hub where it might create an access point for Thurn to enter Valadar's servers.

Just like that, her task was complete. Whether the hack was successful or not now depended on whether the worm could find its way into a data terminal, and if Thurn could get past the company's cyber-security. The only thing she had left to do was talk her way through this encounter with Cyrus and make sure no one swept the room for the next ten minutes while the device was still active. At the end of that time, it would destroy itself, and any trace that she'd ever attempted to hack into the company's servers would vanish with it.

"Admiring the view?" The deep voice came suddenly from behind her. Ora's heart skipped a beat. She hadn't heard anyone enter the conference room. How long had he been there? Was there a chance he'd watched her place the wire?

"Cyrus!" she exclaimed breathily as she spun to face him. She decided to lean into her surprise on the off chance that he'd seen her jump at his first words. "You startled me! Do you always move so quietly?"

"My apologies," he replied, inclining his head slightly. Though his demeanor lent some authenticity to the words, his handsome smirk put the lie to them. "I assure you, it was not my intent." He extended his right hand, palm up, with his left tucked behind his back. It looked like he was making a show of playing the aristocratic gentleman.

Well, it was his house. As far as Ora was concerned, he could play this encounter however he wanted. She decided to go along with it, placing her white-gloved hand on top of his palm. He gripped her gently, bringing the hand smoothly to his lips. "Let us start again. How are you this evening, Ms. Monroe?"

"It's Ora to you, Cyrus. Unless you would prefer for me to start addressing you as Mr. Valadar?"

"No, Cyrus is fine."

"Good, and I am well." She withdrew her hand and leaned back against the table. "How are you? I hope it wasn't too much trouble to fit me into your schedule."

"My schedule?" He laughed. "I requested this meeting months ago. It seems that *your* schedule is the more demanding of the two."

So, he wasn't going to let that one slide. She hadn't been sure if he would bring up the long delay in her response to his invitation. Part of her had hoped that he would neglect to mention it to avoid the risk of seeding conflict in their relationship.

It seemed now she would not be so lucky. She couldn't decide if she respected that or not. "While my itinerary is necessarily rigorous, it is more a matter of optimal timing."

There. Let him chew on that. She had no intention of apologizing. Even an adept actress such as herself would have had difficulty making *that* seem genuine.

Cyrus studied her like a lion making a meal choice. "And what, might I ask, transpired to facilitate this now timely occasion?"

He was coming at her much more aggressively than she'd hoped, yet she was not unprepared for the question. She slipped her MoDAC out of her pocket, loaded a file, and handed the device over to him. "I wanted to discuss the state of the security for your mining operation in the Mythril Cliffs."

He studied the dossier she had loaded up on her device. "What of it?"

"I know who's been hitting your supply convoys on the moon's surface. I wanted to see if you need help addressing that particular problem."

His eyes said he was skeptical. Still, he touched the conference room table, raising a holo-projector at its center. He tapped her device twice before waving it at the projector. Suddenly the dossier was up on the display in its entirety, spread across numerous windows over the table.

Ora wasn't sure how he'd done that. As far as she knew, her device hadn't been set to pair with the table, nor had that information been intended for transfer to any other device. She'd have to have Thurn examine the MoDAC later to figure out what Cyrus had done.

Cyrus watched as various news clips played out in front of him. He waved his hand, causing the files to spread out and cycle in front of him. "And who, might I ask, do you think is behind the attacks?"

"House Tyranus."

"And why would one of the minor houses that have sworn fealty to me now be causing a disruption so close to my base of operations?"

His point was well taken. One could argue that Tyranus might have been better served to hit a target a little farther from the Valadar base of power, but who was she to judge? She'd gotten the Grey Wings their contract by pulling off jobs right here in Valhalla—right under Valadar's nose.

"I can't say *why* they're doing what they're doing. I can only assure you that they are the ones doing it and offer you a solution."

His lips compressed into a tight smile. He raised his right hand, fingers splayed outward, and brought it down in a swooping gesture. All files on display instantly vanished, and the projector sunk back into its hiding place. "I think I can deal with Tyranus just fine on my own, but I do thank you for the information. Now, what will this bit of intel cost me?"

Ora suppressed the urge to sigh in relief. Her intelligence teams had been hard-pressed to dig up the dirt on the mining attacks to provide her cover story. She hadn't been so sure how well she would have been able to deliver on her offer to put a stop to them.

"No charge, I suppose—though I *would* appreciate it if you remembered this when our contract is up for renegotiation next cycle."

"Ora, you didn't need to bring me intel on an unrelated security issue to prove your team's value to me. The Grey Wings have handled security here at NeoGenix remarkably since you've taken over the contract. I've been nothing but impressed with you and your people."

"Thank you. Always nice to hear from a happy customer." Even now, he was all business. This was *not* what Ora had expected.

Part of the reason she'd been so reticent to accept his invitation to meet in person was his openly lecherous implications. Had he grown so truly offended that she had spurned him for this long as to forsake such aspirations?

"Tell me," he continued, leaning casually against the table in much the same manner as she had earlier. "How is it that an organization like the Grey Wings continues to be so effective across multiple systems?"

"What do you mean?"

"I mean that I know you continue to expand your operation on that station orbiting Geb. Obviously, you have forces in *this* system beyond what you've dedicated to my security detail, and rumor has it that your agents are seeking purchase in the outskirts of Helion. All of this takes resources. How deep are those pockets of yours, Ora? What's your secret?"

It bothered her that he mentioned Helion. If there was any truth to what he was saying, that meant he knew about her recent collaboration with Cali and the Marauders. That partnership was only in its infancy, though. How could he possibly have found out? Were his spies closer to her than she realized?

"If I told you all my secrets, Cyrus, then what good would I be to you? A girl has to keep some mystery about her to retain her value."

His smile darkened. "Believe me, Ora, I'm sure there's still plenty of opportunity for us beyond whatever it is that the Grey Wings might offer."

There it was. Finally, a hint of sexual desire gleamed in his eye. Though she was back in familiar territory, she still found herself off-balance under that predatory gaze.

"Careful, Cyrus, that sounded awfully forward."

"Maybe that's because I intend to be forward."

"Oh? And what is it, specifically, that you hope to gain with that kind of tact?"

"Come now, don't be coy: How do you do it? The communication issues alone should be enough of a challenge to disrupt your operations. It can't just be good people. Those in our line of work can't resist the allure of power. Anyone you put in charge of your operations out-system would surely vie to form a splinter group. *How do you do it?*"

Knowing that the hardware in her jewelry was piping back every word she heard and everything she saw, she decided to push for something useful for her true intentions. "All right, how about we make a trade?" She leaned a bit closer to him. "I'll tell you my secret if you let me know what it is you've been diverting so much of your company's resources toward researching here."

His smile dissolved immediately. "Might I ask what it is that you are referring to?"

She suddenly wondered if she had overplayed her hand. Now he seemed suspicious. "I don't *know* what it is I'm referring to. That's the point. I *do* know that the reports I'm seeing about my team's deployments have been out of the ordinary this past week. That screams of a reallocation of assets—something that just might be worth swapping trade secrets over."

Cyrus relaxed, though his eyes remained guarded. "So, not only do you manage across systems, you're able to get detailed reports inside of a week. That must take an awful lot of bandwidth."

"It sounds like you're still trying to get my secrets without sharing any in return." She pulled herself back so that she was now sitting on the conference table. Her legs crossed elegantly as she leaned back. "Come on, Cyrus—if you expect to see mine, you should at least show me yours."

The suggestion was working. Cyrus visibly relaxed. Unfortunately, her little spell was interrupted as Molly appeared once more in the glass doorway.

"Mr. Valadar," she said, anxiety thick in her voice. "I have a message from your sister, Julia. I told her you were in a meeting, but she insisted that it was urgent."

Once again Ora felt bad for Cyrus's young assistant. Though Cyrus was the Don, it wasn't like someone in her position could just ignore the orders from another member of the family. Molly was in a no-win scenario, and she knew it.

The only one who harbored no sympathy for her dilemma was Cyrus. Anger welled up in the man's face so quickly Ora almost flinched. "Is she here?" he snapped.

"No, sir. She's broadcasting a video feed."

"Tell her to hold. I'll be there in just a minute."

"Y-yes, sir." The poor girl was gone as quickly as she had appeared.

Ora snuck a glance at the clock on her MoDAC. More than enough time had passed for the worm to dissolve. Thurn would have gotten whatever he was going to get out of network. Now was an excellent time to take advantage of the disruption and make her exit.

She stood, straightening her white slacks politely. "It seems that you have some important matters to attend to."

"She can wait another few minutes," Cyrus growled. Almost as suddenly as it appeared, his rage dissipated. There was no fury in his look now, just pure animalistic intent. "How long will you be planet-side? Perhaps we can arrange for a follow-up meeting."

It was a good thing that he wanted to meet with her again. Not only did it provide her with another opportunity for gathering more intelligence, but it also served as proof that her wiles were keeping him sufficiently in the dark about her real purpose here.

Still, she found herself strangely uneasy about scheduling a follow-up. "I've made arrangements to remain until early next week."

"How about we meet again tomorrow?" he paused dramatically before adding. "At my manor."

Ora issued a flirtatious chuckle. "Oh, Cyrus. Wouldn't it be proper decorum for you to show me to one of your restaurants before granting a tour of your estate?"

"If it's fine dining you want, I assure you that you will find none better than my private kitchens." He stepped forward, pressing so close that there could be no mistaking his intentions. "Tomorrow. Tell me you can make it."

She reached up and planted her fingertips gently on his chest. It was most certainly a warding gesture, but nothing so assertive as to fully dissuade his advances. "My evening tomorrow is, unfortunately, already spoken for. I have an important business meeting that I must attend to."

"The day after then."

"What if I were to call you? Let me check my itinerary."

Despite how hard she was putting on the breaks, Cyrus had apparently decided he would not let himself get discouraged. "Very well. The offer stands for any night until the end of your trip." He stepped away, reaching to get the door for her. As he motioned for her to make her way back to the elevators, he added, "Please, don't keep me waiting too long this time."

CHAPTER 31

Terra-News-Net Now (TN3)

Headline: BREAKING—Acclaimed Valhalla Restaurant in Flames

Story: Emergency response crews are assembling at New Empire Tower, where the structure's roof-top restaurant—Treskon Fountain—is in flames. Authorities have successfully quarantined the blaze to the structure's upper floors, but the fire still rages throughout the restaurant as the establishment's protective outer dome thwarts efforts to quench the flames. A representative from Valadar Holdings has yet to respond to requests for comment.

Fury barely contained, Cyrus stormed into his office. He tore off his jacket and tossed it onto his desk as he pressed the transmit button on his earpiece. "Put the call through. Main screen." Molly didn't reply as she complied with the directive.

Of his siblings, Julia was definitely his favorite. In fact, she was the one relative that Cyrus was proud to claim. That didn't make her interruption any more tolerable.

Julia's face appeared on the viewscreen. Her expression was calm, cold blue eyes giving nothing away. Despite her assertions that this was urgent, there was nothing to convey that in her features.

"This had better be important, dear sister." Hopefully, his sibling's zero-bullshit approach to conversation would hold today. He wasn't in the mood for small talk.

Julia arched an eyebrow "I'm sorry, Cyrus, were you in the middle of something?" No such luck. She must have been perturbed by how long she'd had to wait.

"No games. Not today. Yes, I was in the middle of something, and if you knew the implications of your interruption you might be a bit less smug. Now, spit it out."

Her eyes narrowed. "So, you haven't heard?"

"Heard what?" He was growing quickly exhausted with this game of twenty questions.

In response, Julia loaded up a clip. The timestamp at the top of the feed told him that it was streaming live. The video showed an aerial view of Treskon Fountain. The drone taking the footage hovered a short distance away, giving the audience a panoramic view of the property.

It was burning.

Flames poured over every structure inside the dome, licking up the charred remains of the walls and the lush interior gardens. The roaring inferno contrasted starkly with the swirling blizzard that engulfed the rest of the city.

Cyrus was utterly bewildered. What could have caused this? "An attack?" he guessed.

"After a fashion."

"Who?"

"Our dear Tessa."

Cyrus let his jaw hang open. "What?"

"Oh, you heard me correctly. This is the work of our little sister. Apparently, she decided she was tired of the restaurant business and has taken up arson as a hobby."

"I recently confiscated her assets."

"Ah… well, there we have it. This is all starting to make sense."

Make sense? None of this made any sense. This was madness. Absolute, utter madness. How could Tessa be so self-consumed as to…?

He stopped that line of thought. It didn't matter if he could understand why she'd done what she'd done. All that mattered was that he find her.

"I'll handle this."

Julia nodded sagely. "I would imagine so. Is there anything you need from me?"

"Do you know where she's hiding out?"

"I do not."

"Then no. Thank you, sister."

"Good luck, Cyrus." The screen went dark as she terminated the feed.

For several seconds he just stood there seething. He flexed his hands rhythmically. He breathed deeply to steady himself.

Everything was going to be fine. He would have someone find Tessa. Then he would bring her in and have another chat with her. He'd get to the bottom of whatever madness had driven her to this and then…

And then, what? What good would it do? The last time he set her down, she'd decided to destroy his office and burn down the restaurant he'd asked her to run. What would make this time any different?

"Molly?" he asked into his earpiece.

"Yes, Mr. Valadar."

"Have Sydney call me. There's someone I need her to find." With that, he spun on his heels and stormed toward his office door.

Right into Dr. Blackwell.

"Damn it, Cyrus! Could you perhaps be a bit more careful?"

He glowered at her. Who had let her in? Why hadn't Molly announced that he had another visitor? "What are you doing here, Lucretia?"

His anger didn't cow the woman. "I've been waiting for you. I was sitting in your lobby when you stormed in here all in a huff. What happened? Did your *date* not go as planned?"

"I really don't have time for this." He started to push past her. If she wanted to hang around and haunt his office, that was her business. Cyrus didn't give a damn at this point.

Her arm shot out and seized his wrist. "Yes," she hissed. "Yes, you do."

He was shocked at her aggression that all he could manage was a dumbfounded expression. "This had better be good, Lucretia. I've had a disappointing evening so far, and you are pushing it."

The doctor didn't even deign to acknowledge the threat. "I think I can cheer you up. What if I told you that I've solved the major problem involving the artifact and the control units?"

What was she talking about? "Which problem?"

She smiled. "The one where you have to be touching the artifact to exert your control over the slave units."

Okay, this was good. "*That* problem? Already? Your new test subjects arrived only yesterday. Don't you ever sleep?"

"No, actually." She brushed a stray lock of hair back behind her ear. "I use a neuro-compiler. It gives your brain all the benefits of a full night's sleep in five minutes."

Was she being serious? It didn't matter. What he needed to focus on now was how to deal with all the fires burning right now. Cringing at the uncanny metaphor, he sighed. "Molly?"

His assistant, sitting meekly at her desk, seemed to be doing everything in her power not to attract attention. "Yes, Mr. Valadar?"

"Tell Sydney to find Tessa. When she does, have her return and give me the location. Nothing else. Understood?"

"Yes, Mr. Valadar."

Good. His initial thought had been to have Sydney kidnap his sister and bring her here, but that wasn't going to help his negotiating position. If he were going to appeal to his sister's better angels, as deficient and neglected as they might be, he'd be best served not to start with an act of aggression.

Yes, this was the better way. All he needed was something else to occupy his mind while he formulated a plan to deal with his sister. Fortunately, Dr. Blackwell had just provided him with the necessary distraction. "Lead on, Lucretia. I want to see the fruits of your labor."

It surprised Ora how hard she had to work not to sprint off the lift and out the front doors of the building. Had it been so long since she'd been directly involved in an operation? She'd never wanted to become that person who sat up in her high tower and told those underneath her how high they should be jumping. In retrospect, it seemed that was exactly how things had turned out. She was rusty.

She fought back against the fear. Her discipline made sure that every step portrayed calculated confidence, from the moment she stepped off the elevator to the second she walked up to the outer door. She spotted a waiting autocar in the valet circle and made her way toward it. At this point, she was finally starting to relax.

"Excuse me, ma'am." A heavy hand came to rest firmly on her shoulder. "I'll need to see some identification."

Ora wanted to jump right out of her skin. Had something gone wrong? She felt the urge to bolt. Instead, she summoned up what resolve she had left to turn and face the man who'd grabbed her.

"Vallus?"

A grin split the Maur's feline face. "I thought it was you."

She punched her old bodyguard hard in one of his massive pectorals, though he probably wouldn't have felt it even without the padding of his security uniform. "You scared the shit out of me!"

"Which makes this quite possibly one of my favorite interactions in recent memory."

"You really need to get laid more," she huffed indignantly before composing herself. "How are you, old friend?"

"Oh, you know—enjoying running the easiest assignment the Wings have to offer."

She eyed him skeptically. "Is it really so bad?"

He waved the comment off. "Not so bad. Things were pretty interesting at first, but they calmed down quick when everyone figured out we were nothing to mess with. Nine hells, what am I telling you for? You've read the reports." Now he was eying her suspiciously. "What are you doing here, Ora? And why didn't we get a little more heads up that you were coming? I hadn't received word until your name appeared on the schedule a couple of days ago."

Realizing that they were still standing outside NeoGenix, Ora glanced around nervously. No one had taken interest in their conversation yet, but that could change quickly. "Do you have time to take a ride with me?"

Vallus glanced over his shoulder and exchanged a look with a rifle-toting guard, who nodded at him. "Looks like I'm good."

"Great. Come with me."

They pressed through the blowing snow and piled into a waiting autocar. Ora gave the vehicle the address for the drop-off point they were using to get to the safehouse: a shopping center a half-dozen kilometers from where they were now.

Sitting opposite Vallus, she activated the jamming application on her MoDAC. "All right," she sighed. "Here's your opportunity. You get to decide whether you want the truth or the cover story. I don't know what kind of scrutiny you're under with your overseers at NeoGenix, and I don't want to accidentally compromise you. If this conversation can't stay strictly between us, I need to know right now."

Vallus didn't hesitate. "We're good, Ora. You can give it to me straight. You, of all people, should know where my loyalties lie."

Ora nodded. "Very well. Here is the full story."

She told him everything: Rico, the Heart, her fake proposition to Valadar, all of it. She was careful not to leave anything out.

Before she'd dispatched Vallus to run the operation on Sif, he had been one of her closest confidants. Truthfully, he was second only to Tashania on the list of people she trusted. Anything short of that and she might have had reservations about sharing this kind of detail. With Vallus though, there were no concerns.

When she'd finished her tale, his first response was, "Why didn't you let me in on this? That stunt you just pulled in there—you have no *idea* how reckless that was. They've got tech in that building like I've never seen. One wrong move and they'd have had you cold."

"I know, but as I told you earlier: I didn't want to compromise your integrity."

"And you think that Cyrus isn't going to hold the Wings accountable when his prized artifact suddenly goes missing on their watch?"

Fair point. Ora hadn't considered that. "Failure to provide security is a little different than conspiring to steal an asset you're charged with protecting."

"I don't think so. The net result is the same."

That was an extreme opinion, but Ora wrote it off to cultural differences. Maybe, from a Maur's perspective, failure to protect something was the same as stealing it yourself. "Terran law doesn't share that viewpoint. You'll have to take my word on this one."

The autocar came to a stop, and Ora waved her MoDAC on the console to pay the fee. She turned to say her goodbyes to Vallus only to find the Maur already out of his seat. "Oh no," he growled, silencing her protest. "I'm coming with you. If you're still planning on going through with this gods-forsaken plan of yours, I'm going to be there to keep you from doing anything completely foolish."

It was a nice sentiment, but not one Ora could abide. "Vallus, if you have any knowledge of this, I can't send you back in there. Everyone on the security detail needs to be well and truly ignorant if it's ever called to question."

"Then reassign me. If you intended to keep me in the dark, you've already told me too much. Besides, do you honestly think Valadar will be interested in maintaining your contract after this?"

Ora honestly hadn't thought that far out. She was just acting on instinct, and that was a good way to end up dead. "Don't you need to be over there running things?"

"I can call my second, and she'll take care of everything. Shit, she'll probably run the show better than me. Besides, I'm overdue for some leave. No one will question it." At least, no one would question it until Valadar started connecting the dots to figure out what went wrong.

Perhaps Vallus was right, though. Ora might have made a mistake in giving all these details to her old friend. That couldn't be undone, but perhaps having Vallus's council would keep her from making mistakes she might otherwise stumble into. "Come on, then. Let me introduce you to the rest of the crew."

They filed out of the vehicle and made their way to the arched entrance to the shopping complex. The whole area could be converted to an open-air market, but—due to the blizzard—a protective covering had been extended over the walkways. It was much warmer under the retractable shelter, not that this did much to attract many shoppers. The weather was keeping most people away, which was fine by Ora. Fewer pedestrians meant a lower likelihood that anyone might be tailing them without their knowledge.

Seeing no need to hide their trail, she led Vallus on a straight path to the safehouse. The most direct path still involved a lot of twists and turns to get to the small apothecary she had purchased in the shopping center. Inside the pharmacy, they took an employee-only stairwell to the private lower level. From there, they slipped into a hidden passage inside the building's storeroom and went a short distance down another tunnel to reach the coded entrance to the safehouse.

"Damn," Vallus sighed. "Do you even need to bother with a passcode on that door? This place is so far out, I'm not even sure I could find my way back if I wanted to."

"That's the idea," Ora agreed. "But yes, I still put a passcode on the door." A light on the keypad turned green in recognition of the code and the metal grated door slid up. They were here.

Markus was the first to greet her. As quickly as he appeared, it seemed that he might have been pacing by the door. The two embraced and he squeezed her tightly, letting out a deep sigh. "You made it back."

"Of course," she said, gently rubbing his back.

He pulled away. "And you brought a friend."

Ora nodded. "Markus, you might remember Vallus."

"How could I forget?" He and the Maur clasped hands.

Vallus chuckled. "Last time I saw you, you were about to lose a leg."

Markus scoffed. "Just a flesh wound. I was up and running before we got back to Sigma-4."

Kadath stepped out of a side room and eyed the Maur. "I was wondering where you'd gone off to, big fella. It's been a while since I've seen you around the station."

Vallus shot a ferocious-looking grin at the mercenary. "Kadath! Ora's still keeping you around? I thought it was just a phase and she might have moved on to someone a little more competent to run her errands."

"Lucky for me there's hardly any talent to be found on the lower tier. As such, I've managed to stick around." The two of them embraced. Ora had no idea they'd managed to get along so well in their short time together. Vallus had been sent over to Sif soon after Kadath's crew first started working with the Grey Wings. It was good that the pair had been quick to establish some camaraderie.

She turned back to Markus. "What's the verdict? Did the hack go through?"

"*Oh yeah.* The hack went through. Thurn's pretty damn good, and not just for an Orchallen."

From the other room, Thurn's heavy voice sounded. "High praise, even if it's comin' from a skinny ape."

Well, it certainly seemed that those two were getting along nicely. "Splendid," Ora said. "Let's see what we've got."

She started to push past Markus to join Thurn at the computer terminal, but his hands on her shoulders stopped her. "Ease up there, boss. He's still going through the files. Let's get you something to eat first. Gotta maintain proper decorum, after all."

Decorum? What was he…?

Oh. It was her last bit of flirtation with Cyrus. Apparently, it had rubbed Markus the wrong way. Well, she was going to accept the jibe to not make the whole thing out to be more than just strategy. "Fine," she sighed. "I'm not hungry, but I could use a drink."

"Wine or water?" Markus asked.

"Do I have to pick one?"

He laughed. "I suppose not." He vanished around the corner into the house's tiny kitchenette while she found a seat in the main room.

Despite her curiosity, she made every effort to let Thurn continue his work. The cyborg's one good eye darted back and forth between the monitors, and his prosthetic whirred and telescoped in and out as data streams slid across his feeds.

Jeagan and Siv joined them in the common area. "How was it?" Jeagan hissed.

"It was about as I expected," Ora replied. She seized the bottle of water Markus brought for her and drained it dry. When that one ran empty, she swapped the container for the glass of red wine in his other hand. "Their tech was a bit more advanced than I expected."

"How so?" asked Kadath.

"He was able to pull the dossier right off my mobile without me granting him access, for one."

Markus grunted. "Yeah, I noticed that. That was quite the trick, there. We should scan your device to make sure he didn't leave any surprises."

"How could he have done that? I was standing right next to him."

"I don't know. How did he send the files over to his fancy conference table?"

"Markus is right," Kadath interjected. "We should scan it as a precaution." He turned to Vallus. "Personally, I'm glad you decided to join us for this little endeavor. More and more it's seeming like we're ill-equipped to break into that facility."

Thurn suddenly spoke up. "Yeah, well, Ah think ya better start gettin' equipped." He pulled up a diagram of the building. A yellow blinking icon appeared at the lower end of the schematic. "'Cause he's got the Heart tucked away at the bottom a the fraggin' thing."

CHAPTER 32

Terra-News-Net Now (TN3)
Headline: Questions Linger After Valhalla Fire
Story: While authorities have been scant on information regarding the fire that erupted this past evening, reports suggest arson is to blame. More scandalous yet, insiders have begun to wonder if Valadar Holdings may be the culprit. Staff interviewed at the scene allegedly reported that they were unceremoniously dismissed by the building's proprietor.

"I was told my services were no longer required," reported one worker who asked to remain anonymous. "I'd just made it to the bottom of the tower when emergency services started to show up."

Allegations of possible foul-play have been denied by both Valadar Holdings and Valhalla city officials. While one might normally be skeptical of such a coordinated response, their stories are supported by the failure of anyone to answer a single question: Why would Valadar Holdings want to burn down the single most successful restaurant in the entire capital?

It was a sad state of affairs when Aaliyah directed the course of a meeting, but that's what things had come to. Eli or Skye would have normally been the logical choices, but they kept getting lost down proverbial rabbit holes. Non-productive conversation was not needed right now.

Sahar might have been a good choice too, but she'd been unusually quiet since they'd gotten back. And then there was Dan, who was more the kind of guy you pointed at a problem and shouted,

"Solve!" His pet android was probably better at managing people than he was.

Well then, here goes nothing. "All right people." She pushed herself into a standing position and rested her hands on the war room table. "We're not gettin' anywhere. Let's rewind this conversation and try again. What do we know?"

Half the people in the room glowered at her sudden interjection. That was fine because they didn't have to like her. They *did* have to quit talking over each other and get this meeting over before she decided to walk out on them.

No one said anything for several seconds. "Fine," she continued. "I'll start. Item number one: The guy running House Valadar has this glowy space-rock. Because said space-rock may have universe-ending special powers, we want to get it back from him."

Argus jumped in. "Item number two: Ryker was negotiating a way to get the artifact away from Valadar and safely into our possession." He paused, dramatically. "Now he's dead."

"Murdered," Amelia corrected.

"Fine," Aaliyah countered. "Murdered. Murdered is a form of dead. We won't get anywhere splittin' hairs. What else do we know?"

Now it was Skye's turn. "We have no way of communicating back to Jocelyn in a timely manner. Mara hasn't answered any of our attempts to hail her. That means we can't check in with coven leadership to get advice on what to do next."

Eli's eyes were downcast as he asked, "Are we all agreed that flying back to the Helion system is out of the question?" Mister play-by-the-rules obviously hated that they were flying blind here.

That was the thing about Eli: He was more comfortable when someone else made the final call. In Aaliyah's opinion, that quality alone was what held him back from his full potential at this whole captain-shtick. He needed to remember he had previously served as the voice of reason, so any opinion he wasn't about to shoot down was probably going to hold up to consensus.

No one spoke up for several seconds. "Looks like everyone agrees," said Aaliyah. "So, we're still goin' to go after the Heart?" She saw a handful of nods—enough, in her mind, to call it a consensus. "Great. So where is House Valadar hiding it?"

Lexa perked up. "That we know, actually." All eyes turned to her. "The information given to us by the Ren'Dahl coven indicated that the bulk of Ryker's meetings with Don Cyrus Valadar were held in his offices at the NeoGenix corporate headquarters. Ryker had reason to believe that this was where the artifact was being kept."

"Not necessarily," Eli interjected. "That also happens to be where Cyrus keeps his personal offices in Valhalla. Valadar Holdings rents the top floor to supply some additional revenue to counteract the exorbitant R&D that goes on at NeoGenix."

Lexa remained unconvinced. "Even so, NeoGenix remains the most well-equipped research facility in all Valhalla. Additionally, we detected an unusual signal emanating from their building. It is reasonable to conclude such a signal would be a byproduct of experimentation with the Heart of Thule.

Now they were getting somewhere. "All right," Aaliyah continued. "That's good enough for me. If that's where they're hidin' the rock, that's where we need to focus our efforts. What do we know about that buildin'?"

"I don't know about the building, but NeoGenix is that company that Ora had us rip-off awhile back," Skye noted. "They use a lot of freelance contractors for things like shipping and security. In fact, I'm pretty sure the Grey Wings run their security now."

NeoGenix was guarded by the Grey Wings? Well, that was a happy coincidence. "So, does that give us an in?" Aaliyah asked.

Eli shook his head. "Not really. Reaching Ora is going to be just as hard as reaching Jocelyn. We've already decided we can't afford the time to go out to the gates and back. They're not going to be of much help here."

"Plus," Sahar added. "We know nothing about NeoGenix beyond what anyone could find on the nets. If they have the Heart hidden somewhere in that building, we're going to need some more information."

"A stake-out then?" Aaliyah asked hopefully. A stake-out meant that they'd be taking the shuttle for a spin. She was getting tired of being cooped up in the ship. "Or maybe some kind of hack?"

Lexa had some reservations about the latter suggestion. "That building doesn't seem to be wired directly into the city's data grid. Assuming they have a network, I would have to establish a connection on-site to access it."

"So that's what we'll do!" Skye exclaimed as she rose to her feet. "We'll scope out the place and look for an opportunity for Lexa to hack the system. Once we do that, we'll come up with a plan to steal the Heart."

"That's the best plan we've come up with so far," Eli admitted. "Tomorrow, though. It's late, and we've had a rough couple of days."

There were no complaints from anyone present. It spoke to just *how* rough these last couple of days had been. "All right then," Aaliyah concluded. "We head out tomorrow."

Markus was more than willing to let Vallus take the lead in the strategy discussions. If anyone knew NeoGenix Headquarters inside-out, it was him. Unfortunately, his analysis wasn't doing much for the team's morale.

"It may not look like a fortress from the outside, but it's one of the most secure facilities I've ever seen." The Maur touched the wire-frame hologram and expanded it, focusing on the lowest levels of the building. "This is where they'll be hiding it. All the firm's R&D takes place on these ten sublevels."

"What are the access points?" Kadath asked.

Vallus touched the central, vertical shaft. "There are technically two, but this is the only one you'll find on the diagram.

They use this freight elevator to get both equipment and personnel down to the labs. That's your only way in."

"What about the second?" Ora asked.

"Cyrus's private elevator. It has only two access points: his office, and the sublevels. That's not going to be of much use." Vallus paused just to see if anyone disagreed. No one did.

"So, we need to penetrate that elevator and get down to the sublevels undetected," said Markus. "What are our options on that front?"

"More like, 'What are our obstacles?'" Kadath corrected. "Assuming we can get to the lift, the first is going to be surveillance, and the second is going to be permissions. Are those things we can hack?"

All eyes went to Thurn. The Orchallen shrugged. "Permissions Ah can take care a'. We got all the codes thanks t' the bug Ora dropped in ol' Cyrus's conference room. Surveillance, though—that'll be a trick. We're gonna need another access point."

"Perhaps I can be of assistance there," Ora suggested. "My meeting with Cyrus got cut short, and he said he wanted to meet again. I can arrange to stop by the building and plant a bug like last time."

Thurn shook his head. "Won' be like last time, boss. Surveillance doesn' run on that circuit. Gonna need t' get the worm right inside the command center."

Vallus furrowed his brow. "That's doable, but Ora wouldn't be the best candidate to deliver the package. I could do it, but that's going to put the Grey Wings fingerprints all over this. We're the only ones outside of Valadar's personal detail that have access to that room."

Both Markus and Ora opened their mouths to object, but Jeagan interrupted. "Perhaps we are looking at this the wrong way. We are thinking of how to get something inside that doesn't belong there. Let us change that approach. How often is that elevator normally in use? What does it typically carry?"

Vallus had to think about that one for a minute. "It's used all the time. It's not the primary bank for guests, but it's the only lift that's big enough to move equipment throughout the building. It's also the only way lab personnel can get down to the sublevels."

Ora asked, "Is there any way we can fake some credentials? Make it look like our team is supposed to be down in the lab?"

"No," said Vallus. "That's another thing that would require security access. Once the discrepancy was discovered, the Wings would be blamed."

Jeagan remained unperturbed. "You mentioned equipment. What kinds of equipment?"

From his increasingly confused look, Vallus had no idea where Jeagan going with this. "That's difficult to say. I'm not in the habit of reviewing the manifests, but I can tell you it's all over the fragging board. Computers, tools, supplies, and dozens of things I've never even heard of."

The engineer's reptilian eyes seemed to glimmer. "Supplies, you say?"

"Yeah, all kinds of supplies. Everything's kept locked up in these big..." The Maur's eyes widened. "*Oh!* Now I see where you're going. That's good. That's *very* good."

Markus arched an eyebrow. "Care to share with the class, you two?"

Jeagan smiled. "If the supplies are stored in large crates, we could intercept one of the upcoming shipments. Then we could use the crates to smuggle in our operatives."

That was the best plan Markus had heard so far. "So, that sounds good, but then how do we get out with the Heart?"

"The same way," said Vallus. "Empty supply crates are taken back up the lift about one hour later. If we stash the Heart in one of those crates, we can have our people ride up with it in the storage containers and no one has to be the wiser."

Damn. That almost sounded too easy. Ora must have thought so too because she quickly pointed out another problem. "We still have to deal with the surveillance issue. Whoever is monitoring the cameras is going to have to look the other way when we're raiding the lab."

"It's a similar problem," Vallus explained. "But it doesn't have the same risk. The Grey Wings don't monitor security in the lab, just the cams on the lift. If there's a problem down there, it'll be Valadar's people who've screwed up. The Wings could reasonably think it's just business as usual."

"Good," Markus said. "So, what kind of manpower are we talking down there?"

The Maur gestured to the first sublevel. "Just one security checkpoint. Though the central elevator can be called down to any of the sublevels with the proper authorization codes, it only stops at this first one. It's the only way in and out."

"Simple enough. What about patrols?"

Vallus shook his head. "No one patrols the area. Cyrus and his security detail are the only ones besides lab staff that venture deeper into the complex."

Markus combed one hand through his beard. "Then we're going to have to figure out a way to keep Cyrus from sightseeing while we're down there. Is there a way to get a look at his schedule? Maybe find some time when he's in a board meeting or something?"

"No need for that," Ora interjected, pulling up a file on her MoDAC. She swiped at the card and a news article appeared on the main display. "We know when he's scheduled to be somewhere. There's a big press conference at the Valkyrie Center tomorrow. The news predicts that the city will renew its contract with V-transit. Cyrus is expected to be there."

"Perfect!" Markus said with a grin. This little raid was starting to seem almost feasible. "Now we just need to figure out how to take down security in the lab before they raise the alarm."

Kadath said, "I may have an option for that. Let's put that conversation on hold for the moment."

"All right," Markus agreed. "Then let's go back to drop off and extraction. How do the supplies get to the building?"

Vallus touched the wire-frame model and pinched his fingers together to zoom out. He tapped the very top. "From the roof, of course."

Terra-News-Net Now (TN3)

Headline: Valadar Holdings Loses Control Over Galacti-Fix Media

Story: After processing several inexplicable stock deals, House Tyranus managed to wrest control of Galacti-Fix Media (GFM-FRV, +66%) from Valadar Holdings. Shares in T-Corp (TCO-FRV, +30.6%), Galvanus PR (GPR-FRV, +26.4%), and Freya Press (FRP-FRV, +56.2%) all rallied today as investors realized that together, the three Tyranus Group companies had amassed a collective 40% stake in the media giant, while Valadar Holdings stake shrank to 36%. Though there is plenty of time for House Valadar to put pressure on the minor shareholders and prevent a hostile takeover, the rapid inflation in GFM's stock suggests it's going to cost them more than a handful of krets to reassert control.

Normally Valadar's investment team is careful to monitor the trading activity of its corporate interests to prevent incidents like this from happening. Recently, however, the firm has been offloading shares in many of its companies to raise capital. Though no one can be certain of the reasons for this, most analysts suspect the effort is to support the massive increase in the NeoGenix (NGX-FRV, -1.25%) research and development expenditures. Combining this fiscal slip-up with the incident at Treskon Fountain yesterday, many are beginning to wonder: What is happening over at House Valadar?

Cyrus watched as the Hissak prisoner made his slave units run the gauntlet Lucretia had set up on the lowest sublevel of the building. Normally this area was reserved for storage. To test their research progress, the company's staff had converted it into an obstacle course.

The Hissak stood with Cyrus and Lucretia at the center of the ring, staring straight forward with casual indifference. Six other test subjects ran the course around the room's periphery. Not a hint of exhaustion registered in their carriage as they moved as fast as their legs would carry them—making death-defying leaps and sliding between burning lasers without hesitation.

"And he has total control?" Cyrus asked.

"Complete and utter," Lucretia agreed. "They will run this course until Geran tells them to stop, or until their bodies are physically unable to complete the task."

Cyrus had no reason to doubt the doctor's assertions, but it was hard to believe. Not only was the Heart currently inactive, but it was in an insulated chamber two levels above them. "Prove it," he said. "Make one of them do something different. Something they would never do of their own free will."

The doctor shrugged. "Very well. Geran?" She pointed at a subject that was ascending an elevated platform. "Break that one's neck."

The Hissak didn't so much as blink. When the test subject made it to the top of the platform, she stopped, walked calmly to the edge, and performed a swan dive onto the concrete below.

A sickening crack echoed across the chamber as her body crumbled on impact. She lay still, and the remaining subjects continued to run their gauntlet, having apparently failed to notice the incident.

"Amazing," Cyrus whispered. "How did you do it?"

Lucretia smiled. "Well done, Geran. Have the remaining subjects return to the lounge area. Explain to them that the one subject suffered an adverse reaction to the procedure. Say nothing of how she actually died."

The Hissak nodded. "I understands. I says nothing."

"Thank you, dear. You've been most helpful."

As the Hissak shepherded his thralls out of the chamber, Lucretia led Cyrus to another door. They entered an elevator, and she pressed the code to return them to the third level.

"It is based on the same technology we used in Mani," she explained as the elevator rose. "When I saw that a charged J-kryst had the same effect as the activated artifact, I hypothesized the same technique should allow the control unit to exert their will onto the slave units. After numerous experiments, I discovered that the problem lay in the quantity needed for the control unit to become active. While a relatively minor amount of radiation is necessary to render a subject compliant, a much larger dose is necessary to exert control."

"But that Hissak, Geran—he wasn't holding a crystal. Not one that I saw, at least."

The elevator arrived, and Lucretia guided Cyrus down another hallway. "Correct. That is because the size of a charged crystal with the necessary power to energize a control unit is too large to be discreet or efficiently transported. At first, I thought we might have to be content with developing a series of control stations away from the artifact, but then I had another idea."

Lucretia led him through a sliding steel door. On entering the next chamber, Cyrus laid eyes on the Heart. The charged artifact glowed within its containment cell, but the equipment surrounding it had changed significantly.

"What is this?"

The doctor smiled. "This is the key to making the artifact work as you desire."

A tangled network of tubes encircled the Heart of Thule. Fluid pumped inside the transparent plastic channels and glowed just as vibrantly as the artifact. The radiant liquid ran over to a larger vessel where it slowly dripped out of the circuit.

Lucretia took great delight in her explanation. "I was able to reduce the crystals to microscopic fragments using the same technology we employ to create nano-machines. Once reduced to that size, the particles are easily suspended in normal saline—the perfect vehicle for injection or infusion into a sapient being."

Cyrus had to force his jaw closed. This was ingenious, even by Lucretia's standards. "You injected the test subjects with liquid crystal?"

"It's technically a crystal suspension, but yes, that's the essence of it."

"And it did not poison the hosts?"

"Not at all. The body seems completely unaffected by the introduction of the particles. Also, the body eliminates the crystal molecules so slowly that it will take nearly three cycles for the dose given to the slave units to wear off."

"And what about the amount given to the control unit?"

Lucretia shrugged. "Hard to say. Without a booster, the control unit's powers may wane after two or three cycles. However, it's likely such a large dose may never fully exit the system."

Cyrus rubbed his jaw, considering the possibilities. "So it can't be extracted?"

"Not without a complete blood transfusion, no."

"Have any of the other psions you've been working with been given the injections?"

Lucretia's eyes drew together in suspicion. "No… Geran was the first. Why?"

"Because I want you to dispose of him. This is too much power for one of the test subjects to have. For your future experiments, I want you to pursue the portable control station idea. No more injections for the control units."

The doctor opened her mouth to protest but thought better of it. "Very well. It will be done as you have asked."

Cyrus's next words were cut off as a new voice sounded from over their shoulders. "So, this is the rock that is taking up so much of your time."

Lucretia whirled on the intruder. Cyrus steadied her with a warding gesture. "Sydney! How did you get down here?"

The assassin smiled, her bushy tail swaying behind her. "If I couldn't sneak down here, I wouldn't be very good at the little tasks you give me, now would I?"

Cyrus still wasn't impressed. "All the same, I would prefer you reserve your infiltration abilities for your targets and approach me using the proper channels."

"Whatever you say, boss." She glanced at Lucretia and back at Cyrus.

The meaning of the gesture was not lost on him. "She can hear whatever you have to say," Cyrus noted. "Have you found Tessa?"

"Yes. She's shacked up with some guy in District 3—one of your low-level dealers if I'm not mistaken."

How did Sydney know who was peddling drugs for his organization? Even Cyrus didn't bother with personnel that far down the ladder.

He supposed it didn't matter. "Good. Thank you for your services."

"Do you want me to pay them another visit? Take out the guy and drag Tessa back here?"

"No, that's quite all right. I'll take care of it myself."

The look on Sydney's face conveyed how she felt about that. Despite her evident objection, she plastered a neutral expression on her face and shrugged. "Suit yourself. Anything else for me this evening?"

"No, thank you. I'll see you back at the apartment." Though the dismissal was clear, Sydney lingered for a moment longer. She cast her eyes warily at the artifact, then back to Cyrus before slipping out the door.

Lucretia waited until the other woman was gone before huffing indignantly. "Anyone else behaving like that around here would find themselves unemployed or worse."

Cyrus chuckled. "Well, she's *not* anyone else. Put it out of your mind. Besides, I need you to hurry and get a new infusion prepped."

For a second time, Lucretia appeared startled. "What?"

"Oh come, now. You didn't honestly expect to show me all of that power and not hand it over, did you?" When the doctor began her stammered response, he pressed a single finger against her lips to silence her. "Why wait?" he whispered. "Let's get this done now."

The setup Cyrus found in the operating room an hour later was far more complex than that. Lucretia hadn't been exaggerating when she said the amount of crystal required for a control unite was unwieldy.

He also wasn't expecting to have to be put under for the procedure. However, at Dr. Blackwell's insistence, he submitted to the anesthesia. He found it ironic that, after a lifetime of never having had surgery, he was about to experience his second procedure within a week.

One added benefit to the anesthesia was the way the procedure seemed to occur instantaneously. One minute he was being strapped into a padded operating chair, and in the next the same technician was undoing those straps. "Done already?"

Lucretia scoffed. "It's been two hours. I do hope you enjoyed your nap, though. How do you feel?"

He flexed his hands as the technician withdrew the intravenous needles from his arms. "Never better." Once he was fully freed from the lab equipment, he stretched his arms and neck. "I wasn't expecting to feel so well-rested. This is far better than the last one."

"Yes, well, that's because we weren't operating on your brain. The sedative was to prevent you from feeling any pain with the infusion. Our first subject said it burned when it entered the veins."

"How thoughtful of him to bring it up. And he's been taken care of?"

"Just like you asked." Though Lucretia's tone was submissive, the look in her eyes bordered on insurrection. The good doctor was getting tired of Cyrus taking away her play-things.

"Aw, don't sulk, Lucretia. It's not your best look. Come now—let us put your procedure to the test."

"Out of the question. I recommend at least a full day before you engage in any kind of psionic activity."

Just to spite her, he extended his hand outward and focused his mind. Everyone in the room jumped as a box slid out of Cyrus's jacket pocket and sailed into his waiting palm.

Lucretia gasped. "You're a *telekin!*"

"That's right." After having the amp installed, Cyrus had read up on every flavor of psionic power to manifest in sapient species. He'd also quietly worked through the beginning steps to test which brand of power had become his.

It had been a pleasant surprise to discover that, like Eva before him, Cyrus had developed telekinesis. He was still practicing with it but had mastered the ability to move small objects with only his mind.

While everyone was watching, he opened the box. Inside was an elegant platinum chain on which hung a slender charm. It was a crystal, emerald in color and slightly luminescent. A serpentine character wrought in silver wrapped its way irregularly around the gemstone. "What do you think?" he asked, extending it toward Lucretia.

"Is that what I think it is?"

"I would guess so. I had it crafted from one of the samples you gave me. Isn't it lovely?" When Lucretia failed to respond, he turned to a lab technician standing to his right. She was a pretty young Terran with the slightest hint of red in her long, golden hair. "How about you, Miss…"

"Renfeld, sir," she replied with a slight blush.

Cyrus's smile broadened. "Miss Renfeld. What do you think of this necklace?"

"It's lovely, sir." Though obviously flattered he would seek out her opinion, there was a level of caution in her expression. Cyrus made her nervous. The woman was a good judge of character.

"Thank you. I have it in mind for a very special someone, but I wasn't quite sure if it would do." He extended the necklace toward her. "Please, Miss Renfeld—would you do me the honor?"

The technician swallowed hard. "Yes, sir." Cautiously, she reached out and took the necklace, and began to fasten it around her neck. As she did so, Cyrus noticed a golden ring on her left hand.

He smiled as his charm fell to rest neatly against the flesh over her sternum. "Just as I thought. It's lovely. Tell me, Miss Renfeld, are you married?"

"Engaged, sir."

"How wonderful. When is the ceremony?"

She smiled at the casual turn in the conversation. "This spring. Just a few months from now."

"Splendid. Just splendid." Cyrus brought his hand to his chin, feigning thoughtfulness. "I tell you what: I feel inclined to give you an early wedding present. That is if you wouldn't mind indulging me in one small request."

Lucretia huffed. "What is it about the phrase 'recovery period' that you fail to understand?"

"I feel fine, Lucretia." Turning back to the technician he continued. "Now, Miss Renfeld, as I was saying: if you would indulge me in one small exercise, I will grant you a one-time bonus of, let's say, twenty-thousand krets. I'll cover the taxes too. That would go a long way to covering those wedding expenses, yes?"

Renfeld beamed. "That's… that's wonderful, sir. Thank you!"

"Oh, it's the least I could do. All you have to do is follow my instructions, okay?" He stood up from the operating table and took a few steps to put some distance between them. "All I need you to do is to stand in that exact spot. Do not move—no matter what I tell you—until you have permission from Dr. Blackwell over there. Do you understand?"

The technician's eyebrows furrowed at the strange request. "Um… okay…"

"Good. The exercise begins now. Come here."

The woman cocked her head, obviously confused. She looked at Dr. Blackwell, then back at Cyrus. "I'm sorry, Mr. Valadar, I don't understand. Didn't you just tell me to stay in this spot?"

Cyrus laughed. "Just making sure you understood the parameters of the exercise."

He drew in a deep breath and closed his eyes. He sent his mind outward, feeling for the energy he knew rested within the charm. A second later he found it, and he opened his eyes. "Now, Miss Renfeld: *come here*."

The woman took a step forward. Then another. And another. As she stood next to him, she blinked uncertainly, as if still confused by the purpose of the exercise. "Ms. Renfeld," he whispered with feigned disappointment. "What were the instructions for our exercise?"

"I'm not to move until Dr. Blackwell gives me permission," she reported matter-of-factly.

"Has Dr. Blackwell given you permission to move?"

"No."

"But you did anyway?"

Confusion swept over her. She blinked rapidly, looking at Cyrus, then back to Lucretia. "I… I don't—"

"It's fine. Let's try again." He paused for a moment, giving her the chance to reset. "Kiss me."

She did so without hesitation. Cyrus felt the softness of her mouth, the warm pressure of her tongue as it probed against his. It was intimate, tender even. Cyrus caught flashes in her mind, remembrances of kissing her fiancé like this, holding him close, making love to him. Every part of her mind was open to him as her mouth worked against his.

He pulled back, breaking the kiss. "Miss *Renfeld*!"

Horror flooded into her expression at the realization of what she'd done. "Mr. Valadar, I…"

He shushed her, pressing a finger against her lips. "It's all right. Now, reach behind your neck and unclasp that necklace. Hand it to me, and the exercise is over."

She did so, though her fingers trembled in the process. He wasn't sure whether it was his power making her do this, or if she was genuinely eager to be rid of the article.

When the charm was in his hand, he smiled. "Thank you, Miss Renfeld. Your fiancé is a very lucky man. I will see that your wedding present is wired into your account tomorrow."

The technician took a nervous step backward. "Th… thank you, Mr. Valadar." Though she managed a semblance of a gracious tone, her eyes did not meet his.

Lucretia cleared her throat. "Well, if you are quite finished, might we call it an evening? The hour is late, and though *I* do not need to sleep, my staff still has that requirement."

Cyrus nodded, completely unable to wipe the grin off his face. "Of course, Dr. Blackwell. Everyone should rest up. I have the feeling that tomorrow will be a *very* big day."

Chapter 34

Terra-News-Net Now (TN3)

Headline: BREAKING—Cyrus Valadar Cancels Press Conference

Story: Valadar Holdings has abruptly canceled the press conference previously scheduled at the Valkyrie Center for early this afternoon. The company instead released a short press release explaining that the conference would be moved to accommodate an "unexpected change" in the schedule of the company's president and CEO, Cyrus Valadar. The release went on to allude to the company's unconventional fiscal moves over the past few weeks, stating, "The Company is restructuring and re-prioritizing its current initiatives. Investors will be briefed on these changes in due course and should expect more announcements soon."

Ora sat with Jeagan and Thurn in the *Basilisk's* hanger. The two of them were quietly playing some dice game she was unfamiliar with. The only time they spoke was when she peppered them with questions about the mission. After having verified everything was in order for about the twelfth time, she'd resolved to stop bothering them.

Instead, she studied the shuttle they were planning to use to extract their team in approximately three hours. They had called it a shuttle, but the damn thing looked more like a heavy-duty skiff. The sides of the craft had massive doors that retracted into the hull. Leather harnesses were bolted into the hull next to the door so the crew could strap in while still hanging out the sides. It would work for their intentions, but Ora would have preferred something a bit more robust.

While Markus, Siv, and Kadath were loaded into cargo containers and delving into the bowels of NeoGenix headquarters, Ora and the others would be stuck waiting. They couldn't risk approaching the building until the team was on their way up the shaft. Any loitering aircraft in the area would draw attention from the city's automated security forces.

The waiting drove her insane. She was so on edge she practically jumped out of her skin when her MoDAC vibrated. She touched her earpiece to pick up the call. "Yes?"

"Package is secure and en route," said Vallus.

"Good."

"Not necessarily. We might have a problem. Have you been watching the news?"

No. Should she have been? "What's the issue?"

"Cyrus just cleared his schedule for the day. He's in the building."

Shit! That meant…

"Affirmative," she replied. "We'll adapt accordingly. Keep me apprised." She ended the call.

Thurn was looking at her, having overheard the exchange. "Somethin' the matter?"

"You could say that. Cyrus just canceled his press conference and is reported to be in the NeoGenix building. That means his *security team* is still in the building."

The pair launched into muttered cursing. Ora snapped her fingers to get their attention. "It's too late to turn back now. Our team is already on its way down to the lab. We're just going to have to call an audible on this one."

Jeagan nodded. "You have something in mind?"

As a matter of fact, she did.

———

"Are ya really plannin' to just stare at the buildin' until ya see somethin' interestin'?" Aaliyah's tone made it obvious to Skye how she felt about *that* idea.

"No," Skye replied with exaggerated patience. "I'm going to stare at the building while Lexa tries to skim off any open-air communications that might tell us more about how to get inside."

"Oh, that's *way* more excitin'. Thanks for clarifyin'."

Eli shot her a sideways glance. "This was your idea, remember?"

"Kind of. I'd been expectin' a little more flyin' and a lot less sittin' around, though. Just give me a minute. Gotta work through the grievin' process, ya know?"

"Way to be a team player, Red." Skye brought her binoculars back to her eyes and resumed her vigil. "Lexa, got anything for us yet?"

The android's voice came over the general channel. "Negative. Although, the news is now saying that Cyrus Valadar has canceled his scheduled appearance at the Valkyrie Center. Based on the communications I've intercepted from the building, Cyrus is now scheduled to remain inside for the remainder of the day."

"So the king is in his castle," Eli mused, drawing his coat tighter around his neck.

"Seems like it," Skye agreed. This development was probably better for them. Word was that Cyrus spent most of his working days at NeoGenix. If they were going to hatch a plan for infiltration, they should do it while observing the heightened security his presence almost certainly guaranteed.

Something caught Skye's eye. "Eli, you seeing this? On the roof." A shuttle—a *large* shuttle—was setting down on top of the building. A squadron of workers and armed guards moved into position as the hatch on the vessel opened and a ramp extended.

"Looks like a supply shipment," Eli noted.

An area in the center of the roof suddenly lifted, exposing an elevator car onto which the workers began loading the cargo they carried off the ship. Skye spoke into her comms again. "Lexa, any chance that elevator goes all the way down to the labs?"

"Affirmative. The building's schematic shows the central elevator shaft as the only marked point of entry or exit to the sublevels."

Then that was their ticket in. "Copy that," Skye replied. "We'll continue to observe."

Aaliyah groaned. "What're ya lookin' for? We were lookin' for the way in, and now we've found it, right?"

Eli was patient in his response. "We should keep an eye out for how many shipments like this show up today, and what their procedure looks like for inspecting and loading the cargo. It's not enough to just get in, Aaliyah. We have to determine how we might get out."

"You don't think Vallus could have found us a bigger crate?" Markus grumbled. The collision of Kadath's elbow with his gut could have been accidental, but he was betting it was not.

"Sorry," the half-breed muttered, as he went back to staring out the one-way peephole they'd installed in the crate. "It appears we have stopped. Masks secure?"

Markus checked the seals on his gas mask for the hundredth time, whispering a quiet affirmative. Siv did likewise, though her shifting had maneuvered her elbow to jam uncomfortably into his back. Markus elected not to complain. Gods willing, they would only be in this crate for a few more minutes.

Everyone was silent for several tense seconds. Finally, Kadath whispered, "Lift is away. Releasing gas."

Here was the moment of truth. If the gas didn't deploy, then it was only a matter of time before the workers pried open their crate. Without their weapons, and in their compromised position, they'd be repackaged and sent to an interrogation room.

Markus needn't have worried. Shouts of alarm sounded briefly in the room outside before falling silent again. Kadath waited several more seconds before confirming, "All targets down. Time to stretch our legs."

He popped open the side of the crate, and the trio practically rolled out into the gray haze that was the room beyond. A dozen bodies in blue coveralls littered the ground, snoozing peacefully thanks to the smoke cocktail Kadath had cooked up.

To Markus's delight, he was able to breathe the filtered air just fine through his mask. He rose to his feet and went straight for the crate containing his weapons. That strangely naked feeling he'd been experiencing abated once his pistol was in his shoulder rig and his rifle was in his hands.

When he'd finished gearing up, Kadath passed him a strip of smoke grenades. "Here we go. It's room-to-room now."

"Sounds like a plan," Markus agreed, accepting the devices. He glanced at the twin doors on one side of the chamber. "Which way?"

"You two go left," Siv hissed. "I will circle around to the right."

"You're going alone?" Markus didn't like the idea of them splitting up.

Kadath chuckled. "She'll be fine. It's us I'm worried about. Come on. We're on the clock."

Progress from that point was steady, if not quick. Kadath and Markus took turns tossing the smoke grenades past each door they opened while the other person covered them with a rifle. Their attack was so quick, and the gas so effective, that they didn't have to fire a single bullet.

They didn't see Siv until they reached the fifth sub-level. The Hissak materialized out of the haze like a phantom with a suddenness that nearly startled Markus into shooting her. "All clear?" he asked.

"Up to this point, yes." She cast her eyes back to the lift. "However, there are still the other five levels below this, and we are running out of time."

Markus glanced at the timer on his wrist. She was right. They'd been down here for over an hour already. They had less than an hour left to secure the Heart and get it prepped for transport. "Ideas?"

"The Heart should be through there," she pointed at the only door they'd yet to clear on this level. "Leave the lower levels to me. You two, secure the package."

It was the best plan. Siv had been effective thus far on her own, and it was better to have two people securing the artifact. Markus nodded and sent her on her way.

He and Kadath approached the door. "You got this one?" Markus asked. With a nod, Kadath plucked one of the grenades from his belt and opened the door.

This room was more crowded than any they'd come across so far. The dozen people in white coats who littered the chamber—busily working at just as many computer terminals—turned collectively to see who was disturbing their work. One woman, a blonde with glasses and a sour expression managed an indignant, "What is the—" before the grenade clattered at her feet.

The now familiar haze hissed from the cylindrical object, rapidly filling the room. The woman in glasses coughed and spun to her right. She stumbled to a nearby console.

Shit. Markus didn't have to think hard about what she must have been reaching for. He sighted down his rifle, but one of the lab technicians stood in the way.

Gods, damn it. He wasn't going to mow down a bunch of lab geeks just doing their jobs. He surged forward, pushing the bystander out of the way. The stunned technician crumbled to the floor, the gas taking effect.

The woman in glasses was within arm's reach of the console. Her hand reached for a lever. Markus body-checked her to the side.

That was all it took. Whatever resolve the woman had left crumbled with her thwarted attempt at sounding the alarm. She was unconscious as soon as she hit the ground.

"Cutting it a little close, there," said Kadath.

"I had it under control." Markus scanned the room to make sure everyone else was out. Satisfied, he turned his attention to the pane of reinforced glass on the far side of the chamber.

Just beyond it, wrapped in a network of transparent tubing and glowing ominously with emerald light, was the prize they'd been searching for. They'd found the Heart of Thule.

CHAPTER 35

Terra-News-Net Now (TN3)

Headline: BREAKING—Valhalla Ends Contract with V-Transit

Story: In the wake of the abruptly canceled press conference from Valadar Holdings, Valhalla City Council has voted unanimously to end their contract with V-Transit (VTR-FRV, -36.6%) for three major mag-rail lines connecting the city to the rest of the continent. Council Chairman and Mayor of Valhalla, Tristan York, explained the decision following the meeting.

"Each of these lines was built by the NTA using tax-payer funds. It is in the best interest of the citizenry to have them managed by a company that's interested in making its service a priority. V-Transit has failed to demonstrate such a commitment and, consequently, the lines will be given to the care of another party."

That other party is Tyranus Rail (TRL-FRV, +60.1%), a company that is wholly owned by the Minor House Tyranus. This is the second consecutive defeat for Valadar Holdings at the hands of Tyranus' companies, making everyone on Sif wonder if they could be witnessing the dawn of the latest collective to call themselves one of the "Great" Houses.

Ora checked her MoDAC as soon as she stepped out of the autocar. Her team had been inside the building for just over thirty minutes. That left almost an hour and a half before they were extracted. She needed to make sure Cyrus didn't take any unexpected trips down to R&D in that timeframe.

She sauntered over to the receptionist in the lobby, plastering her best smile across her face. "Good afternoon. I'm here to see Mr. Valadar. Is he available?"

Though her phrasing should have been enough to answer the question, the receptionist asked, "Do you have an appointment?"

Ora forced a slight laugh. "Oh, no. Of course not. I was under the impression that Mr. Valadar would be at the Valkyrie Center right about now. I heard his schedule had been cleared for the day, and I was hoping that meant he could squeeze me in."

"I can't let you up to see Mr. Valadar without an appointment."

Of course you can't. "I understand. However, I would advise you to let Mr. Valadar know that Ora Monroe dropped by to see him. Otherwise, I could send him a text. I assure you, he will be quite upset if you don't relay the message."

It was a bluff, of course. No one had Cyrus's number. That said, she was hoping that name recognition and the scandalous rumors of the tabloids would be enough to sell her lie.

She wasn't disappointed. "One moment please." The receptionist typed something into her terminal. While she waited, Ora began to contemplate what she might try if Cyrus didn't accept the meeting. Did she have enough political capital to just waltz up there?

Blessedly, she never had to find out. The receptionist smiled up at her. "Mr. Valadar is available and has asked to see you. Please take the elevators to the left up to the top floor."

"Thank you, dear." Ora fought the urge to cheer as she made her way to the lift. Inside the elevator, she adjusted her top and mentally reviewed her strategy.

All she had to do was keep him occupied. If she could get him out of the building, that was a bonus. At the least, she needed to keep him talking. If Valadar's men made their way downstairs, this operation was a bust. No matter how good they were, three operatives couldn't hold off Valadar's detail—much less all the operatives that would be called in for reinforcements. Add in the fact that some of those operatives would be under Grey Wing's payroll and the whole thing would be a shit storm she didn't want on her conscience.

The lift chimed, and the doors opened to reveal the waiting room outside Cyrus's office. Molly was at her desk, as expected. Standing in the middle of an arrangement of furniture was Cyrus himself.

"Ms…" He caught himself. "Ora. What a pleasant surprise. I thought you said your schedule was full for today."

"I could say the same to you. My business in Valhalla concluded this morning, but I thought you would be at the Valkyrie Center this afternoon."

"Yes. Well, plans have changed."

"Obviously. You've made quite the stir with your schedule change. It's all the feeds can talk about."

Cyrus seemed perplexed. "Truly?"

"Absolutely. Haven't you heard? About the city council, I mean." Ora was glad of the fact that she happened to catch the story on TN3 in the cab she'd taken on her way here.

Cyrus's face betrayed more than he intended. "No, I hadn't heard. Molly, what…" He seemed to think better of his query. "Never mind. It's nothing that won't keep until later."

He started to say something else, but a figure emerged from the conference room. It was a Citza woman with long white hair and a tail to match. Her hair and flesh were a stark contrast with the black leathers that covered her entire body. Only a fool would mistake her for one of Cyrus's typical employees.

Cyrus must have noticed how the two made eye contact. "Ora Monroe, may I introduce Sydney Cross? She's a close associate of mine."

Ora extended her hand politely. "A pleasure to meet your acquaintance, Ms. Cross."

After a moment's hesitation, Sydney accepted the handshake. "Charmed, I'm sure." Turning her head over her shoulder, she said,

"I'll be in touch, Cyrus." Without waiting for a response, she walked to the elevator.

When Sydney had disappeared behind the lift's doors, Ora turned back to Cyrus. "I didn't mean to disturb you. Apologies if I'm intruding on something."

"Nonsense. Sydney was just leaving. Your timing is perfect." As he had before, Cyrus clasped her white-gloved hand and brought it to his lips. "Now, where did we leave off?"

Sydney was beyond irritated that her meeting with Cyrus had been cut short. Aside from the sheer fact that they'd been interrupted, *who* had interrupted them that frustrated her all the more. She didn't understand Cyrus's fascination with this Ora Monroe, but it was enough to make him drop everything on an evening he'd specifically cleared for research on that artifact.

Perhaps some of her frustration was due to her jealousy. Sydney had no delusions regarding her place in Cyrus's life. Their relationship was neither loving nor monogamous. Still, she liked to feel she was important to him. Scenes like the one she'd just borne witness to made her feel anything but.

When she stepped off the lift and into the lobby, she suddenly realized that she had left her bag in Cyrus's waiting area. She'd been so focused on portraying confidence in her exit, she'd forgotten her stealth suit behind his receptionists' desk.

She paused for a moment, considering what to do. She could certainly just leave the bag behind. No one would disturb it, and she could retrieve it tomorrow. Then again, she didn't like having any of her assets left to someone else's care.

Frag it. She stepped back onto the lift and stabbed the button to bring her back to the top floor. After an obscenely long series of stops and starts, she finally made it back to Cyrus's waiting room.

Molly seemed a little surprised by her sudden reappearance. "Hi Sydney," she chimed. The look on her face made it clear that she was hoping she wouldn't be asking to interrupt their mutual employer.

"Relax," Sydney said. "I'm just here because I left my bag. You still have it behind the desk?"

"Oh!" Molly's relief was painfully obvious. "Yes. Yes, of course. I've got it right here." She bent down to fish out the backpack from under the desk.

Sydney accepted the bag with sincere thanks. "Sorry to give you a heart attack. No one wants to interrupt Cyrus when he's doing his *thing*." She accompanied the statement with an exaggerated eye-roll.

Molly gave a nervous laugh. "That's the truth." Suddenly she stopped as another thought struck her. "Damn it. I forgot that he had a meeting with Blackwell scheduled in ten minutes. Lucretia has direct access to his office. She's bound to interrupt."

Yes, and wouldn't that *be awkward for all parties involved.* Sydney sighed. "Don't worry about it, Molly. I'll stop by the lab on my way out. I have clearance. I'll let Lucretia know that Cyrus's latest conquest is getting in the way of her scheduled meeting."

"Oh gods… thank you." Molly's smile was genuine. "I wasn't looking forward to that particular rant this afternoon."

Yes, Lucretia would have given Molly an earful. Hopefully, the woman was smarter than to try the same stunt with Sydney. "Don't mention it." The Citza gave her a friendly wave. "Take care, Molly. I'll see you tomorrow."

Back in the elevator, Sydney swiped the badge she'd lifted off one of the lab techs earlier in the week and hit the button for the fifth sublevel. No one must have reported the missing credentials, because the badge continued to function days after it had gone missing. She supposed she couldn't blame someone for trying to cover their ass.

With a priority access code registering in its system, the lift didn't stop at any other floors on the way down. A few seconds later, the door chimed and slid open.

Sydney coughed as a gray haze seeped through the open doors. Not trusting the gas that filled the elevator, she held her breath and reached into her bag. The stealth mask had a filter that should be able to stop any harmful effects of the gas. What had Lucretia and her minions done now?

Securing her mask and stepping out into the sublevel, Sydney quickly realized this wasn't the work of Cyrus's science team after all. The pair of security guards that should have been guarding the lift snoozed peacefully on the floor. Next to them was a small metal cylinder—likely the source of the gas permeating the sublevel.

As inconceivable as the idea felt, the facts were hard to argue with. Someone was assaulting the NeoGenix laboratories.

Sydney scanned the wall and found what she was looking for. Without hesitation, she sprinted across the hall and slammed her fist down on the emergency alert trigger.

CHAPTER 36

Terra-News-Net Now (TN3)

Headline: BREAKING—Valhalla's Automated Security Forces Converging on NeoGenix HQ

Story: Reporters on the scene near the NeoGenix (NGX-FRV, -0.02%) Headquarters in downtown Valhalla are reporting that the city's Automated Security Response has deployed drones to that location. Sources within ASR are reporting that the mobilization is in response to an internal alarm triggered at that location. The situation is continuing to develop. TN3 has reached out to NeoGenix and Valadar Holdings for comment.

The scene playing out through Skye's binoculars went from utterly mundane to insanity-level confusion in a matter of seconds. "Um, Lexa, are you seeing what I'm seeing?"

One side of the building had become a flurry of activity. Automated drones buzzed in a complicated, synchronized sweep around the structure, and people fled from the area in droves. Armored vehicles began to converge on the area, blocking off all roads and skyways leading to the tower.

The android's voice sounded distant, almost distracted. "Yes, the feed from your equipment is coming through. I'm attempting to position some of my drones in that area. One moment please."

Eli watched the scene in stunned silence. "What do you think happened?"

Aaliyah's interest had suddenly been piqued. "What's goin' on?"

"It's Automated Security Response," said Eli. "As far as what triggered it, we won't know that until Lexa feeds us that information. She's sending her drones in now."

Aaliyah snagged a pair of binoculars and brought them to her eyes. "Yeah? She's sendin' her drones into *that* shit storm? Am I the only one who thinks that's a bad idea? ASR is gonna ping them for sure."

Shit. Aaliyah was right. Skye hadn't considered that possibility, but that was why she left things like op sec to the rest of her team.

Lexa must have been listening in on their chatter because she was quick to defend herself. "There is no need to be concerned. The drone fleet is broadcasting an IFF signal on a weakly encrypted channel. I've already isolated the signal and routed it through our drones. Automated Security Response will not see anything out of the ordinary."

"Nice work," Skye muttered. That was some next-level hacking. She doubted even Dan would have been able to pull that trick off on such short notice. Poor kid was probably fuming with jealousy right now.

The android wasn't done showing off either. A second later she came back with the intel they needed. "The drones are responding to an alarm triggered inside the first sublevel of the NeoGenix building ten minutes ago. Currently, their orders are to secure the perimeter and prevent anyone from entering or leaving the building. The assembled force represents only the automated portion of the response. Police forces are inbound and are expected to arrive in thirteen minutes, seventeen seconds."

"The sublevel?" Skye looked to Eli. "That means they're in the lab. You don't think that…?"

"Yes, I do. It's too great a coincidence. Someone must be making an attempt on the artifact."

Aaliyah scoffed. "Sucks to be them, then. With ASR on the scene, there ain't no way in the nine hells they're gettin' that rock out now."

"Don't be so sure," Eli scolded. "Last time we were on Valhalla, we incorporated the automated response into our plans. These would-be thieves may have done the same thing."

"Then we have to get over there!" Skye exclaimed. "If we lose the Heart now, we may never get another shot!"

Aaliyah didn't bother to hide her skepticism. "That may be, Blondie—but ya may have noticed that the scene is swarmin' with city security. Even if we wanted to get over there, ain't no way we're gettin' through all them bots."

Skye wasn't giving up that easily. "No, there *is* a way. We just watched someone use it a little over an hour ago. We just have to get to the roof, then we can take that lift all the way down to the lab."

"And *how*, exactly, are we supposed to get to said roof? I'm assumin' you're talkin' about the one surrounded by a cloud of drones right now."

"We don't need to worry about the bots! Lexa has their IFF codes. She can cloak the ship the same way as she did her drones."

"And if someone looks up and says, 'Gee, that shuttle doesn't look like ASR to me,' then what?"

"No one's there to see us! Valhalla police won't be here for at least ten minutes, and the drones have created a perimeter for us. If Lexa can get us through, no one is going to look at us twice." No one, at least, if they got their asses in gear before the sapient police forces showed up.

The urgency of the situation must have been clear to Eli because he made the call. "Skye's right. We may never get another chance like this. Let's get over there. Lexa, can you fake an IFF signal for the shuttle?"

"Yes, Captain."

Skye was grinning from ear to ear. "You heard the man, Red. Fire this bird up!"

Aaliyah looked seriously stressed as she slid into the pilot's chair. "Y'all are fraggin' crazy, ya know that? Absolutely, certifiably, fraggin' crazy."

"Oh, come on. Weren't you just saying you wanted some action?"

"I never said that!" she protested as she initiated the launch sequence. "I *never* said that!"

Ora preferred wine, but that didn't mean she wasn't versatile. There wasn't a kind of alcohol she wouldn't drink, or a drug she wouldn't take, provided she deemed it necessary. As Cyrus poured her two fingers of whiskey, she definitely deemed this to be one time where drinking something outside of her typical tastes was necessary.

Fortunately, she knew enough about whiskey that she could feign appreciation. It didn't hurt that the variety Cyrus was serving was very good, not to mention very expensive. "Excellent," she said after sipping from her glass. "Black Forest? Imported from Hades?"

"You know your liquor," Cyrus conceded with a grin.

"And my trade agreements. Black Forest only sells in the Helion System and has strict prohibitions on redistribution. It's part of the Hellenic Tourism initiative, and they're paid a lot of money by the NTA to enforce such agreements."

"Then we best not let them find out I have any." He clinked his glass against hers. "Cheers." They drank together and he settled into one of the padded armchairs. "Rumor has it I'm not the only one who can get my hands on embargoed liquor, Ora. Your clubs have something of a reputation for having hard-to-locate beverages."

"I don't know what you mean," Ora said, feigning surprise. "Everything available at my establishments is either widely traded or locally sourced and licensed."

"Indeed, and that's a very nice touch you add to your work. You're not the first to re-brand embargoed food goods, but I must admit that I've never seen anyone do it with quite as much style."

"Then you've seen my ads."

"Yes. And your magazine spreads."

Ora had no idea why men always thought bringing that up was a good pick-up line. She had done dozens of shoots and interviews with media outlets over the years. Somehow, she didn't think Cyrus was referring to her recent work with *Empress*.

"And what about *you?*" she asked. "If you take all the coverage of me and my brands, it's still only a fraction of the press you receive."

"A hazard of the position, as you know."

"Yes, well, I'm particularly excited to read your coverage in *ConneXion* next month. Apparently, you're assembling a harem."

Cyrus laughed. "Oh, that again? I thought those rumors all burnt out last cycle."

"Oh, no. Your eligibility is still quite a hot topic. It's supposed to be quite the list."

"Is that so? Did you make it?"

Ora smiled suggestively into her glass. "Does it matter? We all know you can't believe *everything* these rags print."

"True enough." Cyrus opened his mouth to say something else but was interrupted by the sound of his office bursting open. Three black-clad Terran men, all armed to the teeth, stormed in.

Their apparent leader, a man with olive skin, a shaved head, and a nasty scar over his left eye, spoke first. "Mr. Valadar, an alarm has been triggered in the building. We are here to escort you to the saferoom."

Cyrus stood, his expression wavering somewhere between alarm and indignation. "What are you talking about?"

"Standard protocol, sir. It's written into the corporate bylaws. I apologize, sir, but I must insist."

Ora felt her heart racing. Though there was more than one reason an alarm might have been triggered, she knew the most likely cause. She couldn't give anything away. She needed to calculate her response.

"Is something the matter, Cyrus? Should I—"

"No, no, no." He held a staying hand to emphasize the point. "I'm sure this is all just a big misunderstanding."

The soldier in front of them obviously didn't think so. "That may be, sir, but that doesn't change my obligation. I need you to come with me. Now."

Now Cyrus was angry. "I might reconsider your tone, Mr…"

"Farris."

"Farris. I don't know who you report to, but I guarantee you that they, or one of their superiors, reports to me."

"That may be, *sir*." The man's tone conveyed his obvious frustration. "That still does not change my obligation. I must insist."

Ora was beginning to wonder if the man would resort to carrying Cyrus from the room. With determination like that, she was beginning to think that this Mr. Farris would do whatever it took to get Cyrus into his saferoom, regardless of the consequences.

Cyrus must have come to that conclusion as well. "Fine. I'll come with you. Ms. Monroe will be coming with us."

"No, sir," Farris shook his head for emphasis. "Only you. We can't be certain whether she is part of the security breach. No offense, ma'am."

"None taken," Ora replied. "Cyrus, should I go?"

Cyrus shook his head. "No, that's not necessary. I'm sure this will be resolved momentarily."

"No one is allowed off-premises, ma'am," Farris added. "It would be best if you just waited here."

Just like that they went from "mission accomplished" to "we're fragged." The alarm blared throughout every speaker in the laboratory. The lighting went from sterile white to pulsing crimson.

Worst of all, a metal blast door slammed down to reinforce the one access point to the room that held the Heart of Thule.

"Gods damn it!" Markus roared, pounding his fist against the door. "What in the nine hells just happened?"

"Someone triggered an alarm," Kadath drawled. "Obviously."

"Thanks. How do we get in now?"

"Move." He shouldered Markus aside and pulled something from his belt—a plasma cutter. Carefully, he fired up the torch and pressed the glowing blue tip to the blast door. Though the metal began to melt away under the torch's flame, it did so slowly. That cut was going to take forever, and if an alarm had been triggered, time was something they had very little of.

Markus scanned the room. The throbbing crimson warning lights played off the lingering haze of the gas, rendering the room into a technological hellscape. Even the artifact had gone dark, though Markus could still see the glimmer of the crystal through the other side of the viewing window.

That's it...

He took a few steps back so he was in the center of the room and brought up his rifle. Some kind of sixth sense must have warned Kadath what Markus was about to attempt, because the half-breed managed a shouted, "*No!*" just as Markus pulled the trigger.

The bullets didn't penetrate the window. They didn't even make a dent. They *did*, however, manage to ricochet dangerously all around the little laboratory. Both Markus and Kadath were glad for their static shields because the quick flares of light and energy around their bodies said they'd come dangerously close to picking up one of the bullets on the rebound.

"Are you *quite* done?" Kadath roared.

"Sorry. I thought it was worth a shot." The pun was obviously unintended. "How did you know the window wouldn't break?"

"Because the blast door only covered the entrance. Evidently, the window didn't need reinforcements."

In hindsight, that made sense. Markus had just been hoping it was an oversight by the designers. "Sorry," he repeated. "I'll… uh… I'll watch the door."

For several minutes, nothing else happened. The alarm continued to echo throughout the complex, the emergency lighting pulsing to its beat. The only thing that changed was the slight variation in the hiss of the plasma torch as Kadath continued to cut his way through the blast door.

Then something appeared. In the lingering haze and poor lighting, Markus first mistook it for a shadow. Then it slowly took shape, the shape of a woman. Mistaking it for Siv, Markus lowered the barrel of his rifle.

Only to snap it back up when his mistake became apparent. Though the figure was clad in black leather, she was curvier than their Hissak companion. She also had no cloak, and a fluffy tail swayed casually behind her as she walked. What was a Citza doing here?

"Easy there," Markus cautioned. "Hands where I can see them. Cooperate, and no one has to get hurt."

She complied with the request, raising her hands and placing them on the back of her head. Even so, she did it in a way that betrayed not the least bit of apprehension. In fact, she laughed.

Her voice was calm and smooth—almost sultry. "Excuse me, gentlemen, but I don't think you should be here."

CHAPTER 37

Terra-News-Net Now (TN3)

Headline: BREAKING—Incident at NeoGenix Billed as a Training Exercise

Story: Valadar Holding's CFO Julia Valadar has assured everyone that the current activity as NeoGenix (NGX-FRV, -1.2%) is nothing more than a training exercise and that the appropriate notices have been filed with the Valhalla authorities. "We periodically test the efficacy of our alert system and work with Automated Security Response to improve upon its execution. NeoGenix extends its sincerest apologies to anyone who was unduly disturbed by the training exercise."

Despite Valadar's assertions, TN3 has yet to locate any records indicating previous drills of this type. Valhalla Police Department and the ASR division have yet to respond to requests for comment.

Skye pulled on her helmet as Aaliyah shouted, "Thirty seconds!" Squeezing her shoulders to relieve the building tension, Skye slipped the rifle strap over her shoulder. She preferred handguns, but they had no idea what they were walking into.

She tapped a button on the side of her helmet to patch into the comms channel. Eli's voice came through over the speaker. "Good to go?"

"You know it," she replied, holding up her thumb for emphasis. It had been a while since she'd seen combat, and a part of her was itching for it. Then again, she wouldn't complain if they manage to snag the artifact without firing a shot.

Aaliyah's voice came in over the comms. "Y'all are crazy, ya know that? Really fraggin' crazy."

Through the helmet, Skye couldn't tell whether Eli had rolled his eyes, but his voice sounded like he had. "Maintain a low profile. We'll signal when we're ready for pick up."

"Copy that."

The top of the building zoomed up to meet them. Aaliyah hovered the shuttle just over the roof. When the craft held steady, Skye and Eli jumped to the surface, making straight for the console that summoned the lift. The shuttle was gone before they even hit the call button.

"Picking up any psionic activity?" Skye asked. She figured that if the Heart was active, Eli should feel it.

She was thrilled when he issued a curt, "No." Even though she had no idea what this thing did, she didn't want to find out in the middle of an op they'd taken on an impulse.

The lift appeared, and the pair hastily boarded. When Skye jabbed the button for the first sublevel, a red alert appeared on the display: [ACCESS DENIED.]

"Lexa?" Skye didn't bother to hide the anxiety in her voice.

"Are there any access ports?" the android asked.

None that Skye could see, at least not on top of the console. She felt along the sides, and her gloved hand came into contact with an irregularity in the surface. "Think I might have something." She leaned over to get a better view, knowing that Lexa was monitoring the feed from her helmet.

"I see it. That port should accept a standard data card. I've loaded the program you will need onto your mobile device. Please remove the system card from your device and insert it into the port."

Skye did as she asked, careful not to damage the paper-thin card as she handled it with her gloved hands. Almost as soon as she inserted the chip into the slot, the screen changed. [DESTINATION: SL01.]

"That did it!" Skye exclaimed.

"Excellent. You should now be able to retrieve your data card. I have assumed control over the lift, so you will not need to worry about finding a way out." The card ejected from the port, and Skye slotted it back into her MoDAC. Damn, why hadn't they thought of acquiring a synth before this?

The elevator car descended. "Are you ready for this?" Eli asked.

"Damn right I am!" Skye shot him a smile, even knowing he couldn't see it through the helmet. "Let's get this rock."

Two of them. Just two men had caused this whole mess. How delightful. It had been too long since Sydney had experienced a proper challenge. She'd been getting antsy.

Still, she should probably try to take at least one of them alive. Cyrus would want to find out who they were working for. "I tell you what," she drawled. "How about you lay down your weapons and get on your knees. That way, you can both walk out of here with your lives."

To his credit, the one with the rifle didn't gloat. Instead, he tightened his position and the dot of a laser sight appeared on her chest. "I don't think so."

Oh well. She had tried.

With a twist of her wrists, two smoke capsules popped into her palms. She crushed them in her hands as she flipped back through the door.

The rifleman fired but failed to hit her spinning form as the smoke filled the space between them. She slid twin daggers into her hands. When the gunfire stopped, she sped toward him, as silent as the night.

He didn't spot her until she was already within striking distance. The butt of his rifle swung for her head, but she ducked.

Her off-hand slashed across his stomach, scoring a hit. The pads of his armor were all that kept him from being disemboweled.

She slashed upward with her other blade. The rifle blocked the dagger, but the momentum of the strike sent him stumbling a half-step backward.

Sydney followed with a quick kick to his knee. He twisted at the last second to avoid making it a crippling blow, but it still brought him to the floor. A follow-up kick across his jaw ended the bout.

Verdict: *Disappointing.*

There was no room for taunting, however. The other man had entered the fray, and he was not playing games. He flashed twin blades in her direction, appearing as a whirlwind of silver in the hazy chamber.

Sydney backpedaled, running up against a console and rolling across its length. Her opponents stabbed down where her head had been seconds earlier, sending up a fountain of sparks.

A nice assault. He'd caught her off-balance, but he wouldn't be so lucky a second time.

She dashed right, launching herself up to the far wall. Her feet made contact and she launched herself at her opponent. She closed the gap too quickly for him to bring up his swords.

He abandoned the weapons, pulling up his forearm just in time to block a snap kick from colliding against his skull. He tumbled with the force of the blow, and both combatants rolled across the ground.

When he rose, he was holding a shorter, thicker blade which he employed with no shortage of expertise. The short sword flashed dangerously, again and again, coming within a hair's breadth of Sydney's face.

Then she saw her opening. She attacked the wrist holding his weapon, drawing her dagger deep across his flesh. With a cry, the man released the blade, which tumbled to the floor. Though he managed to dodge the next dagger-strike, he couldn't out-pace her spinning kicks. Two, three, four blows later, he was down.

Damn—she hadn't even needed to kill one of them. What fun was that?

A dark shape blurred at the edge of Sydney's vision. She pivoted just in time to avoid certain death, but the shadowy figure wasn't done. The figure's elbow smashed painfully against her face, followed up by a flurry of blows that would have done any Ghenza proud.

Sydney managed to disengage, and both figures skidded to a stop mere meters apart. She could discern nothing from this new fighter, whose black cloak and armor covered every inch of their figure. Were they part of the same party as the other two? Or some other opportunist, perhaps?

It didn't matter. Sydney would have the answers soon enough. Answers, or their blood. Either was fine with her.

Each passing second frayed Ora's nerves. What was going on? Was Markus okay? Did they have the artifact? Or did Cyrus's men already have them in custody?

Ora hated unanswerable questions. She spent a lot of money on answers for that very reason. Unfortunately, there weren't enough krets this side of Terra to buy her what she needed to know. In lieu of buying a solution, she was going to have to act.

She knew it was a risk to open communications, but she couldn't stand the waiting anymore. Her finger touched her earpiece. "Thurn?"

The cyborg's voice sounded in her ear. "Ya shouldn' be contactin' me."

"I trust you to keep the connection secure. I need to know what's going on down there."

"Yer as blind as Ah am. Ain't no signal traffic down there. Whole fraggin' thing's a black hole."

Not surprising, but still disappointing. If Cyrus had them already, how could she get them out? Was this something she could take on by virtue of their securities contract?

No. There was no way that Cyrus was going to hand over a crew trying to steal the Heart of Thule. More likely he would have questions for her about how they had managed to get past the building's outer security.

Regardless, this wasn't what she needed to focus on. She couldn't know whether Cyrus had apprehended her team. Not yet, at least.

Not without going down there herself.

She glanced around the room. "Any idea where Cyrus's private lift might be?" There weren't any obvious passages, which meant the entrance was probably obscured.

"Ora, Ah ain't the guy t' tell ya what t' do, but Ah—"

"Then don't. Tell me where to look, or I'll start searching myself."

The Orchallen's pause was mercifully brief. "Back corner, to the left of the window."

Ora looked to where he directed. She saw a shelf not so different from the liquor cabinet to its right. She felt around, looking for some kind of switch.

Though she found what she was looking for in short order, it offered little in the way of a solution. Whatever hidden passage lay behind this shelf was protected by a hand-scanner. She reported this to Thurn. "Any ideas?"

"Put yer MoDAC on the scanner an' give me a minute."

Ora did as instructed. The process, praise the gods, took far less than a minute. The shelf sank into the wall and slid into a hidden compartment to reveal the secret lift.

In a last moment of hesitation, Ora glanced over her shoulder. She was gambling with this one. If Cyrus came back and she wasn't here, how was she going to explain that away?

There was no time for hesitation. Now was the time for action. She slid into the lift, performed Thurn's trick with the MoDAC again, and pressed the button for the first sublevel.

As she descended, she pulled an object from a hidden pocket in the back of her top. The flimsy re-breather wouldn't last long, but time was already against her here. Whatever she was going to do, she was going to have to do it quickly.

She pressed the mask up against her nose and mouth. The thing adhered readily to her skin, and she began to breathe normally through the device. Good—one less problem she had to worry about.

Now, on to bigger challenges.

CHAPTER 38

Terra-News-Net Now (TN3)

Headline: BREAKING—Valhalla Officials Confirm Activity Near NeoGenix is a Training Exercise

Story: Valhalla's officials have corroborated the statement issued earlier today by Julia Valadar, stating that the ASR response at NeoGenix (NGX-FRV, +0.5%) is only a training exercise. Councilor Damian Felch insisted that all filings for the exercise had been made appropriately, though there appears to have been an error in the process of notifying other residents in the area. Felch stated that he will personally lead the investigation to discover what went wrong in the city's notification procedure.

When challenged on his assertions, Felch doubled down on the fact that the appropriate filings are in the city's public data system. "Just read the report," he asserted. "Everything you need to know is there." Interested citizens, however, may have to wait to take him up on his challenge. As of an hour ago, all queries related to publicly available filings are temporarily unavailable as the system is currently undergoing maintenance.

The world began to fuzz back into place. The pounding in his head and the soreness in his jaw made Markus feel distinctly like he'd just been kicked in the face.

Oh yeah…

On a positive note, he wasn't dead yet, or at least he didn't feel like it. It also looked like he was still where he'd fallen. So where was his assailant?

Kadath lay sprawled out a few meters away from him and was just beginning to stir. It looked like he'd been no more successful in taking on the Citza woman than Markus had been.

That was when the sound of battle reached his ears. Markus turned to see a pair of dark figures darting in and out of the smoky haze. One of them had to be his assailant. That meant the other form must be...

"Siv!" Markus struggled to his feet.

"She's fine," Kadath groaned, rolling over. "I imagine she's made it a damn spot longer than either of us did. We need to focus on the prize."

He was right. Markus was only going to get in the way if he returned to the fray. "Where's the plasma torch?"

"By the blast door." Kadath tried to push himself into a sitting position before slumping back down. "I'm going to need a minute."

Markus could have used a minute too, but they were running short on minutes. He stumbled over to the blast door, grabbed the torch, and started cutting.

"Holy shit!" Skye whispered. "They've knocked out the whole floor."

"So it seems," Eli agreed. He didn't share Skye's enthusiasm at how well the invading force had handled Valadar's security detail. At least he and Skye had been fortunate enough to keep their helmets on, as the knock-out gas still hung in lazy tendrils all over the sublevel.

Skye shone the light of her rifle on a nearby stairway. "Thoughts?"

"That way is as good as any." They'd covered the whole sublevel by now with no sign of the artifact. The Heart had to be deeper in the complex. "Move out."

Hastily, but meticulously, they cleared every room on the second sublevel. It was more of the same with the eerie haze—made more ominous by the red emergency lighting—and unconscious bodies littering the floor. Still no sign of the Heart of Thule. Though they met no resistance, the situation was making Eli increasingly uneasy.

At the next set of stairs, he closed his eyes and sent a message to Aaliyah. <No sign of the artifact. What's your status?>

<Kinda shitty,> she replied, <It's not just drones anymore. Police just showed up. Y'all are runnin' out of time.>

That was what he was afraid of. He relayed the bad news to Skye. "Do we need to turn back?" she asked.

Eli's hesitation was brief. "No. This could be our best shot. We press forward. Let's pick up the pace."

They moved through the third sublevel quickly and went even faster through the fourth. Still no sign of the artifact. It wasn't until they were at the bottom of the stairs leading to the fifth sublevel that they got their first break in routine.

The sounds of a struggle were audible in the hallway, though they couldn't make out the sounds of the combatants. For some reason, the smoke was thicker here, totally obscuring their vision just a short way down the passage.

"I think we've found what we were looking for," Skye noted.

"Indeed." Eli checked his magazine. "Shoot to wound unless they fire on us first. No need to—" The sound of a cocked pistol cut off his instructions.

"Easy there," cooed a voice just over his shoulder. The pistol pressed firmly against the base of his skull, right underneath the protective covering of his helmet. "Don't try anything foolish, now. Either of you. I'm going to need the both of you to stand down."

Damn it. How had someone managed to sneak up on them?

Even in light of the clear and present danger, something nagged at the back of his mind. The voice was feminine and sounded more than passingly familiar. Where had he heard it before?

It was Skye who placed it first. "*Ora?*"

Though it shouldn't have necessarily surprised her, Ora hadn't expected anyone to recognize her—especially just based on her voice. "You have me at a disadvantage. Do I know you?"

"It's Eli, ma'am. Eli Ren'Dahl."

"*Eli?*" She didn't bother to hide her surprise. "What in the nine hells are you doing here?"

"I might ask you the same question, ma'am, though I suggest we save this conversation for later."

He wasn't wrong, but Ora decided to make an educated guess. "You're after the Heart of Thule."

The Sahaia stiffened as surely as he had when she'd first pulled her gun on him. "How do you know about the artifact?" he asked.

She let out a soft laugh, stowing her weapon. "As you suggested, we'll discuss this later. For now, it is enough to know that our interests are aligned. Though, I would request that you and your companion here adjust your tactics. We have friendlies in there—at least three of them." Ora was putting a lot of faith in the Sahaia. Mostly, she was hoping that they weren't on contract for a faction that would provide her with a problem.

Eli nodded. "Understood." To his credit, he didn't attack her, and he didn't ask questions. He slung his rifle over his back to free up his hands. Then he began to channel.

Normally one couldn't see the way a telekin worked their craft. The haze of gas and smoke, however, created a unique opportunity.

Ripples appeared in the air, emanating from Eli's outstretched hands. They shot forward, winding like snakes toward the shadows of the entangled combatants.

A vibrating tendril of force seized each of them, freezing them mid-strike. With his prey captured, Eli sent rippled of energy outward, clearing the fog so they could lay eyes on the fighters.

Ora pointed to the figure on the right. "She's with us."

In acknowledgment, Eli released Siv and hurled the other figure against the far wall. The Citza woman hit the metal plate with a loud crack and crumpled to the floor.

As a fleeting thought, Ora considered walking over and putting a bullet in the woman's head but decided against it. She was out of the fight for today. No sense in fruitless bloodshed. Ora pushed past Eli and made for the chamber beyond.

Kadath was crouched, ready to shoot the first person to walk through that door—at least until he saw Ora. "Boss?"

There was no time for pleasantries. "Status?" she asked.

The half-breed mercenary lowered his weapon, casting nothing more than a suspicious glance at the two helmeted figures that flanked her. "The alarm deployed a blast door. We're cutting through it now,"—He waved a hand at where Markus was working behind him.—"but it's going to be a bit."

"You're out of time," said Eli. "Valhalla City Police have converged on the building. They're preparing to enter as we speak."

The Sahaia's voice caught Markus's attention. He stopped cutting and turned to face them. "Eli? What the frag…?"

"Later, Markus," Ora interjected. "The blast door—can we force it open?"

Markus kicked the armored panel, more out of frustration than any honest attempt to force it open. "No. It's too fragging thick. Going to take at least an hour to finish cutting it open. It's a bust."

Eli wasn't ready to give up so easily. "Would you mind if I try?"

Ora didn't bother to reciprocate his polite tone. "Yes, by all means."

Markus's posture looked as if he wanted to argue, or at least ask some more questions. Whatever protests he'd been preparing were quickly discarded, and he stepped aside.

Eli extended both hands toward the blast door. The same vibrational lines Ora had seen earlier surged toward the metal plating, which had been scarred with a jagged L-shaped cut. On contact, the Sahaia's power went to work.

It was hard to tell exactly what the Sahaia was attempting, but it seemed like he was trying to force the metal to bend by pounding it on the edge of the cut. When that failed, he shifted the position of his hands, causing the haze surrounding the door to rush back toward him.

He shifted tactics again. Then again. The blast door shuddered. The wall itself quaked, as though he might tear the whole thing down. At length, the entire room seemed to vibrate.

Seconds passed. Then minutes. Finally, Eli relented, gasping for breath and sinking to his knees. "I'm sorry," he panted. "I… I can't…"

Damn it. That was it then. If the Sahaia's power couldn't force the door open, nothing the rest of them could muster was going to fare any better.

They had failed.

CHAPTER 39

Terra-News-Net Now (TN3)

Headline: BREAKING—Valhalla Police Have Entered NeoGenix HQ

Story: "I don't know what constitutes a typical training exercise, but I'm pretty sure this isn't it." This remark from Valhalla Mayor and Council Chairman Tristan York comes as Valhalla Police breach the front doors of the NeoGenix (NGX-FRV, +0.1%) building. Onlookers to the incident could be forgiven for mistaking it for an actual emergency.

ARS drones continue to patrol the surrounding streets, and sniper teams have been deployed to nearby rooftops (though it should be noted that relatively few of the structure's neighboring buildings have line-of-sight to NeoGenix's roof). TN3 will be standing by to report on future developments.

The shock of it all was beyond discouraging. They had been *so* close to securing the objective. Then, out of nowhere, that alarm was tripped, and somehow Skye and Eli showed up. Was it coincidence, or just incredibly poor timing?

Markus supposed the answers to such questions didn't change their predicament. They needed to focus on what to do next. "So, what's our Plan B? We can't just leave it here."

Eli turned to face him. "What are you suggesting?"

"I don't know. Can't we blow it up or something?"

"We can't even destroy this barrier, much less the artifact."

The Sahaia's tone caused something to well up inside Markus. The hostile words that came to his lips were silenced as Ora cut in. "No, we can't destroy the artifact, but maybe we can do the next best thing."

She walked over to a nearby console. Despite all the chaos that had occurred in the room, the terminal was somehow still running. She touched her earpiece. "Thurn? Can you access this terminal through my MoDAC?"

Whatever reply the Orchallen gave her wasn't reported on the general channel. Her earpiece must have established a secure connection.

As they continued their private conversation, Skye cocked her head. "Who's Thurn?"

Markus decided it would be petulant not to answer. "He's our Daniel—except bigger. Lots bigger. He's Orchallen, actually."

"An orc who can hack?"

"That's what I thought, too. But yeah—and he's damn good at it."

As if to emphasize the point, Ora laid her MoDAC on the surface of the terminal. Both devices lit up for a brief second before going dark again. "There!" she said. "Thurn's going to wipe their system. Any data they have on the Heart of Thule will be gone. That will at least buy us some time."

"Nice trick," said Markus. "How's he going to manage that one?"

"By doing the same thing that got me down here. He reverse-engineered the process Cyrus used to port files from my mobile to his conference room display system. It turns out that everything here uses a common protocol." She held up her hands as if to stave off further questioning. "We can discuss the details later. Right now, we need to find a way to get you out of here. Thurn said he can't get the shuttle in here with all the drone pressure. We need an alternate strategy."

"I may have a solution," said Eli. "We were able to match the IFF signal for the drones and pair it to our shuttle. We can extract your team."

The logical question would have been, "How did you manage that?" Markus, however, had a pretty good feeling that it had to do with a certain AI that was likely still working with their team. That AI was one Markus owed a favor to, and Lexa wouldn't appreciate him outing her to a group of people she wasn't sure she could trust yet.

Ora, fortunately, was too glad for the option to question it further. "Perfect. My team will go with you." She glanced at each of them: Kadath, Siv, and finally, Markus. "That works for you?"

She may have addressed the question to all of them, but Markus knew it was intended for him. "That works," he replied.

"Good. Now, get going."

"That sounds like you aren't coming with us," Kadath noted.

"I'm not. I have an appointment to keep." In a sudden moment of tenderness, she grabbed Markus's gloved hand. As she tightened her grip, her eyes met his—quite a trick through the reflective faceplate of his helmet. "I'll be in touch soon."

She may have wanted to say more, but now was not the time or the place. Instead, she turned and disappeared down the corridor.

Skye cleared her throat. "Well, then. Should we get going?"

"Yeah," Markus agreed. "Let's go."

Neither Siv nor Kadath said anything until they reached the lift. Once inside, the latter whispered in Markus's ear. "Ora had a second team on the job?"

"No. They're my old crew. Ora has them on retainer the same as you. I think it's just a weird coincidence that has us all here at the same time."

"Or a dangerous one," Eli interjected. "I didn't know Ora was after the artifact. How did she find out about it?"

Markus started to ignore the question but decided he was being childish. "Rico Chronos—right before he was assassinated. You?"

"My coven has been monitoring it for some time now. We were asked to retrieve it when negotiations broke down."

So, the Sahaia wanted the Heart for themselves. That was going to be an interesting bit of negotiating, assuming they all made it out of her with their skins intact.

"Ten seconds," Skye shouted in warning.

Though it was hard to tell through the helmet, Eli seemed to space out for a second. It was the kind of posture he got whenever he communicated with Aaliyah. "Shuttle's almost here. We'll be cutting it close."

Kadath and Siv exchanged a nervous look. "Don't worry," said Markus. "That's pretty much how all of our extractions used to go."

The lift beeped as they emerged onto the roof. All around them, the nine hells were breaking loose.

Drones buzzed like angry hornets in arching swarms all around the rooftop. Manned aircraft hung in the periphery, and teams of men in black fatigues lined the neighboring rooftops. Every fragging bot, soldier, and police officer opened fire on their position as soon as they emerged.

Eli threw up his hands, creating a protective bubble around them. "Go," he grunted.

Before anyone could ask, "Where?" another object caught their attention. It was the shuttle, swooping in low with its hatch already open.

Markus had never been so glad to see that damned shuttle. He ran forward, careful not to venture too far to the edge of Eli's telekinetic shield. They made it to within a meter of the shuttle before the Sahaia let it drop.

Almost as one, the five of them dove into the shuttle, landing in a pile on its lower deck.

"We're clear!" Skye shouted.

Aaliyah didn't need to be told twice. Immediately the shuttle lifted out of there, hatch closing as they went. "Sixty seconds to the perimeter, and that's only if the fraggers don't try and follow us." Belatedly, she asked, "Who're your friends?"

Eli didn't tell her? So much for avoiding that bit of awkwardness. Markus sighed and removed his helmet. "Hey, Red. Long time, no see."

Captain Farris put his hand to his earpiece. "All clear," he relayed.

Finally. Cyrus stood. "*Now* can you tell me what in the nine hells is going on? Who triggered that alarm? Did they catch them?"

The soldier showed no emotion as he relayed his report. "Your assassin is being debriefed now. She reported three, maybe four operatives. At least one of them was a psion. And no, we did not catch them."

Gods damn it. After all that, they didn't even catch them? "What were they after?"

Somehow the man's solemn expression grew even sourer. "I haven't been told any more than that, sir. The Ghenza—Sydney Cross—was found unconscious in the sublevels if that tells you anything."

A chill that had nothing to do with the winter storm swept over Cyrus's skin. If the intruders had been down in the lab, then there was a good chance he *did* know what they were after.

But how? Who leaked the information? "Were any of the laboratory personnel killed?"

"No, sir. Zero casualties reported."

"Then have Lucretia Blackwell meet me in my office. Immediately."

"Certainly, sir." He paused. "What would you like me to do with your guest?"

Guest? What...

Nine hells. He'd completely forgotten about Ora. "Is she still here?"

"No one has reported her leaving your office, sir."

Cyrus sighed. What had begun as a pleasant surprise had turned into a bit of an embarrassment. Tarrying any longer would do little to mitigate the damage. "Take me there."

Ora stood in the office, as expected. She was looking out the far window, a tumbler of whiskey held casually before her. One of the view-screens chattered softly in the background, displaying a news feed that showed... *gods damn it*. Was that the NeoGenix building?

"Well, Cyrus. Are all of your afternoons this exciting?" She cut him a teasing smile. "I hope you don't mind, but I helped myself to your selection. This whole affair took rather longer than I had anticipated."

Despite himself, Cyrus felt flustered. It wasn't often that anyone had him at such a disadvantage. "My sincerest apologies, Ora. It seems we've had a bit of an incident."

"Oh? The feeds all say that this was just a training exercise. Your sister was on TN3 a few moments ago confirming it."

Was that the story? "Um... yes... well..."

Ora laughed. "Don't waste a good lie on me, Cyrus. I know the importance of appearances." Her eyes narrowed meaningfully. "Did you catch them?"

Cyrus reached for a glass on the shelf to hide his expression. "I haven't been briefed by my security team just yet. I thought it important that we get back to where we left off." He poured himself a drink and took a step toward Ora. "That is, of course, if your schedule still allows."

"Unfortunately, I've just missed my next appointment. If I linger any longer, I fear that I will miss another." She downed the rest of the liquor in her glass and set it on his desk.

Cyrus eyed his own glass balefully, uncertain as to whether he wanted to throw it back or pour it out. "Surely you can make other arrangements. We barely got to spend any time together at all."

"Sadly, you are correct." She reached for his lapels and straightened them. "But that's hardly my fault, now is it?"

Though he didn't see how this incident could rightfully be called *his* fault, he didn't push the point. "Tomorrow, then. Dinner. Any restaurant of your choosing."

She hesitated briefly, taking him in with her eyes. Cyrus, strangely, found himself lost in those amethyst pools. Ora struck him as the type of woman who knew exactly what kind of effect she had on men. At present, she was milking that effect to its fullest.

"All right," she conceded then. "Dinner. But not tomorrow. The day after, perhaps." She leaned in and planted a chaste kiss against his cheek. "I'll be in touch."

Without another word, she pushed past him and out the office door. Cyrus fought the urge to stare as she made her way toward the lift. Her leaving felt like the final note on what had turned out to be an abysmal day. Tomorrow, though, was another story.

Tomorrow, he would take this world, and all the others, by storm.

As much as Cyrus had wanted this day to be over, he had one more task to attend to—one that would not grow more pleasant with waiting.

He'd chosen Farris for the task of driving him this evening. Part of the choice was to force a penance from the guard who had coerced him into safe isolation during the attack on NeoGenix. The other was that he valued the man's commitment to his job.

Such a commitment, including the ability to follow orders to the letter, would be useful this evening.

It might not have been the best idea to deal with this personal problem on the same evening of the NeoGenix fiasco. While the intruders had been denied their objective—the extensive structural damage on the blast door protecting the Heart of Thule told enough to make that apparent—the virus they had introduced into the computer system had wiped away entire cycles worth of research. The total cost of the event numbered in the billions.

The purpose was obvious: if they couldn't steal the Heart, they would do their best to keep anyone else from discovering how it worked. They were too late for that, however. The power of the artifact coursed through Cyrus's very veins. Still, the audacity had him perturbed.

There was nothing to be done for it, however. The attack had been dealt with, and this current matter would not wait. Sydney had tracked Tessa to this location for now, but there was nothing to say she would stay here. He needed to deal with her tonight.

He stared out the window, watching as the persistent blizzard continued to ravage the streets of Valhalla. The cold and precipitation were keeping even the most insensible of the populace indoors tonight. He wondered for the hundredth time if perhaps he should have listened to the urgings of Lucretia and Sydney and waited until tomorrow, or sent someone else to tend to this matter.

The car halted in front of a building that was distinct only in its disrepair. "You're certain this is it?" Cyrus growled.

Farris nodded. "These are the coordinates the Ghenza supplied."

Cyrus looked the building over again. Its face was a faux-brick exterior common in the less affluent parts of town. The facade crumbled away at the corners and near the doors and windows that dotted the building's surface. A rickety metal catwalk zigzagged its way between the entrances at each level. Snow had accumulated on these walkways, though far less than what had piled up on the untended streets below.

"Which level?" Cyrus asked, not bothering to hide his disdain.

"It's the sublevel," his guard replied. "Apartment 0-C." He gestured toward a stairway almost completely hidden by a snowbank.

"Fine. Let's get this over with." They exited the vehicle and approached the entrance to the building. Cyrus tried the handle only to find it locked. Examining the mechanism, he saw it required a physical key rather than a digital access code.

"Allow, me, sir."

Cyrus jumped. He hadn't realized Farris had followed him out of the car. He started to reprimand the guard but thought better of it. "By all means."

His bodyguard pressed the barrel of his pistol close to the locking mechanism. He fired once, and the lock dissolved in a muted shower of sparks. Farris must have used an energy weapon.

Since there appeared to be no deadbolt, the door now swung open freely. Fairly poor security, even for this side of town. Perhaps *especially* for this side of town.

The inside of the apartment building was as uncared for as the exterior. The carpet was grimy with the dirt and slush from outside, and the musty stench of the place seemed to indicate a mold problem. Yellow lighting strips provided just enough illumination to keep them from stumbling into the dirt-smeared walls.

Cyrus wouldn't have tolerated this kind of environment for one of his animals. The thought that his sister was living like this—had *chosen* to live like this—turned his stomach.

A brown door marked apartment 0-C. Cyrus knocked politely as his escort took up a position just over his shoulder. He could hear someone rustling just beyond the door. Several seconds went by and there was no answer. He was contemplating knocking again when the door finally cracked open.

The Terran that appeared in the doorway wasn't exactly muscular, but he was lean. The tattoos on his bare chest and shaved head gave him a menacing appearance. He scowled at Cyrus. In all likelihood, he had been about to tell Cyrus to piss off before he caught a glimpse of Farris standing over his left shoulder. "Need somethin'?" he grunted.

"I'm looking for Tessa."

Recognition dawned in his eyes. "Ah knew ya looked familiar. Ya must be the big man himself: Cyrus Valadar. Tessa said ya might be stoppin' by." He extended his hand. Cyrus looked at the black-gloved appendage disdainfully.

After several awkward seconds, the man got the picture. The smile on his face faltered, and he brought his hand back to his side. "One sec," he said. "Ah'll go get 'er."

He disappeared back into the apartment but left the door open by a crack. It was enough that Cyrus could hear the sounds of raucous laughter inside. It seemed that there were at least two, maybe three more men in the room.

Smoke filled his nostrils and he recoiled in disgust. It wasn't that Cyrus was any stranger to drug use. Far from it, in fact. It was more that only the poorest of users still smoked to get their fix. More efficient delivery mechanisms were way too accessible these days— ones that didn't burn out your lungs inside a couple of decades.

Another figure pushed through the door. It took a moment before Cyrus recognized that person as his sister.

Gone were the expensive stylings Tessa had splurged on when their father's bank account had been open to her. Her crimson-colored shirt—which hung off one shoulder and left her midriff exposed— was slashed in that intentional way that had become fashionable among the lower class once gain. The black pants she wore were cut similarly and failed to completely cover her ass. Her warm brown hair was kinked a tousled, and dark circles spread around her eyes from the long-neglected application of makeup.

It was a disgraceful display—one that made Cyrus's stomach turn.

Her jaw was set, and her eyes were defiant. "Cyrus. What can I do for you, big brother?" Her tone was clipped, leaving no confusion as to how she felt about his presence.

"I've come to take you home, Tessa. You've played in the gutter long enough. It's time for you to resume a composure befitting one of your heritage."

Tessa barked a harsh, cruel laugh. "Frag off Cyrus. You don't get it, do you? This *is* my home. I want to stay here."

"It's not about what you want, sister. It's about family and family honor. You're a Valadar. We can't have you doing"—He gestured in confusion.—"whatever it is that you're doing in there."

"Funny, because what I'm 'doing' is some of the same shit you pay people to do every day. I'm just doing it better. Is dealing drugs only admirable when you do it from your gods-damned ivory tower?"

Tessa was dealing? She must have co-opted part of his existing operation after he'd revoked her assets. That would explain why the oaf he'd met at the door hadn't been surprised to see him. He didn't know Tessa had gone rogue.

"If you want to deal drugs, that's fine. If you want to *use* drugs, that's fine. There is a time and a place for all of that. Just come home and do it with a little dignity."

There—offer extended. He'd thought he was being reasonable, even tolerant. He would accept that Tessa was never going to command respect or build upon their family's empire. She would never be another Julia, but perhaps she could quietly pursue her own interests out of the public eye. Or hells, if she wanted to stay in the public eye, at least show the gossip channels and party feeds that she was better than *this* gutter trash.

What Tessa did next was unexpected. She punched him in the jaw. The blow was strong enough to turn his head. He heard Farris draw his pistol behind him and held up a staying hand.

His sister appeared oblivious to the threat. "Where do you get off?" she shrieked. "You think you can just keep telling me what to do? Is that it? How many times do I have to tell you? *I. Don't. Need. You.*"

Cyrus brought his hand to his lips, and his fingers came away red with blood. Anger flared in his chest. It was not the familiar flame, the raging inferno that he was used to.

No, this was different. This fury was cold, and his heart froze with icy resolve.

He tried one last time. "Tessa, please…"

"No, Cyrus. *No.* Now, piss off before I get my friends involved."

That was it, then. He knew what he had to do. "Very well," he whispered. "I'll grant you your wish, sister."

Tessa faltered, obviously expecting more of a fight. "You will?"

"Yes, it is your life, and these are the decisions you must make for yourself. As much as I might wish it, I cannot make them for you." He paused, feigning consideration. "Could you do me one last favor? A small gesture for old time's sake?"

His sister's eyes grew wary. "Maybe. What is it?"

He reached into the inside pocket of his coat. Slowly, he drew out a small rectangular box. He held it before him, extended slightly toward Tessa. When she did not take the box, he opened it, revealing the platinum necklace with the green gemstone charm.

"I intended it as a welcome home present for you. Presumptuous, perhaps, but I thought that I would convince you to come back with me. I see now that I was wrong, but I would still like you to have it."

Hesitantly, she reached for the necklace. She grabbed its chain and examined the charm dangling at its end. "A snake?" she asked skeptically as she eyed the figure wrapped around the crystal.

"A matter of taste, I suppose." He paused, dramatically. "I would like to see what it looks like on you, Tessa. Would you try it on for me? I swear, it's the last thing I'll ask of you."

The way that Tessa regarded the trinket seemed to indicate that she thought the charm might spontaneously animate and bite her. With a huff, she slipped the chain over her head. The charm came to rest on the exposed skin of her chest.

Cyrus smiled. "Lovely," he purred.

"If you, say so." Tessa remained spiteful to the end. Little did she know that his will had just become hers.

He sunk then into that well of power inside himself, the reservoir he'd built using the amp and the crystal infusion that carried the power of Thule. "Never take it off," he said, infusing each word with intention and authority.

"Why would I take it off?" she retorted.

He couldn't help but laugh. Even under the influence of the artifact, his sister was still an intractable bitch. "Stay here with me for a moment longer, dear sister. Don't move." He turned to Farris. "Can I have your side-arm, please?"

For a second, Cyrus thought the man might refuse him. Reluctantly, Farris released his grip on the weapon and handed it over.

Accepting custody of the weapon, Cyrus thanked him. "Now, go wait outside. I'd like a moment alone with Tessa."

"I'm not so sure that's a good idea," said Farris.

"Please, I must insist. I'll make it an order if I need to."

Farris may have been wary, but he knew better than to push the issue. When the guard was gone, Cyrus returned his attention once more to Tessa.

He drew on his power to silently compel her to answer the questions he was about to ask. "How many men are there in the apartment?"

"Four." Her voice was clipped and mechanical. Though he compelled her to stay with him, her non-verbals still showed how much she wanted to go. "Cyrus, what's wrong with your eyes?"

"Shush now. Only answer my questions. Are these men armed?"

"Probably not."

"Good." He checked Farris's pistol. Finding it loaded, he extended it to Tessa. "Take this. Go inside and execute everyone in there. Be quick about it. Call my name when it's finished."

She took the weapon without comment. Almost casually she marched back into the apartment, leaving the door ajar. Immediately, he heard the sound of rapid gunfire. The jovial voices inside fell silent. It was all over in a matter of seconds.

There was the slightest tremble to Tessa's voice as she called out to him. "Cyrus!"

He pushed his way inside and immediately began to count corpses. As she'd stated, there were four men in the room. Empty bottles were everywhere, along with various powders, patches, and syringes. Half-smoked cigarettes were now burning holes in the tattered couches or on the blood-stained carpet.

Cyrus had never been a candidate for sainthood, but this level of debauchery—this display of *filth*—roiled his stomach. He stepped over to examine the fallen men more closely. "Who was in charge, here? Before you showed up, I mean."

Tessa pointed a shaking finger to the man who had greeted Cyrus at the door. "That's Botch," she sniffed.

Botch? What a name. "And how did you meet him?"

"His guys used to deal to me and my friends."

Cyrus could fill in the rest of the story in his head. Tessa probably asked for an introduction, told him who she was, and took over the operation. He'd have to have someone run the connections to find out who Botch's source was and have them double-check their numbers. He anticipated their revenues were going to be off for this coming period.

"And you two were stealing from me? Siphoning the profits from the drug sales?"

Tessa nodded as she sobbed. Her grief seemed genuine—almost like she'd cared for this guy. Why was that? After everything she had been given, why stoop so low as to mingle with this trash?

Cyrus shook his head. "If you wanted to run the drug ring, why didn't you come to me? I could have made you something. I could have put you over the entire operation. Why didn't you say anything?"

That familiar defiant look slipped into her gaze. For an instant, her brown irises seemed to tint red with the flames of her anger. "I d-d-don't w-want any th-thing f-from y-you."

And there it was. Cyrus closed his eyes and gritted his teeth. It was time to face the reality that Tessa was just too far gone. She hated him so much that she'd rather sink to this level than come to him for aid.

Had this been his fault? Was there something he should have done differently? Some intervention he could have made sooner?

He shook his head again. These were the wrong questions. The only question that mattered was: what would he do about it now?

He walked over to his sister, took the gun from her hand to verify that it still had ammunition. Seeing that it did, he handed it back to her.

"Take the gun, Tessa."

With a trembling hand, she did so. Her sobs grew in intensity. "Cyrus," she pleaded.

"No. No talking now. Take the gun and put the barrel in your mouth."

A pitiful whimper clawed its way out of her throat as she placed the muzzle between her lips. Her breathing grew faster, and her eyes conveyed the extent of her panic.

Cyrus took a steadying breath and then exhaled. Tears burned at the corners of his eyes. He didn't cry for Tessa, though. He knew that he'd written off his little sister long before this.

He wept, instead, for the dishonor she had brought to their House. He wept for the great shame he felt that a Valadar could be brought so low. He wept for the burden that this new secret would carry in his soul for the rest of his life.

A single tear was the only indulgence he allowed himself. As he wiped it away, he stiffened his resolve.

"Pull the trigger."

To be continued.

Hey, reader–thank you for picking up your copy of *Darkest Hearts*. At this point, you are halfway through the Cognis Saga, and I hope you're enjoying every word.

Please take a moment to stop by wherever you purchased this book and leave a review. Honest reviews from dedicated readers are the single most important factor in helping new authors–like myself–expand their audiences. Five minutes of your time makes all the difference in the world.

If you enjoyed reading about Markus, Skye, and the rest of the crew of the *Vandal*, swing by mythicnorthpress.com and pick up a copy of the *Chronicles of Nethra: Origins* eBook for free when you sign up for the mailing list.

Lastly, keep your eyes open for *Chronicles of Nethra* Book Four: *Stardust Grave* coming this fall. If you're interested in getting an early copy of this book and all my future releases, drop me a line at erdonaldson@mythicnorthpress.com.

Until then, swift running.

– E. R. Donaldson